REMEMBRANCE

A NOVEL

SARA HAYES DIETZ

First published by Fire & Feast Books 2025

Paperback ISBN: 979-8-9922008-0-5
EPUB ISBN: 979-8-9922008-1-2

First edition

for mdh

Chapter 1

How did I get here? What is this place?

Condensation gathered on Leah's hands as she cradled an iced coffee that she only half-remembered ordering. The chatter of a dozen conversations filled her ears, mingling with the soft crooning that drifted from the overhead speakers.

I have no idea where I am.

She tried to think back, to review her morning in her mind's eye: she'd sat down at this table without conscious choice, although there were still tables available in less-crowded areas of the cafe; she'd made friendly conversation with the barista who, in retrospect, didn't look at all familiar; she'd been listening to a podcast on the drive over and hadn't used maps to find the location; she'd left her apartment in a hurry.

Bizarre. Why did I come here?

She brushed a strand of brown hair out of her face, frustrated that she'd had it cut so short at her last appointment.

Get a summer cut, they said. You'll feel so much lighter. Never doing that again.

She tucked the flyaway locks back into her headband and looked around again, searching for anything she recognized, any familiar face among the crowd. A redheaded woman patted her baby through the swath of olive green fabric wrapped around them both. Next to her, another mom absentmindedly broke off bites of muffin for her toddler. In another corner, a book club gathered around three tables that had been pushed together. The group was mostly older black men, with a few younger faces, and a lively energy filled their conversation as they laughed and argued. A man in a blue-gray suit and a navy tie tapped away at his keyboard, his hand on his forehead and his eyes tired.

In spite of her confusion, Leah found the coffee shop's ambiance soothing. She took a deep breath. Beneath the obvious bakery scents was a hint of fresh-cut grass, sending Leah back to the carefree summer days of her childhood. Curious, she stood up and made her way toward the door of the coffee shop. As she did so, she made eye contact with another patron, a tall young man with dark hair. He stepped away from the counter, drink in hand, and walking in her direction.

Her heart skipped a beat, and something in her stomach tingled.

He stopped moving, a gasp escaping him before he collected himself and averted his eyes. He brushed past Leah and made his way to the table she'd just vacated.

Do I know him?

She tried to be discreet as she looked back at him, and she was shocked to find him looking at her as well. Their eyes met for another brief moment, and Leah whipped her head around quickly. She felt the color rising in her cheeks as she reached out to grab the open door from another customer.

"Bye, Leah!" called a voice behind her. She turned again to see the barista who'd taken her order—a heavily made-up, bleached-blonde girl who couldn't have been more than nineteen—waving at her from the cash register. Leah waved back, her eyes darting for a split second to the corner booth where tall, dark, and handsome had taken a seat.

He's still looking at me!

A knot formed in her stomach as she made her way out the door onto the patio.

Why did that barista seem so friendly? What's going on here?

The exterior of the coffee shop was as foreign to her as the interior had been. She felt her rib cage tighten around her lungs. Her feet froze in place.

Why is everyone acting like they know me?

The warm, earthy smell of grass was no longer masked by the scent of coffee and pastries, and Leah looked out over a wide open space. The coffee shop's outdoor seating butted up against a field boasting two sets of soccer goals, a walking trail, and a playground. Along one side of the grass was a parking lot, mostly full with plenty of incoming traffic as the Saturday morning crowd picked up.

How did I get here? What is this place? Could this be a dream?

"Excuse me," someone said next to her, and she reflexively stepped aside to allow them to pass. The scent of the man's cologne lingered, and the wind blew around her.

Wait, that's not wind.

Dread filled her stomach as she looked at her arm, searching for the ants she felt crawling on her. She didn't see anything right away, so she pulled her sleeve up over her shoulder and examined the full circumference of her arm.

Still nothing, but the feeling had spread. She swatted at her chest and stomach, dancing as she felt the bugs crawling down her legs toward the ground.

"Ah! Get off!"

People at the tables around her looked up from their conversations, and Leah felt herself blushing.

"Sorry," she said. "Bugs."

But there had been no bugs.

Had there?

She forced herself to take a few steps toward the grass, hoping that her gait didn't give away her discomfort.

She heard someone behind her calling her name. The voice was familiar and sweet. "Leah!"

"Dad?" Leah whirled around in a frenzy, her eyes wide and searching desperately. "Dad!"

There was no one on the patio but the same coffee shop patrons, whose expressions revealed that they were no longer sympathetic.

"Dad!" Her voice sounded hopeful, but she knew he wasn't really there. He'd been gone for years.

What I wouldn't give for one more hug.

Leah's heart pounded as she paced down the length of the field. As she turned the corner, she noticed the young man from the coffee shop exiting through the front doors, a paper cup in his hands. He looked around the field and, upon seeing her, began walking in her direction.

Why is he coming this way? Is he following me?

Leah felt her feet moving faster as she tried to escape the man's notice. An open sidewalk appeared, leading away from the field, and she turned to follow it. The buildings around her looked friendly, if unfamiliar, and a boutique window display caught her eye.

That little elephant would be perfect for Mom's collection!

She looked around until she found the door of the shop, reached for the handle, and pulled the door halfway open. The reflection of the street behind her shifted in the glass as the door swung open.

Suddenly, her stalker's form appeared as if in a mirror.

How did I let myself forget so quickly?

Ignoring the chirpy welcome from inside the shop, Leah let the door slam and sprinted down the street. She turned left, then right, then left again, hoping to dodge or outrun her pursuer.

When she finally slowed down, panting and looking around frantically, a new sense of dread sunk into her chest. There was not a single building on the street that looked familiar. No longer was she surrounded by cheery boutiques and antique stores. Instead, pawn shops and liquor stores sprung up around her, threatening to pounce. The area wasn't busy for a weekend, but the few individuals who did walk past her eyed her with suspicion, and Leah felt herself shrinking under their gaze.

How do I get back to the park?

She spun around, trying to determine which way she'd been running when she'd turned onto the street. She couldn't remember what buildings she'd walked past on her way. Her panting breath shallowed as she turned in circles, desperately searching for any familiar landmark or sign.

A blurry patch appeared in her vision, just below eye level, tracking with her as she looked up and down the street. It was soon joined by another, off to the right. The faintest twinge of a headache began to throb behind her right eye.

Not now! Please, not now.

She continued to plead with her body as she picked a direction and began walking, although the glares of the strangers around her haunted her every step.

Please let this be the way. I just need to get home.

She took a left at a random intersection, no longer deluding herself that she would be able to find her way back to the park. Her eyes scanned the street for any familiar landmark that could help her navigate to a bus station.

Wait, but the car. How will I go get it later if I don't even know the name of the coffee shop I was at this morning?

Without thinking, she swatted at a bug on her arm.

Maybe I remembered to get a text receipt. I could get the name of the cafe there.

Suddenly, a shriek erupted out of her as the sensation of tiny insect legs on her skin overwhelmed her. She felt herself crumbling to the ground.

"Get off me! Get off!"

"Ma'am, are you okay?" The voice was unfamiliar, judgmental, demanding.

"They're all over me! Get them off me!"

"Ma'am, there's nothing on you. I'm going to have to ask you to leave. You're scaring off my customers."

Leah didn't respond. She stumbled to her feet and brushed herself off with trembling hands. Her skin still crawled, but the feeling had begun to abate. The ground seemed to shake under her as she took a few tentative steps down the street before collapsing onto a bus stop bench. She didn't recognize the route number posted on the sign, but it didn't matter.

The bus driver will be able to tell me where to go to get home.

A patter of footfalls drew her attention, and she looked around to find its source.

It was the man from the coffee shop.

How did he even find me he—

Darkness crowded the edges of her vision. Her head spun. The ground and the sky reversed their places, and she knew nothing.

***

Blinking heavily, Leah tried to shake the fog from her mind. Half-remembered dreams echoed in her memory. Her head throbbed. Her shoulder was sore. A high-pitched beeping cut through her groggy thoughts and drew her attention to her surroundings.

Am I in the hospital?

Her heart rate sped up, and she tried to stand. An IV line inserted into her right arm caught on the opposite side of her bed, and she tried to untangle it. Her fingers fumbled and the IV remained stuck.

"Oh good, you're awake." A woman's syrupy voice surrounded her like a warm blanket, and she looked to see a nurse standing in the door of her room. She wore teal green scrubs and a colorful cap.

In her presence, Leah became acutely aware of her own matted hair, her wide eyes, and the ratty blue hospital gown that she didn't remember putting on.

"How are you feeling, dearie? They told me you'd had a rough go of it before you got here, so I didn't know what to expect if you did come to. Looks like you've got yourself in quite a mess here with the IV line." Her words felt cloying, sticky, patronizing.

Leah said nothing in response. She merely watched as the nurse gently unwound the cord of her IV, settling it to rights and draping it over the pole next to her bed.

"Now, I'm sure you'll want a few minutes to wake up, but I know the doctor will want to check in on you the moment he hears you're awake. I'm going to give you five minutes or so, and then I'll send him in."

Leah nodded and tried to thank the nurse, but her throat was painfully dry, and the words barely scraped out.

"Oh, and I'll get you a glass of water right away. You can't be feeling too well after everything that happened."

"What... What did happen to me?" Leah croaked.

"I'll leave that for the doc to explain, dearie. I think it'll be best coming from him."

She handed Leah an enormous clear cup with a blue lid and a straw protruding from the top. Leah took a sip, the cool water shocking her awake.

"Can you at least tell me where I am?"

The nurse started. "Don't you know? You're at the McNeill Institute. Everything's going to be alright."

The nurse stepped out of the room, but Leah barely had time to examine her surroundings before the door burst open again.

"Leah, are you okay? The staff notified me when you were admitted, and I got on the first plane I could to come see you. They won't tell me anything, and I'm not even sure if they'll let me stay in the room once the doctor arrives. They haven't even told me what happened to you."

"I'm—" Leah blinked a few times. "Mom? What are you doing here?"

Her mom shook her short auburn hair as she slipped her glasses up like a headband. "I'm here for you, of course. Do you really think I could stay away after you got admitted?"

"How did you get here?"

"What do you mean? I hopped on an airplane like the rest of the human race and picked up a rental car at the airport." A familiar note of tension rose her voice.

"But you..." Leah decided to let the subject drop. "Thank you for coming."

"That's more like it. Now, how are you feeling?"

"Fine, I guess, just conf—"

She didn't get a chance to finish her sentence. A knock on the door interrupted her, followed by a sliver of light on the floor that grew and shrunk with the door's arc. For a moment, no one walked around the curtain that hung as an entryway in her room.

A voice emanated from behind the curtain. "Ms. Harvey, how are you feeling? I was relieved by the report that you'd awakened."

Leah tensed. The voice was familiar, but she couldn't quite place it. A man walked into her room. His salt-and-pepper hair stood up in the front, and he wore a concerned expression. She recognized him and sighed with relief.

"Oh, Dr. Pierucci, hello. I didn't recognize your voice. Thanks so much for coming by." From her bedside, Leah's mother cleared her throat. "Have you met my mother?"

Dr. Pierucci started, his head tilted to one side as he considered Leah's question.

"Donna Harvey," Leah's mom extended a hand.

If he noticed her, he gave no indication. "I don't believe I have had the pleasure. Perhaps she will be able to join you for a future appointment."

"She's right there, Dr. P," Leah said, pointing to her mom. "You could at least shake her hand."

Confusion melted away as realization dawned on Dr. Pierucci's face. He sighed, pulled his stool up to Leah's

13

bedside, and sat down near her. Gently, he took her hand in his. His voice was barely a whisper. "Leonora, I believe you're experiencing another hallucination."

"No, doc, she's—"

But she was gone. Leah and Dr. Pierucci were alone.

The breath caught in Leah's chest, and she choked on the empty air. She felt her eyes growing larger as panic set in. Dr. Pierucci calmly handed her the large water cup from her bedside table, and she took a long drink, followed by a few heaving, wheezing breaths.

"Dr. P, help me!" A terrified despair clawed at her heart. "What's happening to me?"

He offered her a sympathetic glance and took her hand gently in his. "Do take a moment to breathe, Leonora. There's plenty of time for us to discuss the specifics, but you need rest more than anything else."

She obeyed, making a conscious effort to draw air into her lungs, hold it there for a moment, and expel it slowly. Her frantic heartbeat slowed, and her limbs relaxed. The relentless noise of the monitors in her room receded into the background of her awareness.

"Better." Dr. Pierucci glanced down at his clipboard. "Ms. Harvey, it appears that you've had an... episode. Quite an intense one, to be frank. You were found unconscious at a city bus stop outside a bodega on the southwest side. Eyewitnesses reported that you seemed unsettled: screaming 'get off me' and writhing on the ground in the bodega parking lot. It was a stroke of unbelievably good luck that a friend of the McNeill Institute passed by shortly after you arrived and recognized you. You were immediately transported here and admitted to our in-patient suite for further monitoring."

14

The morning came back to Leah in a flash, and the words spilled out before she could stop them. "That's right, I was at this coffee shop and I couldn't remember how I'd gotten there, and I was so confused, and I kept feeling ants crawling all over me, and I would have sworn I heard my dad there, but he died when I was in high school, and there was this man following me, so I ran away, and then I got lost, and I was trying to find the bus stop, but the shop owner told me to go away, and then the man was still following me, and I guess I passed out..."

She ended her story with a quiet whimper. Dr. Pierucci's face was difficult for her to read.

He probably has other patients that are struggling. And this isn't exactly the progress we were hoping for with this clinical trial.

As if reading her mind, he spoke up. "While this was a frightening incident, I want to reassure you that this is not an unexpected side-effect of the treatment you've been receiving with us for the last three months. We have seen several cases where a patient's condition appears to worsen before showing improvement after the body acclimates."

His words cut her to the quick, and she fought back tears. "You mean it might still get worse?"

"We will keep you here for a few days for monitoring. I make no promises, but I am hopeful that this will be the low point, so to speak, before things begin trending upward." Dr. Pierucci stood up and placed a gentle hand on her shoulder. "Stay the course, Ms. Harvey. We'll get to the bottom of this before too long."

He exited the room, and Leah released a breath she didn't realize she'd been holding. After another sip of water, she picked up her phone. Her most recent notification was a text from her mom.

Why are you at McNeill after hours? Is everything okay?

Leah sighed. She hadn't realized it was already evening, and she wasn't sure whether she was comforted or frustrated by the fact that her mom was actively checking her location from the other side of the country. Setting her discomfort aside, she typed out a quick response and hit send before she could think too much about it.

> I had another episode. Doc isn't worried, says it's normal to see an increase in symptoms in the short term. They're going to keep me overnight and see how I'm doing in the morning.

It's not technically a lie if it's only a half-truth, right?
Her mom's response came through within seconds.

Call me.

Leah braced herself and tapped the phone icon. It had hardly started to ring when her mom picked up.

"Leah, are you okay? What happened?" It was a demand more than a question. "Why are they going to keep you overnight at the clinic?"

"I'm fine, Mom, really. I had a couple of symptoms and ended up getting a little bit lost. Someone from the Institute recognized me and brought me here. I guess they could tell something was wrong."

"Who was it that recognized you?"

Leah grimaced. "I... I don't know. I was unconscious."

"Leah, you passed out?" She could hear the fear and horror in her mom's voice. "That's not fine, Leah! You're not fine if you got lost and passed out in a part of the city

16

you didn't know! How did you even—I mean, are you even supposed to be driving, with the seizures and everything?"

How does she always manage to call me out?

"I don't know, Mom. I guess I just wasn't thinking this morning. It just sort of happened. But I'm at the Institute now, I'm okay. Dr. Pierucci—my neurologist—he's going to monitor me overnight and make sure it's safe for me to go home. I'm in good hands here."

"I know who Dr. Pierucci is, Leah." Her mom's tone was suddenly cold.

That's what she took away from everything I said?

"Okay, sorry Mom. You've had a hard time with names lately. I wasn't sure if you'd recognize him."

"How could I possibly forget him?"

Leah rolled her eyes. "How's home?"

"It's fine."

Why is she upset now?

"Are you doing anything fun this weekend?"

"Not really. I'll go to church in the morning and I think they'll have donuts afterwards. So that'll be nice."

"That will be nice." Leah waited for her mom to offer something—anything—a question, a comment. Nothing. Eventually, Leah faked a yawn. "Alright, Mom, I'm going to let you go so I can try to get some sleep."

"Okay. Sleep well. I'll talk to you soon." Her tone had returned to normal, all trace of resentment gone.

"Talk to you soon. Bye, Mom. I love you."

Her mom hung up halfway through her sentence, leaving Leah alone in her cold, sterile room.

Why did her dementia have to get so bad right at the same time all this was starting? Isn't one crisis at a time enough?

She curled up and closed her eyes. Sleep came quickly.

Chapter 2

"Harvey! A little birdie told me today is your treatment anniversary."

Leah looked up from her Murdle at the sound of her name. She gave an exaggerated eye roll when she realized who'd taken the seat next to her. "Wilder. The whole waiting room is empty, and you chose this spot?"

"So that's how it is today?" He feigned offense.

She grinned, a flutter dancing in her stomach, before shutting her Murdle book and turning to face him. "That's how it is today."

He elbowed her playfully. "For real, though. How are you? You look tired."

Leah smiled at him sadly. "How do you always know?"

"I can read you like a book, Harvey." He winked, his green eyes sparkling. "Tell me what's up."

She shook her head. "No, I'm just tired of having to Uber everywhere. We managed to get stuck behind a wreck on the way here, so I'm super late and hoping they can squeeze me in somewhere."

As if on cue, the door of the waiting room opened and out stepped her usual technician, a redhead with wiry round glasses.

Shoot. I told myself I was going to remember his name.

19

"Leonora Harvey?" he called.

"Over here," she called back, slipping her backpack over her shoulder. "Give me just a second!"

Turning back to Wilder, she held out a fist. He bumped it with his own. "Get here on time next month, Harvey! I miss you."

She tried to hide her smile as she stood up and walked away. Wilder also stood up, making his way over to the reception desk to chat with Shelby, who giggled at whatever he'd said. An unexpected surge of frustration caused Leah to blush.

Keep it together, Leah.

Forcing herself to look away from the desk, she ran a hand through her hair and followed the redhead through the door that led back to the exam rooms, trying unsuccessfully to catch a glimpse of his nametag. He led her about halfway down the hall before opening a door and ushering her in. He slipped her call tag—a bright pink square of paper with her name printed on it—into the clear sleeve glued onto the door before following her inside.

He's been my technician for a whole year!

"Alright, Ms. Harvey. You know the drill. Can you go ahead and confirm your full name and date of birth?"

"Leonora Nicole Harvey. April 23, 1995."

"Thank you. How have your symptoms been lately?"

"Mild. I had a few episodes of anxiety and one auditory hallucination, but I was able to identify it fairly quickly. No migraines or seizures, thankfully. It seems like the treatment has really kicked in now—things have been very manageable. Nothing like last August." She shuddered.

The tech's affect remained flat. "No other new or worsening symptoms?"

"None."

I swear I knew his name when I walked in the front door.

"Do you have any concerns about side effects of the treatment or the medication?"

"None, thanks."

Never have any trouble remembering Wilder's name.

She felt the color rising in her cheeks.

"Any other questions?"

"None."

"Great." The technician looked at his computer. "Looks like this is your one-year appointment, which means that Dr. Pierucci will want to speak with you in a little more detail than usual. I'm going to pop out and see if he wants to chat before or after we run the treatment. His schedule is pretty busy today, and since you were late to your appointment, he may not be able to give you a full half-hour, but I'm sure he'll want to squeeze you in."

"Got stuck in traffic. Sorry. I do need Dr. P to sign off on my paperwork to get my license renewed."

He glanced at her and cocked his head.

Dang it, what is his name?

"I've been seizure-free for three months. I can finally get my drivers' license reinstated if he signs off on it."

"Ah, I see. We definitely want to get that taken care of for you. Let me see if I can grab him right now."

Leah nodded and watched him walk back into the hallway. She pulled out her phone reflexively and found herself scrolling past photos she didn't like of people she didn't care about until something caught her eye.

It was a picture of a young Hispanic man. His huge smile lit up his face as he cradled a laughing child. Intertwined with the two of them were the words "BRING

HIM HOME" in bold orange letters. She leaned forward as she read the caption.

Jorge Rodriguez was wrongfully convicted and sentenced to prison time for a crime he didn't commit. While his innocence has been firmly proven, Scarlett Bay Correctional Facility refuses to release him. Sign the petition today to BRING HIM HOME!

Absentmindedly, Leah clicked the link to a petition and scrolled past the photo and description until she reached the signatures. There were pityingly few, most of them from desperate family members.

A knock on the door of the exam room startled her out of her reading. She set her phone down. "Come in!"

The door cracked open and the redhead stepped back into the exam room, followed by Dr. Pierucci. His salt-and-pepper hair had grayed even more since her visit the previous month, and she noticed bags under his eyes. Even so, he smiled widely as he entered the room. She breathed deeply and rolled her neck, stretching out a tenseness in her shoulders that she hadn't noticed before.

"Ms. Harvey! A pleasure to see you, as always. Did Mr. Bennett inform you that this portion of your appointment will be a little more in-depth today?"

Peter! Peter Bennett. That's it.

"He did."

"Excellent. Well, let's jump right in." He glanced down at the notes Peter had taken. "It appears that your symptoms have improved considerably over the last few months—would you agree with that assessment?"

"Absolutely." Leah nodded. "The migraines and seizures feel like a distant memory now, and the hallucinations have become much less frequent and much easier to identify. I'm really grateful to you and your team."

"We are doing what we can, certainly. Improving your quality of life is, of course, the main goal of our treatment, after pursuing a formal diagnosis." He looked up from his notes. "Would you be so good as to elaborate on how the treatment has helped you in that regard?"

"I mean... I feel like a lot of it is self-explanatory." Leah shrugged. "The biggest thing is that this is my third appointment with no reported seizures, so I can have you sign this and then I can go to the DMV to get my license again."

She handed a pre-written letter to Dr. Pierucci, who signed it without reading it and handed it back to her.

"Just the money I'll save on not having to get an Uber everywhere justifies the cost of this clinical trial." She laughed nervously when neither Peter nor Dr. Pierucci acknowledged her attempt to lighten the mood.

The silence stretched out for a moment before Leah continued. "The migraines aren't a weekly thing anymore, so I'm not constantly checking traffic and ride share rates to see if I could get home for a nap if I needed to. Your team has really helped me develop a specific protocol for medication and supplements, so I'm not juggling eight or nine pill bottles a day anymore, and I have checks in place to ensure I do actually take the things that help me function, instead of just letting the bottles pile up."

Leah closed her eyes, a sudden wave of nausea rolling over her. Dr. Pierucci coughed gently, encouraging her to continue.

"I guess... I'm more focused at work, which is obviously good. And being able to identify hallucinations in real time means I can just let them happen and move on with my day. Does that answer your question?"

"Indeed." Dr. Pierucci looked up from the notes he'd been scribbling in her chart. "Well, that seems to cover 'trust my senses' and 'increased daily function'. The last goal I have written down from your first appointment is 'regaining social confidence'. How have your social interactions been?"

Leah tried to stifle a sigh. "Fine. People at work aren't scared of me anymore, but they don't exactly like me, so it's not great."

He didn't look up from his notes. "And your non-work relationships?"

"There aren't that many." Leah looked at the floor. "Things with Mom are still really uncomfortable. She's got this image in her head of the woman I used to be, and she's constantly sizing me up and comparing me to that version of me. And that's not even going into her memory issues..."

Dr. Pierucci nodded slowly. "Struggling with parents and parental figures is a common theme among individuals with later-onset psychological symptoms like yourself. Are you seeing the therapist we discussed after your major episode last summer? I believe I gave you a referral?"

"You did, and I'm not. I went to one or two visits and didn't get much out of them."

Dr. Pierucci didn't respond; he merely jotted down a note on his paper before resuming his questions. "Any other friendships or relationships you feel have improved with the diminishing symptoms?"

"I don't really have any other friendships." She felt her face redden. "Honestly, the closest thing I have to a friend is Wilder, the guy who usually has his appointments around the same time as mine? We chat in the waiting room. I don't really talk to anyone else consistently."

"Ah, yes, Mr. Frederick is quite the charmer." Something in his voice gave Leah pause, but she couldn't put her finger on what it was.

Dr. Pierucci set his clipboard down and looked back up at her. "Well, it's always gratifying to hear that patients are benefiting from the treatments we offer here at the McNeill Institute. We'll continue working toward some of those interpersonal goals, now that your symptoms are being managed more effectively, and I would highly encourage you to give therapy another shot. I think you would benefit tremendously if you stuck with it."

"Thanks for the recommendation, Doc. I'll think about it." She turned her phone over and over in her hands, carefully studying the posters on the exam room walls.

Like I'm about to go cry in some shrink's office because I don't have any friends...

He watched her fidget but said nothing. Instead, he changed course. "I wonder, would you consider submitting a testimonial for us? I'll have Peter include a link to the form in your visit summary. Patient testimonies are a powerful tool that we use in encouraging others to seek treatment."

"I'll consider it." She shrugged and looked at Dr. Pierucci. "Are you any closer to reaching a conclusion about the cause of my symptoms? I'd love to start focusing on a cure instead of just mitigating symptoms."

The doctor's face changed, a shadow forming behind his eyes. "Regrettably, I am still at a loss regarding the etiology of your condition. The bloodwork we did several months ago illuminated some imbalances; however, it was not conclusive. With your permission, I would like to run some additional tests today to follow up on a few theories."

Leah shivered and sighed. "Do what you need to do. Last time we did bloodwork, Peter was able to wait until after I was masked before doing the blood draw. Would he be able to do that today? I just... needles." She shuddered.

"Of course." He looked back to ensure Peter was listening. Peter nodded, and Dr. Pierucci turned back to Leah. "Well, Ms. Harvey, I do have to depart. I'd prefer to spend a little more time going over your status report with you, but my assistant booked me for back-to-back appointments today."

"Yeah, of course." Leah shook her head. "Peter let me know that you're busy, and since I was late, I would be lucky to get anything at all. Thanks for stopping in. It's always good to see you."

For a moment, his expression twisted into something like frustration, but at what, she couldn't tell. However, as he let himself out the door, his face once again bore its usual smile, and he shook her hand warmly.

"Likewise, Ms. Harvey. Have a good day."

Peter watched the doctor leave, typing for a moment before looking back up at Leah.

"Alright, are you ready to get started?"

She shook her head, grimacing. "Let's get it over with."

They exited the exam room and made their way further down the hall. Peter opened the door for her and helped her get settled in the large orthodontic chair in the center of the room. He slipped a helmet and goggles over her head, and within moments, she felt the tingling begin.

A few minutes later, she felt the telltale prick of the needle as Peter drew blood for the tests Dr. Pierucci had ordered. She whispered a 'thank you' that was inaudible to her, hoping that Peter would hear.

The whole process took the better part of half an hour, and when Peter finally lifted the helmet off, she felt exhausted, as if she'd lived a full month over again. A bright pink strip of soft, supple wrap wound its way around her elbow. On the table next to her, a paper cup containing three small pills sat beside a chilled water bottle with beads of condensation dripping down the side. She popped the pills into her mouth, opened the bottle, and downed all the water, wiping her face with her forearm as she took a gasping breath.

Peter glanced at her briefly, and she took the opportunity to speak up. "This really took it out of me this month. Hoping that medicine kicks in soon so I can get back to work without falling asleep at the wheel."

He responded with obvious apathy. "Should be just a few more minutes. Make sure to pick up your medication on your way out."

"Will do."

Peter clacked a few more keys and left without a word. Leah closed her eyes and focused on her breathing as she waited for the pills to take effect. After a few more minutes, feeling more alert, she packed up her backpack and made her way out to the front of the clinic.

Maybe Wilder won't have gone back yet...

But he was nowhere to be seen. After checking out with Shelby at the front desk and picking up her medication at the en-suite pharmacy, Leah walked out the front doors of the clinic and took a deep breath of the warm spring air. She hopped into her car, the orange bottle rattling in her backpack. The end of the work day was still two hours away, and since her boss hadn't approved her request to take the afternoon off, she couldn't just head home.

She called her mom as she drove away from the neurologist, a monthly ritual that she clung to and dreaded in equal measure.

Her mom picked up on the second ring. "Hi Leah."

"Hi, Mom. How's your day going?"

"Oh, good, good, just spent the morning with Sheila and Margot, and now I'm going to get my haircut."

"That sounds like a good day."

"Good enough. You know how Margot can be sometimes, just the most rotten complainer. But Sheila won't go anywhere without her..."

Leah didn't know what to say in response, but her mom filled the silence. "How did your appointment go?"

"Oh, fine. Just the usual. Things are looking really good, but the doctor still doesn't have a diagnosis for me. Just tests and more tests."

Her mother hesitated before she spoke again. "Have you considered getting a second opinion?"

"Everyone says Dr. P is the best, Mom. I know there are other neurologists in town, but I don't think anyone else would be able to help me more than he has."

"That's not so much what I mean, more just that I would have assumed you'd want a different doctor after everything that happened last year."

Here we go again.

"I know things got worse when I first started seeing him, Mom, but I promise he's done more good than harm in the long run. That breakdown I had last year was tragic and embarrassing, and ending up in the overnight ward was not ideal. I know that. But you don't need to keep bringing it up."

"No, honey, I mean—"

Leah rolled her eyes. "Mom, just let it go. We do this every month, and I just don't want to talk about it."

"Okay."

Another long pause. Leah released a pent-up breath.

"What do you want to talk about, then?" The snark in her mom's voice wasn't even veiled.

"Honestly, Mom, I'm pulling back into my building. I should let you go."

"Okay, bye then."

"Enjoy your haircut." The words felt heavy.

"Will do."

The call ended. Leah had fibbed about her location, and she drove in silence for another five minutes before she actually reached her parking lot.

It's always something with Mom...

She sighed.

But it's not like the dementia is her fault.

No one greeted her as she walked back to her desk, and the last ninety minutes of her day passed in almost complete silence, an occasional email notification the only sound interrupting her focus. She clicked "send" on a minor project moments before its five o'clock deadline, then shut down her laptop and walked silently back out to her car.

Rush hour traffic dragged her ten-mile commute into an hour-long ordeal, and by the time she got to her apartment, the back of her shirt was sticky with sweat. She ran through options for dinner in her head as she parked the car and watered her generously blooming forget-me-nots. It wasn't until she slipped the key into the lock that she noticed the telltale signs of someone moving in a few units down. A young woman about her age, curly dark hair dancing as she walked, passed by on her way back to the moving van in the parking lot.

Don't stop to say hello. Don't stop to say hello.

The footsteps stopped behind her and a cheery voice called out. "Hey! How's it going?"

Leah stifled a groan and turned around, faking a smile. "Hey, doing alright. How about you?"

"Doing great! Super excited to move in and get settled! My husband and I just got married last month, and his lease at his old place ends on Saturday, so we're just taking our time getting stuff over here. This seems like a great place!"

Leah thought about it for a moment. "Yeah, I mean, I guess it is. I've been here for the last year or so and don't have any complaints."

Move along, lady.

"I'm Sarah, by the way! Sarah Winfrey."

"Leah." Her tone was sharper than she meant it to be.

"Nice to meet you, Leah. What fun to have so many neighbors! Everyone here seems so lovely."

Leah shrugged. "I really couldn't tell you. I mostly keep to myself."

Take the hint. Take the hint.

"We'll have to have you over for dinner some time! No need to be lonely in a place like this!" Sarah handed Leah her cell phone, a new text message open on the screen.

Leah forced a fake laugh as she typed out her number and sent a message with her name. "Well, I've got to get dinner started. See you around, I guess."

"See you around! Bye Leah!" Sarah bounded off toward the parking lot. Leah couldn't shake the image of an Irish wolfhound puppy, a prospect that both amused her and filled her with anxiety.

There goes my peace and quiet. It's been nice while it lasted.

She puttered around the kitchen before deciding to take the easy route, heating up some leftover soup and half-watching a sitcom while also checking her email. The promised follow-up email from Peter included a link to submit a testimonial. Leah stared at the prompt for a long time.

The healthy functioning of your brain impacts every part of your life. How has your life improved since beginning treatment with the McNeill Institute?

Chapter 3

Scrambling out of her office a month later, Leah heard a knock on her door. She ignored it as she hastily packed her backpack, tossing her phone and wallet inside.

Her appointment started in twenty-two minutes. If she hurried, she might just make it. She'd lost track of time and had only just realized that she needed to be heading out to the car.

As she slung her backpack over her shoulder and closed her laptop, the knock came again. Behind her, the door cracked open just enough for someone to speak.

"Hello, I'm looking for Leonora Harvey."

Leah whipped around. "Wilder?"

The door opened further, and a spectacled Wilder Frederick walked into her office. His expression was uncharacteristically serious.

Leah's jaw dropped. "What are you doing here? Why aren't you— What is happening?"

"My name is Special Agent Robert McDowell. I'm with the Federal Bureau of Investigation. I'm here about a tip that was submitted last year by a Leonora Harvey."

Leah felt her heart rate speed up. "Wilder, is this a joke? This isn't funny."

He adjusted his glasses. "I assure you, this is no joke."

Annoyed and confused, Leah brushed past him and stepped into the hallway. "You've got the wrong Leonora Harvey, then. I've got to go; I'm running late for an appointment. Best of luck with your case."

He allowed her to shut the door to her office but matched pace with her as she walked out. "Are you certain that you didn't file anything regarding the McNeill Institute for Neurological Development?"

Leah scoffed. "About the Institute? Wilder, this isn't funny. You know I'll see you there in half an hour, and if you keep this up, I'll be late."

Leah pushed the call button for the elevator, but as they waited, she grew impatient and irritated. Wordlessly, she let herself into the stairwell and ran down the two flights to the lobby. Wilder, or whoever he was, did not follow her.

She made it to her car uninterrupted by any other unexpected visitors, but a line at the exit of the garage threw off her timing. She hurried down the side streets until the feeder road appeared in front of her, and then she sped onto the freeway entrance ramp and floored it.

So close. Can't be late again.

Exiting the freeway, she turned onto the clinic's street, its sign beckoning her. She saw the light ahead turn yellow, and as much as she wanted to speed through it, the cameras monitoring the intersection were sure to catch her and send her an automated ticket.

No point trading one fee for another.

Leah checked her clock again as she pulled to a stop at the red light, her left foot tapping non-stop. 2:57. She should just make it.

The light turned green, and Leah eased her foot off the brake and onto the gas. She flipped her blinker on. In her passenger-side window, a truck raced toward her. Her heartbeat quickened.

Is he going to stop?

Her body jerked sideways, whipping her head into the window just as the side airbag deployed. Headlights and brake lights blurred together across her field of vision. The car spun around in the intersection a full rotation and a half before skidding to a stop. Brakes squealed and horns blared around her as other drivers swerved to avoid a pile-up. Dazed, Leah looked around, waiting for the ringing in her ears to cease. Her head pounded, and she could feel her pulse throughout her entire body.

Someone knocked on her door. She jumped. The door began to open next to her and a face appeared. "Are... are you okay?"

Leah paused before responding. "I think so?"

"Oh thank God," the face replied, releasing a huge pent-up sigh. "I am so sorry."

Blinking heavily to clear her mind, Leah turned to see who was standing outside her car. A young man, maybe even just a teenager. Dirty blonde hair. Scared brown eyes. She realized he was still talking. "...going to kill me when she finds out I took her truck. I'm so glad you're okay, I think I would have been grounded for forever if you'd've been really hurt..."

She tuned him out again—his voice seemed so loud—and brought her attention to each part of her body in turn. Her heart pounded in her ears, and she felt cold for such a warm day. But other than the headache and a sore left shoulder, she seemed to be okay.

"... called the police, I think that's what I'm supposed to do, and here's my driver's license and my insurance cards, I grabbed my health insurance and my car insurance because no one ever told me which one, are you okay you haven't said anything and I..."

"I'm okay," Leah interrupted him. "Please stop talking."

"Ah, I'm sorry I'm just really nervous, I've never been in a wreck before, and I just got my driver's license like six months ago, and my mom is going to be furious that I wrecked her truck, she..."

"Please. Stop talking." Leah used her right hand to shield her eyes from the sun. "My head is killing me."

"I've got some ibuprofen in my car. I'll go grab it."

Leah tried to turn and watch as he hopped off. Her neck had other ideas, and she winced in pain before turning her whole body instead. A little smoke rose from the hood of the truck, and she was sure there would be damage to the passenger side of her car.

And all this after I just got my license in the mail last week.

Police sirens wailed in the distance as the teenager walked back to her car with a bottle of ibuprofen. He was on the phone, probably with his mom, if his apologetic tone was any indication. He held up two fingers, raising his eyebrows in a silent question. Leah held up three fingers, and he passed her three round pills before wandering back toward his truck. She didn't envy him the conversation he was having.

The officer asked a few questions about what had happened, noting that it seemed pretty cut and dry. He instructed both of them to take photos of the vehicles involved and facilitated the exchange of insurance information. When the anxious teenager asked whether he meant car insurance or health insurance, the officer suppressed a grin and tried to remain professional. Then, sirens still blaring, he stopped traffic at the intersection to allow both parties to drive off.

Sitting back in the driver's seat of her car, Leah noticed that the pain in her neck hadn't lessened at all. She put the car in gear and righted herself on the road. However, by the time she'd reached the first available driveway to turn off the road again, she'd come to the conclusion it would not be safe for her to drive.

Mom would have told me if she were in town. I don't have Wilder's phone number. If I call an Uber, I'll have to take another one to pick up my car tomorrow. Who else?

Leah sighed, pulled out her phone, and called Sarah. In spite of herself, she whispered a quiet thanks when it was answered on the first ring.

"Leah?" Sarah sounded confused.

"Hey, Sarah. What are you up to?"

"Not much for the rest of the day...What's up?"

Leah huffed. "I got into a car accident. Some dumb teenage boy was texting or something and ran a red light. He hit my car and spun me out... anyway, I've got terrible whiplash and don't think it's safe to drive home."

"I'm there." Sarah didn't even give Leah time to make the ask. "Let me ask Connor when he'll be home from the summer camp he's teaching, and maybe he can drive your car back here. Where are you?"

She looked around, searching for street signs.

Her eyes landed on the sign for the McNeill Institute, and she groaned. "I'm at my neurologist's office. That's where I was headed when I got hit. I'm going to have to pay the no-show fee. I hope they can reschedule... And I missed my phone date with my mom. She's going to be livid, or maybe just really confused and disoriented. I need to get

37

back with her as soon as I can." Leah felt her breath becoming shallow.

"You're spiraling," Sarah interrupted. "You can deal with all of that tomorrow. Text me the address. How far away is the office from the apartment?"

"Maybe half an hour when there's not traffic."

"Perfect. Connor said he'll be home in ten, so we'll head over soon. Sit and rest, but try not to fall asleep. If you've got a headache and whiplash, you might have a concussion, too. Put on an audiobook or something."

"Will do," Leah replied, feeling immensely relieved. "And thanks. I know this is a lot to ask."

"Not at all. What else are friends for?"

We're not friends. Don't go getting any ideas.

The call ended and Leah texted Sarah the address of the office. 4:02. She'd completely missed her appointment. Five missed calls and two voicemails from the office's number confirmed that she would, in fact, be required to pay the no-show fee. Shelby spoke quickly, almost too quickly to understand, and the voicemail felt rambling. It could have just been the concussion speaking, but Leah thought that Shelby sounded... scared.

Sarah's voice echoed in her mind that she could call and deal with it tomorrow, so she put on an audiobook. In spite of herself, Leah closed her eyes.

Another knock on the window startled her awake. Sarah's face smiled at her sympathetically through the glass, her brown eyes framed by her curly dark hair. Connor walked up behind her, still in his button down and tie.

"Hey, girl." Sarah's voice was muffled. Leah opened the door and paused the book, which was still droning on after lulling her to sleep.

"Hi." Leah winced at the evening sunlight and let Connor help her out of her car, handing him her keys. He walked her carefully to the passenger side of their CR-V before hopping into her sedan and adjusting the steering wheel. Sarah slid into the driver's seat next to her, and both cars pulled out of the parking lot.

"I'm going to take you to an urgent care," Sarah said, pulling directions up on her phone. Her tone indicated that this was not up for discussion. "How are you feeling?"

"I mean..." Leah grimaced. "I could be worse, but this headache gives me a bad feeling about tomorrow..."

"Oh yeah?" Sarah looked over at her.

"History of migraines. It's part of what got me coming here in the first place." She gestured to the clinic. "We finally got them under control, and now I'm sure they'll come raging back. Plus, I'm out of medication; I was supposed to get my refill today."

"Medication?" Sarah's eyes stayed fixed on the road, but Leah heard concern in her voice.

"Not really something I want to talk about."

"Fair enough." Sarah sounded hurt, and Leah rolled her eyes.

"I've been coming here for about a year for unexplained psychotic episodes." Leah finally offered. "I was told that if anyone could help me, it'd be Dr. Pierucci. He's got me in this clinical trial that's been helping manage my symptoms, which is great, but no diagnosis yet, which is what I really want. Everything else feels like triage. But I've never missed a session before"

Sarah didn't say anything, but she looked at Leah with pity in her eyes.

I'll tell you what to do with your stupid pity...

"I'm sure it'll be fine, Leah. You can call them tomorrow morning."

"We'll see."

But better pity than disgust, I guess.

They rode the rest of the way in silence. The doctor at the urgent care gave Leah the all-clear to return home, instructing her to ice her neck for a day or so, stay on top of the pain medication, and take it easy. When they finally pulled back into the apartment complex, Sarah walked Leah to the door of her unit.

"Thanks, Sarah." The visit to the urgent care had validated some of her exhaustion and softened her mood. "I don't know what I would have done if you two hadn't been able to come pick me up."

"You'd have figured something out. You're a tough cookie." Sarah winked.

Leah nodded, a twinge of some unpleasant feeling in her stomach.

"Well, I guess I'd better get to bed." She unlocked her door and stepped inside.

Sarah turned to leave. "Good night, Leah. I'll check in with you again tomorrow morning to see how you're feeling."

"Thanks, Sarah." Leah yawned.

The two parted ways, and Leah stepped into the sparsely furnished living room of her apartment. She tossed her backpack on the old gray couch and walked down the hall to the bathroom. While she brushed her teeth, she sent an email to her supervisor explaining that she'd need to take a day off.

Nothing to be done about it, but I'm sure I'll get an earful about it later.

She flicked on the bathroom light and poured herself a glass of water. She tried to call her mom but, unsurprisingly, was met with a notice about a full voicemail box.

Poor mom. She's probably so confused. I bet the rest of her day went totally downhill.

She fell into bed immediately and slept fitfully, tossing and turning all night long, plagued by nebulous dreams that dissipated like smoke from the hood of a pickup truck when she awoke, leaving her with a vague sense of unease.

***

Her head still throbbed when the sun rose, tendrils of soft morning light creeping around her curtains. The clock read 7:53, and for a moment, Leah panicked. Then she remembered that she'd called in sick, so she took another dose of painkillers and went back to sleep. Finally, around 10:00, she awoke. Her headache had subsided—temporarily, she was certain—and her muscles, while still stiff, were no longer screaming in pain.

Leah moved slowly to get out of bed, careful not to turn her neck too quickly or too far. She prepared a cup of coffee and opened the windows along the front side of her apartment, letting in the morning summer air before the heat and humidity became oppressive.

After enjoying her coffee, Leah finally decided to call the Institute.

"Hello, thank you for calling the McNeill Institute for Neurological Development; this is Shelby. How may I help you?" asked a friendly voice on the other end of the line.

"Hi, Shelby. It's Leah Harvey. I was in a car accident yesterday and missed my appointment, so I need to reschedule."

"Oh, yes. I can definitely help you with that. Can you give me your full name and date of birth?"

Leah obliged and steeled herself for the lecture.

"Leonora Harvey, you said?"

"Yes ma'am. I was scheduled for a three o'clock session yesterday and due for a medication refill."

"Yes, I see that." The receptionist paused again. She sounded pensive, and Leah assumed that some distraction in the office was dividing her attention. "Okay, Ms. Harvey, I assume you're hoping to come in as soon as possible to get that refill, correct?"

"Yes. I'm already off next Tuesday for another appointment. Do you have anything that afternoon?"

There was a sound of clattering keys on the other end. "Umm... It looks like we're full on Tuesday... Please hold." A pause. Leah expected to be transferred to a holding line, but instead heard a muffled conversation, as if Shelby had simply placed her palm over the handset. She strained to make out what they were saying.

"...Leah Harvey... monitoring her carefully... Tuesday... cancel the three o'clock... need to prioritize..."

"Ms. Harvey, are you still there?" Leah was startled by Shelby's sudden return.

"Yes?" Her voice wavered.

"I can make Tuesday work. Would three o'clock still be the best time for you?"

Leah hesitated. "I can do another day if you're full on Tuesday."

"No, no, we'll make it work. It's critical that we get you in as quickly as possible."

"Oh, okay," Leah replied uneasily. "Then yes, three sounds good. Is it bad if I'm late on a treatment?"

Shelby sounded flustered. "Oh, well, no, it's just that... well, since you're participating in a clinical trial, Dr. Pierucci wants to make sure we do things by the book."

"I see."

There was a pause as each woman waited for the other to speak. Eventually Shelby said, "Well, I've got you scheduled for three o'clock on Tuesday. Is there anything else I can do for you?"

"I believe I owe a no-show fee for missing yesterday's appointment."

"Yes, I see that here on your account. Would you like to pay now or wait until you come in?"

Leah blinked. "Oh, Tuesday would be better for me, if you're in no rush."

"I'll make a note on your file, then. We look forward to seeing you, Ms. Harvey. Please let us know if you need anything in the meantime."

"I will. Thank you."

The line disconnected. Something about Shelby's tone left a knot in the pit of Leah's stomach. After noting the appointment in her calendar, she tried to return to the peaceful mood she'd enjoyed all morning, but she couldn't shake the feeling that something wasn't right.

She spent an hour puttering around her apartment, alphabetizing books, dusting under the couch, and researching reputable mechanics to repair the damage to her car. Her limbs felt tight, muscles clenched, no matter how hard she willed them to relax.

A knock on the door startled her, and her heart skipped a beat. She wasn't expecting anyone. Who would be coming by her apartment? Who even knew she was home? She crept toward the door and brought her eye to the peep hole. Sarah's wide-eyed face stared back at her through the peep hole. Leah opened the door slowly, her heart still pounding.

"Hey, girl, I brought you some food. I hope you like tacos? My lunch break isn't that long, so I can't stay, but I hope you're feeling be—"

Her voice trailed off as she noticed Leah's pale skin and hunted gaze. "Are you... is everything okay?"

"Yeah, I'm fine. Just still a little out of it." Leah took the bag from her, not wanting to talk about her inexplicable anxiety. "Thanks for lunch."

"Of course..." Sarah's tone was confused, drained of its usual warmth. "Well, I guess just get some rest. I'll plan to come back this evening and check on you. Hope you were able to reschedule your appointment." She offered a half-wave and turned back toward the parking lot.

Leah waved back, closing the door behind her as Sarah walked off, flipping the lock back and forth seven times. She sat down to eat but was interrupted by the buzz of her phone in her pocket. The number wasn't saved, but it looked familiar, and the 'Washington DC' scrolling beneath the numbers jogged something in Leah's memory, but she couldn't quite put her finger on what exactly it was.

Suddenly, as if from a half-remembered dream, she heard a familiar voice in her mind.

"My name is Special Agent Robert McDowell. I'm with the Federal Bureau of Investigation. I'm here about a tip that was submitted last year by a Leonora Harvey."

Chapter 4

As Leah watched the number scroll across the screen of her phone, her vision spun. Her initial sense of unease had been fully replaced by the weight of anxiety constricting her lungs, leaving every breath feeling tight and insufficient. She sent the call to voicemail without thinking.

Was I visited by an FBI agent yesterday? Or was it Wilder? Was the whole thing a hallucination?

The smell of tacos wafted towards her, offering the promise of comfort, grounding her, reminding her that this fear was not normal.

"...Leah Harvey... monitoring her carefully... Tuesday... cancel the three o'clock... need to prioritize..."

The receptionist's muffled words played on repeat in her mind, driving her anxious spiral deeper. Even aside from the possibility that she'd been caught off guard by a very lifelike hallucination, she couldn't shake the feeling that something was deeply wrong.

"There is no FBI Agent stalking you," she said aloud, rubbing her left ring finger with her right thumb until her skin began to feel stretched and warm. "There is nothing sinister going on at the McNeill Institute. You are just recovering from trauma."

Physically shaking her head, as if to dislodge the troublesome thoughts, Leah opened the bag Sarah had left with her. At the very top of the bag was a note scribbled on a napkin.

Leah,
In case you don't answer the door: I got you some lunch and hope you're having a restful day off. I'll check in with you again this evening. Feel better soon.

Sarah

Beneath the note were four tacos wrapped in silver foil, more napkins, and a handful of tiny condiment cups full of salsa. She carefully removed everything from the bag and laid it out on her tiny round table. Leah went to fold the bag flat but was surprised when something bulky still lay in the bottom. She pulled out a sleek black pen with silver accents and laid it out on the table with the food, flattening the bag and folding it over on itself.

I guess Sarah accidentally dropped this in here.

The first taco was gone in moments. Leah hadn't realized how hungry she was. The second taco followed quickly. She carefully removed the silver wrapper from the third taco, ironing out every last crease with her fingers, when the pen she'd found in the bag caught her eye once again. A horrified thought entered her mind.

Can't listening devices be disguised as pens?

A quick search revealed that yes, they could. Furthermore, the images she could find online looked eerily like the pen lying on her table. Her heart rate picked up again and her mind went blank for a moment.

What do I do with this? Could Sarah be bugging me?

She stared at the pen in front of her in disbelief, her heart pounding.

What could she want from me that she can't just ask me?

Her eyes darted around the room, flitting between the photograph of her and her mom at her college graduation and the pile of mail she hadn't opened.

If that FBI agent wasn't a hallucination, maybe Sarah is working with him? What could she want from me?

Without thinking, Leah picked up the pen, opened her front door, and slid the pen into the pot of forget-me-nots on her thin strip of patio. She wanted to break it or throw it away, but she didn't want to risk losing it in case she needed it as evidence.

When she sat back down, she paused a moment before finishing the meal.

There's no way...

She couldn't even finish the thought, but then, she couldn't not.

There's no way Sarah would have poisoned this, right?

Her right leg bounced up and down incessantly on the laminate floor of her dining area.

Surely she doesn't want me dead. We've only known each other for a month. I know I haven't been the friendliest neighbor, but... No, no. There's no way.

Pulling out her phone, Leah typed Sarah's name into her browser and skimmed the search results. Her social media profiles went back ten years, showing graduations and family vacations and engagement photos and her recent marriage to Connor. It didn't take her long to find a post with Sarah's maiden name, which led Leah down the further rabbit hole of her high school and college

47

newspapers. If she was working with the FBI, she at least wasn't using an assumed identity.

After ten minutes of staring into her screen and hoping for peace of mind, Leah glanced back at the two silver wrappers already lying on her table, shiny and wrinkle-free.

Even if they are poisoned, I've already eaten half of them. Might as well enjoy the rest.

She did, and the last two tacos disappeared as quickly as the first two. Feeling worlds better, Leah stepped into the living room and put on a show. She twisted open the blinds to let the afternoon sunlight in, then curled up with a blanket on one end of her couch. The textured gray fabric offered a satisfying scritch-scritch noise as she picked at it with her nails.

As the theme song and opening montage played, she closed her eyes and focused on the rising and falling of her chest.

Breathe in.

Hold.

Breathe out.

Hold.

She felt her muscles begin to relax, and she tucked her blanket under her toes and wrapped it over her shoulders. She nearly jumped out of her seat when her phone pinged a few minutes later, alerting her to a new email. She glanced down at the notification.

Shelby Downs – MIND
Managing Symptoms between Treatments

She picked up the phone, a frown on her face.

Could all of this really be from missing my treatment? Would that short of a delay cause a relapse this intense?

48

She slid open the notification and scanned the email with rabid desperation.

Leah,

I wanted to send over some resources for you in case you experience any withdrawal symptoms due to the missed treatment and medication. This is the best handout I could find. I hope it's helpful. I intended to chat with Dr. Pierucci to discuss specific protocol regarding a delayed treatment or missed medications; however, he will be out of the office and unavailable for the rest of the afternoon. Please call the on-call line if you have an emergency over the weekend, and if not, we will see you on Tuesday.

Sincerely,
Shelby Downs
Customer Relations
McNeill Institute for Neurological Development

Leah sighed. She briefly glanced at the attachment, but none of the information was new to her. Shelby's tone in the email was nothing but professional. Was it possible Leah had imagined the frantic note in her voice on the phone earlier? Could all of this paranoia and anxiety be simply the result of an overactive imagination going through withdrawal?

The possibility was comforting, and she did her best to lean into it, but the nagging voice in her mind refused to let its suspicions drop. Even if she was willing to admit, now, that the tacos were certainly not poisoned, the eavesdropping was still technically on the table. The chatter of the TV continued as Leah set her phone down and slipped into a restless sleep.

When she woke, a text box on her TV asked if she was still watching. The afternoon was almost over, and the light in her apartment was shifting, at once warmer and softer.

She stood up and walked the length of the apartment a couple times, just to get her blood moving again and shake off the grogginess from her nap, checking on things as she did so. The books in her living room were still alphabetized by the author's last name. Her work clothes hung in length order, with shirts on the left and dresses on the right. All the flannel napkins in the basket on the table were facing the same direction. The front door was still locked. She flipped the deadbolt a few times, just for good measure.

It felt like an age had passed since her relaxed morning, and the stiffness in her neck had returned. Blessedly, her headache hadn't reared its head again, a realization that startled her.

Suddenly, the possibility of being bugged seemed much more likely than the possibility of withdrawal. Surely she'd have developed a crippling migraine if she really were going through withdrawal. Or, if not a migraine, then an intense hallucination. Sarah's note still lay on the table, one sentence jumping out at her in a way it hadn't before.

I'll check in with you again this evening.

It had seemed totally innocent earlier; she hadn't thought anything of it. Shortly after she'd first read the note, she'd gotten distracted by the pen-shaped listening device. But now, after the offending writing utensil had been relegated to a safer place, the implications of that line cascaded over her.

Why does she keep coming back? Is someone paying her?

Leah picked up the note and held it up to the chandelier in the dining room, debating whether or not to pull out the blow dryer to try and reveal a secret message. She shook her head to dislodge the thought and set the napkin back down.

Surely she doesn't mean she's just stopping by for a visit, right? It's not like we're all that close...

Leah looked around her sparsely decorated apartment, in no mood for company.

I can't be hosting neighbors for casual coffee chats several times a day! I need to rest!

At that last sentence, her brain paused, forced to wrestle with the reality that she had done nothing but rest for a full day.

When she really thought about the ideas racing through her mind at a million miles a minute, they seemed ridiculous, bordering on insane. The explanation offered by the clinic made sense: she hadn't had a chance to wean off the medication she'd been taking, and the treatment was intended to be administered at particular intervals.

So why can't I shake the feeling that something is horribly, tragically wrong?

As afternoon turned into evening, Leah began to think less about Sarah and more about dinner. She closed the blinds, although the early summer sun was far from set. She opened her fridge several times, peering into it with the halfhearted hope that some new and delightful meal would have spontaneously materialized since the last time she'd checked. Or, at least, that the constellation of unrelated ingredients left from her most recent grocery run might suddenly reveal a recipe to her.

She finally settled on a peanut butter and jelly sandwich. Piling chips on a paper plate beside a handful of baby carrots, she mentally prepared herself for Sarah's visit.

Just as she sat down on the couch with her plate in one hand and the remote in the other, she heard a knock on the door. Once again it startled her, drawing her attention out of her troubled mind and back to reality. She crept over as quietly as she could.

Stupid. You don't need to tiptoe in your own house.

Sarah's concerned face stared back at her through the peephole. Leah paused, debating with herself whether or not to open the door.

The knock came again, louder, followed by Sarah's muffled voice. "Leah, are you awake? Leah, I'm a little worried about you." A third knock, loud enough to rattle the window, finally convinced Leah that there would be no avoiding the conversation.

She took a deep breath and opened the door. Sarah's face looked genuinely relieved.

"Oh thank God. Are you okay? You seemed off earlier. I've been worrying about you all afternoon. How are you feeling?"

"I'm still really stiff when the meds wear off, but no headache or anything."

"Well, that's good, isn't it? You were really worried about that yesterday."

"Yeah," Leah responded, pensive. "Yeah, I guess I was."

The lull in the conversation dragged out, quickly going from tolerable to awkward to uncomfortable.

Sarah eventually spoke up. "Can I come in and sit down? I want to hear how your day has gone."

"What?" Leah's thoughts had been racing again. "Oh, yeah, sure." She led Sarah over to the living room and sat down. With one hand, she picked up her sandwich; with the other, she mindlessly scratched at the couch.

"So... how was your day?" Sarah finally asked hesitantly.

"You're looking at it. Haven't done much. The morning was lovely, but I've been feeling out of it all afternoon."

"I can tell," Sarah said.

A little rude to say the quiet part out loud...

She didn't say anything in response.

"Oh, by the way," Sarah added, her voice stiff. "Did you find a pen in that paper bag when I brought your lunch over? I can't find it and am really hoping I didn't lose it. It was a gift from Connor."

Leah froze.

"Leah? Are you okay? Did you hear me?"

Leah hesitated for a moment, feeling the weight of decision. Mechanically, without actively making the choice, she walked to the door and retrieved the pen from the flowerpot.

Trust it is.

Fear clawed at her throat as she walked back to Sarah.

Sarah is just a neighbor. She's a little friendly and a lot to deal with, but she's not evil.

The affirmations didn't feel like much, but they were a start. Leah handed the pen back to Sarah wordlessly as she sat back down.

"How did it end up outside?"

"So, uh..." Leah said sheepishly. "I hid it in my flower pot because I was afraid you were bugging me."

Sarah burst out laughing, a laugh that broke the tension in the room and acted as a balm to Leah's tired heart.

"A bug? Like, a spy gadget or something?"

A sheepish grin spread across Leah's face and she nodded. "Like a spy gadget or something."

"Leah, that's the most ridiculous thing I've ever heard." Her eyebrows were arched in disbelief.

Leah felt her hackles rise. "Anxiety and paranoia were two of my most constant symptoms before I started getting treated."

"Huh," Sarah nodded. "You thought I was bugging your apartment, and you thought I'd be so obvious as to stick a fake pen in a takeout bag? But you didn't think to take the dang thing apart and check whether or not it had a bug in it?"

Leah averted her eyes, feeling her cheeks flush. "No. I didn't think of that."

"Well, just to ease your mind, go ahead and take it apart. I'm going to give Connor a call and see when he'll be home. Is it okay if he stops by? You seem like you need some real human contact today."

"That..." Leah hesitated. "Honestly, I think I just need to go to bed. I've been... really in my head." Leah continued to avoid eye contact with Sarah, both out of embarrassment and because she was focused on disassembling the pen carefully enough to put it back together when she was finished.

"I can tell," Sarah said again. She didn't call Connor. Instead, she sat in silence and watched Leah take the pen apart, examine its components, and put it back together. They made uncomfortable small talk for a few more minutes until Connor texted Sarah to ask where she was.

As Leah walked Sarah to the door, she mentioned in passing that the "I'll check back in this evening" comment in Sarah's note had triggered the nth anxiety spiral of the day. She immediately regretted it.

"Oh, Leah, I'm so sorry." Sarah's whole face fell.

"No, no! How could you have known?"

"I guess I couldn't have." Sarah had stepped one foot out the door already, and pulled the other over the threshold before offering a quick wave. "Good night, Leah. Sleep well. I'll plan..." She paused pointedly before changing her words. "Let me know if you need anything this weekend."

Leah fell into bed ten minutes later, drained from the demands of the evening.

I never heard from Mom today. I hope she's doing okay.

Chapter 5

Leah awoke to a text message from her mom.

> Hey honey. Sorry for the late reply. I've been busy
> this week and it totally slipped my mind that we
> were supposed to call. I hope you're feeling better
> after your accident.

Classic Mom. Acting like she has a lot going on. Telling me that she doesn't need me.

> No worries, I know how it goes. Feeling better this
> morning. I rescheduled my appointment for
> Tuesday at 3:00, should I call you on my way back
> to work?

> Sure, that sounds great. I miss you and want to hear
> all about the week you've had. Sounds like it's been
> a big one—what a week to miss our regular chat.

She can't tell me that these calls mean the world to her, but I know they do. There's a reason she keeps picking up every month.

***

The next few days exhausted Leah. When Tuesday finally rolled around, her nerves were worn raw from days of intense anxiety, paranoia, and compulsions, and it took every ounce of willpower in her to step over the threshold of the clinic. Her legs were stiff, and her heart thumped in her chest as she approached the check-in desk.

Shelby looked up from the desk. "Hi Ms. Harvey, how can I help you?"

Leah forced a pained smile. "I need to check in for my three o'clock appointment."

A slight pause. Leah's heart stopped. Shelby clicked around her laptop for a moment. "Oh, that's right. Leonora is the first name, correct?"

"Yes."

What does she know?

She smiled. "I've got you checked in. You can go ahead and take a seat, and they'll come get you in a few minutes."

Shelby looked down at her computer, but looked back up in confusion when Leah didn't walk away. "Is there anything else?"

Leah blinked. "Um... I think I owe a fee for missing my last appointment. When we spoke on the phone, you told me that I could wait to pay it today?"

The receptionist paused, her brows knit. "I'm not seeing a balance on your account. Stop by on your way out; I'll double-check that I'm not missing anything."

It was everything Leah could do not to turn tail and race out of the clinic in that moment. She watched, as if at a distance, as her rational mind fought with the paranoia for control of her will.

No late fee? That has to mean something. No one would have just... paid it for me.

Shelby stared at her expectantly. Shaking her head, Leah forced herself to walk to an empty chair in the waiting room and sit down. Glancing around the room, she didn't

58

recognize any of the faces she recognized from her normal Thursday appointments.

I wish Wilder were here.

She felt her cheeks redden and returned her thoughts to her conversation at the desk.

It's probably just a glitch in the system. You're overreacting. You can pay it before you leave. It's not a big deal.

She pulled out her phone and tried to find something to distract her, but nothing held her attention.

But what if it still isn't showing up in an hour? What is she going to do, reboot the entire system?

This internal wrestling hadn't stopped by the time she was called to the back. Glancing around to see if there was anyone watching her, Leah stood up and followed the redheaded technician into the bowels of the clinic. Peter.

Once they'd settled into the treatment room, he unlocked the desktop computer and launched into the same set of questions she'd been asked at every session.

"Good afternoon, Ms. Harvey. How were your symptoms this month?"

"Bad." Peter looked up from his computer, one eyebrow arched. "Well, they were fine until I got into a car accident, and then things got really bad."

He frowned. "Can you elaborate on what you mean by 'things got really bad'? What, specifically, changed?"

"A lot of anxiety and paranoia. Some compulsions," she replied. "It all started after the accident and after I missed my appointment last week, so it's hard to know if it's maybe just from missing the session."

He nodded. "Certainly could be; I'll make a note of it. Have you experienced any other health issues, aside from those related to your car accident, since last month?"

"No." She paused. "Oh wait—I forgot. I did have one incident that I think might have been a hallucination? I'm not sure? It was before the accident. It was super detailed, and it didn't feel like a hallucination, but I was in a rush to get here, so I wasn't paying much attention, you know?" The words tumbled out of her.

She looked up at Peter. He had glanced away from his computer and watched her expectantly.

"You know Wilder Frederick?" She felt the color rising in her face again. "The guy who's usually here at the same time as me?"

Peter nodded. Leah looked away from him, picking at a hangnail as she continued. "You're going to laugh, but I would have sworn that he came by my office asking if I'd submitted something to the FBI about..." She wracked her memory, trying to recall the substance of the conversation. "Oh, wait, shoot, it was about y'all. About this place."

Peter's eyes widened for a moment, but he quickly resumed a bored expression.

She continued. "It was something about a tip from someone with my name about something happening here at the Institute. I can hardly remember it now." She raised her hand to cover her mouth. "Maybe it was just a hallucination after all. I told him I had no idea what he was talking about, and then I got in the car to come here, and that's when the wreck happened... I don't know. It felt super realistic, but that's too outrageous to be true, right?"

"Mhmm," Peter said absentmindedly as he typed away at his keyboard. "I'll get these notes sent over to the doctor while you're hooked up to the console, and he'll be in to see you when we're finished." With a few more keystrokes, Leah watched the screen go blank. Peter stepped over to the orthodontic chair she was seated on, and she felt her heart rate begin to rise again.

Deep breaths. You know this is good for you. You're safe.

The standard blood pressure check reflected Leah's elevated pulse, but the result wasn't high enough to scare Peter out of the treatment. He strapped the cuffs around her wrists, and for the first time in over a year, Leah wondered if she would be strong enough to break free of them.

Breathe in. Breathe out.

He placed the helmet on her head and reclined her chair.

Falling. I'm falling. He's going to kill me.

The falling stopped and the mechanical whirring began. He double-checked her helmet and cuffs, and then he stepped back to his computer.

Calm down, Leah; he's not going to kill you. You've done this a dozen times.

Through the helmet speakers, Leah heard Peter's voice. "Alright, Ms. Harvey, you're all set. Feel free to close your eyes and rest, and I'll be back in about half an hour. You know the drill."

The familiar hum of the console felt comfortable, and Leah began to feel the anxiety's vice grip on her chest loosen. She let out a deep sigh, realizing as she did so how tense her shoulders had been.

But he's a fool if he thinks I'm going to close my eyes.

Her heart slowed. Her breathing deepened. In spite of herself, she closed her eyes. It did feel nice to rest after hardly sleeping all weekend.

The next thing she knew, Peter gently tapped her awake as he loosed the arm restraints.

"I hope you enjoyed your nap, Ms. Harvey," he said. His tone was kind, and the smallest hint of a grin played about the corners of his mouth. "We're all finished here, so I'll go ahead and get you settled in the exam room, and Dr. Pierucci will come and see you in just a few minutes."

Still groggy, Leah nodded. Her mind slowly geared back up, threatening to return immediately to the rapid-fire thoughts driven by the anxiety of the past weekend.

How could I let my guard down that much?

She followed Peter down another hallway and into another room. He held the door for her and followed her in, quietly opening the visit notes on the room's desktop computer while Leah set down her bag and looked around. A moment later—the promptness surprised her—Dr. Pierucci entered the room. He seemed to fill it.

"Ms. Harvey," he said. His face bore a smile, but there was something in his voice that frightened Leah. "I was glad to hear that you had rescheduled your treatment so promptly."

"Yes, Shelby was very helpful in getting me in today." Leah resisted the urge to stretch and roll her shoulders, suddenly aware of how tight her whole body felt.

Dr. Pierucci nodded, observing her carefully. "So how are you feeling? It was unfortunate that you had to miss your previous appointment."

Leah's shoulders slouched. "Yes, I wanted to ask you about that. Is everything going to be okay? How much will this set me back? I felt like it was just setback after setback all weekend, and when I called to reschedule, Shelby sounded anxious to get me in quickly."

Dr. Pierucci frowned. "That remains to be seen. Your case is unique and, therefore, unpredictable. For some patients, a delay like this would be extremely disruptive; for others, it would not be noticed at all. But fear not," he smiled. "We will continue to support you throughout your recovery as much as is needed."

"Fair enough, I guess," Leah sighed. "I've just been so anxious the last few days, and..."

"Anxious?" Dr. Pierucci had never before interrupted her or cut her off.

Leah stared at him for a moment before continuing. "Oh, yeah, I thought I told Peter that. It was really intense."

Dr. Pierucci leaned forward. "You know, Ms. Harvey, perhaps your missing your appointment last week will prove beneficial after all. This is an important note for the research team. Mr. Bennett, ensure that a detailed explanation of Ms. Harvey's symptoms is uploaded to the clinical trial database. You may want to spend some additional time conversing with her about the specifics."

"Yessir." Peter replied without looking up from his computer.

Leah's stomach curled as she prepared to ask her last question. "I did want to ask you: how much longer do you expect I'll need this treatment? Is this, like, a basic maintenance thing that I'll stay on indefinitely, or is there a set end date you have in mind? I guess maybe it depends on the diagnosis..."

A storm grew on Dr. Pierucci's face. His eyes narrowed and his brows knit. "Ms. Harvey, I am certain we discussed this in detail when you began the trial, but I will reiterate. We expect to see you monthly for a full two years before we can even consider spacing out the treatments or weaning you off of your medication. To do so ahead of schedule would be most unwise."

"Of course," Leah said, her tone apologetic. She rubbed absentmindedly at the webbing between her third and fourth fingers. "I'm sorry I forgot what you said before."

"Apology accepted. Now, Ms. Harvey, I have quite a full schedule today and must attend to my next patient. Thank you for your presence, and I will see you next month."

He nodded, stood, and walked out of the room. His exit left a tangible void. Both Leah and Peter watched him depart, pausing for a moment before attempting to resume anything like conversation.

Peter glanced up from his keyboard. "Well, Ms. Harvey, I'll email you that patient survey." He paused, anticipated her objection, and resumed, "Even if it turns out that they're related to your car accident and not to the treatment, it's important that we note everything in real time. Once your participation in the trial has concluded, you'll have a chance to review your notes and add any additional thoughts. So don't worry about editorializing too much."

Leah exhaled. "Thank you, Peter. That's very helpful."

He nodded. "That's all I have for you today; you can pick up your printout at the front desk, and I've gone ahead and ordered your medication refill, so make sure you stop by the pharmacy before you leave. Is there anything else I can help you with?"

"No. I appreciate you all making time for me in the schedule today."

"Of course, Ms. Harvey." He opened the door as he spoke, ushering Leah back into the hallway and gesturing toward the lobby. "We'll see you next month. Stay well."

"Thank you. You too," she replied as she walked away, unable to stop the force of habit.

Behind her, Peter snorted. Leah whirled around, but he had turned to walk in the opposite direction and gave no indication that he was paying attention to her.

Was he laughing at me?

Still lost in thought, Leah followed the hallway down its length and stepped back into the lobby.

Shelby waved her over. "Ready to check out?"

"Yes ma'am." Leah walked over to the desk. "It's Leonora Harvey."

"Of course, Ms. Harvey." She didn't look up from her computer. "I'm glad you were able to make it over today."

"Thank you so much for getting me in so quickly."

"Of course. I know the doctor was anxious to get you in as soon as possible. He didn't stop reminding me about it all of Thursday afternoon."

There was a pause in the conversation as both women tried to act like Shelby's last comment had been left unsaid. She clicked a few things on her computer before standing up and looking at Leah. "Anyway, I'll get your summary printed and you'll be good to go."

"Don't..." Leah hesitated. "Don't I need to pay my fee?"

Shelby glanced down at her screen. "Nope, it looks like it's already been paid."

"I didn't pay it..."

She shrugged. "Do you have auto-pay set up on your account? Sometimes patients forget that they've enabled it. Our system won't let you pay the same bill twice."

Leah grimaced. "That must be it," she said eventually. "I'll double-check my bank statement when I get home."

"Sounds good," Shelby replied, standing up and stepping a few feet away to grab her printout. "Here you go, Leah. We'll see you again soon."

"See you soon..."

Leah tried to keep her steps measured and her expression calm. She fought the desire to sprint out the main exit and bypass the pharmacy entirely. As she waited in line to pick up her medication, her foot began tapping rapidly on the ground in a futile attempt to release some of the nervous energy building up in her bones.

She glanced at her watch. 4:07.

The man in front of her and the woman in front of him both turned around several times, looking down at her feet, their expressions a mix of annoyance and pity.

Another glance at the watch. 4:09.

Phone out. Scroll through social media. Nothing of interest. Phone away.

Watch. 4:11.

Why is this taking so long?

Once again, Leah was ready to abandon the line entirely, but for the minuscule hope that her anxiety and paranoia were symptoms of medication withdrawal. She took a deep breath: in through the nose, hold, out through the mouth. The frantic need to move her body began to subside, giving way, if not to peace, at least to stillness.

4:15.

Finally, after another ten agonizing minutes, Leah walked out the door of the clinic, medication in one hand and notes in the other. She opened the door of her car, threw her things onto the passenger seat, and closed her eyes for a moment. The engine revved and a voice reverberated around her:

"...bringing you the latest update on the case of Jorge Rodriguez, who disappeared from the local Scarlett Bay Correctional Facility last year..."

She pushed the power button for her car's audio system. For a moment, silence reigned. Then, like an addict trying to satisfy a craving, she grabbed desperately for the bag from the pharmacy and ripped it open. As she turned the cap on the bottle, her eyes breezed past the visit summary she'd picked up on her way out.

Written in all-capital letters across the top of the printout was a message that stopped her in her tracks:

DO NOT RESUME MEDICATION.

Chapter 6

Leah did a double-take, almost dropping the bottle in shock. Carefully replacing the lid, she set the orange bottle in her car cup holder and picked up the sheet of paper. A sigh escaped her chest as she began to read.

DO NOT RESUME MEDICATION

Treatment delayed. Several days of medication missed. Intense withdrawal symptoms: anxiety, paranoia, compulsions.
Technician recommended ceasing medication use. Withdrawal symptoms expected to wane within 24-48 hours of appointment.
Participation in clinical trial to be reevaluated at next visit.

"Is... is this my printout?" Leah said aloud, to herself, alone in her car. "None of this is familiar."

She scanned the page, looking for some proof that Shelby had given her another patient's notes, but it was her name listed at the top of the page.

Patient Name: Leonora Harvey
Technician: Peter Bennett
Scribe: Peter Bennett

This is... the exact opposite of everything Dr. Pierucci said to me. Should I call the office back and see if I can talk to Peter?

Her heart rate responded with an emphatic 'no,' and she realized with surprise that the contents of the printout hadn't caused any anxiety at all. Confusion, certainly, mingled with something that might have been relief. It wasn't until she had considered fact-checking that her body had responded with alarm.

Interesting.

Leah meticulously double-checked the lid on the orange plastic bottle resting in her cup holder and slipped it back into its paper bag. She slipped her phone out of her backpack and dialed her mom's number as she pulled out of the parking lot. It rang for a long time, and Leah began to worry, when the line finally clicked.

Leah breathed a sigh of relief. "Mom?"

"Oh, hi Leah! I forgot that we were going to call today, and Linda rescheduled our book club for this afternoon. It's the first time in months that I've actually read the whole book, so I don't want to miss it. Can I call you later?"

Leah blinked and said nothing.

"Are you still there? Is everything okay?" A note of concern crept into her mom's voice.

Leah shook her head. "Oh, yeah, everything's okay. I just didn't remember you joining a book club with Linda."

"Really? We've been meeting every month for probably five years now! I know I must've mentioned it before!"

Dementia is such an odd illness.

"Sounds good, Mom. Well I'll let you go. Tell Linda and the rest of the ladies that I say hello."

"I will. And I'll call you later. Love you, dear. Bye."

The line clicked again, leaving Leah in silence. As she pulled up to a stoplight, she opened her text thread with Sarah, re-reading her neighbor's most recent message.

Leah, I've been thinking a lot about what you said as I was leaving the other night, about my constant checking in and the anxiety it caused. I'm sorry that the sudden attention felt stifling. Connor reminded me today that this isn't the first time I've jumped into 'helping mode' without asking whether the help is wanted. I know you've tried to write off the anxiety as just a response to everything that's happened in the last few days, but I think it's based in a real feeling and I want to be respectful of that. I'm here if you need me, but I'll try to back off a little, especially now that you're doing better.

A twinge of guilt struck her as she remembered Sarah's crestfallen face during their last conversation. She typed out a message to Sarah, but hesitated for a moment before hitting send.

Can I give you a call?

Within a minute, the read receipt appeared, followed by the little bubble that showed that Sarah was typing.

Give me five.

Leah started her car but remained in her parking spot. She scanned the rest of her printout for a few minutes. Sarah called her just as she flipped to the last page. Her tone was quieter than normal. "Hey Leah. How are you?"

Perhaps overcompensating, Leah tried to imbue her response with enthusiasm. "Sarah, I had my appointment for today, and you're not going to guess what just happened."

"No, what?"

"Everything seemed normal while I was in there, but I just sat down in my car and saw that the first line at the top of my printout—you know, the one they give you with the notes?—in big capital letters is 'Don't take your meds.'"

"Wait, what?" Sarah responded quickly.

"Yeah. Every single thing in my printout is the exact opposite of what Dr. Pierucci told me to do."

"That's bizarre." Sarah didn't sound convinced.

"It is." Leah paused for a long moment, weighing her next words carefully. "I'm kind of considering not taking my medication for a few days just to see what happens."

"Leah, that's a really bad idea. Look, I know we've only known each other for a couple of weeks, but..." She exhaled loudly. "You were not stable this weekend."

A guilty half-laugh escaped Leah's throat.

"No, Leah, I'm not joking," Sarah insisted. "Have you called the office to see if they know what's going on?"

"I considered it... Well, I considered calling to see if maybe this printout was for someone else, but then I saw my name at the top of the page. It's the same technician I've had since day one, so it's hard to imagine he'd get me mixed up with someone else."

She paused for a moment, lost in thought. "All weekend, I was desperate to get to this appointment. I was hoping that maybe all my symptoms were just withdrawal from the treatment, and I'd be back to normal as soon as I got back under the helmet. But the treatment didn't change anything, and then to see Peter suggest that maybe it's from missing my medication? I'm already starting to feel more normal... I don't want to be on these pills forever, and I just keep asking myself if there's any chance that this could be real. Even a tiny chance."

"Leah, I'm not qualified to have this conversation. You should, you know, ask your actual doctor."

Leah sighed, struggling to articulate her thoughts. "I should. I definitely should. But... I don't know, Sarah. Something deep in my gut says to follow this one. There's something going on here, and I don't know if I'll be able to stop before I get to the bottom of it."

"What do you mean?"

"It's hard to explain. Just... an intuition. This weekend left me feeling like someone had pulled up my anchor, and with no wind in my sails, I was just floundering. This is the wind I've been waiting for."

"And what if you keep skipping your medicine and then you really go off the deep end? Are you going to have enough wherewithal to get back on it?"

"I mean, yeah." Leah fumbled her words. "If it's nothing, then I'll just resume my medication and nothing will change. But I'll at least have peace of mind about it." She paused for a moment. "And if not? If it turns out that somehow getting off the medication makes it worse... I don't know, Sarah. I don't know what I would do."

Leah shifted her car into gear and eased out of the Institute's parking lot. Behind her, a blue sky shone out, but in her front windshield, the sky began to darken with heavy rain clouds.

Sarah sighed heavily, the sound scratching through the speakers. "Well, at least put a date on the calendar right now so that you know when you're going to call it quits and start your medication again."

Leah sighed. "You're right. I'll put it on my calendar for a week from today. I should be able to know by then."

"If that's what you think is best." She wasn't convinced.

"I think so. If you see me talking to invisible people before then, then I'll call earlier." Leah chuckled at her own comment. Sarah did not.

"Well, Leah, I've got to let you go. I'm actually on my way into a meeting."

"Oh, sorry. I wasn't trying to keep you. I'll see you around."

"See you around."

The call ended.

A week. If I'm not better in a week, I'll start back up again.

Leah woke up each morning waiting for the other shoe to drop, but instead of crumbling into another breakdown, she tied on her running shoes and logged a couple miles before heading into the office. She went to bed each night with the expectation of tossing and turning, but slept more and more soundly.

It defied all logic, all explanation.

This isn't some sort of reverse-placebo effect, right? It can't be all in my head.

But with each passing day, Leah became more convinced that she had made the right decision in stopping her medication. She hadn't felt so good in months, and whatever had changed, she wasn't keen to change it back.

***

As she finished her preparations for a meeting a week after her appointment, Leah felt her phone buzzing in her pocket. She silenced it, wanting to focus on the task at hand. Ten minutes later, as she walked toward the conference room, the phone rang again. She pulled it out to silence it but paused when she saw the caller ID—it was a number she recognized, but not one she had saved.

Washington, DC, again?

Intrigued, she took the call. She hung back in the hallway, holding up a finger to a colleague who looked at her with curious eyes.

A man's voice greeted her. "Hello, is this Leonora Harvey?"

Her stomach flipped, and she forced her voice to remain steady. "Who's asking?"

"This is Special Agent Robert McDowell. We spoke a few weeks ago about a tip you submitted to the FBI. I wanted to follow up with you and see if you'd given any more thought to my question."

What is Wilder going on about? This is so dumb.

"If by that you mean, do I remember submitting a tip, then no, I still don't. You must have the wrong Leonora Harvey."

"I see." He sounded unconvinced. "But you are a patient at the McNeill Institute, if I remember correctly?"

Leah squinted at an abstract painting on the wall and rolled her eyes. "I am."

"Then I think I'd still like to talk with you further. Would you be open to meeting up sometime soon?"

Is he... is he asking me on a date?

Her stomach fluttered. "To talk about what, exactly?"

"I'm not at liberty to give details over the phone. All I can tell you is that my investigation involves the McNeill Institute, and I'm very interested in hearing a patient's perspective."

"You realize that you sound like a stalker, right? How am I supposed to trust that you are who you say you are?" She grinned and hoped that he could hear it in her voice. She expected some cheeky response. Classic Wilder.

"Look me up. Call my senior officer and have him run my badge number for you." His tone had become defensive, and he rattled off a list of numbers before Leah could get a pen to write them down.

"Whoa, whoa, whoa. No need to get snippy," she protested. "Assuming I am open to a conversation, what were you thinking?"

"I'm in town through the weekend on business related to my investigation. Can we meet up on Saturday? I don't know much about the area, but on this most recent trip, I've been to a place called Common Grounds a couple of times—friendly enough, lots of wide open spaces, very public. No need for you to worry about my being a stalker."

She would have sworn she heard a wink.

This has got to be Wilder just goofing off. What a weirdo.

She smiled fondly. "Sure, that sounds fine."

"Ten o'clock?"

"I'm free then. I'll be there."

She hung up without saying goodbye, trying to hide her grin, and slipped into the conference room just as the meeting began. Her presence was mostly a formality, although she was supposed to provide a few project updates at the end. Glancing around to see if anyone was looking at her, Leah pulled up LinkedIn and searched for Robert McDowell.

She'd found him quickly—what was social media for, if not finding random strangers on the internet?—and Wilder's face greeted her. Scrolling through his profile, she noticed that his hometown was listed as Washington, DC.

This seems like a lot of effort to put into a practical joke.

He had 'Special Agent' listed as his job title, and a little gray shield with a check mark greeted her when she clicked through to the Federal Bureau of Investigation page linked as his employer.

There's no way the FBI just lets random people add themselves as employees, right? Let alone as Special Agents? Do they even allow actual Special Agents to do that?

Frowning, she clicked through a few other employee profiles, shocked to find Special Agent as a job title somewhat frequently. She backed up to the Robert McDowell page and read over his educational history. First a bachelor's in international studies, then a graduate program in criminal justice, back to back. The sign of someone who knew what he wanted from life at a young age. His network on LinkedIn checked out, and the tone of his posts matched the self-assured, defensive tone he'd taken on the phone.

But this can't be Wilder, right? Could he have a twin?

She took another glance at his profile picture. Dark hair cropped close on the sides and a little longer on top, those bright green eyes, and a smile that, even over the dim glow of her screen, lit up a room. He wore glasses, which she'd never seen Wilder do, but otherwise, the two men seemed identical.

This has got to be his twin or something.

She glanced around the room. She still had time before she needed to present. She switched over to Facebook, hoping to glean a few more details. The photos that were publicly available were old, probably from grad school, if the timeline on his LinkedIn was accurate. A couple shots at bars or house parties. One of McDowell standing triumphantly on a large rock. A few other hiking photos.

But wait, different last names? Twins separated at birth feels like too much of a stretch.

Having made it through everything she could easily find on Facebook, Leah was about to open Twitter when she heard someone say her name.

"...Leah is going to give us some updates on where the promotional campaign stands."

She quickly closed the browser tab, opened her slideshow, and shared her screen with the monitor at the front of the room. Two images, both of her design, appeared next to one another on the blindingly bright projector screen.

Man, is this all I have to show? I worked so hard on these.

She sighed. Only one coworker made eye contact with her; the rest leaned into their laptops or gazed languidly around the room. Phone screens lit up under the table as a few particularly apathetic colleagues tried to discreetly reply to client texts.

"Yes," she began. "We're still in the early stages, but I've got two mockups for the logo of this year's Fun Run that I need everyone's input on before I can move on." She felt the atmosphere in the room dry up.

Why couldn't Ana just let me do my job? No one else cares about the logo design. This meeting is such a waste of time.

Nevertheless, she dutifully finished her presentation and sat through ten full minutes of critiques on her designs. By the end of the meeting, a vote had been taken, tied, and re-taken. She took notes on everything she'd been asked to change and promised to send out a second draft by the end of the day. They all packed up their laptops and walked back to their individual offices. Seated at her desk, Leah pulled up the design file to make the requested edits. She groaned.

I hate this.

Clicking away from her design software, she opened a new browser tab and pulled up Facebook, typing in "Wilder Frederick" with trembling fingers.

None of the search results even halfway resembled the man she knew from the Institute. She filtered for location, for mutual connections—nothing. She tested different spellings—still nothing.

Maybe he's just not on Facebook?

But that excuse didn't sit well with her. With a queasy stomach, she redirected her attention to the Fun Run logo.

Chapter 7

On Saturday morning, Leah pulled out of the apartment parking lot buzzing with a nervous, excited energy. She hadn't touched her medication since her appointment, and the orange bottle was still nestled in its paper bag on her kitchen counter.

I can't wait to see Wilder. It's been ages since we've actually gotten to chat.

She hadn't recognized the name of the coffee shop when she'd looked up the address, but it wasn't far from her, and she made it a few minutes before ten o'clock. As she approached, a gnawing feeling grew in the pit of her stomach. She glanced up and down the parking lot, along the length of which was a wide open field. Two sets of soccer goals were set up, with some sort of pickup game happening in each. A walking trail surrounded the field, peppered with joggers and bikers. A gaggle of young children clambered up and down a playground on the opposite end of the field from Common Grounds, which had an entrance facing the street and an extensive back patio sprawling out toward the green.

I've been here before. When have I been here before?

She squinted and shook her head.

Maybe not.

Pulling into a parking spot, Leah stepped into the wide open lawn, her eyes drawn towards Common Grounds' patio seating area. As she made her way over, she studied the occupants of each table briefly, looking for Wilder's face among the brunch crowd, but he was nowhere to be found.

Undeterred, Leah entered the cafe and got in line. The interior was crowded, bustling with life and humming with the constant noise of friendships and first dates and folks clacking away on plastic keys. The smell of coffee and citrus wafted throughout the shop.

Leah felt more alive than she had in months, although she couldn't shake the eerie déjà vu that plagued her upon her arrival. She raised herself up and down on her tiptoes, absentmindedly reading the menu. Deciding on an iced latte and a lemon blueberry muffin, she began looking around again. A half-remembered face met her eyes. Dirty blonde hair, high cheekbones, tired brown eyes.

I swear I know her from somewhere.

Leah continued staring from the corner of her eyes, trying to be discreet as she puzzled over the question of where they may have met before.

Natalie.

She didn't know how she knew the woman's name, but she was certain that was it.

Just at that moment, their eyes met across the shop. Natalie raised a hand in greeting, a smile breaking out across her face. Leah waved back, hesitantly, and Natalie pointed over the crowd in the direction of the patio, her lips moving. She was too far away to be heard, but Leah got the gist and gave her a thumbs up.

When she reached the counter, she opened her mouth to order but was cut off.

"Leah, right? Let me guess, you want an iced latte and our seasonal muffin, which today is going to be..." she paused and glanced at the ceiling. "Lemon blueberry."

How did she know?

Leah stared at the barista, a heavily made-up, bleached-blonde girl who couldn't have been more than twenty. When she said nothing, the barista gasped. "Oh my gosh, did I get it wrong? It's been a minute since you were here, and I might have gotten you mixed up with one of my regulars. You look just like her."

"I, um—" Leah stammered. "I've actually never been here before."

The barista's eyes widened in horror. "I'm so sorry. Let me start over." She raised her pitch half an octave. "Hi, welcome to Common Grounds! What can I get started for you today?"

Leah furrowed her brow skeptically but responded nonetheless. "Honestly, that combo you rattled off does sound really good. I'll go with that—what was it, an iced latte and a lemon blueberry muffin?"

"Still got it," the barista whispered under her breath as she rang Leah up.

Have I been here before? She knew my name... and my order?

Leah paid and stepped over to the waiting area as the staff prepared her order. She examined some work by local artists on the wall and picked at a callus on her left hand.

Something about this place is off.

She wracked her brain, trying to remember a previous visit, but came up with nothing. A few minutes later, iced latte in one hand and muffin in the other, Leah made her way back out to the patio. She noticed that the woman she'd recognized—Natalie, if her memory served—had claimed a table. Leah remained standing in one corner, searching for Wilder.

"Leah." She looked in the direction of her name and found Natalie waving at her. "Over here!"

The knot in her stomach tightened, but she nevertheless made her way over to the table. "Hey Natalie, how's it going?" She didn't sit down, but shifted her weight from one leg to the other.

I hope she can't tell that I don't remember anything about her.

Natalie pulled out a chair and invited her to sit down. "It's so good to see you. Thank you so much for meeting us here. Agent McDowell should be here soon."

Leah blinked heavily. Her heart sank. "Wait, you know about that? You're with him? What's going on?"

Natalie exhaled. "I'd rather wait until he gets here to get started."

"Fair enough, I guess." Leah took her seat, her eyes finally breaking away from the crowd to focus on Natalie's face. "Natalie, this is going to sound really terrible, but how do I... how do we know each other? You look so familiar, but for the life of me, I cannot remember where we met. And then on top of that, you're apparently working with the guy I'm supposed to be meeting up with? I don't know... it's a lot."

Natalie took a sip of her coffee. She closed her eyes and breathed deeply. Then she set her mug down on the table and met Leah's eyes. "You know, it's funny. I've visualized this moment so many times. But now that we're here, I don't know where to begin."

Leah chuckled half-heartedly, squirming in her seat. But before either woman could continue speaking, a shadow appeared over their table. Natalie glanced up, smiled, and stood. Leah's heart skipped a beat, and she stood too. The man standing beside her had Wilder's face, but there was no glimmer of recognition in his eyes.

"Special Agent Robert McDowell," he reminded her, offering her a firm handshake. "Good to see you again, Ms. Harvey. Thanks again for agreeing to meet with me. I see you've already met Ms. Bailey."

WHAT IS HAPPENING?

Leah rubbed her forehead. "Yes, I was just telling her—I know her from somewhere, but I can't remember where."

The other two exchanged a pregnant glance. Agent McDowell sat down in the remaining chair, and the women took their seats as well.

"Well, let's just go ahead and jump right in. Ms. Harvey, I have to be honest with you. I did lure you here under somewhat false pretenses."

Leah felt her whole body tense up. She looked around the rest of the patio, tracing paths between the tables in the direction of the parking lot.

"I invited you here to speak with me as a patient of the McNeill Institute, and that much is true. But I also want to speak with you as the woman who submitted the most thorough tip I've received in my entire career."

Leah groaned. "I already told you, I didn't—"

"Let me finish, please."

"But you—"

"Let me finish. Your tip..." He threw up his hands. "Well, a tip came across my desk a little over a year ago. Fifteen months, let's call it. There were two names on the submission: Leonora Harvey and Natalie Bailey." He gestured to each of them in turn. "You were listed as the primary contact, so when I began my investigation last year,

I reached out to you first. You never answered my calls, and due to the sensitive nature of the information, I was hesitant to leave a voicemail. After a few days, I remembered that Ms. Bailey's contact information had also been included, so I reached out to her."

Leah glanced around at the field, something nagging at the back of her mind.

What is it about this place?

"When I mentioned that I had been unable to get you on the phone, she didn't seem surprised. During that conversation, she gave me some important context that has shaped the way I've pursued this investigation over the last year. However, at this stage, Ms. Bailey and I both deemed it appropriate for the three of us to sit down together so that we can be on the same page moving forward."

Leah didn't know how to respond. "Moving forward? Wilde—" She caught herself and huffed. "Agent McDowell. I have no idea what you're talking about, and I'm still not convinced that I'm the woman you're looking for. Surely, I'm not the only Leonora Harvey in Texas."

"You recognized Ms. Bailey when you arrived, did you not?" He raised one eyebrow.

Leah hesitated. "I mean, sort of? She looks familiar?"

"But you've never met her before."

"We're not, like, friends. But we might have met once or twice, I don't know."

His eyes moved to Natalie, and Leah found hers doing the same. Her eyes were downcast, and the corners of her mouth formed a frown. "I don't want to say too much..." Natalie began slowly. "Can't say too much. But it's time you learn the truth, and I suppose this is as good a place to start as any: there is no clinical trial."

She paused, waiting for Leah to respond.

"What?" Leah demanded, processing the sentence and its implications. It took her a second to even connect the dots between Natalie and the Institute.

"There is no clinical trial." Natalie continued. "I know you've been seeing Dr. Pierucci this year for your psych symptoms, and he's told you that you're enrolled in a clinical trial for a new treatment protocol. But there is no clinical trial." Her voice was firm.

Leah's mind reeled. "How do you even know that? Isn't that, like, some sort of huge HIPPA violation? And wait–if there's no clinical trial, what have they been doing to me?"

Natalie nodded slowly. "That's the million dollar question, and I wish I could give you a straight answer."

"But my symptoms have improved over the past year! How do you explain that?" Irritated, she added. "Let me guess, you're going to tell me that I don't actually have any kind of psychosis."

Natalie waffled. "I mean... I think the better question would be why you were having symptoms in the first place."

"That's what we've spent a year trying to figure out!" Leah felt her temper rising. "Everything has gone just like Dr. Pierucci said it would—things got worse for a while, I had a massive breakdown—"

She trailed off mid-sentence.

A tall young man with dark hair and Mediterranean features, coffee cup in hand, walking in her direction. The warm, earthy smell of fresh-cut grass. Her father's voice calling her name. Ants crawling up and down her arms. Boutiques and antique shops and pawn shops and liquor stores. Someone following her. The world spinning to black.

Her eyes widened and she froze in place.

Holy–

A gentle hand on her shoulder cut her thoughts short.

"Leah, are you okay?"

"No, I've been here before." Each quick, shallow breath deepened the sense of panic constricting around her bones. "This is where I– How did you know this place? Why did you pick this place?"

"Leah, Leah, Leah," Natalie's voice cut through the fear. "Breathe with me. Come on, honey. You're safe."

Coming here was a mistake. This whole thing is a huge mistake. I should never have come.

Leah forced herself to match Natalie's breathing. Her heartbeat no longer pounded in her ears, but she found herself looking around the green like a hunted animal. She crossed her arms tightly and looked down at her coffee cup. Her words came slowly. "I've been here before. A long time ago. It's not a good memory."

Natalie gave her a sympathetic smile, but said nothing.

Leah continued. "Why did you bring me here? And why now? Is this because I stopped taking my medication?"

Agent McDowell stepped in. "Sort of, yes. We were already planning to reach out, but your delayed treatment gave us an opportunity we didn't want to lose."

Leah's voice was still quiet. "The HIPPA violations just never end, do they?"

The other two exchanged another meaningful glance. Natalie shrugged and mouthed something that Leah didn't quite catch.

Agent McDowell took a deep breath. "It's not a HIPPA violation, Leah. As part of my investigation, I've been going undercover as a patient at the McNeill Institute named Wilder Frederick."

Leah's eyes widened, her heart sinking as her shoulders slumped. She blinked a couple of times and stared down at her empty plate.

He continued. "I noticed that you weren't at your last appointment, and it didn't take much to put two and two together that you were involved with the wreck down the street. I overheard Shelby on the phone trying to get a hold of you, and I knew this was our chance."

"Our chance?" Leah echoed.

"Our chance to get you out from under Pierucci's thumb."

Leah felt her face flush with anger. "Out from under his thumb? Are you really going to look me in the eyes and tell me that he's committing some kind of, what, medical abuse? That the treatment that's been saving my life is all a lie? That the hallucinations and the anxiety and the seizures are all going away just with a wish and a prayer?"

"Of course not, Leah—" Natalie sounded apologetic.

"Then what do you actually think is happening? I'm not exactly clear on that." She scoffed. "You've made the claim that I submitted a tip to the FBI about a neurology clinic I wasn't even aware of at the time. You've impersonated a psych patient to get close to me. And now you're throwing that persona out the window in favor of one you think I might respect more? It doesn't even make sense! Honestly, if you're trying to scam me, do better."

Agent McDowell's face was grave. He pulled a wallet out of his suit pocket and laid it out on the table, a shiny silver badge facing outward. "I assure you, Ms. Harvey, this is no scam."

She blushed deeper and fiddled with the wrapper of her muffin. "I don't know. This is just a lot to take in."

There was silence for a moment. A bird landed on the patio beside them, searching for crumbs.

"But you still didn't answer my question about the treatment Dr. Pierucci is giving me. If I'm not in a clinical trial, then what have they been doing to me?"

Agent McDowell opened his mouth to reply when fear flashed in Natalie's eyes.

"How did he know we would be here?" she muttered.

Leah looked around, confused. She wasn't certain who Natalie was referring to. The young family—mom, dad, two kids—playing soccer in one corner of the field? The older woman her grandson? The father teaching his daughter how to ride a bike? Then her eyes landed on a young man with dark hair and strong Mediterranean facial features.

A face staring at her from the corner table, mouth half-open in shock. A tall form pacing toward her from across the field.

Feeling another panic coming on, Leah placed a hand over her mouth and turned back to Natalie, who had slipped lower into her seat and adjusted the scarf around her neck.

He wasn't just another hallucination?

Natalie's voice sounded a million miles away. "Leah, I'm so sorry to do this to you, but we're going to have to cut this short."

"Who is that?" Leah barely managed to stammer out the words. Natalie looked back at her but didn't respond. Agent McDowell was tense, his eyes locked forward, his right hand hovering over his hip.

"I'm going to buy you a couple of minutes." Natalie said, her voice firm. "Agent McDowell, Leah doesn't look well. Make sure she gets to her car. Stay out of sight as much as you can."

He nodded as Natalie slipped away. She bobbed around a few tables before making her way over to the young man. Her pace picked up as she approached him, and Leah watched, shell-shocked, as she called a greeting, waving his attention in the other direction.

Agent McDowell's face was pale.

"Come on, then, Harvey." Cutting through her anxiety, she heard the familiar joking cadence of Wilder's voice. "Let's get out of here."

Leaving their dishes on the table, Agent McDowell stood up and helped her do the same. He slipped her arm through his. Her legs were weak, and she leaned on him for support as they slipped through the coffee shop and exited on the street side.

"Who was that?" Her voice was distant and hushed.

"You don't know him?" He seemed genuinely confused.

Do I?

"No." She considered elaborating but decided not to.

Why was he following me the day I had my breakdown? And why is he here now?

"Well, don't worry. I'll walk you to your car, and we'll talk about him another time."

They made their way around to the parking lot in silence. She led the way to her car, and he opened the door for her. She sat down and watched in her rear view mirror as he found his own car and drove off.

Her stomach ached. Her chest ached. She felt the beginning of a headache coming on.

Please not a migraine.

After spending a few minutes allowing herself to calm down, she turned the car on, shifted it into gear, and backed out of her spot. Against her better judgment, she drove an extra lap up and down the parking lot. She had to get one more glimpse of the patio.

As far as her straining eyes could see, neither Natalie nor the young man remained outside.

How did the barista know me? And why did Natalie and Wild—whoever he is... why were they scared enough to leave without telling me anything after all?

Even from a distance, the park was filled with joy, in stark contrast to the clouds gathering in Leah's mind as she tried to make sense of the morning.

There's no way any of this is real.

Chapter 8

The rest of the weekend crept by at an agonizing pace. Leah felt constantly on edge, startled by every sound. She considered taking her medication again—had she not experienced two and a half weeks with no withdrawal effects and no psychotic episodes, she wouldn't have hesitated.

As it was, she felt trapped by her lack of information. She knew just enough to feel uncertain about the best course of action.

No one at the Institute would be able to give her answers about the supposed FBI investigation, and there was no way she was going to call Agent McDowell back to demand more information. She had no way of contacting Natalie, either. She'd never told Leah how they knew each other, and they hadn't exchanged phone numbers.

No matter how much she wracked her brain, she couldn't place Natalie at all. The affection she'd shown for Leah implied that there was more to the relationship than a forgettable one-time meeting, but Leah had no recollection of the circumstances under which they might have met.

And Wilder—Agent McDowell—whoever he really was. A nagging thought at the back of her mind reminded her that she'd done her homework on Agent McDowell and he seemed legitimate.

Could Wilder Frederick really be just a costume he puts on within the walls of the Institute?

***

Monday morning, when it finally arrived, dragged on. The clock read ten past eight as Leah sat at her desk, tapping her foot impatiently. She'd been at the office for all of fifteen minutes, but she already wanted to leave. Her conversation with Natalie and Agent McDowell played on repeat in her mind, like a song she didn't quite know how to sing.

"I don't want to say too much... Can't say too much. But I suppose this is as good a place to start as any: there is no clinical trial."

"But my symptoms have improved over the past year! How do you explain that?"

"I think the better question would be why you were having symptoms in the first place."

She'd been profoundly disappointed in the encounter. Angry, definitely. Confused, to be sure. But mostly just disappointed. Part of it was her fault. She had let herself believe that the whole thing was just an elaborate practical joke on Wilder's part, a chance to make a real friend during a lonely time of her life. She'd been looking forward to that.

Ironically, of course, the exact opposite had happened.

Just my luck.

She didn't want to admit it, but she couldn't seem to shake Natalie's claim that the clinical trial was a fake. After all, if she no longer needed her medication to function normally, then what else could be true that seemed impossible at first?

I could always just fact check it.

The thought hadn't occurred to her before that moment, but it suddenly became as plain as day. At her very first appointment, Dr. Pierucci had recommended enrolling her in a clinical trial—the treatment she'd been receiving. He told her that it was run by the Institute, with participants all over the country, and although the treatment had been originally conceived and approved for another condition, Dr. Pierucci had explained that they were looking into wider applications, certain that they could do some good for other troubled individuals.

There's got to be a website or a database where I can confirm the existence of the clinical trial. Surely that would be enough to prove Natalie wrong.

She stood up and poked her head out of her office, glancing up and down the hallway to see if any of her coworkers were around. No one seemed to be on their way to see her, so she shut the door and set her work status as 'busy.' She pulled up a new browser window and typed a query into the search bar.

how do i see clinical trials for my condition

The first result of her search was a page on the National Institutes of Health website. The teaser included the words "searchable registry"—just what she was looking for—so she opened the page and read the highlighted text."

ClinicalTrials.gov

This is a searchable registry and results database of federally and privately supported clinical trials conducted in the United States and around the world. ClinicalTrials.gov gives you information about a trial's purpose, who may participate, locations, and phone numbers for more details. This information should be used in conjunction with advice from health care professionals.

Leah clicked through the link and was taken to a complex search engine reminiscent of a university library database.

What am I going to do if this doesn't prove anything?

Biting at the inside of her cheek, Leah reviewed the options in front of her. Searching "psychosis" by itself returned over four thousand results, so Leah added additional filters, trying to find a trial that matched the description of the one she'd been participating in. She tested criteria for location, age and sex, the date she'd begun the study. She consulted her most recent prescription and searched for the name of the drug she'd been taking. Nothing turned up that aligned with what she'd been told by Dr. Pierucci.

As a last resort, she searched through her email archive in hopes of finding a digital copy of any consent forms she'd completed when the trial began. There was nothing.

What do I do now?

She hadn't actually expected to come up empty-handed. Natalie's claim had felt like such an obvious falsehood that Leah had been a little insulted by it. Their conversation had been cut short before Leah had been able to get her questions answered to her satisfaction, but it looked like there might be some truth to Natalie's assertions. And yet, everything she knew of Dr. Pierucci by reputation and from personal experience contradicted the notion that was the type of physician—the type of person, even—to make up a clinical trial for any reason, benevolent or nefarious.

Surely there's a simple explanation for this.

Just to satisfy her curiosity, Leah did a cursory search on the neurologist himself. Hundreds of thousands of results clamored for her attention, each eager to be the first to extol the man for his life-changing research, his altruism in making treatments available to individuals in lower-income areas, and his creative genius as manifested in his research.

This glowing portrait, obviously exaggerated and irritatingly sycophantic, nonetheless fit with what Leah expected to see. She'd gotten the impression from Pierucci himself and from other staff and patients that he was a big name in the neurology world.

Would his fame make it better if he were committing some sort of research fraud?

Leah felt the familiar pull of insatiable interest tugging at her mind. The whole situation seemed increasingly like a puzzle, and she could never resist a good puzzle.

I'm not going to be able to let this one go.

A quick glance at the clock revealed that she had already spent an hour of her workday investigating. She sighed and opened up her project inbox, only to close it again immediately and open Facebook.

I know someone said Natalie's last name yesterday. Natalie... Natalie... Natalie Bailey!

She typed the name into the website's search bar and was immediately confronted with a picture of Natalie, smiling, seated next to a bald, bearded man who Leah assumed must be her husband. In front of them, three young children made goofy faces for the camera.

After scrolling through what felt like an endless feed of updates about the Bailey children, holiday photos, and memes, Leah was shocked to find a picture of Natalie and her redheaded technician, Peter. He had posted the picture and tagged Natalie, and Leah recognized the faces of other Institute staff members in the background. Intrigued, she leaned closer to her screen to read the caption.

Nat's last day! This place isn't going to be the same without her.

Leah squinted at her screen and continued scrolling down Natalie's timeline, trying to figure out how Peter knew her. There were several of the "last day" posts, and Leah eventually pieced together that Natalie had been employed at the Institute as a receptionist or office manager.

I guess that's how Natalie was also involved in the FBI tip... if the FBI tip is real.

Leah switched over to LinkedIn. Cross-referencing Natalie's name with the McNeill Institute as her current employer turned up nothing—not a surprise, given the implications of the posts she'd seen on Facebook—but without the employer data, there were over fifty pages of results. After clicking through profiles for a few minutes, Leah found the "past employer" filter, and there was Natalie's face, smiling professionally.

Nothing on her profile surprised Leah. Her listed dates of employment at the Institute lined up with everything she'd seen and heard over the past few days.

So let's operate as if this whole FBI tip story were true, just for the moment. What then?

She wanted to follow that question to its answer, but a glance at the clock revealed that the morning was already halfway over. Before she could talk herself into five more minutes of research, Leah set her status to 'available' and was surprised when, mere moments later, a colleague knocked on her door. She quickly closed all the incriminating web pages and beckoned the other employee into her office.

What should have been a half-hour task quickly turned into an all-out crisis, and by the time Leah felt the issue had been sufficiently resolved, feedback received from all necessary parties, and the graphic in question sent on to the appropriate recipients, it was almost time for lunch. Leah looked sadly at her to-do list, scrawled on a sheet of note paper next to her laptop. She hadn't managed to begin a single item on that list. To console herself, she added one more check box.

[] Confirm Natalie's assertion about the clinical trial

She ticked the box immediately but still felt unsatisfied. She wanted answers, and she didn't want to wait another two weeks until her next appointment with Dr. Pierucci. Leah frowned at her computer, grabbed her backpack, and swung it over her shoulder as she walked to the doors of her office.

"Hey, I'm going to run out for lunch," she called to Ana and another coworker as she made a beeline for the door. They exchanged a pointed glance, but Leah pretended not to notice. "If anyone's looking for me, tell them I'll be back in an hour or so. Busy morning, need some fresh air."

***

Fifteen minutes later, Leah pulled into the parking lot of the McNeill Institute for Neurological Development. She strode in with her head held high. Shelby was nowhere to be seen, but she saw Peter staring down at his phone screen as he waited for a patient near the door to the back hallway. She approached him and cleared her throat. Peter began his speech before looking up, his thumbs moving rapidly across his keyboard.

"Hello, welcome to the McNei— Leah!" His voice dropped to a whisper. "What are you doing here?"

"You're the one who told me to stop my medication." She whispered back, fighting the urge to speak loud enough to cause a scene. "You've got to be in on it. I want answers."

He glanced rapidly around the waiting room. "You can't be here. You don't have an appointment."

"I'm not here for medical reasons," Leah shot back.

"If he sees you—" Peter hissed, "if Jude sees you, if one of his staff sees you—there will be hell to pay."

"Who's Jude? And, wait, aren't all of you his staff?"

"Not like that. This is just my day job."

"Your day job? What does that mean?"

"It means you need to get out of here." Peter's voice was steely. "Now."

"I'm not leaving without answers."

Peter looked her dead in the face. "Take a walk, Leah."

"What?"

"A walk. There's a park down the street. Go take a walk. Clear your head." Peter's tone left no room for negotiation. Leah obeyed, new questions flying through her mind. She lingered for a moment, taking in the waiting room, before exiting out the glass doors at the front of the clinic.

She walked back to her car fuming.

"Go take a walk." What am I, a child? How dare he dismiss me like that.

She opened the door of her car, stepped one foot inside, and sighed heavily.

I can't go back to work like this. I'll bite someone's head off.

Stepping out and closing her car door again, Leah pulled out her phone.

I made it all the way over here already; it'd be a shame to waste the drive. Maybe that new sandwich place around the corner is finally open.

No hours were posted for the sandwich shop, so she assumed it hadn't opened, but as she scanned the map of the area, she noticed the park that Peter had mentioned. It was less than a mile away.

A walk probably would do me good. I hate that he's right.

She locked her car and started walking in that direction. She'd just passed the corner of the building when she heard a familiar voice behind her. "Can you hold the door for me?"

It was Peter. He stepped out of a side door marked STAFF ONLY and carrying a bulging cardboard box, sliding his way through the narrow frame as quickly as he could without dropping his burden or spilling its contents.

Leah froze at his question but recovered quickly enough to hold the door for him as he squeezed through, trying not to scrape his fingers in the doorway.

"How are you today, Ms. Harvey?" he asked as Leah closed the door behind him. He paced slowly toward his car, and she followed along.

"This is ridiculous. What are you doing?" She heard the rudeness in her tone but didn't care to correct it.

Peter feigned ignorance. "I'm taking this big box of papers to the van, and you're holding the door for me."

She glared at him. "You just fussed at me to go away, and now you're out here being all friendly?"

He tried to shrug but strained under the weight of the box in his hands. "I have to put this stuff in the van."

She rolled her eyes. "You sounded awfully smug when you came out here. There's something else going on."

"I'm making small talk. I'm told it's important."

Leah huffed. "Well then, I'm not great, Peter, to tell you the truth."

"I'm sorry to hear that." He sounded much more genuine than she expected, and she felt her face soften.

"Natalie said her meeting with you got cut short on Saturday."

She turned to look at him, eyes wide. "Wait, you know about that?"

Peter barked a harsh laugh in response, then tried to disguise it as a cough. He nodded his head in the direction of a transit van with the Institute logo plastered on its side. "Can you get this door for me?"

She obliged, watching as Peter gingerly set the box down on the floor of the vehicle, wincing as she debated whether or not to offer to help. Eventually he managed to maneuver the box down. He stepped back to admire his work before slamming the van door shut.

"Do you know where the park is?"

"I just looked it up," Leah responded. "But I want it known that I'm going because I think it will be nice to go for a walk, and not because you told me to."

Peter snorted. "Well, either way, I'm headed that way with you. Natalie told me about what happened on Saturday, and she thinks you deserve answers. She asked me to fill you in a little bit if I saw you before she did."

Peter pointed across the street in the direction she'd already been walking.

"Well, I suppose that's better than nothing," she replied sarcastically. "So, Nata—"

He interrupted her. "Let's wait until we get out of earshot of the clinic. I know you've been waiting a long time, but two more minutes won't kill you. I've got," he checked his watch, "just over an hour until my next appointment, so we've got time."

They crossed the street, and Leah glanced over at him as they walked—his hair looked more orange in the sunlight than it did in the fluorescent lights of the clinic. He was taller than she'd realized, and she had to walk quickly to keep up with him. Ahead of them, a well-worn walking trail began to peek through the trees.

"Alright, we should be out of earshot now."

She wished she'd thought to write out a list of questions she'd asked since Saturday. "What did Natalie mean when she said there is no clinical trial?"

Peter drew his eyebrows and flared his nostrils. "She meant that there is no clinical trial."

Leah glared at him. "I confirmed that this morning, as best as I could."

"Then why'd you ask about it?"

"Let me rephrase, then." Leah huffed. "Why do I keep paying to come here and let you crawl around in my brain under the pretense of participating in a clinical trial? What are you actually doing to me? If I'm not getting treated for psychosis then why am I here?" She spat the questions out one after another, her tone harsh. The color rose in her face, and her limbs grew restless. "Who was the man Natalie ran away from on Saturday? What was so important about him not seeing us? Why didn't she give me any way to get in contact with her? Can I trust her? Can I trust that FBI guy? Who even is the FBI guy? Is Wilder a real person? Or is every single thing in my life just a lie?"

A sob caught in her throat, and she paused for a moment to choke it back down. Tears welled up in the corners of her eyes, and she blinked them away. She would not cry in front of this man. She wouldn't give him that satisfaction. Finally, fighting to keep her tone steady, she muttered one more question—the one question that summed up all the rest.

"What's happening to me?"

She sighed as fatigue settled over her like a blanket. Her eyelids felt heavy, and each breath was an effort. Overhead, a blue jay screeched. Peter waited a moment, watching her to see if she was done. His eyes were wide. "Anything else?"

"No." She shook her head, looking at her feet.

"Well then. Let's get started."

Chapter 9

A grimace flashed on Peter's face as he muttered under his breath. "I don't know why Natalie asked me to do this part. Didn't she know there would be feelings?"

Leah hoped he meant it as a joke, but she didn't laugh.

He looked over at her, looking suddenly tired. "Look, Harvey, I'm really not trying to be insensitive, but none of this was ever in the plan. Saturday was supposed to go more smoothly, McDowell was going to explain everything, and Natalie was going to be there to help you process it all. But obviously that didn't happen, and she told me specifically that if I saw you before she did, I had to talk with you. She told me that you deserve answers."

"What's happening to me?" Leah repeated.

"That's... a complicated question, and one that I can't outright answer. Natalie wouldn't have been able to either, so don't go getting yourself worked up about it. There's a lot going on here, and some of it you need to discover for yourself. That's, I think, the most I can say about that for now. But any questions you have about the clinical trial, about me or Natalie or Agent McDowell... that's all fair game."

"So far? What is that supposed to mean? And you know about Wil—Agent McDowell?"

"You mentioned him to me earlier—did Natalie not tell you that I was involved?"

Leah raised her eyebrows. "She literally didn't tell me anything other than the thing about the clinical trial."

Peter's jaw dropped. "So you're just going around telling everyone you meet that you're talking with the FBI about a highly sensitive tip submitted against a nationally acclaimed physician?"

Leah opened her mouth and then closed it again. She chose to stay silent, waiting for Peter to continue.

"If Natalie didn't tell you I was in on this, why did you storm up here and start making demands?"

"I saw a picture of the two of you on Facebook. You were my only link to her. I don't have any way to contact her, and I'm certainly not going to call McDowell back. But I can't just keep sitting on my hands and waiting for y'all to remember that I exist. Plus," she added. "You were the one who wrote on my printout that I should stop taking my medication. That's what started this whole thing."

Peter whistled. "Dang, Harvey. Gotta hand it to you, that's good work." He paused before adding, "And lucky—if the wrong person had seen you in that front office just now, things would not have gone well for you. But I think we're in the clear."

"What?" Leah looked over at him.

"Dr. Pierucci handles your case personally. He always knows when you're supposed to be here. And some of the staff owe Dr. Pierucci a lot. They're willing to go above and beyond the job description for him. If someone were to mention to him that you'd stopped in unannounced..." His voice trailed off.

A knot formed in Leah's stomach. "Then what?"

Peter's voice was grim. "There would be consequences if Dr. Pierucci found out about what we've been doing. I'd get fired, for sure. Who knows what would happen to Natalie and her family, and she doesn't even work here anymore. And you..." He frowned. "You're not exempt from that danger just because you don't know about it."

"Just to confirm," Leah replied, her eyebrows raised. "You're telling me that my neurologist would punish me for talking to my technician."

He glanced at her briefly before looking down at his feet. "I am."

Leah studied the trees for a moment before responding. "How do I know I can trust you and Natalie? I can accept—in theory," she added quickly, "that the clinical trial is made up, but it's hard for me to see how you're not complicit in that deception."

Peter shrugged. "I mean, I'll flip it back on you—how do you know you can't trust us? If we're not careful, this is going to cost us. A lot. So you've got to believe me that there's something more important than my job at stake. Heck, Natalie doesn't work for the Institute anymore, but she and her family have more skin in the game than anyone, and with the kids to put through school, too."

Leah threw up her hands. "Okay, but you won't tell me what's at stake? You won't tell me what's so important?"

"Not yet." He picked at a loose thread on his scrubs.

Their trail culminated in a short loop before sending them back in the direction of the clinic. Leah exhaled and chose a different avenue of inquiry. "How did you and Natalie start working together on this... plan, or whatever it is you want to call it? Clearly you've put a lot of time and effort into it."

Peter grinned, and Leah realized she'd never seen him smile before. It was disarming. "You could say that a mutual friend brought us together. She was—still is, I guess—trying to rectify a lot of injustice and medical abuse, and a little community formed around her—some others who wanted to pursue that goal."

"Injustice?" Leah's interest was piqued.

Peter nodded. "Things like this falsified clinical trial you're participating in."

Leah paused for a few paces. "I'm guessing Dr. Pierucci doesn't know that you're telling me all this."

"No, and we'd prefer to keep it that way."

"Understood. So, what, I just stop the meds but keep coming for the treatments?"

"Yep." He shrugged. "Although, now that I'm thinking about it, I need you to call for a last-minute reschedule for your upcoming appointment. It's good that we can talk about this here so I don't have to make up an excuse on the phone. If you can come in when Dr. Pierucci will be out of the office, I'll have a little more freedom to talk openly. He always knows the date of your next appointment, but if we can throw him off, just for one month, that'd be great. I've got something I want to show you next time you come in, as long as he's out of the office and not breathing down our necks." He glanced down at a squirrel crossing their path.

Dr. Pierucci's face appeared in Leah's mind's eye, and a knot formed in her stomach. "Peter, how can Dr. Pierucci be so friendly with me if he's lying through his teeth and running this fake clinical trial?" She thought for a moment, the implications of her question cascading in her mind. "And what have you been doing to me in that treatment all year, anyway?"

"Most of what I do with the console is purely observation," Peter said quickly. "I go in and see how you've categorized your experiences from the past month, and I do a sweep to see if there are any signs of additional psychotic episodes or symptoms. If I find any, I pull those memories as well so that the doctor can discuss them with you and help you recognize your symptoms more quickly and accurately moving forward. I'm just training your brain in new and helpful habits."

As he spoke, he became more animated than Leah had ever seen him, but when he finished, he blushed, as if embarrassed. His voice dropped back to its usual monotone as he continued. "I'm not sure what I'm going to do at your next visit, because we can't have the doctor seeing any of this conversation. Or anything that happened on Saturday. But I've got time to come up with something." He shrugged and raised an eyebrow.

"He can't see it because you don't want him to know that we've been talking?"

Peter nodded. "Exactly."

"He can see that level of detail?" Leah's eyes were wide.

"Oh, yeah. A month is a super short interval, and you've got such an organized mind pala—" He stopped mid-sentence and bit his lip.

"Have..." Leah hesitated, a gnawing feeling growing in the pit of her stomach. "Have you seen my library?"

Peter refused to make eye contact. "You're not the first person I've worked on—well, worked with—who uses a memory palace, but I've never met anyone whose set-up is as intricate as yours."

Leah felt the color rise in her face. It felt violating. Intimate. Wrong.

For a few yards, they walked in silence, each observing the trees on their side of the path. Squirrels chittered away, and a few birds whistled out their tunes.

Forcing herself to move on, Leah tried to pick the thread of conversation back up. "So what about the medication you've had me on? Is that part of the fake clinical trial too?

"It is a real medication, if that's what you're asking. The symptoms you experienced after your accident were withdrawal from the medication, and for several reasons, it's imperative you don't resume taking it. I hope," he added as an afterthought, "I hope the withdrawal phase has passed?"

She didn't answer his question. "I'm guessing you can't tell me what the medication is supposed to be doing?"

He sighed. "You are correct."

"I kind of hate you for pumping me full of medication and lying to me about what it was doing to my body." She couldn't bring herself to look at him.

"I hate myself for that, too, Leah." Peter's voice softened.

After another few paces, Leah changed the topic again. "Did Natalie tell you about the man at the coffee shop? Why did he scare her so much?"

Peter nodded. "His name is Jude Pierucci."

"Isn't that the doctor's name?" Leah cocked her head. "Wait—you mentioned someone named Jude earlier."

"Yes. Jude is Dr. Pierucci's son."

Leah's eyes widened. "How did he know we would be at Common Grounds on Saturday?"

Peter grimaced. "We're still trying to figure that out. The best case scenario is that it was really, really bad luck;

worst case, our text thread has been compromised and we'll all be disappeared sooner than later."

Leah stopped in her tracks. "Disappeared?"

"Disappeared." Peter did not explain further. He continued walking, and she hurried to catch up with him. They were quickly approaching the exit of the pocket park, and the doors of the clinic were just visible across the street.

"Well, Leah," Peter started. "I probably need to get back to work. My next appointment is coming up, and Dr. Pierucci will start asking questions if I'm gone too long, especially if any of the other techs noticed you stopped by. I..." He paused, clearly debating whether or not he wanted to say more. "We'll be in touch."

She watched as Peter pulled out a business card and a pen out of his front pocket. He scribbled on it before handing it to her. "Here's my cell in case you need to get in contact with me. I don't have Nat's phone number memorized, but I can get it to you. We don't want to leave you in the dark."

She studied the card carefully. "Thanks, Peter. You've given me a lot to think about."

At his request, she stayed back while he crossed the street, only finishing the walk to her car once he'd entered the building.

***

The rest of the day crept by, Leah's mind caught in a tug of war between the projects demanding her attention at work and her conversation with Peter. When five o'clock finally rolled around, Leah eagerly packed up and made her way out to her car. Rush hour traffic slowed to a crawl, and Leah's thoughts began to spiral.

There's just no way that any of this is real. And yet...

When she finally made it home, she unlocked her door and set her backpack down, desperate to get out of her head. She pulled out her laptop and briefly considered working on the project she needed to turn in by the end of the week, which she had grossly neglected during her time at the office.

Instead, she found herself searching for both Peter and Natalie on Facebook, scrolling through pages of photos.

Peter and his German shepherd, Axel. Selfies and photographs in forests across the country. Poolside shots of inner tubes and beer cans. The occasional promotional graphic for the Institute.

Natalie, her husband Matthew, and their three kids. Christmas photos. First and last days of school. Family vacations. They looked happy, although as she scrolled, she noticed a haunted look in Matthew's eyes start to grow and deepen. It took several minutes for her to remember that she was traveling backwards in time, and a wave of relief rushed over her when she realized that what she was seeing was healing, not crumbling.

Maybe one day I'll look back on photos of myself and see the same thing—a little blip of hurt followed by healing.

A weight settled on her chest, and she kept scrolling.

She was surprised to find a photo—several years old—of newlywed Natalie and Matthew grinning widely beside Dr. Pierucci's son, Jude. She clicked through the tag eagerly, desperate for any tidbits of personal information she might be able to glean about the neurologist and his family. She was surprised to see an error message on his page.

Sorry, this content can't be reached right now.

She frowned at her computer.

Could he have blocked me? Maybe he blocks all the clients of the clinic? That seems like a lot of work for very little return.

Out of curiosity, she searched for Dr. Pierucci. For the doctor himself, all she found was a publicity page stacked with professional photographs, quotes from the Institute website, and of course, statistics about patient satisfaction. There was no personal page, as far as she could tell.

Deciding that there was nothing more to be gleaned from glowing marketing posts or a decade of Bailey family photos, she turned her attention to the Institute itself. The searches flew off her fingers without her conscious thought: "McNeill Institute fraud" "Jude Pierucci Sr lawsuit" "falsified clinical trial psychosis". Before she knew it, she had fifteen tabs opened.

Clicking back through to decide where to start, she was startled to see a string of terms she didn't remember typing: "McNeill Institute prison disappearance".

Intrigued, she scrolled through the search results, trying to discover what train of thought had led her to that query. She muttered aloud as she skimmed each headline, grateful for the sound of her voice breaking the heavy silence of her apartment. "Dr. Jude Pierucci delivers inaugural 'State of the Prison' address. McNeill Institute, under Pierucci's leadership, kicks off Rehabilitation Research Program in Scarlett Bay Correctional Facility. Jude Pierucci, MD, is a murderer..."

This looks interesting.

Leah clicked through the last link with curiosity piqued. The web page assaulted her eyes. A pale red background, large black text with apparently random bolding, italics, and capitalization. A handful of blurry photos featuring orange shapes that could have been people. Nothing definitive. Mostly conspiracy theories. Lots of hyperbole.

Never mind.

Rolling her eyes, she clicked back to the search tab. Nothing else in that search really called out to her. The other searches yielded interesting facts, and she lost herself in consuming them, occasionally jotting down a note or a reminder.

She glanced at the clock. It was a quarter to midnight.

Shoot. I need to get to bed. Ana won't be happy if I'm too tired to function tomorrow.

She ran a toothbrush over her teeth as quickly as she could, changed into her pajamas, and set her alarm for six o'clock.

I should get up earlier and do just a little more—No. If I let myself start reading this stuff again before I go to work, I won't get anything done all day. It can wait until I get home.

She flipped off the lights.

Sleep was a battle. Fears and frustrations clamored into her mind, elbowing one another for space and attention. When she finally fought them off and slipped into a fitful slumber, her dreams were restless.

Chapter 10

The rest of the week passed monotonously, and as it wore on, her attention became focused more deeply on a looming deadline at work, which came and went with fanfare and rejoicing. She moved on to the next project, and the next, and the next.

After another week of receiving no word from either Natalie or Peter, Leah's motivation to continue her research was waning. She hadn't been able to find the answers she'd been hoping for. Boredom crept around the edges of her mind like clouds covering a full moon. As the date of her next appointment approached, Leah received the standard confirmation text.

> Hello, your upcoming appointment with the
> McNeill Institute for Neurological Development is
> scheduled for Thursday, July 13, 2023.
> Reply Y to confirm, N to cancel. To opt out of
> receiving text messages, text STOP.

Leah confirmed the appointment and quickly received the follow-up message.

> Thank you for confirming your appointment. We
> look forward to seeing you.

Leah set her phone down and turned back to her computer, glancing through the twelve or so tabs she had open. Email. Calendar. An article that a client had asked her to read. Six or seven references for the project she was working on. The McNeill Institute website. An anonymous piece written two years back about a man named Jorge Rodriguez who had been incarcerated at Scarlett Bay Correctional Facility.

Her research had led her to Rodriguez, and she vaguely remembered hearing about his trial when it had been happening, and a few times since on social media. She hadn't been able to find much beyond the official story, parroted and sometimes outright copied from one news outlet to the next, and a dramatic petition full of upset friends and family. She felt a twinge of guilt at the sight of the tab in her browser.

Rodriguez is a dead end.

Her phone rang next to her. She glanced at it out of habit but didn't pick up. She closed the tab about Jorge Rodriguez and opened her current project—

Wait, that's Peter's number.

She picked up the phone. "Hello?"

Peter didn't waste time on pleasantries. "I just confirmed that the doc will be out on Tuesday to present at a conference. I know that's a couple days early. Any chance you can reschedule?"

A quick glance at her calendar reminded her that she had an important meeting on the books for most of the morning, and another in the late afternoon.

She gritted her teeth. "I could do after lunch if we keep it quick."

"I can't promise quick."

"Well, how long is not-quick?"

"At least an hour."

Leah looked back down at her calendar. "What time are you open?"

"Any time after two. I'll clear my schedule. We won't get this chance again."

She exhaled. "I can do two o'clock, but I have to be back at the office with time to prepare for a four 'o'clock meeting."

Peter scoffed. "You scheduled a meeting at four o'clock?"

"It's with a cl—" Leah tried to respond.

"See you at two o'clock on Tuesday. Don't be late."

***

As Leah pulled into the parking lot of the McNeill Institute a few days later, her phone pinged with a text from Peter:

don't come in the main door. meet me at the back.

She parked at the far end of the lot and walked around the side of the building. Peter's head—red hair and round wire glasses—peeked out from behind an unmarked metal door along the back wall. He waved her over, and she half-skipped, half-ran the rest of the distance. He ushered her in and closed the door behind them as quietly as he could. His voice barely rose above a whisper as they made their way to one of the treatment rooms.

"Thanks so much for coming on such short notice, Leah. We were able to get your appointment rescheduled without the doctor noticing, so we should be in the clear, but I don't want anyone seeing you if we can help it. The fewer people know about this, the better. I'll get you settled in the room and then go check you in at the front desk."

He pointed towards the room—one of the furthest away from the reception area. Not for the first time, Leah wondered if Peter really could be trusted, but she stepped inside and sat down on the orthodontic chair. He shut the door on his way out.

Leah studied the peeling leather of the chair until she heard a gentle knock on the door. When it opened, Peter stepped in first, followed by a middle aged woman who Leah thought might be Nigerian. Her hair, graying at the roots, was pulled up into a puff on the top of head, and her eyes looked tired.

"Leah, this is Valerie DeLeon." Peter gestured to each of them in turn. "She's an expert in the console technology, and even though she's no longer employed at the Institute, she agreed to come in and help me with a little demo."

Leah offered her a handshake. "Nice to meet you."

"Of course. Very glad to be here." There was a heaviness in her voice that startled Leah.

Peter stood at the desktop in the corner of the room as Valerie pulled up a chair in front of Leah and sat down.

"So, Leah," she began. "Peter tells me that you've had some experience with the MentaLink console, although none with the simulator."

Leah nodded. "That's right."

"Well, you're in for a treat." Her eyes lit up. "The MentaLink console is capable of a wide range of functions; today, we're going to introduce you to a few of them."

"Thanks, I think?" Leah glanced at Peter, but his nose was buried in his computer and he didn't look up. Only his red hair was visible above the monitor.

"Well," Valerie said, the tiniest hint of a grin playing at the corners of her lips. "Peter and Natalie are correct in their assertion that there are some things you need to discover for yourself. But there's nothing stopping us from helping to get things going."

Leah's eyebrows knit together, an unspoken question on her face.

Valerie stood up. "You'll see what I mean shortly."

She pushed a few buttons on the wall, and the whole room came to life with a symphony of whirring fans, blinking lights, and dissonant tones as different instruments turned on. As the chaos settled into a consistent background noise, Valerie gently placed the helmet over Leah's head, fastening it under her chin. She pulled the mask down over Leah's eyes, and for a moment, the room was shrouded in darkness.

Through the headset speakers, Leah heard Valerie talking to Peter. "Go ahead and run a scan for some basic information and images. I think running through the standard pitch is going to be our best bet. Do you remember it?"

"Enough for today, at least, although it's been a while since I was in sales."

Valerie chuckled. "Well, we aren't trying to sell her a simulator, so it's okay if our presentation isn't timed to perfection." The heaviness in her voice was back.

"Never again." Peter, too, had a shadow in his voice. "I'm glad those days are behind us."

Leah didn't have much time to wonder what shared history they were referring to—Valerie lifted the goggles and helmet off Leah's head and replaced them on their shelf as she began speaking to Leah again. "The MentaLink console, created by McNeill Institute co-founders Dr. Jude Pierucci, Sr, and Dr. Arthur DeLeon—"

Leah interrupted her. "Didn't you say your last name was DeLeon?"

Valerie gritted her teeth and nodded slightly. She did not offer a further explanation. "—is a revolutionary piece of technology that can give your neurology team unprecedented insight into the human brain. Whether you are seeking a more comfortable high-resolution imaging experience, more detailed brain activity scans, or more precise delivery for a range of important therapies, the MentaLink console is the tool for you."

Peter jumped in, his voice teasing. "Val, you don't literally have to recite the speech verbatim! We're not selling her a console, remember?"

Val raised her eyebrows and looked over at him. "Do you think I could ad-lib this after fifteen years of reciting it from memory?"

"Fair enough," he laughed. A bell chimed on the desktop computer, and Peter gave her a thumbs up. "It's ready."

He stepped over to a pair of heavy metal doors at the back of the room. Leah had hardly noticed them before; if she'd thought about it at all, she'd assumed it was a storage closet. Peter turned the handle of the right-side door and pulled it a crack. Leah craned her neck to see inside, but nothing caught her eye.

Does my normal treatment room have one of these?

Peter looked at the two women with an excited smile before opening the door. He nodded to Valerie, who led Leah through the doorway and into the room beyond.

Valerie grinned. "This is my favorite part."

The door closed behind them, and Leah thought she heard the click of a lock. She looked around at the underwhelming second room: large gray tiles lined the floor, walls, and ceiling. There was no obvious light source, but the room wasn't pitch black, and Leah searched up and down for the solution to the paradox.

A wind picked up in the room, like a sudden tornado, with pieces of some unknown material whirling around them. Leah ducked and jumped to avoid getting hit. Valerie stood eerily still, watching with quiet awe. Leah's stomach churned, and she began to worry she might vomit, when she noticed that the flying... things around her were beginning to coalesce. Within moments, the room had been transformed from a boring gray box to a living, breathing scene. Leah inhaled sharply when she realized it was the scene of her accident.

"But where the console really shines," Valerie said, continuing her monologue, "is in its unique connection to the MentaLink simulator. Simulators have already been installed in select beta-testing clinics across the country, and the results have exceeded our wildest hopes. Simulator technology allows treatment teams to create quasi-physical, immersive experiences for their patients. The possibilities are, truly, endless."

The crumpled side door of her sedan and the smoking hood of the truck looked real, and Leah couldn't help herself—she reached out to touch her car door. When her fingers didn't pass through the handle, she gasped. "How did you—"

"On the therapeutic front, ease into exposure therapy in a simulation that gradually increases in intensity as the patient displays readiness to proceed."

As Leah tried to open the door of her sedan, the scenery around them changed again. Leah wanted to close her eyes to steady her churning stomach, but she was too fascinated by the process unfolding in front of her. Her car and the smoking pick-up trick crumbled to dust, which swirled around in the air before coming together in a new shape. Once again, Valerie stood tall in the midst of it, and Leah tried to imitate her confidence. Somehow the particles did seem to pass around—or through—the two women.

Valerie continued her speech. "Allow patients to relive key moments of their lives in vivid detail, giving them the chance to change how they see themselves in their story."

Laid out in front of them was the wide open green space by Common Grounds. Leah bent down to run her fingers through the grass. It felt soft and warm, just as she would have expected, and she marveled at the way it moved under her fingers. She gasped as she saw herself sprinting off away from the coffee shop, Jude Pierucci not far behind her. Just as her ribs began to tighten around her heart, the scene began to shift again. Leah watched, mesmerized.

"Previously unimaginable treatments for trauma, grief, and relational conflict can be conjured up instantaneously."

She recognized the kitchen of her childhood home before the pieces had finished falling into place, and her heart broke as she saw her mother silently removing a third setting from the table. Every detail about the scene was correct, nothing out of place.

I'd forgotten about that huge fight we got in. What I wouldn't give to do that moment over.

Lost in thought, Leah didn't notice as the kitchen melted away.

"Bring your visual metaphors to life as you allow patients to physically release damaging thoughts and emotions into a river, to be carried away by the current."

A brook babbled cheerfully past their feet as wide birch leaves floated down around them, only to be carried downstream. Leah was surprised to see words written into the leaves. She reached out to grab one and stared in disbelief as she recognized her own handwriting:

What I wouldn't give to do that moment over.

Leah held the leaf out to Valerie, who smiled, dropped it into the river, and watched it until it was out of sight.

Turning back to Leah, she concluded her speech. "MentaLink—if you can imagine it, we can make it real."

The wind blew again, this time as gently as a summer breeze, clearing the particles from the room entirely. The gray tiled walls looked as if nothing had happened, and Leah stood for a moment, taking it all in.

When she finally spoke up, her voice was quiet. "Valerie, that's all fascinating, but I don't see how that's going to speed up any kind of process of discovery. I mean, at the risk of sounding ungrateful, is this all you wanted to show me?"

"No, no," Valerie said. "All of that was just prelude to this." As she spoke, the whirlwind began again. Leah's stomach churned, and she screwed her eyes shut.

Her legs felt shaky as she opened her eyes again, just a peep at first, to make sure everything was still. She gasped, eyes wide, as she recognized where they were standing. She wasn't sure what she had expected to see, but it certainly wasn't the library. Her library.

She looked over at Valerie in shock. "How... how did you do this?"

Valerie winked, a wide smile on her face. "If you can imagine it, we can make it real."

Chapter 11

Leah gazed down the central aisle of her library, noticing that all the little details were exactly as she'd imagined them. The beloved scent of old books filled the room. The flickering candles cast dancing shadows all around them.

"But Valerie, this... this is my memory palace. This isn't a real place. It's based on a real place, but it doesn't actually exist." She couldn't help but laugh.

There was a spring in her step as she made her way up and down the stacks, running her fingers along the spines of the books. She pulled one out at random, opened it, and inhaled deeply. She immediately felt her heartbeat and breathing slow. Her muscles relaxed. Her eyes closed. She replaced the book on the shelf and walked to the end of the stack, where a staircase spiraled downward.

"That's where all the information is stored," she mentioned to Valerie. "This library is just the central hub where I can get to everything else. All the good stuff is downstairs, you know? And of course it's organized in its own way. But the library is the place I'm most proud of. I spent a lot of time visualizing the little details. I wanted it to feel like home."

They walked out of the aisle and into the central space of the library, where a large desk sat, littered with papers.

"It's certainly beautiful," Valerie said.

"It's amazing to be able to walk around in it like this. I could easily see myself wanting to spend every waking moment here." Leah looked up at the ceiling, turning in a circle to take in all in. "I never thought I'd be able to do something like this."

"You're not the first to feel that way. The simulation feels very real." She raised her eyebrows as she watched Leah take in the scene. "It's intoxicating—addictive if you aren't careful. Addictive and dangerous."

Leah pulled another book off the shelf and was amazed to realize that there was writing inside. She flipped through a few pages, glancing quickly at the text as she did so.

Evening sunlight peeking around blackout curtains. Her mom, twenty years younger and with anxious tear-stained eyes, crouched at her bedside. A throbbing pain behind one eye.

"Oh wow," she mused aloud. "This is wild. This isn't a piece of information that I actively memorized. This is just... a story. A random, normal day in my life. I wonder if all the books are like this."

Intrigued, Leah replaced the book in her hand and pulled another down.

An empty notebook on a crowded classroom desk. Nervous, excited energy in her stomach. A middle-aged professor using a laser pointer to circle each part of the brain on her slides.

"Is this just... my memory?" The sheer number of volumes in the library began to impress upon her. "What else can this thing do?"

Leah slid the book back into its place and turned to find another. Valerie stood in the library's main aisle a few feet away, and Leah jumped when she saw her. She'd forgotten that she wasn't alone.

"It's incredible that the simulator was able to incorporate things in here that I wasn't even aware of," Leah mused as she wandered over to a different stack.

Pulling another book down, Leah leafed through it.

Butterflies in her stomach. A large dining room table. Eggplant Parmesan and white wine.

She was surprised to see that significant portions of the book had been run through with a black sharpie.

"How odd..."

Her brow furrowed as she scanned the few words and lines that remained. She was unable to make sense of it. Closing her eyes, she tried to recall the rest of the scene.

Nothing.

"What is it?" Valerie asked.

"If all these books contain moments that I didn't consciously commit to memory, why does it look like some of them are... redacted? Like you see on classified documents or blackout poems. It just strikes me as odd." She paused for a moment, lost in thought.

Looking back to Valerie, she continued. "I suppose if this space is a physical manifestation of my memory, then maybe they're just things I forgot?"

She pulled a few other books off the shelf at random, skimming their pages, dog-earing one.

Soulja Boy blaring through gym speakers. Parents and teachers chatting near bowls of candy and punch. Crepe paper jellyfish hanging from basketball goals.

Then another.

Her father's hospital bed. His face contorted with a pain he tried to mask while she was in the room. A frail hand in hers, dry lips pressed to her forehead.

And another.

Blazer and pencil skirt. Hair tied back in a tight bun. Practice answers to practice questions on repeat in her mind. "Thank you for coming in today."

Leah felt Valerie's eyes on her as she worked, at least for the first minute or two, but as her focus deepened, she lost all awareness of her surroundings, like a bloodhound seeking out a scent. Her steps quickened as she paced from stack to stack, rifling through books she selected on instinct. Soon she had fifteen or twenty books out, leafing through each one with intense interest. The dog-eared pile grew, and Leah soon chose to move the books to the desk in the center of the library. She lowered the slant-top surface to lay flat, spreading her haul out in front of her.

She opened all the books back out to the pages she'd marked. Most were heavy-laden with black lines, only a few words still visible. She set these on the left hand side of the desk, stacking them in chronological order with shaking hands. On the right, she piled the few that had only one or two black lines streaking across the pages.

Valerie approached Leah and stood silently beside her. Leah glanced over, then back at the books, and sighed. She leaned over the table and shook her head.

"What is it?" Valerie asked.

"This stack over here..." Leah gestured to the smaller pile of mostly intact books on the right side of the desk. "These are things that I remember. The handful of details that are blacked out are probably just little things I've forgotten over the years. Names of kids I went to grade school with, restaurants we went to for my parents' wedding anniversary, that kind of thing."

Valerie nodded. "And the other pile?" Both women glanced at the stack of books to their left.

"Those scare me," Leah responded quietly. Her teeth chattered, and she clenched her jaw to stop them. "I hardly remember anything in these. Clearly the bare bones are there, but... nothing else. It's just random details with no context. But based on those little details, I have to assume that I'm an adult in most of these. You'd think I would remember more of things that happened more recently, right?" She glanced at Valerie, fists clenched at her sides.

Valerie met her gaze, her eyes deep and still. After a moment, she said, "Why don't we keep walking around?"

Leah shrugged, gave one more long look to the pile of books on the desk, and ran a finger along the edge of the wood surface. She gestured to Valerie to lead the way.

They wound their way through the majority of the building until they found themselves in a back corner. Leah stopped in her tracks, blinking heavily. Her chest tightened. Her heart beat faster. Her muscles tensed.

A towering iron gate covered the span of what should have been the back wall.

"Valerie..." A sense of dread filled Leah's whole body. "What's this?"

Beside her, Valerie remained silent. Leah approached the gate cautiously, peering through the wrought iron bars into a dark room. Dust gathered on half-empty shelves, and the air felt cool and heavy. Books law strewn around the floor, their pages bent and stained. Signs dangled from single cables. Lamps lay sideways on the floor surrounded by broken glass.

Leah gasped and stepped back. An ancient, rusted lock hung on a hefty chain around the center of the gate. Leah reached out and touched it, lifted it, felt its cold weight in her hands.

"I don't know this. I didn't..." Her voice trembled. "I didn't make this. What's going on?"

Valerie laid a gentle hand on Leah's shoulder. "I believe that Natalie told you there is no clinical trial?"

The truth landed like a weight on Leah's chest. Her breath caught in her lungs. "But Peter said he was just observing!"

Valerie frowned and said nothing.

Leah's mind raced. "But wait—what's actually back there?" She rattled the iron bars. They held fast. "Is this related to the blacked out parts of the books? Are there... are there memories behind this gate?"

Valerie's deep brown eyes were heavy as she offered a sad half-smile. "We can only guess. We have ideas, of course. But nothing certain."

Sweat beaded on Leah's hairline, and she felt her face flush. "Are you saying that Dr. Pierucci... what, wiped my memory? That he somehow moved stuff around? Is that—" She pointed at the gate. "Is that me back there? My memories and my knowledge and my life that he's just taken from me?"

Tension built in Leah's limbs as she processed the full implications of her question. She wanted to throw something. She wanted to break down the gate and put things to rights, to tidy and repair and discover what had been moved without her consent.

She assumed it was without her consent.

Could there have been something so horrible that happened to me that I asked Dr. Pierucci to take it away from me?

Before she could follow that train of thought to its natural conclusion, a siren began to blare and a red light flashed around them. Valerie's body tensed, eyes wide.

"We have to go." Her voice was barely a whisper. As she spoke, a crack of light appeared in the gate in front of them, quickly expanding into a right angle and then a doorway. A man's silhouette appeared in the midst of it. Peter.

"This way, Val. You're safe. I won't cut the sim until you're both out here with me. Just needed to give you the warning because my next appointment starts in ten minutes."

Leah watched as Valerie's frozen body relaxed. "Thank you, Peter." She turned back to Leah and gestured toward the door. "Leah, our time has run out. We can continue to talk in the console room, but the simulation cannot run without Peter present."

"Of course." Leah followed Valerie out of the simulation chamber, shivering. As she stepped back into the harsh fluorescent lighting of the console room, her stomach turned sour.

Peter waved a hand towards the orthopedic chair, and she silently resumed her seat. He gave her a moment to get settled before speaking in a gentle voice. "Like I said, I do have to go soon; I have an appointment I wasn't able to cancel, and I know you have to get back to your office for that meeting. But are there any questions you feel like you need to ask now?"

Leah bristled, forcing herself to measure her tone and choose her words carefully. "Valerie and I saw a huge locked section in the library. There were memories behind it—things that Dr. Pierucci had moved out of place so that I couldn't remember them. Explain."

Peter glanced toward the ceiling as he gathered his thoughts. "The long and short of it is that the MentaLink console allows Dr. Pierucci—allows us," he added sheepishly, "—to locate specific memories or bits of information within the brain. As I said last time we talked, the level of detail is really remarkable, and it's come a long way in the last few years. But anyway, once the console has created a map, if you will, of the patient's brain, there's a lot we can do. In some cases, we rewire the neural pathways to rob certain items of their context, and because everything in the brain is interconnected, the loss of context makes recall super difficult." His expression was animated. "It's not technically wiping memories, at that point. It's more like... suppressing them, I guess?" He shrugged.

Valerie coughed pointedly. Peter grimaced and rubbed his forehead slowly before continuing in a less enthusiastic tone. "Your memory palace was a blessing and a curse. It made it easy for Dr. Pierucci to find the specific memories that he was looking for, but it made it much more difficult for him to put those memories somewhere else. In less-orderly minds, it's harder to find particular memories and information, but it's easier to hide them again."

Leah closed her eyes and clenched her fists, taking a long, slow breath.

Peter continued to speak but avoided Leah's eyes. "Since Dr. P essentially had to work within the existing structure you'd set up, there was nowhere that he could 'hide' them, which is why he had to create the... the locked section, as you put it. He was counting on the fact that you wouldn't know about it, so you would never try to access it, so it would stay hidden in plain sight."

Leah raised her eyebrows, leaning forward in her seat. "So all you had to do was show it to me."

"Exactly!" Peter's face lit up. "And now that you're aware of it, your brain will start to push back. The human brain is comfortable with a lot of ambiguity, forgetfulness, contradiction, even outright falsehood... But we've found that it does not appreciate being meddled with. It's kind of like a scab that your subconscious can't stop picking at. Once you're aware that things have been 'rewired' up there, your brain starts trying to restore order."

Leah nodded slowly. "I understand." Something gnawed at the pit of her stomach. The lights seemed brighter. The sounds seemed louder.

I need to get away from here.

"It's a lot to take in," Valerie added. "And you're not alone."

Leah nodded again, her mind racing. She couldn't focus on anything as Peter excused himself to prepare for his next appointment and Valerie walked her to the back door of the clinic. Before she knew it, the heavy metal door clicked behind her, leaving her alone with a large blue dumpster in the dusty back alley. She kicked a rock, watching as it tumbled across the concrete and thudded into the metal dumpster. The noise reverberated around her, filling the alley.

Peter is complicit in this. And he enjoys it. How could he do this to me?

She started walking back around the building to the main parking lot, questioning how and why she'd let herself be dismissed from the back exit.

Everything about this whole situation just screams criminal activity.

A flock of whistling ducks flew by overhead, their bright orange beaks barely visible from the ground. The sight filled her with a deep ache.

I wish Mom still lived in town.

If she heard the creak and click of the door, she didn't think anything of it. But the sound of shuffling steps behind her drew her out of her thoughts.

Could Valerie have come back through on her way home?

The back of her neck tingled. She blinked heavily. Time slowed down.

"Leah?"

She recognized the voice. A shiver crawled its way up her spine, and her stomach flipped. Leah turned around slowly, her heart pounding in her chest.

Jude Pierucci, Jr. stood just behind her, his eyes wide and his mouth agape.

Chapter 12

"Leah!" Jude called out again. He took another step in her direction.

"Make sure she gets to her car. Stay out of sight as much as you can."

She felt herself shrinking, her heart pounding.

Pounding feet racing toward her as she sat at a bus stop in a strange part of town, the world spinning to darkness around her.

"I'm sorry—it seems I've startled you." He began, taking a step back. "I should have introduced myself. I'm Jude Pierucci. I'm Dr. Pierucci's son."

"If Jude sees you—there will be hell to pay."

"Hi." Leah glanced around the back lot, wishing anyone else was there.

Jude raised his eyebrows. "Seems like you're a little lost. Did you get turned around inside? I know that back hallway can be a nightmare to navigate."

Do I play dumb? What'll he do to me if he thinks that no one else knows I'm here?

"I guess so," she said with a tittering laugh. "I've been coming here for over a year now, but I still get lost so easily if Peter doesn't have me in the exact same exam room."

Don't mention Peter! But wait—he's gotta know that Peter is my technician, right?

He chuckled. "I know what you mean. My father's been working here since I was a child, and there are still days where I get distracted and have to wander around for a minute or two to get my bearings. It really is a maze."

Leah laughed back, half genuinely and half as a survival mechanism. It sounded hollow, but if Jude noticed, he said nothing. Instead, he turned around and gestured back toward the building, clearly intending for her to follow him.

Here goes nothing.

She took a step toward the building, wishing she had some way to let Peter know what was happening. As a desperate measure, she pulled his contact up on her phone as discreetly as she could, clicking "share location indefinitely" before sliding it back into her pocket.

I hope Jude didn't catch that.

He had swiped his staff badge on the pad next to the door and held it open for her, watching her and waiting.

"Oh, thanks! Sorry about that—got a text from the client I'm meeting with this afternoon. Got to hurry back to the office to finish up a project for them. It's already a little behind schedule, and they'll be livid if I miss the meeting."

I'm expected somewhere. If anything happened to me, someone would notice. I would be missed.

"Another meeting this late in the day? Working hard, I guess." It wasn't the response she expected.

Could Peter and the others be wrong about him?

She shrugged. "They're over in California, so they just finished lunch. You gotta do what you gotta do."

"That you do," he replied, nodding. "That you do."

See, someone gets it!

Jude ushered Leah in through the back door, closing it behind them before taking the lead. Leah watched him, noting the strength in his arms and back, obvious even through his dress shirt.

"So, how did your appointment go?" They were walking towards the main lobby of the building. "You're here earlier than we were expecting you."

Leah's eyes widened. "Um... it was fine, I guess? I had something come up at the last minute and had to reschedule." She heard the fear in her own voice and hoped that he didn't. "Another work project. But the treatment is going fine. Just more of the same."

She desperately wished she could see his expression, and she picked up her pace to walk next to him instead of behind him.

Jude glanced over at her as she matched his pace. "I know my father will be disappointed to have missed you. He enjoys seeing you each month. Your case is fascinating, and it eats away at him that he hasn't been able to get you a diagnosis. He tells everyone that he's in medicine for the good he gets to do, but between you and me?" He opened the door to the main lobby. "It's really about the puzzles. And you, Le—Ms. Harvey... you are a puzzle that has been unsolved for too long."

She didn't like his tone. There was a note of finality in it that scared her, but before Leah could bolt out the front door, he spoke up again. "How have you been lately?"

"Not bad, I guess?" She shrugged. "Lots going on." They lingered in the waiting room for a few seconds before Leah realized her mistake. "Oh, you meant all this! Great, honestly. The treatments have really hit a good stride, and my symptoms have been super manageable."

He chuckled again, warmly. "Well, I did mean more generally than just your symptoms, but I'm glad to hear that they're not bothering you as much. And I'm glad that you're doing well." He glanced around the room, but it was mostly empty. "Oh, by the way—am I mistaken, or did I see you at Common Grounds a few weeks ago? I would have sworn it was you, but an old coworker wanted to catch up, and by the time she'd walked away, you were gone."

Leah froze. She nodded slowly.

He saw us that day after all? How much does he know?

"I'm sorry–I'm not trying to frighten you. I only ask because I thought I saw you with another patient of ours, and I was wondering what the two of you were doing out together. I hope I'm not being too forward if I express a little anxiety on that front, assuming that I'm not misreading the situation. He... of course, I can't say his name, but I'm sure you know who I'm talking about." He met Leah's gaze. "He's not entirely safe. In fact, I'd go so far as to say that he's quite dangerous... I'd really hate for some harm to come to you that I could have prevented. Please, do forgive me for being so cryptic. HIPPA prevents me from saying more... from saying everything I'd like to say."

"Thanks..." Leah's stomach dropped. She wasn't sure what response he expected, but she didn't want to risk angering him.

Relief washed over his face. "No, thank you for understanding. Patient relationships can be so delicate, and I'm still working to master the art of it." Jude looked out the window, intently studying the cars in the parking lot. "Father is ready for me to take on a little more leadership here at the Institute, but if I'm being honest, I'm a little nervous about it. He always expects so much of me, and I so rarely feel confident that I'm living up to his expectations." He met her gaze, his deep blue-gray eyes drawing her in.

"But of course, he knows that. No one can keep secrets from Father for long."

She didn't respond.

"It's really good to see you." He smiled.

That was the last straw. "I'm sorry, do we know each other? You're talking as if we're close friends or something, but I don't think we've ever actually met."

Jude froze, just for the tiniest fraction of a second, before leaning his head back and laughing. "I am so sorry, Ms. Harvey! Would you believe that I do this all the time? As my father's executive assistant, I know all the patients here at the clinic, and I sometimes come to feel a sort of affection for you all. I forget that so much of my experience with you is one-sided." He shifted his weight to the other foot. "And with you being in the clinical trial and all, I know my father has a particular attentiveness to your case, which means that I do as well."

Leah wasn't satisfied, but she also wasn't going to press the issue. "I see."

He opened the front door of the clinic for her, and she stepped out into the hot, humid afternoon. It felt refreshing after the chill of the clinic's interior.

"Wait!" A tiny crack appeared in his suave air. "It really was good to see you, Leah. And... I'm sorry. For everything. I hope you can forgive me."

Her heart stopped, and she slowly turned back around to face him. She felt the muscles in her arms and legs loosen, ready to run if she needed to.

A subtle sadness had come into his voice that concerned her, but more frightening was the look in his eyes: hungry, almost. She would have described him as awestruck if she hadn't known better.

I need to get out of here right now.

Leah laughed, hoping that her discomfort wasn't too obvious. "Don't worry about it, Jude. We all overshare sometimes."

"Of course. Goodbye, Leah." He raised a hand to wave.

"Goodbye." She made her way down to her car, steeling herself for her phone call with her mom. A thought had crossed her mind during the aftermath of her appointment, and she hadn't been able to let it go.

I've been telling myself for so long now that Mom changed after her stroke... but what if she's not the one who changed?

She started her car and called her mom, who picked up right away.

Leah put on her most cheerful voice. "Hey Mom!"

"Well hi, Leah! You sound like you're in a good mood."

"Just glad to talk to you. Although I don't have too long—my appointment today ran long, and I have to rush back to the office for a meeting with my California folks."

She sighed. "I know you're busy."

Come on, Mom, there's no need to get defensive about it.

Leah swallowed down a lump in her throat as she turned out of the parking lot. "What have you been up to?"

"Oh, not much. Just getting ready for my trip to go see my sister next week, which will be lots of fun. She said she's going to try to get the grandkids to come over to play in the sprinklers. Apparently they love that and they just laugh and laugh. So it should be good."

Leah could hear the smile in her mom's voice, and she laughed at the thought of cousin's kids. "Yes! Give Kathy and her family my best. You're going to have so much fun with them."

"I hope so!"

The light ahead of Leah turned green, and she put her foot on the gas pedal. "Oh, by the way!" She screwed up her courage and spat out the next sentence before she could talk herself out of it. "I had the most bizarre dream last night, Mom, that you'd had another stroke."

"Another?" She laughed. "The first is news to me!"

Leah played along, her mind reeling. "Oh gosh! Was that also part of the dream? I guess it must have been—I was so certain in the dream that it was your second stroke. I guess it really got into my head that you'd had one in the last year or so. How wild. It felt so real!"

"No, Leah, I think I'd remember if I'd had a stroke. Heck, I'd probably go see Dr. P, just for old times' sake. But no, no strokes here."

Leah forced a laugh.

Go see Dr. P for old times' sake??

She reigned in her confusion. "Well, isn't that a relief."

"You're telling me!"

Leah changed lanes and got on the freeway. "Dreams are funny things, aren't they?"

"You can say that again. And always so hard to remember what's real and what isn't."

"Absolutely."

She heard her mom bustling around the house. She had to work to recall what the house looked like—she'd only visited a few times since her mom had moved back to be closer to her own parents. A homesick ache settled across Leah's shoulders as she remembered her last visit to her dad's last home, right before her mom had moved.

"Well, honey." Her mom's voice cut her thoughts short. "I need to start a load of laundry, so I'll let you go. It's been good to chat with you."

141

Leah sighed. "Alright. Bye, Mom. Love you."

"Bye, Leah."

The call ended.

That felt... weirdly normal? Is it possible that Mom is right? There's no way... she just doesn't remember her stroke.

She shook her head as she stepped out of the car. A notification sounded on her phone—a reminder of her upcoming four o'clock meeting. The sound both startled and grounded her.

She tried to avoid eye contact on her way in from the parking lot, only offering the smallest of half-smiles to the few passersby who insisted on being seen. She closed her door, locked it for good measure, and sat down at her desk. Her laptop was still open, a pop-up reminder on screen. She opened the video conference but didn't begin the meeting yet.

Deep breath in.

Deep breath out.

She shuffled through the pages of her legal pad, looking for the notes she'd need.

Deep breath in.

Deep breath out.

Her phone rang. Peter's name appeared on her screen. She hadn't thought of him or Valerie since encountering Jude, and seeing his name added a new layer of worry to her situation. She typed out a short text message.

Going into my four o'clock. Will call ASAP.

She silenced her phone and placed it on her desk screen down. No need for further distractions. One more deep breath. The clock turned four, and Leah started the meeting.

Halfway through her call—she'd given all her updates and was trying to focus on what her clients were asking for—she peeked for the tiniest moment at her phone. Set it back down. Picked it back up. Tried to balance it in front of her computer screen so she could see it without appearing to ignore the others in the meeting.

Four missed calls from Peter. A voicemail. Two text messages. Another call from an unknown number that Leah hoped was just a notice about her car's extended warranty. And one call from the Institute's main line. The last one worried her—there was no way for her to know who from the Institute was calling.

"—isn't that right, Leah?"

Leah's eyes shot back to the video call. Three other sets of eyes stared back at her expectantly. In the minute that her attention had been diverted, she'd lost track of the conversation, and no one offered a hint of what they'd been discussing.

"I think so, but I'd love to hear any additional insights you have," she replied, crossing her fingers under her desk. The line was a go-to in these meetings, and she hoped it wouldn't let her down this time.

The client resumed talking, and she nodded along for a few seconds as she reoriented herself. Once she'd gathered enough context clues to feel confident in speaking up, she rejoined the conversation, setting her phone down next to her once again.

Peter will have to wait.

When the meeting wrapped up, Leah wished her clients goodbye with a forced smile. The second the video conference closed, she let her face drop and massaged her tired cheeks. The clock read ten minutes to five. Leah placed a hand on the back of her laptop to close it for the night, but something stopped her. Staying in her seat felt safer. Her blood still thumped in her ears, not allowing her to forget the game of three-dimensional chess that had been her conversation with Jude just an hour or two before.

She flipped her phone over again, allowing the screen to light up and reveal an additional call and text from Peter, and a voicemail from the Institute's main line.

I'm not ready for this yet.

She picked up her water bottle and mechanically walked down to the water fountain for a refill. Passing the coffee maker on the way back, she fixed herself a cup of decaf with two packs of sugar and a splash of cream before making her way back to her office.

One thing at a time.

First the text messages.

Call me as soon as your meeting is over.

Eight minutes later.

Shelby told me she saw you and Jude walking out together. Call me when you can.

And finally, just before her meeting had ended:

How long is this meeting? Call me. Urgent.

Peter's voicemail was more of the same, although his breathy whisper and quickened pace made his words hard to understand.

The second voicemail, from the Institute line, gave her pause. It looked longer than Peter's, and while it was theoretically possible that he or even Valerie had used

Shelby's desk phone to try and reach her, something in her gut told her that wasn't the case.

After staring at her phone for a long minute, she worked up the courage to hit play.

"Good evening Ms. Harvey. This is Jude Pierucci, Jr. from the McNeill Institute for Neurological Development. I just wanted to call and follow up on our conversation this afternoon, which I'm afraid I let get out of hand. I wanted to apologize for my lack of professionalism, and particularly for my indiscretion in bringing up some rather sensitive topics that were not related to your treatment. Anyway... The real reason I called is to let you know that since Dr. Pierucci didn't get to see you today, I anticipate he'll want to get you on the phone soon, just to touch base with you about the study. I'll try you again in a couple days when he's returned to the office so that we can find a time that works for everyone's schedule. Thank you so much. Goodbye."

What the...

She closed her voicemail and returned Peter's call.

He answered on the first ring. "Leah, thank God."

"I saw your texts. Fill me in."

Peter exhaled heavily. "Not two minutes before my appointment started, Valerie let me know that she'd almost walked straight into Jude Pierucci on her way out of the clinic. Jude knowing that she'd been there would have been catastrophic for several reasons, but Val isn't who I'm worried about, I know she can hold her own. She ducked into a side room, it all turned out fine."

"Of course."

"But Shelby told me she saw Jude walking you out together—is that... I mean, did that actually happen? Because if so, we're in big trouble."

Leah inhaled sharply and heard her voice waver as she responded. "How much trouble?"

A few choice words on the other end of the call gave Leah all the answer she needed.

"He thought I'd gotten lost and ended up in the back on accident." She gritted her teeth, waiting for Peter's response. "When he first walked out, I thought about running, but I wasn't sure if that would cause more trouble. So I just played dumb and went along with it."

She heard Peter breathe on the other end of the line. "I'm going to do some investigating. I'll call you back by ten o'clock. Stay safe, Leah. We can all hope this will just blow over, but I'd feel better knowing you had an overnight bag packed, just in case..."

Her eyes widened. "In case of what?"

"I don't know." He paused. "In case I can't delete your address from your patient file quickly enough."

The words sent a chill down Leah's spine.

"Peter—"

"What is it?"

She found herself hesitating again, resistant to the idea of telling him about her conversation with Jude and the voicemail he'd left for her. She must have paused for longer than she realized, because Peter asked again. "What is it, Leah? Is everything okay?"

"Yeah." She shook her head. "Thank you, Peter. Please let me know as soon as you know anything."

"Of course. Stay safe. I hope I'm overreacting."

"I do, too." The desperation in her voice surprised her.

He ended the call without saying goodbye. Leah packed her backpack with trembling hands and slowly made her way out to her car.

"I hope I'm overreacting."

She repeated the words under her breath, alternately terrified and comforted by them.

Back at home, Leah threw some pizza rolls in the oven for dinner and sat down to wait for them to finish cooking. In her mind, she stood in lobby of the McNeill Institute, pondering the look in Jude's eyes and the fondness in his voice. Out of nowhere, she heard that same voice, laced with intense desperation, echoing back from somewhere deep inside her, as if a book in her library had been picked up and the black lines swept back.

"Could we not suppress her memories, and then replace them with our own stories? If the attempt fails, more extreme options are never off the table."

The thought took her by surprise. It felt real. Solid.

I've never spoken with Jude before today... when would I have heard his voice before?

A sobering thought dawned on her as she remembered the redacted books she'd piled high in her library that afternoon.

Did I know Jude before whatever happened to me?

If that thought really was a memory—if it really was something Jude had said to her, or at least said in her presence—then he might be a major player not just in the cover-up and the falsified clinical trial, but also in whatever had gotten her there in the first place. The possibility both intrigued and scared her. Her heart sank as she considered how little she really knew, but she was increasingly certain of two things: Jude Pierucci, Jr. knew something about her memories being removed, and she would do whatever it took to find out what that was.

147

Chapter 13

Leah awoke the following morning to a voicemail from Peter. He hadn't called until well after ten o'clock, but she hadn't noticed. The message was short and to the point.

"Leah, sorry to call you so late—I think we're in the clear through the end of the week. Dr. Pierucci decided to extend his trip, and that all of his appointments should stay in place. Seems weird to me, but I'm not going to look a gift horse in the mouth. Call me tomorrow."

Leah listened to it but didn't respond. She felt a twinge of guilt for not having told him about her conversation with Jude, but she was certain Peter would have told her not to investigate further, and she wasn't willing to do that. There were a few things she wanted to look into, questions she needed answered without anyone else's comments clouding her judgment. Once she was satisfied on those—or once she reached a dead end—she'd consider touching base with Peter again.

Random pieces of conversations from the previous day were swirling uncontrolled through her mind. It was like trying to complete a jigsaw puzzle with no reference image and half the pieces missing.

"I hope you can forgive me." "Shelby told me she saw you and Jude walking out together." "If you can imagine it, we can make it

real." "We can only guess. We have ideas, of course." "The human brain does not appreciate being meddled with."

Perhaps most haunting was the memory that had resurfaced, unbidden, the previous afternoon. Jude's voice—she was somehow certain it was his—saying words she remembered but couldn't remember.

"Could we not suppress her memories, and then replace them with our own stories? If the attempt fails, more extreme options are never off the table."

Jude having blocked her on Facebook suddenly seemed much less like standard practice and much more like a personal choice. In her search for answers, his profile was tantalizing—close enough to grasp but just out of reach, almost certainly a step toward clarity but definitively inaccessible.

I wonder if his profile is public... I could ask someone else to take a look at it for me.

After a brief moment of hesitation, she typed out a text message and hit "send".

> Hey Sarah. Long time no chat. I'm working from home today, are you around? Got something I want to talk about. I've got a dozen muffins with your and Connor's name on them.

She reread her message and set her phone down before pulling out the ingredients and organizing them on her kitchen counter.

Work from Home Wednesdays was a gimmick Ana had initiated for the team a few months back, hoping to raise morale. So while "I've got a dozen muffins with your and Connor's name on them" wasn't yet strictly true, it would be within the hour.

As she prepared her batter, her mind never stopped rotating puzzle pieces, trying to fit together something—anything—that might point her in the right direction. She kept returning to Jude's Facebook page as the most logical next step.

I hope Sarah responds soon. If his profile isn't public, we can figure out what to do after that. But best to at least give it a shot before getting Peter involved.

Just as Leah put the muffins in the oven, a ping sounded from her pocket.

Lunch? I need to leave by three.

A quick affirmative ended the conversation. Lunch it was. Leah's stomach squirmed at the thought.

I hope this works.

***

An hour or two later, Leah stood on the doorstep of Sarah and Connor's apartment, muffins in a bowl, stomach in knots. She had just raised her hand to knock on the door when it opened without her touching it.

Sarah greeted her. "Hey! Welcome!"

Leah smiled. "Hey, Sarah."

"What's up? Your text seemed kinda out of the blue." Sarah shrugged.

"I..." Leah swallowed hard, steeling herself for a lecture. "I just hadn't heard from you in a while and thought it might be nice to catch up."

She grinned. "And you brought muffins!"

"I did." Leah handed the bowl to Sarah, who took it and stepped out of the doorway, allowing Leah to enter.

The sun peeked in at the corner of the window, a large square of light dancing on the floor.

"Well, come on in and let's eat. How have you been?"

Leah laughed nervously and raised her eyebrows. "You go first. I've got a story for you on that front."

They ate and chatted and, all things considered, it felt good. That realization was comforting and confusing to Leah, who had half expected to be chided for not checking in sooner or for only reaching out when she wanted something. As Sarah brought her plate over to the sink and returned to the table with a glass of water, she brought over a muffin for each of them.

She sat down and leaned forward in her seat. "So then, what's this story you've got?"

All of the sudden, Leah felt a squirm in her stomach. "Do you remember a couple of weeks ago, the whole drama with my medication?"

Sarah didn't respond, but her expression told Leah that she did. She carefully broke her muffin into four pieces and took a bite of one.

Leah left her own muffin sitting on her napkin untouched. "I can't remember how much we've talked since then, but it turns out that this clinical trial I'm in isn't a clinical trial at all. It's a long story. There was this FBI agent at this coffee shop, and another woman who I sort of knew? And then this creepy guy came, and we had to—"

"Leah, Leah, Leah, Leah." Sarah waved her hands, shaking her head rapidly. "Back up. Back up. None of this is making any sense."

Leah groaned. "Sorry. There's a lot. I should just start at the beginning, shouldn't I?"

So Leah told the story from start to finish: Agent McDowell's visit to her office; the car accident; the meet-up at Common Grounds and Jude's presence there; her investigation into the clinical trial and the fallout of what she'd learned. She felt herself falling into the role of storyteller, encouraged by Sarah's expressions of curiosity and, at times, concern. The muffins lay on the table, half-eaten. Eventually she caught up to the rescheduling of her most recent appointment. "So then Peter—the guy I've been talking to—"

"Talking to?" Sarah grinned widely.

"Not like that!" Leah felt her cheeks redden. "He's just the guy from the Institute who's been walking me through all this stuff. My technician."

"Oh. Just a guy. Sure." Sarah winked.

Leah stuck out her tongue.

If there were going to be 'just a guy', it wouldn't be Peter.

She paused for a moment, lost in thought.

"I wasn't trying to make it weird," Sarah chimed in, worry in her voice.

"Oh, no, yeah. Sorry, I got distracted." Leah shook her head. "Anyway, Peter was insistent that I come in when Dr. Pierucci was out of the office because he wanted to show me some of the stuff the Institute tech can do—which," she pointed at Sarah with her fingers crossed, "don't let me forget to tell you all about it because it's incredible—but one of the things Peter showed me yesterday was that the Institute hasn't actually been treating me for symptoms... It looks more like they've been altering my memory."

Sarah's brows furrowed. "Altering your memory? Like, what do you mean, changing your memories into things that didn't happen?"

"That's what it seemed like." Leah nodded, gritting her teeth. "Removing old memories, at least, and letting my brain make up stories to fill in the gaps."

"What the... Leah, are you sure about all this?" Sarah's tone was skeptical. "You had all that paranoia, and then someone told you to stop taking a prescription medication, and now this? I don't know... this is starting to feel like a poorly written science fiction show."

Leah chose not to engage with Sarah's comment, hesitant to say something that might hurt her chances of carrying out her plan. "So I was leaving my appointment, and I ran into Dr. Pierucci's son, Jude. That's the guy Natalie was surprised to see at Common Grounds. And Jude was clearly surprised to see me—which seemed weird in and of itself, since I'm a patient there, and it's not like we've met before—but I don't know..." She looked around Sarah's kitchen. "We talked for a while because he thought I was lost and he wanted to show me the way out, and he seemed... kind of nice? I guess I just imagined that if Natalie was so frightened of him, he must be horrible."

Probably best not to mention that Jude was at Common Grounds the day I had my breakdown.

Sarah nodded, her eyes narrowed slightly.

Leah looked back down at her muffin, still only half eaten. "But I also felt a little bit like I was playing a game of chess. Part of me wants to believe that it was just all the secrecy Peter had about rescheduling the appointment, you know? Or maybe it is just still paranoia, and it's all in my head. But some of Jude's comments left me... worried."

"Hm," Sarah huffed. "Comments like...?"

Leah wracked her brain for the specific phrasing Jude had used. "Oh, it was something like... 'You can't keep secrets from Father for long.' That might not have been exactly how he said it, but it was along those lines."

"Okay," Sarah cocked her head to one side. "I mean, I can see how that could sound threatening."

"Exactly. And then... I don't know, he was talking about one of the other patients, who I'm kind of... well, friendly with, I guess. Called him dangerous. Said he wouldn't want me getting hurt by this guy." The thought of Wilder made Leah's stomach ache, and she kept talking before Sarah had time to ask any questions. "Right as we were parting ways, he started apologizing for something, but he didn't say what. And then he called an hour later and left me a voicemail where tried to play the whole thing off as professional indiscretion? I don't know, it just felt... off. Honestly, let me just play it for you."

Leah pulled out her phone and played the voicemail. As they listened, Sarah opened her mouth, as if to make a comment, but closed it again, gesturing for Leah to continue her story.

"Later that afternoon—yesterday afternoon, I guess—a memory... or, at least, it really felt like a memory, but I don't know... anyway, it was Jude recommending that they—whoever 'they' are—replace my memories, and it just suddenly clicked that maybe the reason he acted like he knew me was because... he did know me."

Her voice had gotten smaller throughout the last sentence. Hearing herself say it out loud really brought it home. Her shoulders slumped, and she tore off a small bite of her muffin and popped it in her mouth. Sweat beaded on her hairline, and she couldn't stop fiddling with a bit of loose skin on her lip. Sheepishly, she looked toward Sarah, who met her eyes with quiet compassion.

After a few seconds, Sarah spoke up. "That sounds really hard, Leah. Whatever's going on, I'm sorry that you're going through it."

The sentiment took Leah by surprise. Sympathy hadn't been on the list of expected responses. The two women sat in companionable silence for a little while, each expecting the other to speak first.

Well, it's now or never.

"So, I have a weird favor to ask. It sounds a little crazy, but at some point recently I realized that Jude has me blocked on Facebook. I assumed it was just an overly cautious professional policy, but now I'm not so sure. I don't have any idea if his profile is public or not, but could we..." Leah pulled off another piece of muffin. "Could we check if you can see his page from your account?"

Sarah had pulled her laptop out before Leah even finished her question. She turned the screen towards Leah, who typed Jude's name with trembling fingers.

His profile was, indeed, public. She glanced through the sparse posts and photos he had shared over the last two years and didn't see anything that stood out. Switching over to posts and photos he had been tagged in, Leah began to lose hope that his profile would lead anywhere.

And then she saw it.

There, staring back at her through the screen, was her own smiling face. Her hair was shorter, her makeup heavier. She looked tired.

The photo was dated from two New Years' Days ago—eighteen months had passed since it was taken. She didn't recognize the name of the person who had posted it, but a little gray arrow with Jude's name appeared under his face. No tag appeared under hers.

She wore a diamond ring on her left hand.

"Holy cow, Leah. Is that you?" Sarah asked. Her voice was hushed. "That looks like an engagement ring." She zoomed in on the photograph, trying to get a closer look.

Leah nodded, her hand over her mouth. "That definitely looks like an engagement ring. And it does look like the kind of ring I'd want. Not that that proves anything, I guess." Her heart sank. "Was I engaged to...?" The question died in her throat.

Sarah slid the laptop back towards herself, clicking through a few more photos and posts as Leah sat in stunned silence. A clock on the wall ticked out the seconds, and a bird outside trilled its repetitive song.

Sarah looked up from her screen. "Leah, I'm not going to lie to you. This definitely looks like the remnants of a relationship he tried to scrub off his profile." Leah opened her mouth, but Sarah wasn't finished. "And before you ask, no, he isn't on Instagram, so there's nothing we can find over there."

Leah leaned back in her chair, sobering to the reality of what they were seeing. It didn't feel real, necessarily, but it also didn't feel so far out of the realm of possibility that she could dismiss it out of hand. It felt... heavy. Tired.

A knot began to form in the pit of her stomach. "Sarah, I think I need to go."

Sarah reached a hand out toward her. "Are you okay?"

Leah's hands remained under the table. "I'm not sure. But I need answers. I'm sick of just uncovering more questions."

"Okay." Sarah nodded slowly, her eyes wide. "I don't quite understand what's going on, and none of this makes any sense to me, but... I'm with you."

Leah looked up and met Sarah's gaze. "Thanks, friend. That means a lot."

As she walked back to her own apartment, Leah typed out a text to Peter, hoping to get his attention quickly.

We need to talk about Jude. Call me.

There would be no turning back now.

Chapter 14

Less than two minutes later, Peter's name appeared on her screen. Leah was at her door, but as she answered the call, she chose to keep walking, hoping that doing so would still her pounding heart.

"What happened?" Peter's voice was tense.

Leah didn't waste time on pleasantries. "Was I engaged to Jude Pierucci before his father removed my memories?"

"Um—I—" Peter stammered. "How did you—? What?"

"Is that a yes?" she demanded.

He inhaled deeply. Exhaled. "Can we meet up tonight to talk about this? I can't have this conversation over the phone."

She felt her eyes roll but tried to keep her irritation out of her tone. "Fine. Where do you want to meet?"

"Would you be okay with going over to Natalie's house? I need to make sure she's free tonight, but I don't think this is a conversation for me to be having."

Leah breathed out, her cheeks puffing up as she did so. "Fine. Just have her text me the address."

"Will do. And Leah?" He paused. "Thank you for your patience. I know this can't be easy for you."

"Bye, Peter." She hung up.

So that's a "yes" then.

Leah took another lap around her complex, allowing herself to work up a sweat. Her heart beat faster and her breaths stayed shallow, but as she approached her door and slowed back to a walk, she felt invigorated by the exercise. She let herself back into her apartment, walked back to her desk, and pulled out a sheet of paper. She started writing, the questions piling on top of one another.

- How and when did Jude and I meet? How long did we date? How long were we engaged? When and why did we break up?

- How much did Jude know about or play a role in removing my memories?

- Did Dr. Pierucci know about my relationship with Jude? Did Dr. Pierucci remove my memories because of my relationship with Jude? Could my relationship with Jude have been so traumatic that I asked his father to make me forget it? Is Jude dangerous?

- Is Wilder/McDowell actually dangerous? Is it possible that he has some sort of split personality disorder, or some kind of delusions? Or does Jude have some other reason to drive a wedge between us?

- How has no one ever said anything about the fact that I used to be engaged? About any of it?

The last question dropped like a bounder on her chest, pushing away any other thoughts.

- I've been in this 'clinical trial' since last May. I signed my apartment lease last May. I started my job last May. Is there anything in my life that has been part of my life longer than this treatment I've been receiving?

She wracked her brain for a long moment before the answer revealed itself.

Mom.

Her heart pounded. Her chest began to tighten.

I'm not ready to face that.

She shook her head to dislodge the thought, glancing instead back to her page. As she read over her own words, her fingers reached for the ring on her left hand. Her mindless fidget.

Her ring was gone.

Her heart skipped a beat as she looked down at her hand. Empty. Her eyes flew around the room, scanning her desk and the floor. Nothing.

She stood up and walked around her apartment, checking in all the usual spots. Had she left it in the kitchen? In the bathroom? By her bed?

Standing in the doorway of her room, Leah came to a startling realization.

There was no ring.

She wasn't engaged.

What just happened? That muscle memory of reaching for my left hand—the certainty that I'd lost something—where did that come from?

She looked down at her hand, then back around her room. A queasy feeling arose in her stomach and she thought she might vomit. A glass of water and a lone peppermint—leftover from some holiday and dug out of the back of the pantry—steadied her stomach enough to get her out of the bathroom, but she didn't feel well enough to sit at her desk and putter through whatever series of minuscule changes her clients would demand.

Work isn't going to happen.

Curled in the fetal position in her bed with the blanket up to her chin, Leah sent a quick email to her supervisor.

Ana,
I'm feeling ill. Mostly finished my tasks this
morning, but probably not going to get any more
work done. Can I take the afternoon off?

Sincerely,
Leah Harvey

Planning to ask for forgiveness if permission was not granted, Leah closed her eyes and tried to drift off to sleep. She felt herself doze in and out before a notification sounded on her phone and woke her back up.

Slacking off again, Leah? Kidding, of course. Hope
you feel better. See you tomorrow.

Ana

The tone was friendly enough, but she was sure Ana would fuss at her in the morning.

Nothing to be done about it.

Setting an alarm for an hour later, Leah curled up and closed her eyes. It wouldn't do to go to Natalie's house feeling terrible, or worse, to have to cancel.

***

When she woke, the nausea had subsided. The sky was gray with cloud cover, and the dull light barely illuminated her room. A group text had been started during her nap, containing Natalie's address, their family's usual dinner time, and Peter's offer to bring dessert. Seeing the logistics laid out in front of her brought home the reality—and absurdity—of her situation.

I need a cup of tea.

She watched the water bubble and hiss in the electric kettle before pouring a generous splash into her empty cast iron teapot. As she waited for it to get warm, she rifled through her cabinet and settled on a mango black tea that had been a pantry staple since her undergraduate years. She measured out the loose leaves and filled the mesh basket sitting on the counter.

She tapped the side of the teapot and drew her hand back in surprise at how quickly it had heated up. Pouring the first pot of water down the sink, she placed the basket into the teapot and refilled it, breathing deeply as the steam rose.

After a few sips of tea, Leah pulled out her phone and began typing a message to Sarah. The process of writing the text felt like wrestling, as she went back and forth on what specifically she wanted to say and whether she even wanted to send the message at all.

> Sarah, thanks again for this afternoon. I'm going to meet up with Peter and Natalie from the clinic tonight to talk about Jude. Thought you might want to know. I'm kind of scared about it.

I guess I am a little scared, aren't I?

She read the message back to herself, biting on her lip. Her finger hovered over the 'send' button as she debated whether or not to include the last sentence.

She sent the message and set her phone down. Picked it back up. Set it back down.

Why hasn't Sarah responded yet?

Annoyed, Leah tossed her phone onto the couch and sat back at the table to finish her tea. The nausea had passed. She had the afternoon off. Dinner wasn't for a while. She stared into space, her mind racing.

Engagement. Maybe a wedding website? Maybe an announcement in the paper? Who was the person that posted the photo of me and Jude—maybe they have more photos I could find.

Sarah's reply came as Leah was opening her computer:

How are you holding up?

Leah hesitated for a moment before replying.

Not great. Took the afternoon off because I was feeling nauseous. Took a nap. Feeling better now. Trying to find something to research.

She was about to pull up Facebook and see if she could find some mutual connections between herself and Jude when one more text from Sarah arrived. She knew what it was going to say before it came in.

Stay off the screens. Go take a walk.

Leah rolled her eyes, a half-smile on her face. She changed into a t-shirt, laced up her sneakers, and stepped outside.

Forty-five minutes later, Leah arrived back at her door drenched in sweat. A shower filled the rest of her hour, and once she was dressed and ready, she hopped in the car. Her stomach churned as she pulled up the directions.

***

Natalie and her family lived in a modest house on a cul-de-sac in a suburban neighborhood, and the small fleet of wheels littering the yard—a scooter, a tiny green bike with no pedals, a red and yellow plastic car, and a kid-size bicycle—attested to an active family life. In the warm evening sunlight, it seemed idyllic. Worlds away from the confusion and suspicion in Leah's mind.

Another sedan pulled up behind her as she opened her car door. After a moment, Peter got out and began walking up to the house. The door opened, and light spilled out onto the walkway. Natalie's silhouette stood in the doorway to welcome them. A cacophony of whoops and hollers wafted out with the smell of hamburgers on the grill. Leah followed Peter up the walk, but he didn't have time to greet Natalie before one of her kids grabbed him by the hand and dragged him inside.

Natalie watched with a tired smile as her son ran off with Peter. She ran a hand through her hair as Leah approached and offered a quiet greeting. "Leah, so good to see you again. Thanks so much for being willing to come to our place—Matthew does most of bedtime with the kids, so we should be able to talk freely after dinner."

Matthew's arms were full of a giggling child who might have been five or six. He set her down and she ran back into the house squealing.

Matthew greeted Leah warmly. "Leah, it's so good to see you. How have you been?" He offered Leah an arm, as if to give her a hug. Natalie's eyes flashed, and the offer turned into a handshake.

"Matthew!" Leah said, pulling him into a hug anyway. "It's been forever! How's the job search going? Are you still staying home with the kids?"

She pulled back, blinking in shock at her own warmth, but there was no time to reflect more deeply. As if on cue, three small bodies came barreling out of the house, surrounding Leah, tugging at her clothes, clamoring to be picked up.

"Auntie Leah!" "Did you bring cookies?" "We've missed you!" "Will you hold my stuffie?" "Look, I lost my tooth!" "Where have you been?" "I learned a new song at school!"

"Josie! Victor! Rosie-roo!" Her heart swelled as she knelt down and hugged each child in turn, commenting on how much they'd grown. When she finally stood up, smiling so widely that her cheeks hurt, she met Natalie's shocked eyes, brimming with tears.

"Leah, you remember them?"

Once again, a wave of nausea rolled over her, threatening to bring her back to knees. Something buckled, and she found herself falling toward the ground, saved from collision only by Matthew's quick reflexes. He helped her steady herself and waved Peter over to support her other side. Together, they walked into the living room, followed by a reverent procession of Natalie and the children.

"Peter," Natalie ordered quietly, while Matthew got Leah settled on the couch. "There are some peppermints by the front door. Grab a couple and bring them here."

He obliged quickly, his eyes wide.

Matthew handed Leah a blanket, and she closed her eyes and gratefully accepted the handful of peppermints from Peter. A moment later, Natalie appeared with a glass of water, dimming the lights as she came back into the living room.

"Auntie Leah, are you okay?" whispered one of the children.

"You need some medicine?" asked another, shoving a bottle of some vitamin in her face.

166

"Mom, I want a peppermint before dinner," demanded the third, following Natalie closely.

Grinning, Matthew herded the children into the kitchen, whispering promises of dinner and maybe even the dessert that Mr. Peter brought.

"What's happening to me?" Leah croaked out around the feeling of bile rising in her throat.

Natalie's eyes were full of compassion and pity. "You're remembering."

"Is this... this is normal?"

"We think so. But, truthfully, we don't know."

"What?"

Natalie smiled sadly and placed a hand on Leah's shoulder. "Just rest, Leah. You should feel better in a few minutes, and we'll explain everything over dinner. The kids should be ready for bed in," she glanced at her watch, "the next hour, give or take, and there will be plenty of time to answer all your questions."

Leah nodded almost imperceptibly, her eyes shut and her stomach still churning. She felt someone place a stuffed animal next to her head and didn't notice the sudden absence of voices.

Chapter 15

She awoke to a little face mere inches from hers. "Her sleepin, Mommy! Can I wake her up? I wanna say goodnight."

"No, Rosie, let her sleep. She's not feeling well." Natalie's soft laugh and gentle rebuke were met with a tiny disappointed groan, the sound of which brought a smile to Leah's face in spite of herself.

"Mommy, her smiled!" Small arms wrapped themselves awkwardly around her shoulders and a wet pair of lips found her cheek. "Goodnight Auntie Leah! Love you! Miss you! Come play with me soon!"

Leah felt tears gathering in her eyes as she propped herself up on one arm, returned the hug and kiss, and watched Rosie leap and twirl off to bed behind Matthew. Josephine and Victor, upon learning that Rosie had gotten to say goodnight to Auntie Leah, came running back for a hug before racing one another down the hall.

Natalie sat next to her on the couch, her eyes damp.

"How are you feeling, Leah? I think I've got some ginger drops left over from my last pregnancy if the peppermints aren't helping."

"No, I feel so much better." Leah blinked heavily. "I'm sorry to have slept away the rest of the time the kids were awake. But thank you for letting me rest. I don't know what hit me." She stifled a yawn.

Natalie smiled. "It was probably enough excitement for them just to get to see you again. They were so happy when you got here."

"It's so good to see them." Leah said, eyebrows raised. "They've grown so much."

"They really have. Victor is eight now, if you can believe it. We're a year and a half away from double digits. They've missed you a lot." Natalie's gaze grew distant and her voice quiet, but she stood up and offered Leah a hand to help her to her feet. "Let's sit down and eat, and we can talk more. I want to hear everything that's been happening, and everything you can remember, as long as it doesn't make you feel too sick."

Leah steadied herself and took a tentative step toward the kitchen. "Of course."

A plate was already set for Leah, french fries piled high beside a burger, and she was relieved to see that the rest of the group had not waited for her to eat. Half of Matthew's burger still sat on his plate, and Peter served up slices of pie for himself and Natalie, who had finished already.

"This looks delicious, Natalie. Thanks for dinner."

She smiled as she sat down and refilled her glass of iced tea. "Anytime, dear. Eat, and then we'll chat."

Leah took a few bites in silence, conscious of two pair of eyes on her. Eventually, she cracked a grin. "Alright, y'all can't just watch me eat! Someone talk about something!"

After another moment of awkward silence, Peter asked in a half-joking voice, "So, how's work been treating you?"

"Ha," Leah snorted. "It's so boring. I don't know what originally drew me to it, but it all feels so pointless now.

And it doesn't help that I'm distracted by all this." She waved her hands around nebulously.

Peter chuckled. "I bet it doesn't."

"Yeah. I hardly even remember applying, honestly, it was back when things were really bad. I remember being surprised they wanted to hire me." She paused for a moment, staring at the crown molding. "I wonder what I put on my resume for that application."

The table went silent for a moment, and Leah regretted her last sentence. Desperate to regain the conversation's momentum, she looked over at Natalie. "What have the kids been up to recently?"

Natalie smiled and told few stories, giving Leah a chance to finish her dinner.

"Alright," Leah said when the conversation lulled. "I think I'm ready. What's the deal with Jude?"

Peter and Natalie exchanged glances. Peter raised his eyebrows and threw up his hands.

"Leah," Natalie smiled sadly. "If you're asking the question, I think you already know the answer."

Leah nodded. "We were engaged." Her voice was quiet. "It... wasn't always happy. The photo I saw on Facebook, the feeling when I think about it... It's all heavy, and tired, and sort of melancholic."

Natalie's eyes were downcast. "You fought a lot, especially towards the end."

Her words tied Leah's stomach in knots. "It's funny. He walked me through the clinic yesterday—like I told you, Peter, after he found me in the back and thought I was lost—and I..." She looked down at her empty plate, poking at it with her fork. "I guess, I see what I saw in him."

No one said anything.

Leah looked up, making hesitant eye contact with Natalie. "But I also saw something in him that scared me. Something about the way he talks about Dr. Pierucci."

The corners of Natalie's mouth lifted just a little, but her eyes remained half closed. "That's Jude in a nutshell."

Leah looked away from her, turning toward Peter. "So, why is it so bad if he sees me? Or, I guess, bad that he saw me?"

Peter grimaced. "The long and short of it is that Jude, perhaps more than anyone else, is in a position to make or break the suppression. And since he's a bit of a wild card, we have to assume that he'll choose to support his father, no matter the costs."

Leah's eyebrows furrowed. "What do you mean?"

"Well, okay, this is going to require just a tiny little bit of suppression theory." Peter held out his thumb and pointer finger, almost touching them. "So bear with me."

Natalie groaned.

Peter rolled his eyes. "I haven't even started yet!" They both laughed, and he continued. "So, Valerie showed you the place in your mind palace... library... where Dr. Pierucci is trying to keep the suppressed memories. And as I told you, the neural pathways leading to those memories have been severed, forcing your brain to reroute. In other words, you either forgot or you came up with new stories and told yourself they were true."

Leah nodded along, her head already swimming.

Peter glanced around the room, squinting. "Did I already tell you why we're showing you all this?"

Leah shook her head.

Peter took a deep breath. "I guess, first of all, and probably obviously, we want to help undo the effects of your suppression. I don't know that it needs to be said, but there it is, just in case. It sucks that Pierucci did this to you, and we don't want you to have to endure it any longer."

Leah felt the telltale pressure of tears welling up behind her eyes. Natalie rested one hand on top of Leah's, giving Peter a tiny thumbs up with the other.

"Second of all—and not to negate the first thing—is that, from a research perspective, you are a landmark case." Peter tapped the table emphatically. "We don't want to miss our chance to understand exactly what can help or hinder the recall process. Dr. Pierucci has been using the memory suppression technique for several years now, but he's done basically no research on reversing it."

Beside Leah, Natalie gave Peter a pointed look. He blushed. "Sorry, I get a little carried away sometimes."

Leah scoffed. "So you're just stabbing in the dark, hoping something works? Watching me like a lab rat while you've got the chance?" Her cheeks warmed and her heart sank. "That's... frustrating. And it sounds kind of hopeless."

"Not exactly..." Peter rubbed a hand over his cheek. "We have theories. Direction. We know that we can't just tell you everything, for example. We can't just lay it all out there and trust that your brain will reconnect those lost pathways. So what we're doing is trying to feed your brain those prompts that will get the gears turning, and then it's up to your subconscious to rewire the pathways and start to break down that gate. And once that happens, we move forward with—"

Natalie coughed quietly a couple of times.

Peter's eyes widened for just a split second. "With recovering and rebuilding your real memories."

There's something else going on here.

Leah fiddled with her utensils for a moment, pretending she hadn't noticed the glance between Peter and Natalie. She brought the conversation back around. "So that's where Jude plays into this. You're worried that if we were to talk, he'd screw something up?"

Peter nodded, his eyes alight. "Oh, yeah, Jude. Exactly. What little research we've been able to get our hands on suggests that you're in a particularly vulnerable position, especially right now. So, here's an example: Jude was at Common Grounds the day you were meeting with Nat and Agent McDowell. You had a suspicion that something was up, but you didn't really know what. If Jude had seen you and had, I don't know, referenced your engagement..." Peter shrugged. "Basically, your brain might have responded by processing that information in the same way it processes a story, rather than an experience. Or you'd've assumed he was crazy, and then there would be a bias to overcome before you could accept the truth."

Leah scratched the back of her neck, her stomach churning. "Versus how it actually played out, where I just sort of tugged at the loose thread until it unraveled."

"Exactly." Peter glanced at Natalie for a moment, then looked back at Leah. "I would love to hear about that, by the way, if you don't mind my asking."

Leah shrugged. "Sure, I mean it hardly feels real. A few weeks ago, when we all first met—" She looked at Peter and Natalie. "—well, when Natalie and I first met—okay, I guess I must have known you before if I know all your kids' names..." She paused. "Anyway, I was on Facebook looking all of you up, trying to see if you were real people or scammers. And at some point I realized that Jude had me blocked on Facebook. I guess this must have been after you

174

and I went for that walk, Peter. But I didn't think much of it at the time—Jude having me blocked, that is. I figured that maybe it was just the Institute's standard policy to, I don't know, maintain professional distance. But then after my conversation with him yesterday, I started to wonder if maybe there was something else."

She looked back down at her hands, which were fiddling with her utensils again. "So I asked my neighbor if I could use her profile to look him up. And there wasn't anything on his profile about us, but there was a picture that someone had tagged him in, and he and I were in it together. That was the sort of intellectual realization, I guess." She looked up from her utensils and studied the floral wallpaper. "But then I got back home and was going about my day, and all the sudden I had this sinking feeling in the pit of my stomach that I'd lost my engagement ring. I looked all over my apartment for it and was on the verge of panic when I realized that I... well, that I don't have a ring."

Peter leaned forward with such force that his chair scraped backward. "So it really felt real in that moment, then? You went from that intellectual knowledge to the more visceral experiential knowledge without even noticing?" He made no effort to hide his excitement.

Leah squirmed in her seat. "I guess so? It doesn't necessarily feel experiential, or whatever, anymore. It did in that moment, but it not as much now."

"Fascinating." Peter looked over to Natalie, his eyes wide. "Holy smokes, Nat, this stuff is cool."

Natalie's gave him a look.

He covered his eyes with his hands. "I know. I know. I'm sorry. I need to be more sensitive. But Natalie, this is incredible! And a good sign that we're on the right track."

Natalie raised her eyebrows a fraction of an inch in response, saying nothing.

Peter sat back and scooted his chair back in. "But yes, Leah, to go back to your question. Being force fed the truth would lead to a very different experience, at least as far as we know. So we can't let Jude or Dr. Pierucci force our hand... can't let them disrupt the natural process of remembrance. I know it sounds a little fuzzy, but this isn't just mine and Matthew's best guess. This is the Institute's research arm's official theory. And Jude knows that. We can't let him use it to his father's advantage."

"Matthew?" Leah piped up. His name tickled an itch in her mind that she couldn't quite scratch.

"Yes?" he responded, walking back into the dining room and rubbing his eyes.

"A question for another day," Natalie interjected, giving Matthew's hand a squeeze as he sat down next to her.

Leah's gears had been turning while Peter had been talking, and she started speaking before she fully knew where her sentence would end. "Peter, for all your talk about it being so terrible for me and so interesting for you, about reversing the memory suppression..." The bitterness in her voice surprised her. "I don't know, I get the sense that there's something else going on. Is there... I mean, is something you guys or Agent McDowell want from me?"

Peter glanced at Natalie and Matthew as Leah paused, but she kept going, unsure if she was talking to herself or to Peter. "I guess that would answer a lot of the 'why' questions I've had—why the FBI is involved in this whole situation, why you've gone to such lengths to keep everything hidden from the staff at the clinic, why you even care in the first place... I don't know, there's just been this air of urgency and fear, and I don't understand it. But I guess if there's some bigger thing, then that might make sense of it..." She trailed off.

Natalie looked at her for a moment before responding. "Yes, you're onto something. There's definitely a bigger picture here—that's part of what Peter was alluding to when he said that Jude telling you everything upfront would be problematic. There are certain things that we need you to remember. Wrongs that only you can right."

Leah's lips were pressed tight as she considered her next words. "I guess my next question would be, how do you know that it's what I want? What I would have wanted before or what I want now?" She looked around the room. Her eyes landed on a pair of antique bird sketches in little round frames.

"Leah—" Natalie started, but Leah cut her off.

"I keep wondering if there's any possibility that I asked Dr. Pierucci to suppress my memories, you know? But I also think that might just be a sign that I don't want to shake things up too much. This year has been hard. Really, really hard. And it was finally starting to get better when all of this started. What proof do I have that it's not going to get worse if I go along with whatever harebrained scheme you've cooked up?" Leah felt her pulse rising and her voice speeding up. "Do any of you understand what it's like? Knowing that there's basically a separate person inside your head threatening to break out? You're telling me that it's important to you that I remember these things, but... who are you working for? What's your goal? And is my good even part of the calculus?"

Her eyes shot fire around the table. Peter and Matthew exchanged glances with one another. Peter mouthed the word 'feelings' and shrugged sheepishly. Matthew rolled his eyes. Both men looked to Natalie.

After a long moment, Natalie spoke up. "Leah, your good is central to the calculus. Your good is the calculus. I wish I could say more, but I promise that everything we're doing is... guided? inspired? by someone you trust."

"I don't know who I trust anymore." Leah looked around the table, making eye contact with each of them.

"I know," Natalie responded sadly. "To answer your question a moment ago, I can't fathom experiencing what you're going through right now. But Leah, we—Peter and Matthew and I—we knew you before. And even if you don't fully remember us, heck, even if you only ever remember my kids and never remember me at all, I hope that you can believe me when I tell you that everything we're doing now is for you and for your good."

Leah didn't respond, and a weighty silence descended on the room. The sun had fully set, the darkness outside held at bay only by the thin slats of the open blinds.

"You know what will help everyone out?" Peter's voice was cheery—too cheery—as he stood up from his seat. "Pie!"

Although he'd plated a slice of pie for each of them just as Leah had started eating, he hadn't passed them out. All four pieces were still clustered all around him, although one had clearly been nibbled on. He passed out the plates and watched with eager eyes as everyone took their first bite.

Leah closed her eyes and savored the taste of the fresh berries and the homemade crust. "Peter, this is delicious, as always. Is this the same recipe you made for that random Fourth of July party at the office?"

A huge grin broke out across Peter's face, and he threw his head back with laughter. "Yes! That time we filled all those latex gloves with water and left them all over the office! Who were we even trying to prank, do you remember?" He sighed contentedly. "Gosh, that was fun."

It was the stomach ache that tipped her off. She pulled a peppermint out of her pocket and popped it into her mouth, but the nausea wasn't as intense as before.

Peter looked apologetic. "Ah, shoot, I'm sorry. I didn't know when I made the pie that remembering things would make you feel sick. I just thought it might be—"

"Hold on a second," Leah interrupted. "I worked with y'all! At the Institute. Is that how we all know each other?"

"Atta girl." Matthew nodded, his voice filled with pride. "I guess I probably shouldn't say more... but you'll see more soon enough."

Natalie reached behind her and grabbed an orange shoe box off a sideboard along the back wall of the room. She handed it across the table to Leah. "I think you're ready for this now."

Leah lifted the lid slightly and peeked inside the box. It seemed to be full of random trinkets—pamphlets, some folded sheets of loose leaf paper, a rubber banded stack of photographs, and what might have been a small book. She shut the box quickly and tucked it under her chair.

Just the thought of it left her queasy. "I'd prefer to look at this on my own time, if you don't mind."

"Of course," Natalie said, shaking her head.

"Leah," Matthew spoke up. "It sounds like Nat and Peter have already covered the basics, and I'm sure you got more of a technical lecture than you wanted from this nerd." He gestured toward Peter with his thumb. "But I guess I just wanted to reiterate that we only want what's best for you. We're with you in this. You might not know it yet, but you were there for our family through the hardest things we've ever faced, and there's no way that we're going to abandon you now."

Pain flitted across Natalie's face, and Matthew squeezed her hand tighter. But his words settled like a warm blanket across Leah's chest, and the tension gripping her heart like a vice relaxed. "Thank you, Matthew."

"Oh, and by the way." Matthew grinned. "Did I hear you say that you asked your neighbor to Facebook stalk Jude, and that's how you figured this whole thing out?"

Leah nodded sheepishly, stifling a laugh.

Matthew chuckled. "Gosh, some things never change. Can't suppress that curiosity, no matter how much they want to." He smiled. "It's really good to have you here, Leah. I know this isn't easy for you, but we've missed you."

"Well, I haven't missed you one bit." She said it with a smile and a wink, but her heart was heavy.

After another half hour of conversation, Leah decided it was time for her to head home. She followed the walkway back towards her car, the warm light of Natalie's house casting her shadow long and faint in front of her. As she pulled away, Leah couldn't help but watch the door shrink in the rear view mirror until it finally disappeared around the corner.

The shoe box suddenly felt heavy in her lap, and a sense of dread overtook her.

Chapter 16

At exactly five o'clock on Friday afternoon, Leah closed her laptop and slipped out of the office. She waved goodbye to Ana without stopping to chat and made a beeline for the parking lot. The bag of peppermints she'd purchased at a gas station early Thursday morning was already half empty. She popped one in her mouth on the way to her car, and there were another four or five in her backpack. She patted the side pocket, just to double check.

Sitting on the beach next to her mom, both of their heads thrown back in hysterical laughter. The sun beating down. The salty spray of the waves. Sand between their toes.

The end of the week had been brutal. Since dinner at Natalie's house, the memories had not stopped coming back. Most of the time, they had still been accompanied by a crippling stomach ache.

Babysitting Natalie and Matthew's kids while they went out for their anniversary. Kid Charcuterie for dinner—salami and cheese sticks and grapes and crackers. Singing Kenny Loggins' House at Pooh Corner for a full forty-five minutes until little Rosie finally drifted off.

Sometimes the images appeared out of nowhere, interrupting her day and forcing her to pause her task until her stomach settled.

Ice skating with Jude at the outdoor skating rink just before Christmas, bundled up in sweaters and scarves, enjoying the cold front while it lasted.

Other times, she found herself deep in thought, reminiscing about the past, only to realize later it was a memory that had been hidden away.

Her mom and her Aunt Kathy flying in every second of November to visit her dad's grave. Sipping on hot chocolate until late into the night, reminiscing about his life.

There was little relief in the prospect of the weekend. Driving home, all Leah had to look forward to was going through the box that Natalie had given to her. She was dreading it. Not only for the inevitable illness it would provoke, although that alone was enough to give her pause. But as the memories had slowly trickled in over the last few days, challenging deeply held beliefs and assumptions, a growing sense of unease had begun to build in her chest.

What if this whole ordeal doesn't... fix me?

She pulled the car to a stop at a red light and reached for her phone. When the screen unlocked, her most recent internet spiral greeted her—the psychology department page on the Swarthmore website. She'd been looking for a familiar face among the faculty, trying to confirm whether or not she'd actually earned the degree listed on her resume.

Does it really matter if I can't remember the specifics of my college graduation? Is it actually important that I remember whether I went to college and where? Do I—did I—have friends from undergrad who think I've ghosted them?

A car behind her honked. The light had turned green. Leah set her phone down and eased her foot onto the gas, still lost in thought.

What must Mom think of me because of all this? Maybe she's been right all along... maybe I really have become a totally different person over the last year.

She turned into her apartment complex and navigated to her unit, but her usual spot was taken. In her search for an open space, she had to drive all the way to the opposite end of the complex.

I hate Friday nights. Stupid parties. All these spots will be empty by morning, and I'll still have to do this walk.

She pulled her car into the parking space, turned it off, and stepped out. Slipping her backpack over her shoulder, she began the long walk across the complex.

And when... when I'm Mom's age and forgetting things because that's just what happens when you get older...

She didn't want to finish the thought, but she couldn't stop it from unfolding.

...will I get to 'just' forget things? Or will is just be this... over and over again... until I just...

When she finally stepped inside her apartment, it was almost six o'clock. Prime dinner time on a normal day, but Leah could hardly stand the thought of food and felt certain she wouldn't be able to stomach anything. Instead, she put on her favorite sweater, made a pot of ginger tea with honey, and curled up on her bed, blankets and pillows piled around her.

She picked up the shoe box from Natalie and looked at it. The bright orange of the cardboard felt jarring. She set the box down and picked up her phone again, scrolling through Facebook and then Instagram for a while. But even her social media account was bleak, full of breaking news stories that sunk her further into despair. A serial killer who had been dormant for a few months seemed to be active again. A teenage boy killed in a shooting on the south side of town. An armed bank robbery by a man who was released on parole for armed robbery.

It's now or never, Leah. You've got to do this.

She set her phone down and ran her trembling fingers around the box, feeling the rough edges of the cardboard. Taking a deep breath, she lifted the lid and examined the contents with anxious resignation.

The first thing she picked up was an ID card clipped onto a lanyard, and when she removed it from the box, she noticed that it wasn't the only one. There were three in total, all bearing the McNeill Institute logo. They had clearly been printed in three different years, as evidenced by the different designs and the fading and peeling on two of the cards. She selected the oldest one and was surprised to find a picture of herself as a child. Her name, her parents' names, and her mother's phone number were listed on the card, alongside the word PATIENT. On the back was a barcode and a small map labeled 'McNeill Institute for Neurological Development—Children's Ward.' A faded red dot, drawn in permanent marker, marked one of the rooms. A hot pink Lisa Frank lanyard was clipped through the hole, and faded childish scribbles overlapped the already colorful design.

The second card also contained her photograph—a teenage Leah with side-bangs, a feather crimped into her hair, and a wide grin that betrayed more excitement than angst. The word INTERN was printed in large letters across the short end of the card. The lanyard on this card looked handmade, woven of embroidery floss and seed beads, worn down over the years. It was wide and long, and an intricate design bookended the words 'MIND Intern Squad'. On the back of the card, a neon green brain-shaped rubber band hung from the lanyard clip, and two signatures covered the barcode and map. Leah studied the handwriting carefully but was unable to make out the names.

The third card was in pristine condition—the photograph looked maybe five years old, if that. Leah noticed that her full name—Leonora Harvey—was printed on the card, with 'Marketing Specialist' written beneath in slightly smaller letters. Along the short edge of the card was the word STAFF, and the back of the card was filled with phone numbers. A small heart had been drawn in one corner. This card was attached to a retractable badge holder, as if it belonged on a blazer or a purse strap.

For a long moment, Leah held the cards in her hand, waiting. The nausea didn't seem to increase at all, and nothing presented itself to her memory yet. The three versions of herself looked at her, smiling widely, full of a hope and excitement she didn't share. Eventually, she carefully wrapped each card in its lanyard and placed them back in the shoe box.

The next stack that Leah picked up consisted of a couple of pamphlets advertising different services that the Institute offered. Some of them she recognized, having seen them a dozen times in the brochure racks at the clinic, but there was one in particular that caught her attention. It was steel blue with large white text reading 'Rehabilitation Research Project'. On the front was a photograph of Dr. Pierucci and two other men standing in front of Scarlett Bay Correctional Facility.

The design was pleasing—if Leah hadn't known better, she'd have said that it was one of hers. She turned the pamphlet over and found a QR code and a contact email for the Institute. As she opened it to read the inside, she found herself whispering something.

"These criminals have been taken off the streets for public safety, and the McNeill Institute is working with the justice system to streamline rehabilitation while improving inmate quality of life at our very own Scarlett Bay Correctional Facility."

To her surprise, the same sentence was typed out across the center of the trifold, surrounded by other text and more photographs.

How did I...?

A new memory hit her.

An argument in a large corner office. Her blood pounding in her veins, her face flushed. "I wrote that statement; you don't need to quote it back to me. But that's not the whole story, and I won't remain complicit while lives are being ruined."

A voice responded—she couldn't quite decipher whose voice, but they were clearly annoyed. "Leonora, that is irrelevant to this conversation. We are here to discuss your behavior, as well as your future at this company..."

The image faded.

Maybe I really did design this one.

She closed her eyes tightly, willing the scene from her memory to return.

Dark clouds gathering out huge windows, a wind whistling past the building. The first tiny drops of a freak summer storm. A deep mahogany desk, on which a glass plaque sat. She could only barely make out the letters carved into it.

McNeill Institute for Neurological Development
Jude Pierucci, Sr, MD, PhD
2018 Employee of the Year

Her heart sank.

Dr. Pierucci.

It wasn't a question so much as a statement of fact.

What could possibly have happened that left him feeling so threatened by me? If that really is what happened...

Unable to remember anything more, she placed the brochures back in the box and turned her attention to the stack of photographs. The rubber band holding them together was old and crumbling. It snapped when Leah gingerly tried to remove it, and the photos sprawled out on the bed in front of her. The one that caught her attention first featured her and Natalie's three children, all a couple years younger. Rosie wore a party hat, icing smeared all around her wide grin.

Another photograph appeared to have been taken at the McNeill Institute, showing Leah smiling and holding a small bouquet of flowers. A few others—some faces she recognized, some she didn't—were holding up the number one with their fingers. There was a selfie of Leah and Peter, each wearing a star-spangled paper top hat, holding water-filled latex gloves. Herself and Jude at various locations.

She stopped dead at an image of herself and Jude standing next to her mother in front of a "she said yes" banner. It must have been before the stroke.

Mom never really had a stroke.

The thought haunted her as she mulled over the phone call with her mom after her most recent appointment. Her face flushed and her head spun.

How dare they steal my life from me. My mother. My family. My friendships. What could possibly justify doing something so horrible to someone Jude supposedly loved?

She threw the loose photos back in the box. The circumstances surrounding her engagement were still so fuzzy, both its inception and its conclusion, and it was infuriating to know about its existence without any details to color in the outline.

Forcing herself to move on, she glanced at the photo album, which was mostly empty. Some sheets of colored paper had been tucked inside the back cover, and one solitary photo had been slipped into a sleeve. She and Jude stared up from the page, a proud smile on his face and a tired one on hers, his arm around her waist, her left hand held forward to show off an engagement ring. A hand-written little note on a scrap of paper read, "Will you be my forever?" and taped around the edge of the photograph were a dozen tiny scraps, each with a little heart.

Leah picked up the staff badge and compared. The hearts were the same.

On the next page of the scrapbook was a note.

Leah,
It's been a week, and I still can't believe you said yes.
You are everything I could have hoped for in a wife.
A dream come true. I thought it might be fun for us
to fill this photo album with pictures from our
engagement, and we can have our family and friends
sign it at the wedding. What do you think? I'm the
luckiest man in the world.
Love, Jude

Tears welled up in her eyes, and for a few minutes, she allowed herself to grieve. She wept for the loss she remembered, and for the loss of what she didn't, and for the life she'd never have.

Her heart fluttering as Jude, all braces and acne and way too much cologne, handed her a valentine in their high school hallway.

Shouts of "surprise!" as he walked into a birthday celebration she'd put together when he turned twenty-five. Fabric swatches and paper samples and tiny slices of cake.

When the tears slowed, she wiped her eyes, closed the photo album, and set it back in the shoe box with an unexpected reverence. All that remained in the box was a folded stack of loose leaf paper.

The first page was clearly old, perhaps decades old, lined with grade school triple-score and filled with the stilted hand of a new writer.

Printed at the top of the page was Leah's name, followed by the question, "What do you want to be when you grow up?" The words had been carefully penned, likely by a teacher, and were answered by her own messy scrawl.

When I grow up, I want to be a nurolojist! They are docters who help people and fix their brains.

My brain doesn't work, because its my grain, and my doctor is helping fix my grain. I want to help peopel too!

Leah couldn't help but grin. She studied every letter on the page, reaching back in her memory for any recollection of the assignment, of getting her picture taken at the Institute, of knowing what a neurologist was by the time she was eight years old.

"Heck, I'd probably go see Dr. P, just for old times' sake."

She set the yellowed paper down and thumbed through the rest of the pages, which generally seemed to consist of short stories, poems, and essays, with the occasional letter thrown in. It was fascinating to watch her handwriting mature and her spelling become more accurate. At the very back of the stack was a letter in Jude's handwriting. She pulled it out and smoothed the creases from the page.

Sweet Leah,

We've been fighting a lot lately, and I miss the days
when we could just go see a movie or a play without
it being a big thing. Let's go on a date next week.
What do you say?

All my love,
Jude

Clipped to the letter were two unused paper tickets to
Fiddler on the Roof. If the tickets had been purchased but not
used, was it possibly because of their break-up? The date of
the show was listed as Saturday, April 30, 2022, and
although the letter was not dated, Leah could put the pieces
together enough to calculate a possible range. The
certainty—relative as it was—gave her some comfort.

Rummaging around in her desk, Leah pulled out the
planner she'd used the previous calendar year. Hesitantly,
curiously, she opened to the April spread. It was blank.
Every page before it was blank too. By the middle of May,
each day was filled with her careful notes in her neatest
handwriting, as if she'd just purchased it and wanted to
make sure every detail was recorded. Over the course of the
year, as her habitual use of the planner had become less
habitual, the handwriting became messier and the entries
less consistent.

So that's it happened. Sometime before April 30.

Part of her was afraid to spoil the notebook, as if she
could hinder the return of her memories by tampering with
its pages. But she needed to see things laid out if she was
going to make any sense of them.

Glancing around her desk, she found a pad of sticky
notes and a permanent marker. In large letters, she wrote

'break-up?' and stuck the note squarely in the last week of April. Another sticky note, this one bearing the words 'theater date' was placed directly on April 30. She flipped back to the previous week and added a note reading 'letter sent/received?'

Picking up her phone, Leah carefully paged through the planner with one hand while searching her email archive with the other. She added sticky notes for each event of which she was certain, as well as for the things she suspected. The day she started her new job. Her first treatment session at the Institute. The date she'd signed her lease and the date she'd moved into her apartment. The New Year's Day party she'd discovered on Facebook, where she'd seen the engagement ring.

Half an hour later, her phone buzzed. Sarah.

How ya doing?

Setting down the pen and the planner, Leah responded to Sarah without thinking too much about it.

Ha. Sick. What a week.

The two women exchanged a few text messages, and within another half hour, somewhat begrudgingly, Leah found herself seated on Sarah's couch, a steaming mug of rich, milky hot chocolate cradled in her hands and a plate of "very mild, I promise, please just give them a try, you really should eat something other than peppermints today" shortbread cookies next to her. Connor flicked through the available movie options while Sarah bustled around the living room distributing blankets, turning off lights, and placing the dinner dishes in the kitchen sink.

Feeling brave and nervous, Leah said aloud, to no one in particular, "I feel like Frankenstein these days."

Connor wordlessly switched off the TV and set the remote down on the couch.

"Frankenstein's monster," Sarah countered with a wink and a half smile.

Leah wasn't sure how to respond. Part of her wanted to chuckle and respond in kind. Part of her wanted to cry. "It's like there are two half-people living inside my head, and I don't know which one is really me."

Connor nodded, offering a quiet encouragement for her to continue.

The words tumbled out like water bursting through a dam. "I feel like a tool that they're trying to use, and it's so hard to know if I can trust them. And they have these perfect, clean explanations for why they can't tell me anything, but meanwhile I'm left wondering if my mom really did suffer a debilitating stroke last year, because apparently I received treatment for migraines at the Institute as a child, but the stroke is tied too closely in my head to the fake clinical trial for me to be certain whether it really happened, but if it didn't really happen, then have I wasted a year of our lives tiptoeing around the subject for nothing?" She choked on her own words and sat in silence for a few minutes.

Sarah took the opportunity to top off Leah's hot chocolate and refill her plate, which was mostly empty. When she sat back down, Leah continued.

"I called Mom after my last appointment, and she didn't remember having a stroke. And that's part of the issue, see, some stroke survivors don't remember it. And I've had in my head that she's got early stage dementia, so

I've been talking around her and making all these assumptions about what she needs in terms of routine and kid gloves and whatnot. And I've doubted everything she says, because people with dementia struggle with memory loss, you know? That's, like, the big thing, but... but what if she's been right the whole time? What if I'm the crazy one? You know?" Leah sniffled and rubbed at her watery eyes. She looked around the room for a moment before continuing. "Apparently I interned at the Institute, too, and worked there for a while. The roots just seem like they go so deep, and I have no idea how I'm supposed to untangle these threads of reality and fiction, and no matter what Natalie says about it, it just feels impossible to believe that..."

Leah paused, choking back a sob and offering her friends an apologetic glance.

Connor's voice broke the silence. "Why don't you just call her?"

Leah blinked back tears. "What?"

"Your mom. You seem really beat up about her. Why don't you just call her and ask her?" Connor's voice was matter-of-fact, as if he couldn't believe that this very simple step hadn't occurred to Leah.

She hesitated for a moment, an excuse brewing on her lips, "Well, I would, but with this dementia or whatever she's got, she doesn't always remember things, and she doesn't really do well with changes to her rout—" She didn't finish her sentence.

Connor gave her a little half-nod, as if to say, "See?"

Leah gave half a smile, her eyes half-closed with exhaustion and grief. "I'll call her in the morning."

"Good."

Two hours later, Leah made her way back to her own apartment. Her jaw was no longer clenched; her breathing came easier. She walked slowly in her bare feet, feeling the cement and the mud and the grass beneath her toes. A tiny sprinkle of rain drifted lazily earthward, not enough to soak her but enough to shield her head in a helmet of minuscule droplets.

When she finally curled up in bed, she silently thanked Sarah for convincing her to eat something. Although she wasn't feeling back to her best, she noticed a definite improvement in her mind and body from the days before.

Chapter 17

As Leah made breakfast, she held her breath and called her mom. She picked up on the first ring.

"Leah, is everything okay?" Her voice sounded urgent, even scared.

"Yeah, Mom, everything's fine. I'm just calling to chat. I've been feeling nostalgic lately."

An audible sigh of relief scratched its way through the phone. "Oh, thank God."

"Did you expect something to be wrong?"

"No, it's just that you never call me much, other than our usual day, so I always worry when you do."

A pang of guilt shot through Leah's abdomen. "Ah, I'm sorry, Mom. Everything's okay. I'm sorry I haven't been calling much lately."

"Well, it's good to talk to you now." Utensils clinked in the background. "How have you been? What's got you feeling nostalgic?"

Leah closed her eyes and took a deep breath. "Oh, I found my old patient card from the McNeill Institute, and I've just been thinking about all the time we've spent there over the years." She paused, adding as an afterthought, "Gosh, I must have been so young when we first started going there."

For a moment, there was only silence on the other end of the line.

This was such a huge mistake. What have I do—

Her mom's voice was filled with compassion. "Oh, you were. You can't have been more than six or seven. It was so hard for me to watch you suffering. I was so grateful to Dr. Pierucci for everything he did for you to help manage those horrible migraines more effectively. It really did seem to work, even after your father died. I thought for sure they'd come back with all the stress we were under."

They both paused for a moment. Leah brought her plate to the table and sat down.

Her mom spoke up again before she could reply. "But I don't remember you having more than one or two a year for so many years... really, up until maybe two years ago? It seemed to go hand in hand with you and Jude fighting more" Her mom's voice was timid. "How is Jude doing, by the way? Do you ever, I don't know, see him around when you go for your appointments?"

Leah blinked heavily, her mind reeling. She stared blankly out the window of her apartment for a long minute.

Her mom fussed over the silence. "Oh, I'm sorry, honey, I wasn't trying to make things awkward."

Leah shook her head, her voice quiet. "No, no, it's not that. I was just trying to remember—I've seen him once or twice lately. It seems like he's doing well enough, I guess. We don't really stop to chat or anything." She tried to play it cool, but heart raced.

"You know, Leah," her mom began. "I'm not sure I've ever told you this—and I'm not totally sure I should—but I'm glad that the two of you broke up. You never seemed happy with him... Right after you broke up, of course, I didn't want to say anything because it was so clear that you were grieving, but then I guess you never really recovered, and it never seemed like the right time."

She knows about Jude? Knows him? How could she possibly...?

Leah could picture her mom glancing around the room and shrugging, lost in thought, as she continued. "I suppose he was a fine enough young man, although he was a little more... ambitious, I guess... than I'd expected you would go for, but generally polite enough and clearly head over heels for you... it just never seemed like a good fit." Another pause, followed by a halfhearted, "But I'm glad to hear he's doing well."

All Leah could muster was a quiet affirmative noise.

"That's not so much what I mean, more just that I would have assumed you'd want a different doctor after everything that happened last year."

"Well, Leah, if that's all..." For a moment, the two women sat in silence, neither sure what to say next.

"It's really good to chat with you, Mom." Leah swallowed down a lump in her throat. "I'm sorry I've been distant lately."

"I know you're busy, dear. Anyway, I've got to go, thanks for calling."

Leah smiled sadly. "Love you, Mom."

"Mhmm, you too, dear. Bye now."

"Bye."

The call ended and tears streamed down her cheeks.

How many times has Mom brought up Jude and I dismissed her as delusional? How many times has she tried to talk about something in the past and I assumed she was making it up?

The dissonance was too much for her to bear. It welled up inside her, behind her eyes and deep in her chest, and for a few minutes, all she could do was cry and scream until her voice was hoarse.

What have I done? What have they done to me?

Her tears eventually slowed back to a trickle. As she wiped her puffy eyes and blew her nose, Leah tried to think of someone who might be able to tell her definitively whether her mom had experienced any relevant medical events or received any diagnoses in the last two years.

She considered Sheila and Linda, her mom's closest friends, but they would probably share the conversation far and wide and create a whole new drama for her to deal with. Aunt Kathy might be more discrete, but Leah didn't feel ready to answer all the questions she'd ask.

There wasn't anyone from childhood or undergrad she'd really kept in touch with, as least as far as she knew, so that was off the table. And she didn't trust Peter or Natalie or anyone from the Institute—people she might have known before—to give her an honest answer, if they knew even knew anything in the first place.

Having considered all the possibilities, she came to a startling realization.

There was no one.

Leah's chest felt hollow.

How did I get here? How did I get to a point where there is not one single person in my life who would be able to answer a basic question about my family?

She looked around at the walls of her apartment, still largely bare. When she'd moved in, she hadn't wanted to get in trouble for holes, especially since she didn't have all that much artwork to hang in the first place. But the walls felt oppressive now, closing in on her with blank stares that she couldn't escape.

Desperately, she made her way over to the shoe box and pulled out the photograph of herself and the Bailey kids. She looked around for a thumbtack and, finding one, promptly hung the photograph on the wall in front of her desk.

It looked small and frail there by itself, curling at the corners with the thumbtack in the center of the top edge. She hadn't realized it as she was hanging it, but the nail was placed right in the center of her forehead.

Right through her brain.

Her brain that had been broken, locked up, transformed without her consent.

She lay back on her bed, fighting back tears again, staring up at the endless spinning of her ceiling fan. Unease settled over her like a sheet, curling around her rib cage, ringing in her ears, aching all up and down her back. Her limbs itched to move—to throw punches, to sprint around the block, to do anything—but she couldn't muster the willpower to get up, let alone go for a run.

Jude.

His name popped into her mind in spite of herself.

I know things have been rough lately, and I'm sure he's tired of hearing me complain... but maybe he'd be willing to listen while I rant for a little bit. I could make his Nonna's lasagna for dinner in exchange.

The lasagna was certainly work-intensive, but it was one of her favorite dishes, and more importantly, it was one of Jude's favorites. She picked up her phone and opened her list of starred contacts. Jude's number was missing. Flipping to the list of all her saved numbers, she searched for him by name and was surprised to find that his number wasn't saved in her phone at all.

Weird. Must have gotten deleted somehow.

She tapped over to the phone screen, typed in the number from memory, and saved and starred the contact again. Returning to the phone, her thumb hovered over the green "call" button, her mind still debating whether or not to make the call.

I really need to talk to someone, and if it has to be Jude, it has to be Jude. I just don't know that there's anyone else...

And then, small and whispered, even in her thoughts:

I hate that this is how I feel about talking with the man I'm going to marry.

A motorcycle raced down the street, its engine rumbling the floor. She looked up, briefly, before glancing back down at her phone. Jude's name and phone number stared back at her.

What am I doing? I can't call Jude! That could ruin everything!

She shook her head to dislodge the thought... although, if she were perfectly honest with herself, she wasn't quite sure what everything referred to—was it something about the prison? something about her library?

She closed her phone and put it in her pocket.

So there's no one to talk to. Nothing to be done about it. Best find something else to do so there's no risk of calling Jude again.

Without thinking, Leah slipped on her sneakers, grabbed the grocery list off the front of her refrigerator, and hopped in the car.

The grocery store was, as always, both overwhelming and calming. Parking was a mess, par for the course on a weekend, and the entrance was packed. Trying to navigate her cart up and down each aisle felt like driving a bumper car, so she stashed it in an out-of-the-way spot and darted in and out of the produce section, grabbing a couple of carrots and onions, a bunch of celery, plenty of tomatoes. She stopped to pick out some fresh herbs and a large bag of peaches for her lunches over the coming week. Next was the meat section—ground beef, ground pork, some lunch meat—and then the dairy. Leah picked up the usual and deliberated over several brands of ricotta, parmesan, and mozzarella cheese. Eventually settling on an option for each, she grabbed a tub of mascarpone, too, for good measure. She stopped for her favorite red wines—one for cooking, one for drinking—before making her way up and down the center aisles of the store, grabbing broth, noodles, espresso, and ladyfinger cookies, as well as an assortment of pantry staples.

As she stood in line at the checkout counter, Leah surveyed the contents of her cart. Like waking from a dream, she stared for a moment, confused, at the obvious collection of ingredients for a dish she wasn't sure she knew how to make.

Lasagna? Tiramisu?

Her list and her cart did not match. She thought back through the morning, wondering when she had decided to make lasagna, when a memory presented itself.

Standing next to Jude in a spacious kitchen. Tattered off-white aprons over their Institute polos. Jude waving a wooden spoon around, tomato sauce splattering everywhere, a goofy grin on his face. Leah's stomach hurt from laughing so hard.

A twinge in her stomach grounded her.

That was the day he taught me how to make his Nonna's lasagna.

She tried to focus on the nostalgia of the dish, which she could almost taste, rather than on the beat that her heart skipped at the memory, but she couldn't stop the half-smile that formed on her face.

I hope I can remember how to make it. I miss those days.

The thought startled her. She'd grown accustomed, in the last week or two, to seeing Jude through Peter's eyes—his father's watchdog, always on the prowl, at once charming you and stabbing you in the back. But her Jude was different: confident, silly, even sweet. He was excited to bring her into his life, into his family, to show her these people and places and foods that he loved so deeply.

I miss being in love. Just enjoying being together. I miss the days before we fought all the time. I miss the days before I had this image of him in my head.

The dissonance hurt viscerally, deep in her gut.

I don't know if I can say that I want to go back to those days... but I do miss them.

She grimaced at the clerk, trying to force a smile but thinking she probably looked as sad and sick as she felt. The clerk's pitying glance confirmed this suspicion, and Leah felt her cheeks flush as she slid her card into the machine.

On her way home, she ran through her to-do list. The lasagna was, if she remembered correctly, something of an all-day affair. That was good. She needed the distraction, needed the comfort that came with a busy body and a focused mind.

After I get the sauce going, I'll make the tiramisu and pop it in the fridge. Then I can get bills paid and make a couple of phone calls... and I need to follow up with Matthew about that interview we did about the prison... I may even have time to watch a show before it's time to put the lasagna together and get it into the oven.

She exited the freeway and sped up at the sight of a yellow light ahead.

It'll be good to have a full day of getting things done around the house. I've been so busy late—

The light turned red just as she passed underneath it.

The interview with Matthew about the prison?

A snippet of conversation from the dinner at Natalie's house came back to her.

"This isn't just mine and Matthew's best guess. This is the Institute's research arm's official theory."

"Matthew?"

"A question for another day."

She filed the conversation away in her mind, debating whether it would be worthwhile to give Natalie and Matthew a call while she was cooking. But as it turned out, just the act of recalling the recipe was a Herculean effort, and she had no time for anything but chopping and mixing and stirring and remembering.

It was well worth it, and self-satisfied photos were sent to her mom and Sarah. Then she poured herself a glass of wine, turned off her phone, and indulged the bittersweet nostalgia that had been clamoring for her attention all day. Dwelling on those memories—a father-daughter dance in middle school, before her dad's cancer had come back; high school debate club; Jude standing next to her at her father's funeral—both satisfied and deepened the ache she'd been feeling. A sinking feeling in the pit of her stomach grew until it became all-consuming.

Eventually, realizing that dwelling on the past was doing her more harm than good, Leah stood up from the table. She put the leftovers away. She washed the dishes. Then she turned out the lights in the kitchen and headed back to get ready for bed. She pulled her phone out of her pocket, her finger hovering over Natalie's name.

I'd love to get some more information out of her and Matthew about this loose thread about the prison.

But she couldn't bring herself to make the call. Instead, she finished brushing her teeth, turned out the lamp in her room, and slipped into bed.

Jude's spot-on but unflattering impression of his father. The way she had to stifle a giggle when Dr. Pierucci said something that Jude had mimicked earlier that day.

The memories were crowding her mind now.

Sitting across from Matthew at Common Grounds. Fear and shame and regret in his eyes. Her heart pounding as she took notes on his story.

She could picture the books in her library as the redaction lines were wiped away, text typed over text on the pages, volumes lying helter-skelter on the floor as she tried, futilely, to reorganize things based on the new information available to her.

Blaring the soundtrack to Hamilton in her car on her first day of work at the Institute.

The worry that one set of memories would feel fictional seemed like a wished-for dream now, rather than a danger. Anything to help her distinguish between what was real and what wasn't.

But does 'real' even matter? Does it matter what did or didn't physically happen to this body?

After tossing and turning for what felt like hours—she'd used decaf espresso in the tiramisu, but the insomnia was mental more than physical—Leah groaned as she felt the nausea return. She groped around her bedside table, only to find that her bag of peppermints was empty.

Stomach still churning, she stood up, pulled her hair back with a stray ponytail holder, and made her way over to the bathroom. Her mouth filled with hot saliva as she knelt down on the tile floor, dreading what she knew was inevitable.

Let's get this over with.

Chapter 18

Leah woke up on Sunday morning drenched in the ache of nostalgia. She'd slept well after finally throwing up, and the nausea hadn't returned. The anguish of holding two identities at once had subsided and had given way to an intense desire to relive the past. Combing through old, returning memories in her library, Leah compiled a playlist of beloved songs, which she listened to as she whipped up some breakfast tacos. Half-remembered lyrics tumbled off her lips and tears pooled in the corners of her eyes.

Who's cutting onions?

Leah smiled wryly at her own joke before realizing that she was, in fact, cutting an onion. She chuckled aloud at the irony.

Jude would get such a kick out of this.

For a moment, it was as if nothing had changed.

Well... he would have gotten a kick out of it.

She sighed. Muscle memory guided her cooking, and when she finally sat down to eat, she found herself seated in front of the iconic tacos from the dumpy-turned-famous Jalapeno Joe's Taco Corner not too far from the clinic.

Dang, I didn't know I knew how to make these. When did I find a copycat recipe? I bet this is the real reason Jude wiped my memory—he got paid off by Jalapeno Joe.

Leah chuckled and took a bite, savoring the flavors of the eggs, onions, peppers, chorizo, and salsa.

I wonder if that place has been renovated yet... I'm sure they'll ruin in when they do try to "fix it up." Although, it had certainly seen better days back when Jude and I started dating.

The memory of their first date—a last-minute plan for Saturday brunch at the as-yet-undiscovered Jalapeno Joe's—was a sweet one. Thinking back, Leah could almost feel the butterflies that had fluttered in her stomach as she'd walked up to the dusty outdoor seating. It had been late spring, and the anticipated summer's heat had made itself felt in the midmorning sunlight. The place had been empty, just one or two other picnic tables occupied as they'd talked in hushed voices. Jude had showed up in a button-down shirt, and Leah couldn't help but notice the way it fit him in all the right places. She'd been unable to suppress a grin at his formal attire, secretly feeling a little flattered that he thought she was worth dressing up for.

They had stayed for five hours. Around two o'clock, Jude had ordered a second round of tacos for a late lunch.

The memories were sickly sweet and shadowed with shame. Shame for not having seen sooner than Jude wasn't right for her in the long run. Shame for letting herself fall in love at all. Shame for not being able to let go of the 'what if' questions that peppered her constantly.

Was it worth spending all that time with him?

She wasn't even sure if this shame was from before, or if it was new, imposed on her by Natalie and Matthew and Peter's opinions of Jude. Her mom's, too.

I wish I could form my own judgment about him... again, I guess. I'm not sure I want to know what I thought right before my memories were suppressed. I remember fighting a lot.

The end of their relationship—at least a few weeks, maybe as long as a few months—was still fuzzy in her mind. It lay just beyond her reach, a secret or a problem or a conflict. The discomfort of that time, although cloudy, crowded her chest, tightening around her lungs and tensing her muscles.

I need to get out of this apartment. Just to get some fresh air and a change of scenery. It doesn't even matter where.

Before she could convince herself otherwise, she grabbed her keys and hopped in the car. Nostalgic tunes blaring through her speakers, Leah pulled out of the parking lot. She didn't know where she was going, but she soon found herself parked in front of Jalapeno Joe's.

A sad smiled played on her lips as she stepped out and walked around. The main shopfront had been repainted, possibly renovated, since her last visit, but not much else had changed. The picnic tables were clearly the same ones that had been in place since they'd first opened. The ground was still littered with fallen leaves from the wide-spreading trees that shaded much of the gravel-dressed yard. Dust swirled in the air, stirred up by the wind and the constant footfalls. Grainy, tinny music blared through half-blown speakers, and much of the perimeter fence had seen better days.

Leah breathed deeply, enjoying the smells and the feeling of the air in her lungs as she meandered around the yard. Most of the tables were empty—it was still early on a Sunday, and the crowds usually came at dusk.

A small carving on one of the back tables stopped her in her tracks.

JP ♡ LH

209

Jude's hand carving the characters into the old wood. Her own laughter—a guilty, nervous giggle she hardly recognized—quiet as a whisper. Her left ring finger felt heavy. Her heart felt heavy, too, although the laughter did a good job of hiding it.

As she walked back out through the opening in the fence, a familiar but long-forgotten weight settled on her chest. A phrase, part memory and part thought, ran through her mind over and over again like catchy lyrics to a song she didn't quite know.

Did I really say yes to this? Am I really ready for this?

She turned down the nostalgic music as she as she drove away. She put on a podcast instead, although she hardly heard a word of it.

I should have gotten an extra tub of salsa. But it's not worth going back. Good riddance.

Before she knew where she was going, she hopped onto the freeway. A part of her wanted to go back home, curl up on the couch, and cry. But another part nudged her to keep driving past her normal exit. She watched as it came and went, the decision having more or less been made without her active consent. Instead, she found herself getting off at an exit that she didn't not remember. Left. Right. Left. Left. She pulled the car to a stop on a row of houses, shuddering at the realization that she may have just arrived unannounced at a now-stranger's home. Or worse, at Jude's home... or his father's.

A glance up and down the street revealed few other cars parked in driveways, and it didn't look like the lights were on in many—if any—of the structures.

Is this neighborhood abandoned?

She breathed a heavy sigh—she hadn't realized she had been holding her breath—when she saw business names affixed to each home. Perhaps a residential area that had been converted to commercial use. Whatever its story, the street was not well-maintained.

The paint was chipped and peeling on the sign of the home she'd parked near.

The Children's Ward
McNeill Institute for Neurological Development
Welcome, families. Healing lives here.

A smile formed on her lips. The house was old, with peeling paint on the shutters and overgrown bushes along the porch. There were no cars in the driveway, and no lights on inside. Her heart lightened as she walked across the brown grass of the lawn, shrieks of delight sounding in her imagination and two or three children playing ball in her mind's eye.

She tried the door, certain it would be rusted shut but unable to stop herself. To her surprise, it creaked open at her touch, admitting her into a cobweb-draped foyer. A large mahogany desk had been placed along one wall, its surface covered in a layer of dust that must have been a quarter-inch thick. A cracked and faded bulletin board hung beside it. The paper on the board had clearly once been golden yellow, but after years of patchy sunlight, it was barely off-white. Childish signatures littered the bottom half, and the word WELCOME had been stapled along the top in once-glittering navy letters.

Her own name, scribbled in her characteristic childhood way—Le♡n♡ra Harvey—was off to one side. She remembered scrawling it there: large, proud, excited. She'd been thrilled to belong.

This place seemed like a wonderland.

Leah closed her eyes, picturing the room as it had been. A large fish tank in the center of the room, surrounded by benches, had provided hours of fascinating observation. The buzz of friendly voices and soft music. Toys and games, movies and stuffed animals. Coloring pages, markers, and sometimes snacks. There were children who were waiting, or struggling, or even staying the night at the Institute's guest house.

Blinking the memory away, she wandered around the room, peeking down the two main hallways and swinging open each creaking door. For the most part, the house was stripped bare, although a few pieces of furniture remained: a paint-stained kids table in the dining area, the large desk in the entry, and—to Leah's surprise—a child-size orthodontic chair in one of the back offices, its faux leather exterior cracked and peeling. Upstairs, a jumble of mattresses, disassembled cribs, and pieces of at least five board games were scattered across the three bedrooms.

This place used to be so special.

The memories she had here were faded, like the discolored paper on the bulletin board, weathered not only by the effects of the suppression, but also by the inevitable passage of time. Life had been simpler back in the days when her parents brought her here.

Ghosts from her past seemed to walk the rooms, although she knew it was just in her memory—most of them were anonymous, unrecognized individuals. But a few stood out. Dr. Pierucci, of course, his eyes less creased, his smile less forced, his hair much darker. A loud child playing around his ankles—Jude Junior, or JuJu—always willing to pull a prank or crack a joke to get a laugh. A young black woman, her hair in long braids down her back. Leah struggled for a moment to remember her name, when it suddenly came back to her.

Valerie? Valerie DeLeon?

She couldn't help but smile.

I guess if her father was one of the founders, it makes sense that she'd have been around... Gosh, I thought she was just the coolest when I was a kid. I wish we could sit down and chat now.

She made a mental note to ask Peter for Valerie's phone number.

Wandering back out towards the door, Leah was struck with a bittersweet longing. This house existed somewhere between memory and fairy tale, and seeing it in such disrepair was sobering. A piece of her childhood that was definitively gone. Her newfound desire to connect with her past added another layer of grief—this was a piece of herself she might never fully recover.

Tears filled her eyes as she climbed back into her car, and for a moment, she couldn't see enough to drive. When her vision cleared, she sniffed and wiped her eyes before shifting the car into gear and navigating back to the freeway. Lost in thought, she meant to go home, but when the car came to a stop, a standalone building greeted her.

Is this a bank? Why did I drive here? This isn't even my bank.

She stared at the facade of the building, which was closed and locked for the weekend. She could remember walking through those doors, could picture the interior lobby, the tellers' desks, the high ceilings and intricate moldings. It was a grandiose building, more like a modern-day palace than a modern-day bank.

She approached a teller, a friendly Hispanic man with salt-and-pepper hair and a huge grin. His name tag read "Pio". Her hands were full of papers that she'd carefully organized inside a manila file folder. Her heart was racing, and she glanced around, wanting to ensure that no one had followed her.

She scrunched up her eyes, trying to remember the conversation. It was just beyond her grasp until it wasn't.

"How can I help you today?"

"I need a secure place to store some important documents. Do you all have safe deposit boxes on-site?"

"Of course we do! I'll get that paperwork out here for you momentarily."

The memory faded, and Leah felt exhausted by the sheer effort of recalling it.

A safe deposit box? What could I have needed to store?

Without thinking, Leah pulled her keys from her bag, fidgeting with the buttons of her gate fob. Her eyes glazed past the actual keys, moving towards the bank, before darting back. She counted out the keys—apartment, gate, mailbox, office building, office room...

There was one additional key on her set—a small brass key with a round head and a short blade. She'd always assumed it locked her main desk drawer, but she'd never bothered to test it out. Perhaps...

I know where I'll be over my lunch break tomorrow.

Chapter 19

The heavy wooden doors stared down at Leah as she approached the bank on Monday. She opened them, and the building's interior was quiet and solemn. There was no one else in line, which surprised her, but she stepped between the stanchions to wait for an available clerk.

"Next!" The voice came from the far end of the line of desks, and Leah hurried to avoid keeping the teller waiting. As she approached, she saw an empty space in front of a friendly Hispanic man with salt-and-pepper hair.

"How can I help you today?" He didn't look up from his computer.

Here goes nothing.

"I need to access my lockbox, please."

"Number?"

Leah grimaced. "I'm sorry. Could you look it up?"

He grumbled, still focused on his screen. "I'll need your driver's license and key, please."

She slid the two items through the small hole, hoping that she wasn't wrong about the key. The man picked up her driver's license and began entering some information on his computer when he did a double-take.

A huge grin broke across his face, and he finally looked up. "Leah! *Mijita!* It's been too long! How have you been?"

Leah froze.

His eyes widened. "Are you okay? You look like a deer in the headlights! Sorry for being so unfriendly just now, it's been one of those days, and I was absolutely not expecting you! It's been over a year since you were here, I think?"

She recovered just enough to stammer out a reply. "Something like that, yeah. How have you been?"

His face fell. "Oh, same old, same old, you know. It's been boring around here lately. I feel like all my regulars stopped showing up. Now it's just people who are angry about their financial decisions and try to take it out on me." His face lit up. "So you're a very welcome sight!"

He typed a few more things into his computer, handed Leah her license and key, and looked back at her. "Well, hey, I've got that box number so let's go ahead and hop on down there."

He stood up and met her on the outside of his desk, she noticed his nametag. Pio. Her eyes crinkled in a smile. She and Pio walked together to the elevator, and memories began to shake loose. How many times had they done this before? She could picture at least half a dozen occasions.

What is in this lockbox?

"Are you still seeing that boy? Last time you were here, I think you said y'all were fighting a lot. I got worried about you when you stopped showing up."

Leah frowned, although her eyes were affectionate. "You're sweet, Pio. We broke up a little over a year ago. Not too long after the last time I was here, actually."

He held the elevator door open as she walked in. "I'm sorry to hear that, but when it's time, it's time."

"Yeah." Leah was silent for a moment. "How's your family?" It felt right, although she couldn't remember them.

216

"They're doing okay, *mija*, thank you for asking. My dad's been in and out of the hospital, but he's home right now and seems to be doing alright. My little girl is going to be ten soon, and my son just turned five." Pio laughed. "They keep us busy, that's for sure."

He opened the door to the vault, and rows and rows of lock boxes surrounded them. "You're number 42, right there on the right, about eye level."

"That's right. Thanks Pio." She slid her key into its lock and watched as he did the same. Together they turned the keys, and the door of the box swung open. Leah tugged on the drawer and was shocked to find a huge stack of papers stuffed tight inside. The top pages crinkled as she strained to open the drawer all the way.

"You're really getting your money's worth out of that box, aren't you?" Pio teased.

"Sure looks like it." Leah spoke without thinking as she thumbed through the pages. "Pio, can I hang onto these for a few days?"

He furrowed his eyebrows. "It's your stuff, *mijita*, you can do whatever you want with it. The box can be empty forever if you want, it doesn't matter to us."

Leah chuckled. "I guess that's true. I'll bring it back in a couple of days, once I've had some time to look through everything I've got in here."

He shrugged. "All the same to The Bank, but I know it'd brighten my day to see you around here more often."

Leah smiled at him. "It's good to see you again, Pio."

The two made their way back up the elevator, the contents of the lockbox tucked safely into Leah's backpack. Her heart raced, and her mind tried frantically to anticipate what she would find inside. Pio walked her to the door of the bank, told her to come back soon, and gave her a hug. The smell of his cologne lingered as she slid into her car.

Is this what it's like to belong somewhere?

***

Back in her office, Leah pulled her lunch out and dropped the stack of papers on her desk. It had taken a superhuman act of the will to refrain from reading them in her car, but she knew it would be useless to try to wait until the end of the workday. Maybe she would be able to satisfy her curiosity and then cut herself off after she finished eating, to be able to get some amount of work done before leaving for the day. Either way, she couldn't let Ana see her distracted.

A nagging familiarity bounced around in her mind as she stared at the stack of papers.

This is it. I don't know what it is, but this is it.

A sticky note stapled to the top sheet of paper read, in her handwriting, "The Harvey Files." She had to chuckle— she had a recollection of writing the note, trying to break the tension in her own mind, before one of her last times visiting the lock box.

She carefully removed the sticky note from the top page, which appeared to be a letter, printed on the Institute's letterhead.

To whom it may concern,

I am an employee at the McNeill Institute for Neurological Development, and I have recently become aware of human rights violations happening under the umbrella of our Rehabilitation Research Project, hosted at Scarlett Bay Correctional Facility.

Attached, please find all the supporting documentation you will need in order to understand the nature and scope of the crimes being committed. These issues run deep, into the very heart of the Institute itself, and it will not be easy for you to address them without a complete assessment of the situation.

I find it extremely likely that I will lose my job over this report, so I have done my best to be thorough in walking you through the case step by step; however, if upon receipt, you have questions about any of the attached documents, you are welcome to reach out to me directly. If I am unavailable, my colleague Natalie Bailey will be able to assist you.

Sincerely,
Leonora Harvey

The mention of the prison began to trigger new memories in Leah's mind. She could almost taste it. The thrill of research. The horror at what she'd found. The heavy weight of a responsibility to do something with the information.

Driving through the main gate of Scarlett Bay with a videographer in her passenger seat. Haunted eyes refusing to meet her gaze.

She set the letter to the side and opened a manila folder on which she had written, in large capital letters, INTERVIEWS.

The very first page in the folder was a sheet of notebook paper, the curly holes along the side carefully removed, covered in the scrawls of secretarial shorthand. Leah skimmed the page with a measure of surprise—she hadn't been aware that she could read or write shorthand—before noticing that, just behind the notebook page was a typed transcription.

She read the heading and stopped cold.

Matthew Bailey
Former Research Technician (2016-2021)

I need to follow up with Matthew about that interview we did about the prison.

She studied the page more carefully.

This is that interview.

Her hands trembled as she read through the transcript of their conversation. It horrified her. The Institute described the Rehabilitation Research Program as an opportunity to minimize the costs of long-term incarceration and maximize successful rehabilitation by helping inmates to break out of destructive patterns. In order to accomplish this, Matthew claimed, the program was using the MentaLink technology to remove the inmates' memories related to their criminal experience, and then offer them simulated real-world scenarios to test whether or not they committed the same crimes. After sufficient proof of rehabilitation, the inmates were released early, equipped with any vocational training they had completed during their incarceration.

But it went deeper: Matthew shared that it wasn't only memories related to the inmates' criminal experience that were suppressed; sometimes, it was vast portions of their lives, if not the majority of their memories. Where the statistics claimed that under 20% of inmates experienced any form of relapse after their first session, Matthew alleged that half of those tested were "terminated from the program" after the first round of simulation testing due to immediate violation. Matthew's elaboration sent a shudder down her spine:

> L: Terminated? What happens to these folks?
> M: They leave in a body bag.
> L: They're killed? Are you sure?
> M: I saw it myself. That Jorge Rodriguez fellow they keep talking about on the news? I was one of the last people to see him alive.
> L: He's dead?
> M: Oh. I assumed you knew. I'm sorry, Leah. He died almost a year ago.
> L: But his family—the petition I keep seeing everywhere—isn't it all branded "bring him home?"
> M: They probably don't know. I certainly haven't been brave enough to tell his family. I can't think of anyone who would take that risk.

Leah set the paper down, taking a moment before she could continue reading. The rest of the interview was equally disturbing, and Leah couldn't help but project her own experience onto the stories Matthew related. What shocked her was his comment that side effects often extended beyond the treated inmates to the prison employees who worked with them, including Matthew himself.

> M: And gosh, Leah, Nat was always so kind to me when I would come home from work fuming, mid-migraine, irritable like you wouldn't believe... I can't do that to her again. Can't do that to our kids again. I walked out from that job six months ago and haven't looked back. I feel like a totally new man, or like I've returned to the man I was when I married her. I don't know why she didn't leave me, but I'll never betray her trust like that again.

221

Reading that paragraph, a realization struck Leah like a bolt of lightning.

This was why Jude and I broke up.

She wasn't sure if this realization filled her with pride or shame—she'd come to believe that they had parted ways over the interpersonal differences that she now saw as glaringly obvious. Was this better or worse?

It would have been something else soon if it hadn't been this.

She rubbed the empty space on her left hand where her engagement ring had once been.

We weren't going to make it to the wedding.

There was a strange comfort in that certainty.

A few minutes passed before Leah jogged herself back to the present moment. Shaking her head, she opened her laptop and responded to an email, only to get distracted by the contents of her lockbox within a minute or two.

Before she knew it, the clock read 5:30. She had accomplished maybe three tasks all afternoon, checking her laptop notifications when they came in, looking up from her papers when someone walked past her door. The office was hauntingly quiet—she hadn't stayed late at work in weeks and wasn't used to the silence. Hurrying to pack up, Leah noticed her hands shaking as she shut her laptop and tucked it into her desk.

"If the attempt fails, more extreme options are never off the table."

Bile filled her throat. She took a long drink from her water bottle before exiting her office, but even after the acrid taste receded, her stomach churned.

She nodded at Ana as she left, rubbing her arms as if she were cold, although the summer air was sweltering.

Pierucci is going to kill me if he finds out I'm remembering.

222

The thought presented itself out of nowhere. She slid into the driver's seat of her car but didn't start it. Natalie's pained expression filled her mind's eye, and a horrible question dawned on her as if for the first time.

Who else is in danger because of me?

She drove home without knowing how she did it, and when she got home, she went straight to her desk and pulled out the stack of papers again.

She shuffled through a handful of letters and cards that she'd found in the middle of the pile. They seemed personal, unrelated to the rest of the contents. A performance review from her first year employed full-time at the Institute. A birthday card that everyone in the office had signed. The initial notes for a marketing campaign that Dr. Pierucci had penned on a piece of hotel stationary. General nothings from her life. Her chest ached as she leafed through them.

At the very bottom of the stack was the steel-blue Rehabilitation Research Program brochure she'd seen before, stapled to a couple folded sheets of printer paper. Once again, the line on the center of the brochure stood out to her.

These criminals have been taken off the streets for public safety, and the McNeill Institute is working with the justice system to streamline rehabilitation while improving inmate quality of life at our very own Scarlett Bay Correctional Facility.

Once again, she heard her own voice echoing from the past.

"I wrote that statement; you don't need to quote it back to me. But that's not the whole story, and I won't remain complicit while lives are being ruined."

Snippets of that conversation had been returning all weekend, but she couldn't yet recall it start to finish.

Hands trembling, Leah removed the staple from the brochure and unfolded the pages attached to it, flattening out the deep creases before beginning to read.

I don't know what I'm supposed to do. Dr. Pierucci asked me to create a marketing campaign to build (rebuild?) public trust in the Institute in light of some rumors that have circulated on the internet recently. Things that started out on conspiracy websites and gradually made their way to more mainstream human rights' pages. Stories of torture and death, not only under the noses of Institute employees, but at their hands. Abuses of the prison system, of the rehab program... Things I don't even want to repeat because they make me sick to my stomach.

But I think the rumors are true. What do I do next? Where do I turn? How do I stop this madness? I don't know who to tell.

I've continued to work on the campaign, even going to print on some brochures I designed to explain the benefits of the Program. But I'm secretly doing more research. I'm keeping my statements vague and as factual as I can, although I'm sure I'll have to answer for the harm I'm perpetuating while I try to figure out my next steps.

This all started out so innocent, even pointless. Conspiracy theorists are going to theorize, and it's not worth listening to them. That's what I told myself at first. But then their information... wasn't wrong. There was enough truth in their crazy rants to draw me in, and I had to know who their sources were. I hacked into the project database—an offense

I'm certain would get me fired if it were found out, given that I have nowhere near the security clearance to access those files—I don't know how far I'm willing to go for this, how much I'm willing to risk. But I have to know the truth. And if it is all true, if people really are suffering and dying at the Institute's hands, I can't stand by and remain complicit. I don't want this blood on my hands.

I couldn't live with myself knowing that human beings are experimented on, tortured, even killed... in the name of what? Progress? Science? The common good?

The text soon changed to more of a note-taking format, lists dated and bulleted, as if to ensure that every detail got written down. But as she read the words on that first page, everything fell into place. She could feel the iron lock and rusty chain on the gate in her library falling, thundering as they hit the floor and shattered into a thousand pieces, throwing up a cloud of dust. In her mind's eye, she watched as books and papers flew past her, reshelving themselves. A tremendous weight lifted off her shoulders as the thick black sharpie lines receded, rendering visible the text they'd covered only moments before.

It was chaos. It was freedom. It was everything and nothing like she'd expected.

Chapter 20

The streetlight blazed through the window of Leah's office, muddling her sense of time. The sun had dropped beneath the horizon hours ago, and a late spring chill had settled on the streets. Leah sat at her desk, illuminated by the light of her laptop screen, a horrified expression on her face.

Surely there was no way this was true. But there it was, a video of a McNeill Institute employee and a Scarlett Bay employee talking about the things they'd seen while working at the prison: Weeping spouses. Blank stares through plexiglass windows. Cultivated amnesia. Malnutrition brought on by unchecked nausea.

And the body bags. So many body bags.

The faces of the employees in the video were blurred out to protect their identities and their families and perhaps even their lives, but Leah recognized their voices. She'd interviewed both of them herself within the last week as part of this public image crisis. Their answers to her questions had been banal, but she'd noticed a hint of something in their eyes... had it been terror?

The gravity of the situation slowly imposed itself upon her, settling like a weight across her shoulders. If she accepted that these stories were true, what responsibility did she have to make them known to the public? The haunted look of the men she'd interviewed took on a new significance as she began to see her own fears reflected in their eyes, the same questions gnawing away at them from the inside.

What was there to do? If the Institute was willing to murder patients in cold blood, and could do so with impunity, then what safety was there for a whistleblower except in anonymity?

* * *

Hands shaking, Leah tested the doorknob. Locked. She produced a single key, palmed off of Jude a few minutes previously. The key turned in the lock, and she slipped into the office, closing and locking the door behind her. As quickly as she could, she inserted a flash drive into the computer and navigated to the files she was looking for.

It didn't take her long to find them. She copied the files to her flash drive, tugged it loose, and let herself back out of the office. No one had seen her enter or leave. The key would be back in Jude's pocket momentarily.

She was in the clear.

For now.

* * *

Skimming the project files she'd stolen from Dr. Pierucci's computer confirmed her worst fears. Memo after memo discussed strategies, next steps, and test results without so much as a moment of silence for the vast human cost of this horrific experiment.

Her conscience was wracked with guilt as she considered the lives lost during the time she'd spent hemming and hawing, let alone the time she'd spent researching and creating materials to rebuild trust in the Institute she no longer trusted herself.

Was this the right way to go about it? She was never certain, and the "what if" questions plagued her mind constantly. The list of dead lay at the top of her papers. Just one page among hundreds. Their bodies laid to rest in unmarked graves, their families left wondering why they'd stopped returning calls...

* * *

She didn't hear the door open. Her back was turned as she hunched over the filing cabinet in the back of her office. Hands on her waist stopped her heart, and she whirled around, ready to throw punches if it came to that.

Jude's smiling face greeted her, his self-satisfaction turning to confusion at the panicked look in her eyes.

"Woah, Leah, are you okay? I wasn't trying to scare you." He paused, waiting for her to respond, but quickly spoke up again to fill the resulting silence. "What are you working on?"

She stepped over to her laptop again, hurriedly bringing up her email to hide the document she'd been updating. If Jude found out about the research she'd been doing—about what she'd done to accomplish it—there was no telling what would happen. She knew he loved her, but even so...

"Just more of the same," she said eventually, trying to still the tremor in her voice. "Wrapping up the Scarlett Bay campaign and starting to put together some materials for the gala."

"Gala already? I feel like we just did that." He shook his head. "How has the campaign been going, by the way? Father always seems anxious about it. I guess yesterday I mentioned something to him in passing that I'd seen you working on, something in the project files, and he looked really worried. Everything okay on that front?"

Her shaking hands brushed against yesterday's mug and sent it spinning. The remains of her coffee, now tepid and stale, splattered in a dramatic arc. Liquid pooled around the wilted alstroemeria petals littering her desk before drip-drip-dripping to the ground. For a moment, Leah just stood and watched. Jude appeared at her elbow with a napkin. She took it and mechanically began to wipe up the spill. Her thoughts spun out in a half a dozen different directions, and she struggled to focus on the conversation.

"You told your father I'd been looking at the project files?" She tried to force her voice to remain neutral, grateful that Jude couldn't see or hear the intense ache in her stomach.

Jude shrugged, nonchalant. "Oh, yeah, I mean, I'm sure you were just looking for photos or something to use, and that's exactly what I told him, but he started grilling me about exactly what files you'd been looking through. I told him I didn't know, and eventually he dropped it. I don't know. I'm sure it's nothing. You know how he can be sometimes." He exhaled, something between a laugh and a huff.

Leah knew exactly how he could be.

The two chatted for a few more minutes while Leah tried to figure out how she could politely ask Jude to excuse himself, when his phone buzzed in his pocket.

He groaned. "I'm sure that's Father. I think I'm supposed to be in a meeting with him. Anyway, gotta go. See you after work." He kissed her softly and let himself out of her office.

"Hey, Jude?" For the tiniest moment, she considered bringing him into her confidence. It might not change anything—the cards had already begun to fall—but it might bring her some comfort.

He turned around and looked back at her, his sleeves rolled halfway up his forearms, a tiny fleck of salsa in the corner of his mouth. He must have stopped for tacos that morning. She thought better of her plan. The desperate grasp of a person tumbling into a chasm. It wouldn't do either of them any good.

He stared at her, waiting for her to speak.

"You've got salsa on your face." She pointed to the corner of her own mouth.

He whispered "thank you," wiped his face discreetly, and raised his eyebrows. She nodded, and he walked away. She closed the door behind him and immediately pulled out her phone. Matthew Bailey's phone number wasn't saved, but she easily located the intentionally vague message thread they'd used a few weeks previously, when she'd interviewed him about his time at Scarlett Bay. Her fingers flew across the screen, still shaking, as she typed out the message.

> We need to talk ASAP. What are you doing tonight?

His response was prompt. The children must have been napping.

> Come by for dinner. I'll tell the wife. No need for you to
> say anything at the office. I'm making a huge dinner.

She heaved a sigh of relief.

* * *

Dinner at the Baileys' house was all business as Leah laid out the whole situation to them. It was comforting, in a way, to share the details with people who weren't shocked by them. Matthew's work at the prison had scarred him. Leah could still see the weight in his tense shoulders and his lightning-quick startle reflex at every little noise. But they were the same, in a way, as they grappled with questions of complicity and responsibility, and Leah knew she could count on these two if her life depended on it.

"I don't see this ending well for me," she admitted quietly. "I wasn't able to find everything I wanted, but it'll have to be enough. There isn't time for anything else."

Matthew nodded grimly. "What do you need from us to get this into the right hands?"

Beside him, a petrified look came into Natalie's eyes. He squeezed her hand. "It's going to be okay, sweetheart. This isn't going to be like before."

Natalie didn't look convinced.

Leah was adamant that the Baileys keep themselves out of harm's way. "If something happens to me, I don't want you two to get hurt, and I don't want you to do anything that would put the kids in danger."

"Of course." Natalie was no longer hiding the fear in her voice. "But Leah, there's no one else at the Institute who could convince the press to run this story. It's you, or it's us."

Matthew chimed in, a quiet and steady presence. "The press isn't the answer, and neither are the cops. I'm sure I told you this, Leah, but some of them are on his payroll. We can't risk it."

A lump formed in Leah's throat. "So what do we do?"

He looked her in the eyes. "We go to the FBI. They've got an online tip submission form. I've flirted with the idea before, but I haven't had enough evidence to feel like it was a compelling case. This, though?" He gestured to the chaos of papers laid out on his dining room table. "This is compelling."

Leah nodded. "FBI it is. I'll take a look at it tonight."

"List me on the tip, as well, Leah. Just in case..." Natalie didn't finish her sentence. She didn't need to. Leah nodded, gulping down the bile rising in her throat.

Matthew placed a strong hand on Leah's shoulder. "We have your back here, Leah. And God forbid something happens to you, we'll... we'll make sure justice is done."

Leah nodded slowly, trying to numb herself to the gravity of Matthew's words. "I stand by my statement that this won't end well for me, but... I have an idea. I don't like it, but it's the best I can come up with."

In spite of the tension in the room, Matthew grinned. "There it is. I knew something was brewing. Hit me with it."

Leah grimaced. "Basically... if everything at Scarlett Bay hinges on temporary or permanent memory suppression..."

Matthew's smile faded. "Leah, you don't mean—"

She threw up her hands, her eyebrows raised. "Do we have another choice? It's not like Pierucci's going to let me walk free

232

after this. It's suppression or a body bag, Matthew, you know it is. You know it better than any of us."

He sighed. Natalie chimed in, "Surely, he'll have some mercy on you. His own son's fiancé? His future daughter-in-law?"

Leah bit her lip and shrugged her shoulders. "I don't want to count on that. Jude and I... I don't know. If it were up to him, it might be different. But Dr. Pierucci doesn't see things like that..."

Matthew chimed in. "But how are you going to convince Pierucci to go with the suppression? If you suggest it, he'll just shoot it down that much faster."

Leah looked at the table, rubbing her forehead with one hand. "I know, I know. That's where I keep getting stuck."

Natalie raised a hand tentatively. "If things would be different with Jude... I mean, is there any way you could talk to him and see if he'd suggest it?"

Leah scoffed. "And trust him to keep his trap shut for who knows how long until we see if we can undo it?" She rolled her eyes. "Yeah, right."

Matthew glared at her.

Leah sighed. "I'm sorry, Natalie, that was rude. It's not a bad idea, but I don't think it would help to talk to him. He'd never go against his father like that."

Natalie raised her eyebrows. "You really think he'd let you...?"

"Well, no, but..." Leah scratched at her neck. "I mean, if it comes down to me or his father, I know who he's going to choose." Leah felt her eyes glaze over. "But what if I just... I don't know, make lots of references around him to memory and forgetfulness and amnesia." A single desperate laugh escaped her. "Could I just subliminally suggest it and hope for the best? It's a long shot either way, but at least there'd be no chance of him turning on us later down the road."

Matthew shrugged. "I mean, it might be the best we've got."

233

Leah nodded, her mind still racing. "We'll need a tech on our side if we're going to pull this off. Who do you think is trustworthy? Natalie, you probably see them most often."

Natalie didn't hesitate for a moment. "I know just the guy. You've met him—I think I remember you two goofing off at an office party one time. Total nerd for the MentaLink stuff, but not overly popular with the rest of the staff."

Leah gave two thumbs up. "Good enough for me. Don't tell me his name—the less I know, the better. If you trust him, I trust him. Can you try to find a time to speak with him this week?"

Natalie nodded, "I'll schedule him an appointment with a fake client. That'll give me about half an hour."

"Perfect. And Natalie, please please please promise me—" Leah's voice was desperate. "If anything happens to me, get out. I don't want y'all risking more than you already have."

"We'll take each day as it comes, Leah. You got us through Matthew's rehab. We'll get you through this." Her words were confident, but her eyes told a different story.

Adrenaline coursed through Leah's veins as she struggled to remain focused. Natalie poured her another cup of chamomile tea and changed the topic. "You need a break, Leah. Your mind needs a break. You're not a machine."

The gentle rebuke stung more than she wanted to admit. When she finally left the Baileys' house, long after midnight, she didn't feel at peace, exactly, but she did feel less frantically anxious. It was a start.

* * *

Pierucci's retribution was swift. Within two days of learning that she had been accessing the files, he had put a meeting on her calendar. While the subject of the discussion was not stated, it was anything but ambiguous. Leah was mildly surprised to see Jude *included on the calendar invitation—was Pierucci trying to throw her off her game?*

***

When she walked into his office that day, gray clouds were just beginning to gather in the otherwise crystal-blue skies around the clinic. Jude was seated across from his father, and Leah availed herself of the empty chair next to Jude. The deep mahogany of Dr. Pierucci's desk seemed to stretch for miles between them and the doctor. Muted sunlight streamed in from the floor-to-ceiling windows of the corner office.

After a moment of heavy silence, Dr. Pierucci began to speak. "Jude," he began, nodding to his son. He turned to her. "Leonora."

"Dr. Pierucci," Leah responded, her hands shaking in her lap.

Jude grinned and elbowed Leah. "Gettin' the full name treatment today, eh? At least we're not back to 'Ms. Harvey.'"

Leah rolled her eyes.

Dr. Pierucci looked disappointed, although which of them was the target, Leah couldn't tell. "I expect you know why I've requested this meeting?"

"I believe so," Leah responded. She felt her voice shake, and she willed herself to remain strong.

"Leonora, it has come to my attention that you have been... how do I put this delicately? ...making some imprudent inquiries into certain projects with which you are not involved. This, of course, would be absolutely unacceptable behavior for any employee of this organization, but for one so closely connected to my own family," he gestured to Jude, "it would be a scandal beyond belief."

Leah sighed, twisting the engagement ring on her left hand and glancing at Jude. His confusion grew into a squirming discomfort, and he turned away from her. She followed his eyes to the plaque on his father's desk.

McNeill Institute for Neurological Development
Jude Pierucci, Sr, MD, PhD
2018 Employee of the Year

Dr. Pierucci continued, "I do not need to tell the two of you that this company is involved with several projects for the national government, knowledge of which is restricted to those with top security clearance. Accessing–or attempting to access–project files without clearance is not simply a betrayal of this organization, but a breach of national securi–"

"If I may, sir," Leah interrupted. "The projects to which you are referring are only tangentially related to national security, but more importantly, they are concealing egregious human rights violations from a deliberately misguided public."

Her voice shook, the way it did when she and Jude fought and she was trying to sound more confident than she felt. She hoped that Jude didn't notice. She needed him to take her side on this.

"Wait, what?" Jude demanded.

Dr. Pierucci ignored him, making eye contact with Leah. "Then you are guilty as charged?"

Leah took a deep breath. "I am."

Jude's tone was frantic. "You did what? When? Why didn't you tell me?"

She turned to him, indignant. "How could I have told you? What would I have said? 'Oh, six months until the wedding, how exciting, also today I discovered that your father is murdering patients at Scarlett Bay.'"

Jude furrowed his brows. "Leah, what are you talking about? These criminals have been taken off the streets for public safety, and Father is working with the justice system to streamline our prisons while improving inmate quality of life." He rattled off the script, his fingers tapping away at his pant leg non-stop.

236

Leah only rolled her eyes in response. "I wrote that statement; you don't need to quote it back to me. But that's not the whole story, and I won't remain complicit while lives are being ruined."

Before Jude could respond, Dr. Pierucci interjected, clearly irritated. "Leonora, what you discovered is irrelevant to this conversation. We are here to discuss your behavior, as well as your future at this company... and with this family."

Jude burst into the conversation again. "Would one of you mind telling me what the heck is going on here?"

Leah and Dr. Pierucci exchanged glances, but neither spoke. The light from the window danced and shifted as the sky darkened with the weight of an incoming storm.

Jude's voice was hushed as he spoke into the silence left by his outburst. "Leah, what were you doing snooping in Father's stuff? And Father, are you trying to say that you're going to forbid me to get married?"

Dr. Pierucci scoffed. "Do you mean to say that you are unaware of Ms. Harvey's actions over the last three months?"

Jude spoke slowly, each word weighted. "I have no idea what either of you are talking about."

"Jude," Leah's voice was softer now. "A few months back, I started hearing rumors. We all did—torture chambers in the prisons, living quarters the size of a bathtub... At first, I thought they had to be false and just laughed them off. They were so ridiculous. But then I was asked to create that marketing campaign to rebuild public trust in the Institute, so I needed to understand what exactly was being said."

Across the desk, Dr. Pierucci remained silent, his lips pursed. The room had darkened significantly, and the first drops of rain were pattering on the window, racing downward and gathering speed as they did so. Leah glanced at him before continuing. He nodded, frowning.

She looked back at Jude. "This might be hard to hear, but when I was researching the rumors and the folks who were publicizing them, I came across some interviews with anonymous former employees of the Institute and of Scarlett Bay."

Now it was Jude who sounded skeptical. "Unnamed employees? Leah, you've gotta be kidding me. That stuff's always fake."

"That's what I assumed too, but there was a nagging doubt at the back of my mind. And you know me—I don't know when to stop. Before I knew it, I'd swiped clearance codes and logged into the project database." Her voice faltered again as she held back tears. She closed her eyes and spun the ring around on her finger as she waited for him to respond.

"It's true, then." Jude said coldly to no one in particular.

Leah steadied herself. "It is. The technology he—we—sent to the prison is being used to conduct illegal experiments on the inmates, and the results of the research are being presented as the cutting edge of neurology. Conferences, papers, articles... and your father can stand back and watch his business thrive, fill his pockets, and suffer no consequences for his cruelty."

Shock and sadness mingled on Jude's face. His wide eyes darted between her and his father, and Leah looked away.

Eventually, his voice interrupted her thoughts. "Father, why didn't you tell me?"

Her heart sank.

There was an insufferable pride in Dr. Pierucci's voice as he responded. "I have merely been waiting for the appropriate moment to onboard you. The project is still in its infancy, but believe me, I have been looking forward to bringing you on as a cooperator."

Outside, a torrent of rain filled the sky. The antique lamp on the doctor's desk enveloped them in a circle of warm light, shrouding the rest of the room in darkness by contrast.

"What type of research are you doing?" Jude asked, his voice faltering. Leah wished she could speak to him alone for just a few minutes.

For the first time, Dr. Pierucci beamed. "An excellent question, son. We are using the MentaLink console and simulator technology to test the very limits of the human mind. If we can suppress the memories of violent criminals, replacing them with a carefully-crafted past of our own choosing, we can reduce the likelihood of a repeat offense by over 60% and subtly shift the thinking of the population at large, without wasting funds on inefficient prisons and ineffective political campaigns."

Jude nodded along. "That's incredible. An elegant solution to some age-old problems."

Leah cut in, unable to help herself. "He's spinning it, Jude. He's chosen pretty words, but you have no idea how ugly the reality is. The side effects of the memory suppression are nauseating, even to those who haven't received it, and his stats are skewed because he has the prison guards execute anyone who commits a repeat offense in the simulation."

Dr. Pierucci avoided her gaze, continuing to make eye contact with his son. "My methods are unorthodox, I acknowledge. But desperate times, as they say. And my results speak for themselves. Wouldn't you rather have well-adjusted school teachers and salesmen living in a hundred neighborhoods, instead of a hundred violent wretches living under one roof?"

"Unorthodox? You're murdering them in cold blood. Jude, these people are spouses and parents and friends, and he isn't even giving them the dignity of a proper burial! I don't think he's even telling their families that they've died!"

Dr. Pierucci leaned back in his chair. If he was fazed by the conversation, he gave no sign of it. Jude, on the other hand, squirmed in his seat, looking around the room frantically. His eyes didn't rest for more than a moment on anything. His fingers tapped restlessly on his pants legs.

Eventually, he offered a hesitant response. "You're right, of course, Father. I'm hurt that you didn't think I was ready to tackle this project, but I must say I'm impressed by what you've accomplished so far."

Leah's heart fell and her shoulders slumped. Hoping that no one had noticed, she took a deep breath, straightened her back, and set her face like flint.

Dr. Pierucci smiled, and the sight sent a chill down Leah's spine. "I'm glad to know that you approve. I look forward to further conversation on this topic–perhaps we can meet late next week? We will be rather tied up until that time." He glared pointedly at Leah.

"Tied up?" Jude sounded genuinely confused.

"Well of course. We must deal with Ms. Harvey's betrayal of us and of everything that this Institute represents."

Jude rolled his eyes. "Father, are you still going off about the engagement? I know this stings, but surely-"

"Jude, if you persist in even the consideration of a union with this woman, I will never speak with you again. I can no longer see her as a member of our family." Jude opened his mouth to respond, but his father cut him off. "But no, I am speaking of punishing her for her actions as an employee. I cannot allow her to continue. She must be terminated."

"Terminated? You mean fire her." Leah heard the panic in his voice, and she allowed herself to hope. "Terminate her contract."

"I do not."

Jude was speechless. He breathed deeply and clenched his fists. "You would... kill someone over this? Kill Leah?" She could tell that he was struggling to keep his voice measured. Leah realized, not for the first time, how dramatically her opinion of her future father-in-law had shifted in recent weeks. Her heart pounded in her chest, but his words did not surprise her in the slightest.

Dr. Pierucci shrugged as if to ask what other option he had. "Capital punishment is the appropriate response to an offender who cannot be prevented from harming the community. I have full confidence that Ms. Harvey would find a way to continue spreading misinformation from any prison unfortunate enough to receive her."

"I..." Jude trailed off. Leah would have given anything to know what was going through his mind.

She screwed up her courage and turned to face him. "You don't have to agree to this, Jude."

"Silence, Ms. Harvey." The doctor's voice was sharp. "This discussion no longer concerns you."

She could have hit him. "It concerns me quite intimately, Dr. Pierucci. And while I am fully prepared to accept the consequences of my actions, I think it's important for your son to keep in mind that you are not a law enforcement agent, and any punishment you administer beyond firing me is, once again, an egregious human rights violation."

Jude's eyes widened. "Leah, you would give your life for this?"

"Absolutely." Her voice was sad, but calm.

Dr. Pierucci cut in. "Well, son, do you have an alternative suggestion regarding an appropriate punishment?"

Jude hesitated. "Father, surely in light of her years of service to the Institute, and her connection with our family, perhaps we could consider a more... fitting resolution."

"Fitting in what way, may I ask? What punishment do you believe fits this crime, if not death?"

Jude's words came tumbling out. "Could she not become a test subject? Could we not suppress her memory and replace it with a past of our own crafting? After all, she is no use to us dead..." He paused before adding. "And if the attempt fails, more extreme options are never off the table."

He sounded just like his father: the tone, the inflection, even the hint of malice crouched beneath the surface. Leah shut her eyes tightly for a moment, her stomach in knots. When she opened them again, a cruel grin played on Pierucci's lips. "An intriguing concept. Please do say more."

Jude leaned forward in his chair, placing his forearms on the desk. "If we could create a past for her that includes a neurological diagnosis, we can ensure that she comes to the Institute for treatment. We can conduct regular scans of her brain to monitor the effectiveness of the memory suppression, as well as any side effects. I assume your inmates are being tested in the simulator; well, a real-world subject is the natural next step. And she has no violent past, so she's no threat to the public."

For a moment, the doctor said nothing. When he did speak, his voice was quiet. "Very well. I accept your proposal."

Outside, a bolt of lightning snaked across the sky, followed by a peal of thunder that shook the building.

"Spooky," Jude said in a goofy voice, a habit he had been unable to break. His face reddened. Both Leah and Dr. Pierucci rolled their eyes. For a fleeting moment, Leah felt a sense of kinship with her future father-in-law.

But then he stood up, and the feeling vanished. Slowly, methodically, he walked around the desk and placed a heavy hand on Leah's shoulder. "Well then, Ms. Harvey, I believe it is time for us to go."

Jude made a noise as if he wanted to speak, but he said nothing. Leah stood and turned to him, fighting back tears. "I'm not sorry, Jude. This is why I didn't tell you what I found. I knew you wouldn't care. I knew you would side with your father."

"Is that so wrong?" His voice was desperate.

She didn't respond. She wanted to feel something toward him—anger, sorrow, disappointment, anything. Instead, she just felt numb. The first tendrils of post-rain sunshine crept into the room.

Leah slipped the engagement ring off her finger and held it out to Jude, "I suppose I won't be needing this anymore." He took it.

She opened the door and didn't look back.

Dr. Pierucci walked through the door and took the lead. She followed him out of his office and down the hall. Her mind raced, trying to ensure that everything had been hidden adequately. She pushed Natalie and Matthew out of her mind, hoping against hope that this last desperate effort would keep them safe. Had it been the right choice to get them involved? Would she ever get a chance to find out?

Her heart pounded, her breathing shallow and rapid.

Dr. Pierucci sat her down on the orthodontic chair without a word, strapped her arms and legs down tightly, and clipped a pulse oximeter to her finger. He tied a tourniquet around her upper arm and inserted a needle into her vein. The sight of the injection left her feeling light-headed... or was that the result of the drug he'd given her?

As she began to fade, she heard his voice, as if from across the ocean.

"You know, Leonora, I always knew you were too good for that son of mine."

The anesthesia took hold of her, and there was nothing.

***

Leah's eyes shot open. Her heart pounded in her chest.

"I need to call Natalie."

Chapter 21

"Hey, Leah, what's up?" Natalie's voice was sleepy, and Leah suddenly became aware of the darkness pressing in through her windows.

"Ah, shoot. Did I interrupt bedtime?"

Natalie yawned. "No, no, they've been asleep for a while. I was in Rosie's bed, but I think I was out too." She paused. "What's up?"

Leah's heart skipped a beat. "I remember, Natalie. All of it. The prison, the engagement, Dr. Pierucci threatening my life, Jude doing nothing to stop him... It all came back this evening, and I don't know what to do with it." Her words tumbled out as panic set in. "I need you to tell me that everything's going to be okay."

Natalie didn't respond, and Leah desperately wished that that they were in person so she could read Natalie's body language.

The pause lengthened.

Did she fall back asleep?

"Did... did you hear me?"

"You remember everything?" Natalie's voice was little more than a whisper.

"I do." Leah still struggled to gauge Natalie's reaction. Was she surprised? Confused? Scared? "It's a lot."

When Nat spoke again, her voice was hushed but excited. "Leah, that's amazing. I can't believe this is happening. I didn't really think it would work! I mean, I didn't not think... well, you know what I mean."

Leah nodded to herself, tracing figure-eights on her leg to guide her breathing. "I do, I do. It's crazy. I... I'm sure we'll find places where everything is still a little rough around the edges, but it worked. And I'm... it's a lot to take in all at once."

If Natalie noticed the strained tone of Leah's voice, she didn't let on. "I'll call Agent McDowell right now! I know he'll want to get together with you to talk about next steps."

Next steps?

Leah felt a twinge in her stomach.

Before she could respond, Natalie's voice turned to unabashed joy. "And I need to tell Matthew—oh, Leah, Matthew is going to be so relieved; he's missed you so much. I don't know if he ever got a chance to tell you, you know, before it all went down, but you changed his life with that interview. You gave him and so many others a voice. He really... well, I know he'll have a lot to say. I'll tell him, of course, but please do come by tomorrow evening if you're able. We'll make dinner. I'll invite Peter, and maybe Agent McDowell too. We can make plans. It'll be good!" Natalie spoke so quickly that Leah had a hard time following what she was saying.

"Yeah, sure, I should be free for dinner. That sounds good." She shoved down the discomfort that gnawed at her. "It'll be good to see Matthew again."

"Great, well, I'll let you go so I can make those other phone calls," Natalie chirped. "I'm looking forward to seeing you tomorrow!"

"See you tomorrow. Bye." Leah's voice was barely louder than a mumble, but Natalie didn't seem to notice.

It really will be good to see Matthew again.

The call ended, and Leah looked around her apartment as if with new eyes. The windows were dark, blinds open, street lights standing sentry. Business as usual. The clock on the wall read half past nine, and Leah decided to make her own announcements in the morning. If Natalie got to it ahead of her, so be it, but otherwise there would be plenty of time for reunions after a good night's rest.

She slipped into bed a few minutes later, but her nerves left her unable to fall asleep quickly. In her mind, she wandered the halls of her library, running her fingers along the spines of books as if she were greeting old friends. There were certain volumes that called out to her, and unable to pass them by, she carefully slid them off their shelves, perusing their pages with fondness, reveling in the stories they held or the information they contained. The process was comforting, and she noticed her breathing slow down and deepen.

Everything is going to be okay.

***

She woke the next morning still tired; she'd tossed and turned for most of the night, only falling into a deep sleep around three or four. After her second cup of coffee in under an hour, with a bowl of instant oatmeal steaming in front of her, she typed out a text to Peter.

I'm baaaaaack!

Just for good measure, she also sent a few of her favorite GIFs bearing the same words. About ten images in, his

247

response came through, a single line of text amidst a wall of color and motion.

No freaking way. It worked?

They exchanged messages for a few minutes. As she expected he would, Peter demanded all the details but remained unsatisfied with what Leah was willing to share over text. She knew he'd want the detail of a peer-reviewed journal article, so she cut herself off and promised to tell him all about it at the Baileys' house that evening. As an afterthought, she invited him to the Baileys' house that evening, just in case Natalie forgot.

A restlessness filled Leah's heart and limbs as she drove to the office. Like Natalie, Leah hadn't been fully convinced that her memories would ever return, in part or in full. She hadn't really expected to make it out alive at all. None of them had been certain. There was no precedent. There was no guarantee.

Frankly, it's half a miracle that Jude suggested the suppression in the first place, although I suppose Natalie was right that he couldn't just sit by and watch his father murder me.

But it had worked. Her memories were back. She was back, in a way that felt real but didn't fully make sense. When lunch time finally rolled around, Leah ate quickly and excused herself to go for a walk. There wasn't much green space around her office, but over the course of the year, she'd perfected a thirty-minute trail that would have her back at her desk by one o'clock. She stayed in the shade of the ancient oak trees, trying to avoid the sun beating down on her. A pair of grackles cawed back and forth. The joy in her chest tightened into anxiety as she remembered Natalie's comment about inviting Agent McDowell.

248

Am I really willing to risk everything a second time? Now that I know what it's like?

A ringing interrupted her thoughts, and she slipped her phone out of her pocket. The number wasn't saved in her contacts, but it looked familiar. She answered it without thinking.

"Hello, is this Leonora Harvey?" Valerie's voice was hesitant.

Leah was overjoyed. "Valerie! What a surprise! I guess Natalie filled you in on everything that happened?"

"Peter did." She paused. "I'm not sure Natalie knows that I've been involved."

"Oh," Leah felt her brow wrinkle. "Well, I'm not sure when you got brought onto this whole project, so I'm not sure how much you know, but frankly, I can't believe it worked."

Leah wished she could see Valerie's face. "Peter opened up to me about it fairly quickly. He needed someone to talk to about it. We have a lot in common, Peter and I, and this year wasn't easy for him... But of course it worked. It was always going to work."

Curiosity won out over politeness. "What do you mean, it wasn't easy for him?"

Valerie's voice sobered. "Peter has a lot of passion for the MentaLink technology, but... well, he didn't join the Institute to suppress healthy minds. And then, of course..." She trailed off.

Leah's feet slowed as she approached a bench, and she took a seat. She could sense there was more that Valerie wanted to say. "Of course what?"

"It's really not my place to talk about it," Valerie replied. "I'm sorry. I shouldn't have brought Peter up."

More evasion? After everything that's happened?

"You said that you and he are very similar," Leah prompted.

"Oh," Valerie said after a moment's pause. "Well, I left the Institute because how my father's technology was being used. He would have been horrified, especially in light of my mother's accident."

Accident?

Leah wanted to press her further, but Valerie changed the topic before she could ask another question. "So, how does it feel to have your memories back?"

"Oh, it's amazing," Leah sighed, watching a sparrow peck at the dirt. "I finally feel at home again. I hadn't realized how much I was missing, but now that it's back, I can't fathom how I functioned for so long without it..."

Valerie chuckled. "I can already hear the questions Peter is going to ask when you tell him that."

Leah laughed aloud, reveling in the warmth of the sunshine on her face. "Oh, he's going to demand a dissertation, I'm sure. I'm already steeling myself for tonight." She added quickly, "Did Peter mention dinner at the Baileys' house tonight?"

"He did, although I asked him to make sure I would be welcome. I don't want to presume on Natalie's hospitality."

"Of course." Leah nodded. "Well, I hope you'll be able to make it. It'll be like a little reunion!"

Valerie hesitated. "A reunion, I suppose. But you know that Natalie has asked the FBI Agent to come as well."

A cloud floated in front of the sun, casting a shadow across the sidewalk.

"Oh yeah, that's probably just because he was doing some undercover work while I was in treatment at McNeill.

We're kind of buddi—well, it's complicated." Leah laughed, hoping Valerie didn't hear the tremor in it. "But I've got a year's worth of stories to catch up on, and I can't wait!"

A warm smile grew in Valerie's voice. "You know, Leah, you and Peter give me a lot of hope for the Institute. I often wonder if I made the wrong choice, leaving when I did. But you two give me hope that things will get better."

A question arose in Leah's mind, and she voiced it without thinking. "Valerie, if Dr. Pierucci weren't at the Institute anymore, would you come back?"

For a moment, there was silence. A sparrow hopped over to Leah's bench, searching for crumbs. Leah held her out her empty hands and shrugged. The bird hopped away.

"I'm sorry if that's an impertinent question." Leah added.

"No, it's not that." Valerie's words came slowly. "I've asked myself the same thing. And I don't think I have an answer yet. It's not off the table completely, but there's so much history there."

"Mmmm," Leah affirmed. "I understand."

There was another pause, heavy with the weight of untold stories, before Valerie spoke up. "Well, Leah, I have to go. It's been lovely speaking with you"

"Likewise, Valerie. I hope to see you this evening. And thank you... for everything."

"Of course, Leah."

The call ended, leaving Leah once again alone with her thoughts. The image of Valerie as a young woman was seared into her memory. As a child, Leah had adored her for her gentleness, her fierce protectiveness, and her obvious investment in the children at the Ward. As an adult, though, she could see there was more to Valerie than her younger self had been able to perceive: anger, grief, even fear, tucked beneath the surface.

I wonder if I'll ever get to know her whole story.

Taking another deep breath of the sweltering summer air, Leah stood up and began her walk back to the office. By the time she sat down at her desk, she was drenched in sweat. She downed a glass of water and refilled the cup before pulling out the backup stick of deodorant she kept in her backpack.

She opened her laptop and logged onto Facebook. At the top of her feed, Natalie had shared a picture of Rosie, whose wispy strawberry-blond hair curled out from under a sun hat, her grin contagious.

I can't wait to see those kids again. Maybe I can get to Nat's early so we can make cookies before dinner.

She scrolled further until she saw a long post that her Aunt Kathy shared.

I should call Mom.

She closed the browser and pulled open her project management program. A list of her overdue tasks greeted her. Overwhelmed, she opened Facebook again.

But how am I going to explain all of this to her?

She scrolled through her feed, chuckling at a couple of reels, until a bright orange ad caused her heart to skip.

BRING HIM HOME.

Her thumb hovered over the picture of Jorge Rodriguez and his son as she debated whether or not to click on the image. A knot had suddenly formed in her stomach.

No use feeding the guilt trip. It is what it is.

The afternoon crawled by. A few hours later, Leah pulled up directions to Natalie's house and was dismayed to find that driving straight there from work would save her forty five minutes of car time. She wrapped up her projects for the day and decided to kill the extra time with a TV show. Grabbing a sparkling water from the fridge, she closed the door of her office and opened a new browser tab.

Forty-five minutes... What do I want to watch?

Nostalgia won out, and she selected a show that Jude had introduced her to. She hadn't seen it in well over a year, but she found she could still recite the opening montage from memory.

Everything is going to be okay.

Chapter 22

The golden-hour sun shone through her car windshield as Leah pulled up to the Baileys' house, trying to calm the knot in her stomach.

There's nothing to be nervous about! This is going to be a fun reunion—you know and love all these people.

"There she is!" Matthew's voice rang out from the doorway as she made her way up the walk. He wrapped her in a hug and ushered her into the entryway of the house. The air smelled of rosemary and red wine, and the atmosphere was unusually calm.

"Where are the kids?" Leah asked, glancing down the hallway and hoping for the patter of little feet.

"They're with Nat's parents for the night. She thought it'd be better to have fewer distractions." Leah tried to mask her disappointment as Matthew rummaged around in his pockets. "But Josephine did specifically tell me that I have to give you this."

He pulled out a beaded bracelet and dropped it gently into her outstretched hand. Colorful round beads were interspersed between small white circles, each with a letter, spelling out 'Auntie Leah'.

Leah cracked a huge grin and slipped the bracelet onto her wrist. "Please thank her for me!"

Matthew assumed the wide-eyed childish pout he always wore when quoting his kids. "She said to tell you that the pink and purple beads are for her and Rosie, and the orange ones are for Victor, and the green ones are for you since she didn't know your favorite color, but she thought it might be green."

"Oh, of course," Leah replied, smiling fondly. "Well, you can tell her that she guessed correctly." She spun a few of the beads between the fingers of her other hand. "I'll treasure it forever."

Matthew smiled. "Well, hey, come on in! I think the roast should be just about ready, and everyone else is here. I know they'll be excited to see you!"

Leah followed him into the living room, where Peter and Valerie were chatting amicably. Peter nursed a beer and Valerie a glass of wine, and they looked up as she walked into the room. Peter raised his bottle in greeting, and Valerie smiled.

Leah joined their conversation as Matthew walked toward the kitchen. "Good to see y'all! Where's Nat?"

"She's talking with Agent McDowell." Peter gestured with his bottle again, this time toward the kitchen. Glancing over the bar, Leah could see Natalie's blonde hair and some of Agent McDowell's face.

Her heart skipped a beat, and her stomach squirmed. She dropped her voice to a whisper. "Is it just me, or is it kind of weird that he's here? I mean, like, we were friendly enough at the clinic, but it's not like he's part of the group or anything."

Peter shrugged, looking in the direction of the kitchen. Valerie cocked her head slightly, looking at Leah with wide brown eyes.

Leah continued, still whispering. "It's not even like he's really my friend... I got to know his undercover persona, not him. And honestly, I don't know, it feels like he hasn't done anything with the information I sent in. You know? It's been a year. Shouldn't they have made an arrest already? Why drag all of us back into it?"

As she spoke, Leah watched Agent McDowell notice her. He offered a slight nod in her direction, then said something to Natalie, who turned around and spotted her. Natalie's eyebrows shot up, and she waved Leah over.

"I'll be right back," Leah sighed to Peter and Val before stepping into the kitchen. She tried to keep her voice casual as she approached. "Hey Nat, how's it going?"

She extended an arm to offer Natalie a hug, but Natalie didn't notice. After a long moment of waiting, Leah lowered her arm back to her side and turned to Agent McDowell. "Good to see you again."

"Good evening, Ms. Harvey. Thanks for coming tonight." His voice wasn't cold, but it contained no trace of the warmth she'd come to expect from Wilder.

Was all of Wilder's personality just a lie?

"Can I get you a drink or anything?" Natalie asked, turning toward the oven and shuffling some carrots and celery off a sheet pan.

It took Leah a moment to realize that Natalie was addressing her. "Oh, a glass of wine would be great."

Natalie started to turn away from the stove, but Agent McDowell stepped in. "Let me get that for you."

"Thanks, Robert," Nat replied, turning back to her pan.

Oh, Robert? So we're on a first name basis now?

Agent McDowell poured Leah a glass of wine and handed it to her before picking up his own. Natalie continued to bustle about the kitchen and dining room as she got the food on the table.

"So, what have you been up to lately? Anything new?" Agent McDowell's voice interrupted Leah's thoughts. She thought he sounded uncomfortable.

"No, just the usual." She felt the stiffness of her response. "Work. Going for walks. Whatever."

They stood in silence, each examining different items of Natalie's kitchen decor. Leah's eyes landed on a ceramic goose—or, at least, the upper body of a goose—next to the oven, a kitchen towel draped over its neck. She stole a glance at Agent McDowell and followed his gaze to a collection of dessert plates mounted on the wall. Leah shifted her weight to her other foot, swirling the wine around in her glass.

"What about you?" Leah asked him.

"Work." He shrugged.

Matthew popped his head in to let them know that everything was just about ready. He noticed a basket of rolls next to the stove, stepped in to grab them, and darted back into the dining room.

Natalie's voice snapped in the other room, followed by a quiet whisper from Matthew.

Leah watched through the doorway as Natalie forcefully set a glass down on each place mat. "Poor thing, she's probably just starving." She glanced up and made eye contact with Agent McDowell, feeling a need to make excuses for Natalie's mood. "I know I am."

"Alright, everyone, come and eat!" Matthew's voice was strained. Natalie brushed past Leah and Agent McDowell as they stepped through the doorway from the kitchen. Peter and Valerie wandered around from the living room. Leah claimed a seat and flushed when Agent McDowell chose the one next to her.

Come on, really? Not even going to let me sit by my friends?

As Natalie brought the last few items to the table—a pitcher of water, a couple serving spoons, and a stack of paper napkins—the atmosphere in the room dropped a few degrees. Her chair scraped when she pulled it out and again when she pulled close to the table.

For a minute, the only sound in the room was chewing.

Eventually, Leah spoke up, her voice sticky with forced cheeriness. "So, how's everyone's year been?"

No one responded.

"I feel like y'all know what I've been up to, but I want to hear how things have been for you guys." The more she tried to save it, the deeper she felt herself digging. "I guess I know a few things, but come on! Give me all the details!"

I thought this was supposed to be a fun get-together.

"We've been fine." Natalie replied, her tone icy.

Leah raised her eyebrows. "I mean, you left your job at the Institute! That's a big deal, right? Is Matthew back at work full-time?" Something in Matthew's eyes as she spoke warned Leah not to say anything else. She looked back to her plate and took another bite, her leg bouncing rapidly under the table.

"I am," Matthew replied. "We were just ready to be done with the Institute. It was a long time coming."

Leah nodded, shuffling veggies around on her plate. "I'm glad it worked out. What have you been doing, then?"

"I'm working at the kids' pediatrician's office, actually." He nodded. "It's been good. Very low-key."

"Oh, that's amazing!" Her enthusiasm felt out of place amid the relative silence of the rest of the table.

Valerie chimed in when Matthew didn't say anything else. "I've been doing pediatric neurology research since I left the Institute."

Peter looked over at her. "How's that study going, by the way? Did you guys end up getting funding for it? It sounded really neat—I'd hate to hear that it fizzled out."

She shook her head back and forth. "We got enough funding to get started. It'll be an uphill battle once this grant runs out, but we're hoping to have some preliminary results by that point. Who knows?" She shrugged, and Peter did the same.

Agent McDowell remained silent, his eyes glazed over. The scrape of a knife on a plate startled him, and he looked around the room. He made eye contact with Natalie, who gave him a pointed look before asking him a question. "So, Agent McDowell. Why don't you fill us in on your year? What have you been working on?"

He nodded, glancing briefly at Leah before responding. "Of course. Well, I think you all know the story better than I do up to the point when Ms. Harvey got the tip submitted through the Bureau's online form. Shortly thereafter, it landed on my desk, and I won't lie to you all, I wanted to whoop for joy. Not that any of it was particularly... uplifting, of course. It's just that most of our tips are low quality, just half-forgotten circumstantial information. But this? This was the tip every agent wants to receive."

He nodded toward Leah, and she had the thought that if he'd been wearing a hat, he'd have tipped it to her. She sat back in her chair, took a sip of wine, and gave him her full attention.

He gestured with his hands as he continued. "Once I'd familiarized myself with the basics, I started investigating. I knew that it wouldn't take much to get this Pierucci guy under lock and key if even half the allegations were true. I just needed to confirm it for myself, so I went undercover as Wilder Frederick, a newcomer to the area suffering from epileptic seizures—"

"Seizures? Is that it?" Leah broke in. "No delusions of grandeur or violent tendencies or anything?"

Agent McDowell looked at her, his eyebrows raised in an expression of genuine confusion. "What do you mean?"

For a split second, Leah saw a shadow of her friend. But she blinked, and it was gone. "Well, it's just that when Jude walked me out of the clinic last week, he told me you were dangerous. He did see us that day at Common Grounds, and he was acting all worried that I was spending time with you. I figured you'd given yourself some exotic condition just to be... well, I don't know, Wilder always just struck me as being kind of like that." She blushed, much to her own horror, and reached for her left ring finger, twisting the skin for a moment before realizing what she was doing.

"Like what?" Wilder—no, Agent McDowell—asked.

Leah looked at the wall behind his head. "Like... dramatic, you know? Flamboyant." She paused, waiting for a reaction from him. None came. "I don't know... Epilepsy doesn't seem dangerous enough for someone literally named Wilder."

"Ms. Harvey, you do understand that I was trying to remain as under the radar as possible. I wasn't trying to be interesting. I wanted to observe Dr. Pierucci, and I wanted to get to know you."

She nodded, avoiding his eyes, and her stomach turned.

He glanced over at Natalie, then back at Leah. "I knew about your situation early on, and frankly, it horrified me.

The first time I met you in the waiting room at McNeill, I was certain I had the wrong person. There was no way that this woman could have written that tip. And yet... Ms. Bailey assured me it really was you."

Matthew's hand wordlessly reached toward Natalie's and gave her a gentle squeeze.

Agent McDowell continued. "There's not much else to say about my undercover work. And then, of course, you know just about everything since our meeting at Common Grounds. We're working on a case against Pierucci, and probably his son and the warden as well," Agent McDowell concluded. He looked around the table, ending with Leah.

A swell of anger surged in her chest. "So why haven't you done anything yet?" She spat out the words.

He blinked a few times. "I—"

Peter groaned. "Nat, surely you told her..."

"Told me what?" Leah demanded.

Natalie threw her hands up, her voice defensive. "Peter, I told you that I didn't get to cover any of it at Common Grounds! You saw her first. It was your job to explain it. Don't put this on me."

Peter rolled his eyes and started to say something in response, but Leah interrupted him. "Can someone please tell me what's going on here?"

All eyes turned to Agent McDowell. He exhaled slowly through puffed cheeks. "Ms. Harvey, the evidence you sent me is extremely thorough. As it stands, we definitely have enough to convict Pierucci for the breach of research ethics, and probably enough for assault charges. And he's the ringleader—it's almost a guarantee that taking him out of the picture will collapse the entire operation. That's a lot of good we'd be doing."

"But that's not..." Leah trailed off as she realized where Agent McDowell was going. She picked up her knife and ran her finger gently along the ridges. "You never found the bodies." Her voice was quiet.

Agent McDowell nodded slowly. "I've combed through the prison's records dozens of times. Every inmate death that was reported to the coroner's office has the relevant death review paperwork turned in, and there's no sign of any deaths in the research documentation itself. Not even the language of termination comes up. There's no evidence of any inmates failing out of the study."

Leah glanced at Matthew, who sat with his eyes screwed shut and his face downward. His fists were clenched on the table, and one of Natalie's hands rested on top of one of his.

I cannot imagine what this is like for him.

"But we know for a fact there were deaths." Leah's heart pounded in her ears. "You can't honestly tell me that they'd literally get away with murder just because they threw away the research files and dumped the bodies in a river somewhere. Surely the testimony of half a dozen eyewitnesses would be enough to convince a jury beyond a reasonable doubt?"

Agent McDowell spoke up again, changing the topic slightly. "Ms. Harvey, there seems to be some misunderstanding. I thought you were aware of all of this. I was led to believe that your active participation in this investigation was a motivating factor when you were trying to ensure that your memories would be suppressed instead of..." He didn't finish his sentence.

"You were misinformed. Self-preservation was the motivating factor." Leah's voice was terse. She glared at

Natalie, then turned back to Agent McDowell, gesturing toward him before realizing she still gripped her knife. "So you've spent a year investigating, and you haven't managed to find anything more than what I uncovered in three months?" She bit down on her tongue to keep herself from saying everything that she was thinking.

"Leah, that's not fair and you know it," Peter's voice was desperate, defensive.

"Oh, like you're one to talk about fair," she shot back.

Peter glared at her. "What's that supposed to mean?"

"At the park that day, you told me all you were doing was training my brain in helpful little habits." Her voice was mocking. "You conveniently left out the part where you were actively reinforcing the memory suppression!"

Peter opened his mouth, then shut it again. Leah took that as her cue to continue. "And you, Natalie-last time I was here, you told me that this was all for my good. You knew from the beginning that I thought I was going to die that day in Pierucci's office. I sent off my research knowing that I wouldn't see it through—I never intended for you to wait for me! All of this," she gesticulated wildly, knife still in hand, "trying to suggest the memory suppression to Jude ahead of time, planning for any kind of a future? This was all just a wild hope that maybe I'd make it out alive." She slammed her knife on the table. Everyone jumped. "This wasn't, 'get Leah's memories back so that she can swoop in and save the day.' This was, 'hey, it'd be nice if I didn't get murdered next week.' How could you do this to me? To the people who are dying at Scarlett Bay because Agent Ronald McDonald over here didn't do his job?" She threw a hand toward Agent McDowell and tried to ignore the fact that it was trembling. "How could you tell him that the reason I wanted my memories to come back was so that I could jump right back into the lion's den? Have I not sacrificed enough already?"

The table was silent for a moment. A fly buzzed around the room before zipping into the kitchen.

"Sacrifice!" Natalie began, her eyes wide, her tone full of disbelief. "You want to talk about sacrifice? You want to play that game? Do you have any idea what the Institute has cost my family over the last ten years? My children? The only reason we still live in this city at all is because of you! You asked me and Matthew to be there for you if you didn't get terminated. That was all you asked." Her voice had lowered to a simmering rage. "You just assumed that we'd be willing to take the lead on a federal investigation into the organization that ruined our lives. But I've done my duty to you, and I'm out. I'm not staying close to that man any longer than I have to."

Natalie glared at Leah, daring her to respond.

"Ms. Harvey, I know this is a lot to take in," Agent McDowell started, his voice quiet and slow. "I'm sorry for the way I've handled this situation. I should have been more tactful in bringing it up."

Leah turned on him, her heart pounding in her ears. "No, I don't want to hear it from you, either. You don't get to act like an innocent bystander here, Mister Big Shot FBI. You're no better than the rest of them—you've done nothing but lie to me from the beginning. You knew I was in a vulnerable spot, and you manipulated me into thinking that we were friends!" She screwed her eyes shut. Everything felt out of control. "Dammit, Wilder, I trusted you! You were the only person I thought of as a friend this whole year. And then you turn around and go all cold and professional, and you tell me that all of it was a lie? That our whole friendship was just you playing pretend?"

She stood abruptly. Her chair toppled backward from the impact, thumping into the wall behind her. "I'm done," she said quietly. "I'm just done. With all of this. You're all a bunch of liars. Best of luck with everything."

She walked to the door, grabbed her backpack, and let herself out.

Chapter 23

A late summer twilight greeted her, and she forced herself to inhale the warm, humid air. Halfway down the walk, she looked up and saw the familiar stars of Cygnus the Swan winking down at her from a moonless sky.

I cannot believe they tricked me into trusting them.

Behind her, the door clicked again. Still fuming, Leah refused to turn around.

Natalie had better not come out here and try to convince me that they're in the right.

But it was Valerie's voice that filled the night air. "Leah, can we talk?"

If it were anybody else...

She almost said no, just on principle. But she had no grief with Valerie.

Still, she couldn't hide her frustration. "Did they send you out here to try and change my mind?"

Valerie made her way around to face Leah, her movements gentle and her voice soft. "No."

Her answer surprised Leah. "Then why did you come?"

"Because I get it." A sad smile played on her lips. "This started as your personal thing. You did as much as you could, and then you passed it off to people who could do more. You thought you were done with it, and you were

267

ready to walk away. You've had time to slow down and gain some distance, and it's shocking to be thrust back in."

Leah nodded slowly. "I was willing to die over this, Valerie. I didn't expect to come out of it alive, but I did. And then they pulled the rug out from under me, and it turns out I'm just a pawn in their stupid chess game." She scuffed her foot along the concrete walkway. The sun was quickly setting, dousing the street in darkness.

Her voice was quieter when she continued. "I thought they cared about me. But I was wrong. They're just using me to get what they want."

Valerie didn't say anything for a long moment. The streetlights flickered on, and Leah could see tears pooling at the corners of her eyes.

"You're not the only one who's felt like that around the Institute," she said softly. "It's a heavy burden to carry, and it's not fair to you."

"Thank you." Leah felt her shoulders slump, as if Valerie's words alone could release all the evening's tension. A lump formed in her throat.

"But the fact remains that you are the case here. Agent McDowell might feel more official, but we have no loyalty to him. We're here because of you, and we're here for you." Her voice was firm. Not unkind, but firm.

Valerie's words landed like a knife in her heart. Leah felt her chest constricting. Her arms grew restless. Her thoughts clouded over.

Not Valerie too.

"Valerie, I can't do this. Not with you, not with them. All I ever wanted was to get my life back. I didn't want to be the superhero here. I'm not like you." Leah's voice faltered. "I just didn't want to die."

"Like me?" Confusion washed over Valerie's face. "Leah, if you run away from this, you're exactly like me."

"But you're..." Leah tried to protest. "I always looked up to you. Why do you get to run away and I don't?"

A rare flash of anger filled Valerie's face. Clenching her fists and her jaw, she took a slow, deep breath. Her face fell.

Leah's heart sank. "Oh, Valerie, I didn't mea—"

"Good night, Leah." Valerie stepped past her and walked slowly back toward the house.

A lump formed in Leah's throat, and she tried to croak out a goodbye. Valerie didn't seem to hear. The door clicked behind her once again, this time with a depressing finality. Tears began streaming down Leah's face as she walked to her car and slipped inside.

For a few minutes, she could only weep. A truck turned onto the street, its headlights twinkling in Leah's blurry vision, before finding a driveway and shutting off. Crickets chirped and cicadas sang around her, filling the night air with a symphony of sound. She thought she heard an owl hoot as she took a deep, gentle breath and wiped her eyes.

She wasn't sure how much time had passed before a crack of light appeared in her peripheral vision. The front door opened again, and Peter stepped out. A panic filled Leah's mind as she fumbled with her keys, started the car, and pulled away from the house.

I hope they didn't see me just sitting here and crying.

A podcast began to play after her phone connected to the car. The host's voice was grating, and Leah shut off the audio. Silence pressed in on her from every side, her memory filled with harsh words given and received.

She turned the car's sound system back on and clicked through her queue, eventually settling on an episode of

Myths and Legends that she'd started earlier in the week. But she couldn't force herself to focus on the story, and she quickly turned the podcast off again.

When she pulled into her apartment parking lot, she got out of the car and knocked on Sarah and Connor's door. It was late—almost ten o'clock—but she didn't want to be alone.

She waited, counted to twenty, and knocked again.

No one answered.

Of course they're not here. The one time I really need them, and they're out on a date night or something. Go figure.

She unlocked the door of her apartment and stepped inside. The blinds, still open from the afternoon, let in slats of light from the parking lot. She closed the blinds, slipped off her shoes, threw her backpack onto the couch, and walked back to her room.

What a waste of an evening.

Without even changing into her pajamas, she curled up on her bed and went to sleep.

***

She awoke the next morning with a stiff neck and the seam of her jeans imprinted on her leg. She pulled herself out of bed, yawned, and wandered into the kitchen to make a cup of coffee.

At least it's Wednesday, so I don't have to look presentable.

She slipped her laptop out of her backpack and plugged it in at her desk while her coffee percolated. Above her screen, the Bailey children smiled at her. She glanced down at her wrist and found Josie's bracelet, spinning the beads with her fingers as she waited for the computer to unlock and start up.

The smell of burning coffee wafted toward her, and she hurried to the kitchen to take the moka pot off the stove. She grabbed a tumbler and filled it halfway with milk before pouring the espresso and adding a handful of ice. She swirled the drink and watched the ice clatter around as she made her way back to her desk.

I should eat something for breakfast.

She sat down, took a sip of coffee, and opened an unread email.

The rest of the morning flew by, and Leah was surprised to see the clock turn eleven. She was about to send the final version of the Fun Run logo to the team when her phone rang.

Jude Pierucci's name scrolled across her screen.

"Since Dr. Pierucci didn't get to see you today, I anticipate he'll want to get you on the phone soon, just to touch base with you about the study."

Dread filled Leah's stomach.

Do I have to pick this up?

The phone continued ringing.

Why is he calling from his cell?

Panicking, Leah picked up the phone, answered the call, and took a deep breath.

Play it cool, Leah. You don't want him to suspect anything.

"This is Leah Harvey," she said, trying to sound neutral.

"Hi Ms. Harvey, this is Jude Pierucci, Jr. from the McNeill Institute for Neurological Development. How are you doing this morning?"

"Um—fine, thanks. How can I help you?"

If Jude noticed her discomfort, he didn't let on. "I wanted to go ahead and get a phone call on your calendar. I believe I shared with you that the doctor will need a few minutes of your time to touch base about your symptoms over the past month?"

"Oh, that's right." She didn't dare say anything else and risk giving herself away.

"I'm so sorry for the delay in following up. My father was out of the office for his conference last week, and we spent the past few days catching up from his absence."

Leah stammered a response. "I underst— I mean, that's fine. Do I... do I really need to talk with him before my next appointment? It's got to be just around the corner at this point."

"It's in..." Jude trailed off and Leah could hear papers shuffling in the background, "three weeks. And I know it seems like overkill, but it is actually quite important that he speak with you directly." She could picture Jude's expression just from his tone of voice: an indulgent smile, a sympathetic shrug. "He's always been a stickler for the rules, and he'd be risking your spot in your clinical trial if he didn't have notes from each visit."

"I see."

Does he know that I know? How could he possibly?

Jude continued, undaunted by her terse response. "So, is there a time this week that would work for you? I know you're quite busy, so I hope you can manage to fit us in." He chuckled. The sound squeezed Leah's heart.

She hoped that he couldn't hear the sadness in her voice. "Well, I'm free any time today. Tomorrow and Friday I've got meetings all morning, but the afternoons are open. So just have him give me a call whenever, I guess."

"Wonderful, I'll let him know. Thanks so much, Ms. Harvey. It's been great to chat with you, and we'll see you in a few weeks."

"Goodbye," she replied as the call ended.

"Just have him give me a call whenever?" So he can catch you off guard again?

She slammed her phone down. The impact was louder than she'd expected, and when she turned it back over, one corner of her screen was shattered. She groaned and stared at her laptop. Her hands found one another instinctively as she rubbed the base of her left ring finger. She was haunted by the fear that Jude could see her in his mind's eye as clearly as she could see him in hers.

Does he know? Can he tell just from the way I sound?

Her stomach burbled, and she remembered with surprise that she'd never eaten breakfast. Her empty coffee cup still sat beside her on the desk, but she'd gotten too sucked into her work to get up and grab anything to eat.

It's Work from Home Wednesday. I don't have any meetings. Who's going to care if I take an early lunch?

She pulled a loaf of sourdough out of the fridge, balancing the peanut butter and jelly in her arms as she shut the door with her foot.

A dark-haired boy with a goofy grin approached her. "Hi, I'm Jude Pierucci. Who are you?"

She looked at her shoes. "Leonora Harvey."

"Leonora is too long of a name. Can I call you Leah? I've never seen you before. Are you new? Why are you here?" He cocked his head.

She tapped her temple a few times. "My mom said this doctor can help with my headaches."

"The doctor's my dad, you know." He said it like it made him the coolest boy in the world.

She spread the peanut butter slowly onto one slice of bread, savoring the memory of her first meeting with Jude.

I can't have been more than seven or eight when we met.

A glob of peanut butter slipped off the bread and onto the counter. She did her best to scoop it back up and glom it back onto her sandwich before wiping the knife clean and opening the jam.

"I got two tickets to junior prom... want to go with me?" Jude's voice was nonchalant, but his fingers tapped restlessly at his side.

She blushed, nodded, and wrapped her arms around his neck. He wrapped his around her waist, and she felt the color rise in her cheeks even more. When she pulled away, he grinned at her and ran a hand through his bangs. "Well, cool. I'll pick you up for dinner at five?"

"Yes! I'm so excited!"

She couldn't wipe the smile off her face for the rest of the day.

The jam had clumped up in the fridge and refused to spread. Forcefully, she ran her knife over it until the globs were at least evenly spaced on the bread.

The knife clattered as she tossed it into the sink, and she slapped the two slices of bread together.

He's been a part of my life for twenty years now.

She rinsed out the last ring of milky coffee at the bottom of her tumbler, refilled it with water, and sat down at the table.

Her phone rang again, and she jumped. It was the Institute's main line.

Already? I bet Jude could hear it in my voice.

She answered the phone with trembling fingers.

Shelby's voice greeted her. "Hello, this is Shelby Downs with the McNeill Institute. Is this Leonora Harvey?"

"It is."

"Hello, Ms. Harvey. I have Mr. Pierucci on the line for you. He said you'd be expecting him."

Mr. Pierucci?

"Uh, yes, I am," Leah bluffed. "Thanks so much."

"I'll transfer you to his office." A few notes of a plinky elevator song played before the line clicked again.

"Hello Ms. Harvey, this is Jude Pierucci again."

"Oh, hi Jude." She tried to steady her voice.

I cannot let him see what's really happening here.

"I'm sorry to bother you again so soon. My father's calendar for the rest of the week booked up more quickly than we expected, so he asked if I would do the touch-base with you. Just this once."

"Father is ready for me to take on a little more leadership, but if I'm being honest, I'm a little nervous about it."

"Oh, okay." Her thoughts were racing too quickly to formulate a less awkward response.

"He always expects so much of me, and I so rarely feel confident that I'm living up to his expectations."

"Is that okay? Do I have your permission to go ahead and proceed with the interview?" Something was off about his tone.

"No one can keep secrets from Father for long."

She stood up and paced the hallway of her apartment. "Oh, yes, of course. Go ahead."

"Well, why don't you start by telling me about how your symptoms have been this month?"

"Oh, sure," She gave a fake laugh. "I mean, I'm really feeling pretty good. Things have been good lately."

Peter never told me what he was going to do to my treatment readout. I really hope I'm not giving myself away here.

She heard the scratching of a pencil on paper from the other end of the line. "Your readout from last week looks remarkably clear."

275

If I get outed because of Peter, I swear I'm going to lose it...

"Yes, like I said, this was a good month." She felt the sharpness in her voice.

"It seems that you've had quite a few good months now... Ms. Harvey, I'll be honest with you," Jude's tone dropped, becoming confidential. "I obviously can't make any promises, and your situation with the clinical trial is quite unique, but... if this were another patient's file, I'd consider you cured."

Cured? What is he trying to get at here?

"Cured?" she replied. "What does that mean, exactly?"

Jude backtracked. "Well, again, I'm not your primary care provider, so I can't do or say anything official, but I'm going to make a note here on your chart recommending you be released early from the clinical trial."

Leah's jaw dropped. She stopped pacing.

"Ms. Harvey, are you still there?"

Get it together, Leah. You can't blow this.

"You mean you'd let me go without a diagnosis or anything?" She squinted and gritted her teeth, hoping that putting up some resistance was the right move.

She heard Jude falter. "As I said, I don't have the authority or expertise to make any official changes, but I..." He caught himself, assuming a tone that sounded dangerously like his father. "If a diagnosis is still important to you, that's obviously something you can discuss with the doctor at your next visit. I was merely observing that the treatment itself seems to have accomplished its objective."

Leah was stunned by the change in his voice, and she blinked a few times before responding. "I see. Well, you've given me a lot to think about. Is there anything else you need from me, Mr. Pierucci?"

"I think that'll be all for today. I'll let you go. And please," he added, falling back into his normal tone. "Call me Jude. Mr. Pierucci was my grandfather."

She rolled her eyes at the line, which she'd heard a thousand times. "Thanks, Jude. I l—" She caught herself before the words 'I love you' slipped out by force of habit.

Please tell me he didn't hear that.

"What's that?" he asked.

"Nothing, sorry. I was talking to..." Her eyes widened in panic. "A coworker."

"I see." Was that a squint she heard in his voice? "Well, have a good rest of your day, Ms. Harvey."

He hung up. Leah threw her phone onto the bed and bent over, placing her hands on her knees and breathing deeply.

This is bad. This is really bad. He must have figured it out by now. He's going to tell his father, and they're going to come find me, and they're going to...

In spite of her best efforts, her breathing became shallow and rapid. Her eyes darted around the room, desperate for something to focus on. She shook her head, trying to dispel the spiraling thoughts racing through her mind. With trembling legs, she stepped over to the window and looked out, listening to the chittering of two squirrels as they chased each other around the trees. Watching five mockingbirds fuss around for food in the bright green grass. A single gray tabby cat sauntered past, on his way to the bowl of cat food Sarah left on her patio. Slowly, she felt herself calm down.

There's no way that Jude is actually serious about pulling me from the trial... right? Could Peter have done his job so well that they'll let me go, blissfully unaware that I remember everything?

She stepped away from the window and walked back to the table, where the last bite of her sandwich still sat. She chewed absentmindedly as she refilled her water and rinsed off her plate.

Or is Jude just playing with me, hoping that I let my guard down and say something I shouldn't?

The soapy plate slipped from her grasp and fell into the sink, cracking into pieces with a loud crash.

Chapter 24

The next day, Leah waited with restless superiority for any kind of contact from anyone—Peter, Natalie, even Agent McDowell—but no one reached out.

Are they really going to just let me be? They're not going to try and convince me?

The weekend came and went. Leah checked her phone compulsively, unlocking the screen and scrolling through notifications she'd already seen.

Surely, someone is going to say something. Anything. Even just a "hey, how's it been going since your memories came back?" They wouldn't just abandon me, would they?

Over the course of the next week, she worked on promotional materials for the Fun Run, tinkered around with some social media graphics for her clients, and designed a survey for a conference she'd helped promote. She ate at her desk and left right at five. More and more, she noticed her leg bouncing under her desk. Several times, she bumped an elbow into her coffee cup, sending it tumbling to the floor. She couldn't bring herself to focus on anything, and each day crawled past.

I thought we were partners, Nat and Matthew and I. Friends, even. But they're no better than Dr. Pierucci. I'm only worth keeping around as long as I'm willing to be used.

In the evenings, Leah started running more consistently, clocking a couple of miles and enjoying the way she slept so soundly after a run. She reached out to Sarah and Connor a couple of times, trying to find a time to hang out, but their schedules seemed to conflict every night, and dinner never happened.

I thought this whole memories returning thing was supposed to make everything better.

***

Two full weeks passed until, early in August, her phone buzzed with the standard appointment reminder.

> Hello, your upcoming appointment with the McNeill Institute for Neurological Development is scheduled for next Tuesday, August 10, 2023. Reply Y to confirm, N to cancel. To opt out of receiving text messages, text STOP.

Shoot. What am I supposed to do about this?

On the one hand, skipping her appointment was out of the question. After so many months of showing up late or rescheduling, yet another missed visit would be sure to arouse suspicion. It wouldn't do to set Dr. Pierucci on edge. There was too much at stake.

But on the other hand, how could she possibly go and face him in person without letting on that her memories had returned? Her phone call with Jude had been hard enough, and she hadn't had to worry about controlling her body language.

But there's nothing to be done about it. I can't put everyone at risk by not going.

She pressed the Y key and clicked send.

A confirmation arrived within moments.

Into the belly of the beast it is.

***

Leah had to steel herself just to walk across the threshold of the clinic a week later. Her jaw and fists were clenched as she approached Shelby's desk. Shelby handed her the usual pink call slip and grinned at someone behind her. Before Leah could turn around to look for a seat, a familiar voice called out.

"Is that Leah Harvey?"

Her heart leapt. She whirled around.

Wilder?

Special Agent Robert McDowell sat in his usual seat, a huge grin on his face. He stood up and gave her a side hug, and Leah's stomach did an uncomfortable somersault.

"Leonora Harvey, in the flesh. I haven't seen you in forever—I figured they kicked you outta here!" He walked back to his chair and sat down, patting the seat next to him.

"Hey Wilder," she finally responded as she sat down. "How's it going?"

I hate this. This is so weird. Why did he have to be here?

"Oh, I've been great! Went mountain climbing up in Colorado last week, got this gnarly scratch on my arm." He rolled up his sleeve to reveal a scab that reached from his wrist to his elbow.

"Oh my gosh—are you okay?" Leah gasped with genuine horror, her eyes wide.

"Oh, yeah, it's nothing. My buddy got me stitched up right there on the mountain, and we still summited." He rolled his sleeve back down. "The scar's gonna be epic. How about you, what have you been up to?"

He looked at her with those bright green eyes, and Leah couldn't help herself. "It's been tough lately." She frowned. "I had some friends... some people... who I thought really cared for me, but they did something that really hurt. And I'm still trying to figure out what to do now."

A pained expression crossed his face. He looked away, glancing toward Shelby's desk. "I'm really sorry to hear that, Harvey. That really sucks."

"Yeah," she replied. "It does."

Before she knew what was happening, she felt his arm around her, pulling her in. She rested a heavy head on his shoulder, feeling the rise and fall of each breath. She closed her eyes and felt her muscles began to relax.

A moment later, reality came crashing down around her again. She pulled away, shaking his arm off and glaring at him.

How dare he act like we're still friends.

"Harvey—" he started, his voice apologetic.

She turned in her seat so that her back was toward him and pulled out her phone.

Absolutely not.

A notification appeared at the top of her screen. Agent McDowell. She clicked it.

> I know you're having a hard time, but S is already
> keeping a close eye on us. Please don't give her any
> more reason to be suspicious.

S? Who's S?

Leah looked up and glanced around the room to see who Agent McDowell might be referring to. She was surprised to find Shelby at the reception desk furtively looking over her computer screen. They made eye contact for the briefest moment before Shelby turned back to her work and began typing rapidly.

"If he sees you, if Jude sees you, if one of his staff sees you— there will be hell to pay."

Leah felt her eyes widen.

Shelby wasn't at her desk the day I came to talk to Peter. Is that why he was in such a hurry to get me out of the office? He knew she would be back soon?

With a sigh, Leah turned back to Agent McDowell. "So Wilder, I don't know much about Colorado mountains, other than Pikes Peak from the time I visited it as a kid. How crazy was this climb you did?" Her voice was stiff.

This is why I never did theater growing up.

"Well, we're working our way through the highest peaks in Colorado, but we only get to do a couple a year. This one wasn't much higher than Pikes, elevation wise, but a lot more dangerous. We had a blast."

Leah faked a laugh and rolled her eyes.

"Thank you," he mouthed silently.

Leah nodded as slowly as she could, her eyes darting to the reception desk, where Shelby no longer seemed to be watching them directly.

When Peter finally came to call her back to her exam room, his voice was steely. They proceeded down the hall in silence. Peter shut the door behind them and helped Leah get situated before speaking a word.

"So, you decided to show up." He said it quietly, with his eyes fixed on his computer, but his tone was knife-sharp.

"Of course." Leah heard the defensiveness in her own voice. "I wouldn't do that to you guys."

"Do what to us, Leah?" He glanced up from his screen and looked her in the eyes. "Force us to take the heat from

Pierucci for you? Leave us to deal with the problem you created?"

She studied the pharmaceutical ads plastered on the walls. "Peter, I—"

He cut her off. "I don't want to hear it, Leah. It was very considerate of you to come, but I'm not going to pat you on the back as if it was some grand gesture of detached goodwill."

An exasperated sigh escaped her. "I never said I expected that."

"No, you never said anything. You walked out and didn't look back." He looked back to his computer. The clatter of keys filled the room.

Leah's face reddened and her heart raced. "It's not like any of y'all made an effort to hear me out, or even check up on me and see how I was doing. You guys started all of this, only to leave me in the lurch when I needed you most."

"I told you I don't want to hear it." There was a finality to his voice that frightened her. "Just shut up and let me figure out how I'm going to simulate your treatment readout today because I clearly can't run anything on you."

"Can't you just tweak the readout from last time?"

He rolled his eyes. "That's what I did last month, and Pierucci was already getting suspicious. He was livid that he didn't get to see you personally, by the way, so you're in for a real treat when he gets here. Hope you're ready."

Leah clenched her jaw and swallowed down a lump in her throat.

Silence reigned for a few long minutes, with Leah seated on the orthodontic chair and Peter standing at his computer. The only noises in the room were the whirring of the hard drive fan and the clacking of keys; the only visual distractions Leah could focus on were a few posters she'd long memorized, including one she'd designed. Her hand reached for her phone instinctively, but she stopped herself. Scrolling social media felt sacrilegious, an offense against the chasm that already existed between her and Peter. Instead, she fiddled with the beads on her bracelet, anxiously waiting for Peter to say something.

This isn't at all how I wanted things to go.

Without warning, Peter stepped over to her chair and slipped the helmet off its hook. "I think I figured it out."

She allowed him to place the helmet on her head and lean her back into the recline of the chair. He strapped her wrists down beside her before pressing a few buttons. The chair flattened and lowered beneath her. Beeps from the console alerted her to the fact that something was happening, but whatever it was, he didn't explain it.

Time ticked by—ten, fifteen, twenty minutes of silence and darkness as Leah waited for the treatment to end. She tried to pick up on what Peter was doing, but her library felt vacant and sterile.

After he finally unstrapped her wrists and hung the helmet back on its hook, Peter moved her to the consultation room and went to get Dr. Pierucci, leaving Leah alone with her thoughts. The knock on the door a moment later sent her anxiety into overdrive, a flurry of butterflies squirming throughout her lower abdomen.

"Come in." She hoped they didn't notice the anxiety in her voice.

Dr. Pierucci entered with a storm cloud on his brow, angrier than she'd seen him since her memories had been suppressed. He tried to soften his expression as he entered, as if to give the impression that she wasn't the object of his ire. Before, she might have fallen for it. Not anymore. Much to Leah's shock, Jude walked in behind him. He raised a hand in greeting before silently taking a seat in the back of the room.

Dr. Pierucci wasted no time. "Ms. Harvey. Thank you for coming in today. I am pleased that you were able to be present at your originally scheduled time. I was quite disappointed to miss you last month." Leah opened her mouth to respond, but he wasn't finished. "Our touch-bases are, as you know, essential in my ability to monitor your condition and progress towards our mutual goal of a diagnosis."

Leah put on her best apologetic face. "Yes, I'm sorry I had to reschedule last month. Something came up at the very last minute, and that was the only opening Shelby had." She reached for the bracelet Josie had made her, spinning the beads between her fingers.

Dr. Pierucci scowled, glanced at her wrist, and continued. "Very well. I hope you don't mind if my assistant joins us as part of his training." Clearly not looking for a response, he continued. "How have things been for you of late?"

Leah froze. "Things have been..." She felt the pause in her words stretch out like a rickety old bridge between them. "...rough. Last month, like I said over the phone, was really good. The anxiety I'd been experiencing after my car accident had worn off, and other than that, I really didn't notice anything particularly out of the ordinary. But this month has been hard. Out of the blue, I started feeling really nauseous, and while I think it was just a bad stomach flu, I feel like I can't even remember half of what's happened since my last visit."

Wait, Jude said they were going to discharge me because things were going well. I can't make it sound like I'm regressing.

Dr. Pierucci cocked his head to one side. "I'm sorry to hear you've been ill. I hope you've made a full recovery. Your readout for this month looks exceptionally clear, which is an encouraging sign."

Leah glanced at Peter, but he wasn't looking at her. "Like I said, I haven't really noticed any psychotic episodes since my last visit. It's amazing how quickly things have progressed once they really got moving."

"Indeed." He nodded, his eyes distant. "I wonder—are there any changes in your environment or your habits lately that may have contributed to this rather shocking lack of symptoms?"

He knows. He has to know.

"Not necessarily. I'd hate to think the cure for this whole mess has been a bad stomach flu!" She forced a chuckle, hoping to divert the conversation.

Dr. Pierucci did not laugh. He sat, silent and pensive, watching her carefully.

"But really," she continued, hoping he couldn't hear her desperation. "Other than the nausea, things have been pretty normal. I'm starting to feel more like myself than I have in a long time."

"Is that so?"

Shoot.

Her fingers continued to spin at the beads around her wrist. "I mean, just worrying less about having an unexpected episode has helped me to feel more confident in how I'm interacting with people. My mom and I have been talking a little bit more, and it's been hard, but it's been good, too. I'm even starting to make real friends!" She looked down at her feet, kicking them restlessly. "And work has been less tedious and terrible the last couple of weeks."

She felt Peter's eyes on her, his gaze heavy. As best she could, she tried to flash him an expression of confusion, unsure what he was trying to communicate beyond his general anger with and disappointment in her.

His lips formed the word that he didn't speak: bracelet.

Eyes wide, she pulled her hand away from her wrist, hoping the action wasn't too abrupt. Her mind raced, trying to assess the situation.

"Is everything okay, Ms. Harvey?" Jude's voice, laden with genuine concern, drew her out of herself and tossed her back into the orthodontic chair in the treatment room.

"Oh, yes, everything's fine. I just, ah," she hesitated, weighing a gamble in her mind. "I think I just started my, you know..." She glanced downward as pointedly as she could, trailing off and hoping that the implications would be enough.

His eyes, gray-blue and anxious, widened. He squirmed in his seat and looked away from her.

Some things never change.

Jude grimaced. "Ah, I see. Well, we'll detain you no longer if you need to, ah, attend to that. Take your time packing up your things, of course, but that's all we need from you today." He looked at her sadly for a long moment. She thought she saw him steal a glance at her wrist, and she quickly adjusted her position to hide it from him.

Dr. Pierucci said nothing, the storm still brewing in his face. He sat perfectly still, watching her.

"Thank you." She let her face show just a fraction of the exhaustion she felt in her bones, hoping that Jude wouldn't be able to somehow see the truth in her face. The two men stood up, and Jude opened the door while Dr. Pierucci shook her hand. They stepped out silently and turned to walk down the hall.

"You didn't take it off?" Peter hissed the moment the door clicked shut. "How could you be so careless?"

Leah cowered. "Do you think he noticed?"

Peter glared at her over the screen of his computer. "You know him better than that, Harvey."

She furrowed her eyebrows. "The letters are so small, and it's not like 'Auntie Leah' necessarily means anything."

"I can read it clearly from here." Peter said, his voice heavy with disdain. "And exactly how many other people call you Auntie Leah?"

She looked down at her hands.

Peter continued. "Do you know how quickly the Bailey kids stopped calling him 'Uncle Jude' after you were out of the picture?"

An unexpected lump rose in her throat.

"You have got to be more careful, Leah." A note of camaraderie had entered into Peter's voice, and Leah allowed herself to look up and meet his gaze. "We cannot let our guard down even for a minute. I know it's a lot to keep in mind–believe me, I know it better than anyone. But it's no more than you asked of us last year. We're all in this together, whether you want to be or not."

His last sentence brought her frustration racing back. "Can you lay off me for one minute? All you've done since my memories came back is bark at me, and that's supposed to convince me to be on your side in this?"

"My side? What's your other option?" He gestured toward the door. "Theirs? And why should I have to convince you of anything? This whole thing was your idea!"

"Not dying was my idea," she hissed. Her voice barely rose above a whisper, but it carried the force of a shout. "This wasn't a glorified Witness Protection Program! I just didn't want to get murdered by my future father-in-law. You have no idea what this has been like for me." She held a hard stare, daring him to cross her.

Peter's face softened. "I do. Not exactly, of course. But I do know."

Leah furrowed her brows.

He better not try to make this all about him.

But in spite of herself, she felt her own expression soften as well.

"My brother used to work at Scarlett Bay." Peter studied his screen intently. "He was good friends with Matthew. He killed himself about two years ago. He had it all: the migraines, the anxiety and depression, paranoia, delusions, hallucinations... Eventually he just couldn't take it anymore. He wasn't married. He had no one other than me and Matt. We were close, but he didn't tell me he was struggling that badly until... well, until it was too late."

Leah fought back the urge to stand up and embrace him. "I'm so sorry. I had no idea."

"I asked Matthew not to mention it to you when you interviewed him because I wasn't ready to talk about it, and I knew you'd come asking nosy questions."

"Oh, Peter." She didn't know what else to say.

He looked up at her. "So don't go giving any of us that line that we don't understand. We might not have the same story as you, but we all have stories." He shut down the computer and stepped toward the door. "See you around."

She watched him walk away. After taking a minute to compose herself, she followed him out the door, making her way down the hall and into the waiting room. There was no sign of Wilder, and Shelby didn't look up from her computer. She stopped by the pharmacy to pick up her medication, although she had no intention of taking it, and then stepped out into the humid summer afternoon.

Peter's words echoed in her mind as she slipped into her car and pulled out of the parking lot.

"Don't go giving any of us that line that we don't understand. We might not have the same story as you, but we all have stories."

Chapter 25

As Leah pulled out of the parking lot, she called her mom. Her fingers trembled.

Her mom picked up right away. "Hey, how was your appointment?"

"Oh, Mom..." Tears filled Leah's eyes and she stifled a sob. She breathed heavily and blinked so she could see.

"Leah, are you okay?" Her mom's voice was suddenly concerned. Leah felt like a child again, in the thick of a headache. The tone surprised her, but it wasn't unwelcome.

She a tear off her cheek. "Mom, the last few weeks have been so hard. I don't even know where to start."

Her mom waited for her to continue.

A heavy sigh escaped her. "I guess this is as good a place as any: do you remember when I called you and told you I'd had that dream about you having another stroke?"

"Yes." It was just as much a question as a statement.

"I..." Leah bit her lip. "I really thought you'd had a first stroke. Not just that day after the dream—I made the dream up, honestly—but for a long time, I really did think you'd had a stroke. I thought a lot of things were true that aren't true because when Jude and I broke up, Dr. Pierucci..." She sniffled. "Well, he suppressed my memories. I had discovered some horrible things happening at the Institute, and he didn't want it getting out, so he used the console at work to make me forget."

"Leah," her mom scoffed. "What are you talking about? This doesn't make any sense."

"I know, Mom!" Leah gripped the steering wheel and took a moment to compose herself. "I know. It doesn't make any sense. But bear with me, I just... You've told me so many times this year that I seem distant, that I seem different, that it seems like I've changed..."

"You have changed," she agreed hesitantly. "And you're right that it started right before Jude broke up with you. You never really recovered."

"That's exactly what I'm saying." She heard the desperation in her own voice. "But it's not the break-up that changed me. It's because I didn't remember the break-up. Or Jude. Or working at the Institute, or even going there as a child. I didn't remember so many of the things that make me, well... me. I just had these sort of fuzzy and grainy and unconvincing memories, and I just thought that was how everyone felt all the time... I didn't know what I was missing." The words had tumbled out of her, uncontrolled.

"Because Dr. Pierucci wiped your memories?" The concern was gone, replaced by skepticism. "Leah, are you okay? Is this another episode? I really think you need to see someone else about a second opinion. I know Dr. P is highly respected, and I know you have a lot of history with him, but... I don't know, maybe another doctor would be able to find something he missed. It just doesn't seem like you're getting any better."

As she turned a corner, Leah grasped for anything that might convince her mom that she wasn't totally losing her mind. "That's exactly my point. I haven't been getting better because they were the ones doing it to me. All the psych symptoms I've had this year are side effects of the stuff they were doing in my brain. They made me forget everything, and as my subconscious tried to fill in the gaps, it just made stuff up to connect the dots. Anything that fit with the information I still had."

She sighed. "And, of course, you were talking about Jude a lot right after we broke up—you were asking if I was okay, you were trying to make sure that I was getting over him... and since I didn't remember him, I just assumed that you'd made him up somehow, that you were remembering something that hadn't really happened. I just assumed that you'd had some sort of medical crisis that changed the way your brain worked, and I guess what I want to say is that I'm sorry." She heaved a deep breath. "I'm sorry. I have been really distant and really patronizing and really rude to you this year, and I'm only just now coming to realize how horrible it must have been for you to see this happening without knowing what was going on."

Leah stopped at a red light and stared at the crepe myrtles outside her office, reds and pinks and whites like fireworks in the median. "What are you thinking, Mom? Are you still there?"

Her voice was hesitant. "I'm still here. This is a lot to take in. Are... are you sure you're okay?"

Tears welled up in the corners of Leah's eyes. "I'm okay, Mom. I'm just stressed. Some friends of mine helped reverse everything, which means I'm feeling like myself again for the first time in forever... but it also means that I have to face some things I'm not ready to face yet. And I'm scared." She pulled into a parking spot and let the car idle.

"What do you need from me?"

"I don't know. I just..." she wiped her cheeks. "Can you tell me that everything's going to be okay?"

Her mom sighed. The sound scratched through the car's speakers. "I can't promise that, Leah." Leah felt a lump in her throat. Her finger hovered over the 'end call' button. "But I can tell you that I'm not going anywhere. Whatever you've been through this year, we've made it through that, and we'll make it through this too."

Relief spread through Leah's whole body, out from her heart and down her limbs. "Thanks Mom. I love you."

"I love you too, Leah." It sounded like a reproach. "I'm going to see if I can get a flight down to see you soon."

"You don't have t—"

"I know I don't. But I can, and I think we're overdue for a visit."

Leah breathed slowly, feeling the air move deeper into her lungs than it had in hours, days even. "Thanks Mom."

"I'll talk to you later, honey. I've got to go now, but please let me know if you want to call again soon."

Leah smiled, her eyes still red. "I will. Bye, Mom."

"Bye honey."

The call ended, and Leah shut off the car's engine. She walked into her office feeling hollow. Opening her laptop, she set her status as 'busy' for the rest of the day. No one came in to bother her, and her eyes eventually stopped feeling so dry. She stepped out shortly after five, avoiding eye contact with the rest of her office, and headed home.

"Agent McDowell might feel more official, but we have no loyalty to him. We're here because of you, and we're here for you."

Valerie's words haunted Leah as she pulled out of the parking garage.

"If you run away from this, you're exactly like me."

"You say you're all here for me," Leah muttered as she turned onto the freeway. "But what exactly do you think I can do better than the FBI?"

She knew the answer. She'd been running from it since the moment her memories had returned.

I don't want to be the bait.

The thought presented itself before she was able to escape it, but once she'd acknowledged it, the floodgates opened.

I don't want to be the bait. I don't want to put myself in harm's way again. I don't want that responsibility—can I make him say all the right things, all the damning things that need to be said? And what happens to me if things go wrong?

Traffic was stop and go, and the drive stretched to fill the better part of an hour.

I don't want to face them at all, honestly. Today's appointment was more than enough to convince me that I'd rather never step foot inside the Institute ever again.

She buzzed in at the gate, parked her car, and walked inside her apartment. Setting her bag down, she grabbed a coffee mug from one of her drawers and made her way over to the kitchen.

A cup of tea would do me good. Just something to get me through the evening.

As she stood waiting for the electric kettle to heat up, she sifted through the bin of tea bags in her pantry, wishing it were better organized, and eventually settled on a decaf ginger peach. She tore open the package and placed the bag in her mug, looping the tag around the cup's handle. The water began to hiss and bubble in the kettle, and she covered the bottom of her mug with honey before pouring the water in.

On her way back to her room, the navy and gold text on her mug caught her eye. It was the Institute's logo. She shuddered as a sinking feeling grew in her stomach. She set the tea on her nightstand, still full, and curled up in bed.

***

The rest of the week was uneventful. The following Tuesday morning, she awoke from a dream in which she was being chased, although she couldn't tell if it was the Pieruccis or the Baileys chasing her. Adrenaline coursed through her veins, and try as she might, she couldn't get back to sleep. The clock read ten till six, so she pulled herself out of bed and stretched her stiff muscles.

She arrived at work earlier than usual, and it felt like the office was stretching its own muscles. The lights were on, but the place felt abandoned. Leah couldn't help looking over her shoulder as she set her laptop down and made herself a cup of coffee.

Over the next half hour, the rest of her team slowly trickled in. Ana expressed visible surprise to see Leah already at her desk, but said nothing. Leah spent a good forty-five minutes cleaning up her inbox, and she was about to dive into her first project of the day when a knock on the door shattered her focus. Her brow furrowed.

I'm not expecting anyone. Maybe just a polite coworker?

"Come in?"

The door opened a crack, and Leah was surprised to see Natalie. Her heart sped up. "Hi Natalie. What's up?"

"Do you have a few minutes?" Her voice wavered, and Leah's ribs tightened around her lungs.

"Of course. Can I get you a bottle of water or a cup of tea or something?"

"Water. Please." Natalie nodded, looking for all the world like a deer in headlights. "Thanks."

Leah stepped out to grab two bottles of water as Natalie sat down in Leah's guest chair and placed her purse on the ground beside her. After both women got settled, they sat in silence for a moment.

"So what's going on?" Leah hoped the question didn't sound accusatory, but she was still keenly aware of her rapidly-beating heart.

Natalie's voice was barely above a whisper. "Peter told me about what happened at your appointment last week."

Leah's face fell. "I'm so sorry, Nat. I wasn't at all prepared for what that visit was going to entail, and I feel horrible about it."

She waited, wide-eyed, for Natalie to respond, but instead, a single tear slid down Natalie's face, and her shoulders trembled.

She leaned forward in her seat. "Natalie, are you okay?"

"Of course not!" Nat snapped. "How can you even ask me that?"

Leah blinked, shocked. "What happened?"

"Peter said he was going to text you."

Leah shook her head, concern in her eyes. "I haven't read any of my messages."

Natalie rested her face in her hands, saying nothing. Fear and confusion gripping her heart, Leah pulled out her phone and opened her text thread with Peter.

> Call me ASAP. Matthew arrested. Nonsense
> charges. Suspect Pierucci is behind it.

Leah's heart stopped. "Oh my gosh, Natalie. I'm so sorry. Tell me everything."

Nat barely looked up. "I mean, what did Peter already say? I don't feel like there's much to talk about."

"Just that Matthew was..." Leah could hardly bring herself to say it out loud. "That Matthew was arrested."

For a moment, neither woman spoke. Leah could sense Natalie's hesitation... and her pain. It took all her self-control not to launch into a lengthy apology.

Don't make this all about you, Leah. She'll talk again when she's ready.

The silence—and the tension—stretched out between them until Natalie said, as if she couldn't hold it in any longer, "Can I play you the message he left me?"

Leah nodded. "Of course."

Nat pulled out her phone and navigated to the voicemail.

"Hi, honey, it's Matthew. I hope you're doing okay. I... Well, I don't really know how to say this, but I got picked up by the police on my way to work today, and they're not really giving me much to go on as far as what to expect, or even what they want me here for. I've been trying to get someone to tell me how long I'll be here, but no one is giving me a straight answer. I'm really hoping this is just some parking ticket I don't remember, but I... well, I love you, Natalie. And I love the kids. And I never want you to forget that. They've taken away my cell phone, and I'm not sure if I'll get another chance to call you. I was hoping to have an update before I used my one phone call or whatever, but since I probably won't make it home for lunch, I didn't want you to worry about me too much. I love you. Goodbye, sweetie."

The weight of his unsaid words was palpable.

"Oh, Natalie. I'm so sorry."

"Any other day," Natalie said slowly, "I would've said he was overreacting... we've all been tightly wound lately. I'd expect him home for dinner with a slap on the wrist about that forgotten parking ticket or something equally trivial. But I think we both know that's not what this is, and I didn't give him a hug this morning before he left because I was tied up with Rosie, and I can't stop thinking about what I'm going to do it the last thing I ever said to him was 'get out of here before I make you change her sheets.'" Natalie choked up, tears streaming down her face, and Leah found herself on the verge of tears as well.

"And this is all you've heard? Peter said it's possible that Pierucci's behind it?" She swallowed hard.

Natalie's eyes flew to Leah's face, rage hiding just behind the surface. "I know you're not that stupid."

Leah winced. "I'm so sorry, Natalie. I wasn't trying to be insensitive. I guess I just hoped that... that it might be something else."

"What else could it have been? We have been beyond careful this year, making sure our conduct was absolutely blameless, even though neither of us even works for him anymore. I quit my job after your memories were suppressed because I thought he might figure out that you and I had become friends and come after me. There was no way I was going to let him touch my family. And then to end up here after all..." Natalie buried her face in her hands again, sobbing.

Leah's heart sank in her chest, and her fingers reached automatically for her 'Auntie Leah' bracelet. "I'm sorry. I should have been more careful at my appointment. I just wasn't thinking. I really didn't mean to put you or anyone in danger."

"I never thought you did it on purpose," Natalie said through tears. "But you were careless, and we're facing the consequences."

"But surely once the police see that he's innocent, they'll release him? They can't hold him indefinitely. There are laws about this kind of thing!" Leah knew she was grasping at straws.

Natalie looked at her with red eyes. "Don't you get it? It doesn't matter whether or not he did whatever nonsense they brought him in for." She wiped her cheeks with the sleeve of her cardigan. "They'll have him spirited away, memory wiped, and back on the streets within a month if Pierucci is really convinced that we're a threat." She sighed. "And that's the best case scenario."

For a moment, her eyes glazed over, fear written plainly on her face. She looked up and made eye contact with Leah before continuing. "Maybe you're just being hopeful, or maybe your brain isn't quite on straight yet, so just in case, let me lay it out for you in words you can understand: Pierucci tells himself he's immune to fear. He has nothing to be afraid of, and it would be irrational for him to experience fear. But he does get scared. Terrified, even! He just masks it as anger so his self-image can remain intact. And that makes him so much more dangerous... because he's always convinced that his anger is just and that his punishment is mercy."

Leah nodded, unsure what to say.

Natalie continued, holding Leah's gaze. "And he knows that I won't see things his way, but he's too self-absorbed to care. He'll tell me, and the staff, and the world that he's doing us a favor by dealing with Matthew. And at the end of the day, it doesn't really matter whether or not he actually believes it, because he acts like he does… and no one can stop him."

Natalie crushed her empty water bottle. Leah waited for her to continue, but she said nothing more. Ana walked by Leah's office again, raising her eyebrows at Natalie's presence. Leah shook her head as discreetly as she could, and Ana kept walking. The air conditioner switched off, leaving the room absolutely silent.

Leah muttered quietly. "I can stop him."

For the tiniest moment, something softened in Natalie's face, but before Leah could respond, it was gone.

"You could," she said coldly. "But you've made it fairly clear that you're not willing to take any more risks right now, so I didn't think it was worth bringing up."

"Natalie, I—" Leah closed her eyes and breathed deeply. "You're right. And I'm sorry. I wish I had seen things more clearly before… before it came to this. But I won't sit by and let him harm Matthew or your family."

Natalie shrugged, and Leah's heart sank further. "Okay, Leah. Whatever."

"I'll be careful," Leah said, immediately overthinking it.

"That's what we said." Natalie frowned.

Leah watched, her brows knit, as Natalie stood up and stepped toward the door in silence. Desperation clawed at her chest, and Leah called after her. "Do you need anything? Can I grab you something to eat?"

Natalie didn't turn around. "I'm not hungry. I've got some errands to run before I have to pick the kids up."

"Please keep me updated," Leah pleaded. "I'll do the same if you'd like."

Nat shook her head. "Not really. I just want Matthew to come home." She opened the door and let herself out.

"Goodbye," Leah said as the door clicked shut. Her ears rang in the silence created by Natalie's absence.

"I'll be careful." Isn't that what I said about my research last year? And we all ended up here anyway.

The thought was sobering, and Leah felt herself shrink.

It was stupid of me to even get Natalie and Matthew involved in the first place. I knew how much they were hurting. I thought maybe I'd feel less alone... but at what cost?

She exhaled deeply, letting her cheeks puff out, before turning back to the project she had open on her laptop. The flow she'd found early in the morning was gone, and she clicked between windows for a few minutes, halfheartedly trying to recover her interest in her work.

I should have just kept my trap shut. I would have figured out eventually that the FBI was the way to go. If I hadn't roped them into this, they could have gotten out of Pierucci's web so much sooner.

She opened a drawer on her desk and looked inside. Her mind was foggy, and she flipped through her hanging folders without seeing them. Sitting back up, she closed the drawer and stared at her laptop again.

But it's too late for that now. The damage is already done.

She shoved the thoughts down and picked up her phone, scrolling through her voicemails to find Agent McDowell's number. Her stomach fluttered as she clicked the 'call' button and raised the phone to her ear. The memory of his arm around her shoulders haunted her.

Which version of him am I going to get?

After three rings, Leah began to despair that she had alienated him as well as the others. But just before she ended the call, Agent McDowell's voice startled her out of her thoughts. "Hello?"

"Hi Agent McDowell. This is Leah Harvey. I'm... I'm ready to work with you. I'll do whatever you need to take the Pieruccis down. But first, I need your help with something."

His tone was cautious. "What's that?"

"Matthew Bailey was just arrested, and my gut says Pierucci's behind it. I slipped up at my last appointment, and I think he figured out that my memories are back. I can't stand by and let Matthew and their family be punished for my stupidity."

"What exactly are you asking me to do?" He gave her no indication of what he was thinking.

Leah picked at a loose flap of skin around her thumbnail. "I need to get Matthew out of custody and help his family lay low until all of this blows over. I'm not sure where he's currently being held, but if Pierucci really does have him, we don't have much time before things escalate." A shiver ran down her spine.

"I see," Agent McDowell said matter-of-factly. "You said you think Pierucci knows your memories are back. Why would that lead him to Matthew?"

"I..." Leah hesitated. "It's a long story. Their kids call me Auntie Leah, and when we were all over there last, Josie had made me a bracelet that says Auntie Leah on it. I didn't think to take it off before my appointment, and I saw both Jude and his father notice it."

Agent McDowell didn't respond.

"The Baileys are the only people who call me that, and Jude knows it. I don't have any siblings, and I've been very upfront at my appointments that I don't have any friends, either." She paused, her heart aching as she recalled her words to Dr. Pierucci back in May.

"Honestly, the closest thing I have to a friend is Wilder, the guy who usually has his appointments around the same time as mine? We chat in the waiting room."

Agent McDowell's voice cut through her thoughts. "So you think he arrested Matthew because...?"

"Because if I've been seeing Matthew and Natalie, then my memories are back. And if my memories are back, then I'm probably plotting to take him down." Saying the words out loud hurt viscerally, deep in her gut. She continued. "Matthew went through a lot when he was working at the prison, and I think Pierucci knows he can leverage that trauma to his advantage."

"I understand," McDowell said curtly. "I'll make some inquiries and see what I can do. But Leah—"

"Yes?"

He sighed, and her heart dropped. "I don't want to make any promises. If Pierucci can convince the cops to arrest Matthew, then they're probably not filing their paperwork. I'm going to do my absolute best and find out everything I can, but I'm not a magician."

"I understand. Thank you for trying."

He ended the call, and Leah wanted to cry.

Not yet. You don't get to cry until you've cleaned up the mess you've made.

Chapter 26

Tuesday afternoon and evening crawled by as Leah waited for any word from Natalie or Agent McDowell. She called Peter several times, hoping that he'd heard through the grapevine that she was going to step in after all, hoping that he'd forgiven her and would be willing to share some details about what was going on. But he never picked up, and her phone never rang.

The next day was a Wednesday, so she let herself stay in bed a little longer. Finally pulling herself up five minutes before she was expected to be online, she threw on a blouse and logged onto her laptop.

Well, if no one's going to tell me what's going on with Matthew, maybe I can at least get some work done today.

She knew it wasn't true even as she thought it, but she opened her inbox all the same. Her heart sank when she saw an email from Ana.

Good morning Leah,
I'd like you to come into the office today for a little bit. I took a peek at your schedule, and it looks like you're free for most of the day. I'm in meetings all afternoon, so I'd appreciate if you could come in around 9:30 or 10:00. Please let me know when to expect you, and plan to bring your laptop.

It's Work from Home Wednesday! Are you even allowed to ask me to come in?

Nevertheless, she dutifully traded her pajama pants for a pair of slacks, packed her laptop into her work bag, and hopped in the car. As she drove, she passed the exit for the Children's Ward.

Such a shame. But I know Dr. Pierucci hated having to go back and forth between the two offices... and I'm sure he saw it as a total drain on the budget.

She stayed lost in her thoughts until she arrived at the office. Although she was still uncertain why she'd been called in, she didn't really care. Her thoughts were elsewhere.

Ana waited for her near the door when she stepped inside. "Leah, good to see you. Come right in. No need to set your things down. Let's chat."

She ushered Leah into her office and gestured to the guest chair. Leah set her bag down and began pulling out her laptop as Ana closed the door and sat down.

Ana shook her head. "There's no need to get your computer out, Leah, I just wanted a chance to talk with you. You've been really struggling lately, and I wanted to see how you're doing. I thought it would be best to have this conversation on a day when the office is empty, just to maintain your privacy."

"Thank you...?" It was just as much a question as a statement.

Ana looked at her, eyes expectant. When she said nothing, Ana sighed. "Leah, I've noticed a drastic decline in the quality of your work lately, and I want to talk with you about your future here."

"Oh." What else was there to say?

Ana leaned forward, placing her forearms on her desk. "We were very impressed with your portfolio when you applied last year, and you've gotten us through a number of tight spots. You came here and showed us from day one that you're a hard worker, a dedicated employee, and an insightful observer of individuals and trends." Ana shuffled uncomfortably in her seat, and a sinking feeling in Leah's stomach filled her with dread. "That's why it's been very difficult for me to watch you... unravel over the last few weeks."

Leah looked away.

Ana fiddled with a stack of papers on her desk. "You were upfront with us in your application that your mental health was in a fragile place, and we've done our best to accommodate that when it's been necessary." She looked up, as if expecting some sort of affirmation. Leah nodded slowly, still feeling lost.

Ana mirrored Leah's nod. "I don't know if this is the same issue, or if it's something else... I know you were in that car accident a few months ago—I don't remember you mentioning any ongoing health issues as a result, but if I had to pinpoint when things started to go downhill, that would probably be the easiest mile marker. At first, I just chalked it up to the accident. You had to take a day or two off for the whiplash, and it seemed reasonable that you'd need some time to get back on your feet. But I don't think I've seen any improvement in your performance since then. If anything, you've continued to slip."

She spread the papers in her hand out across the surface of her desk, revealing some projects that Leah had recently submitted for distribution. Immediately, her eyes found a dozen mistakes: misspelled words, incorrect punctuation, mismatched branding between clients, even swapped logos on a couple of images.

Leah felt her face redden, and she brought her hand to her forehead. "Oh, gosh, I'm so sorry. This is mortifying."

"This isn't like you at all." Ana's expression had shifted to one of concern. "I'm worried about you. Are... are you doing okay?"

Leah leaned back in her chair. "I've just had a lot going on lately. It's a long story and not one I'm ready to share, but I've been really distracted... Obviously." She gestured again to the papers laid out in front of her.

"I understand." Ana's hands trembled ever so slightly as she gathered the pages back up. "And how long do you think this... distraction... is going to last?"

Leah sighed, trying to find the words, but Ana continued before Leah could speak up.

"Like I said, you've been a valuable member of this team, and if you're just going through it and need support, I'd be happy to connect you with someone in HR who could help you find a therapist or a doctor or someone... We can even work out some kind of long-term leave if we need to. But at a certain point, I can't keep fielding emails from your clients and editing your work. I was told earlier this week that our team is going to have to do some downsizing this month—budget cuts, lower workload, just bad timing all around. I don't want to have to let you go, Leah, but based on your recent performance, I'm not sure I have a choice."

"I understand," Leah said again, her voice hollow. Her eyes glazed over as she stared at the wall.

"Do..." Ana hesitated. "I guess, do you have any idea how long this distraction is going to last? Is it from some sort of situation, or is it something deeper than that? I know you said you weren't ready to talk about it, but I don't know how to help you if you're not going to..." She trailed off.

Leah blinked and cocked her head to one side, confused by the question. "I'm not going to share more, if that's what you're asking. It's not something I'm interested in discussing in a professional context. I don't expect it to last forever, but it's hard for me to put a timeline on it—a couple of weeks, maybe a few months?" She pursed her lips.

"Okay... I..." Ana raised a hand to her face and groaned. "Leah, I'm sorry. I should have just led with this, but I didn't want to jump right in, only for you to tell me that your mother had just died or you'd been diagnosed with a terminal illness." She sat up taller and straightened the pile of papers in her hands. "Leah, I'm going to have to let you go. You're not the only one—I was told that I need to cut a full five percent from the budget—but your performance lately hasn't been up to the standard we need, and it's taken too much of my time and energy to cover for your mistakes... I don't have another choice. You can go ahead and clean off your desk. Leave your laptop there, and please don't forget to write down your password before you go. I'll have some paperwork and your last paycheck for you when you're ready to leave."

"I, um..." Leah blinked. "Okay, then. Thank you."

Leah walked out of the room reeling. She grabbed a cardboard box from the work room and began to gently clear items off her desk and set them in the box. A framed photograph of herself and her mom. Two coffee cups—a generic one she'd been given on her first day of work, and one bearing the logo of Common Grounds. She smiled when she saw it: Jude had given it to her on their first dating anniversary, in honor of all the Saturdays they'd spent there together. She'd just assumed it was an office mug that had taken up permanent residence at her desk.

A handful of birthday cards and thank you notes were sorted into a "keep" pile, and the rest were thrown away. Unused takeout utensils and sauces were left in the break room, and the scant paper files she'd maintained were left for another employee to sift through later in the week.

Finally, Leah connected a USB drive to her laptop and saved the personal files she'd collected over the course of the year. She carefully copied her relevant passwords onto a sticky note, which she left with Ana on her way out.

And just like that, she was gone. All trace of her removed from the building, as if she'd never been.

Her heart was heavy on the drive home, with her box full of desk junk on the passenger seat next to her. Her face was red with shame and frustration.

Can I even be mad about it, though? It's not like this was some big surprise...

The car in front of her screeched to a stop, and Leah slammed on her brakes. She braced herself for impact as the contents of her box went flying toward her windshield. When she stopped moving, her front bumper was mere inches away from the other car. Her heart pounded in her ears as the brake lights dimmed and the cars ahead of her began to trickle forward.

It feels so petty to even care—so I got let go, what of it? Matthew is probably being tortured, and I'm moping because my boss told me that my bad work was bad?

She drove the rest of the way home in silence, both physical and mental. She eased her car into a spot, shifted it into park, and stepped inside. The emptiness of her apartment felt oppressive. No longer facing a long to-do list, Leah changed back into her pajamas and crawled back into her bed.

If I were half the woman they all think I am, I wouldn't need a personal reason to get involved. I'd do it because it's the right thing to do.

She shivered, although the morning sun had filled the room with warmth. Shadows of crepe myrtle branches danced on her wall. She shut her eyes tight.

But I'm not. I'm not even close. I'm just the same as Pierucci— only willing to protect things that matter to me.

She spent most of the rest of the day in bed, scrolling through social media, looking for something to distract her. She tried to read a few pages of a novel, but it didn't grab her attention, and she set it down. When her stomach growled, she poured herself a bowl of crackers, only to eat a few and leave the rest on her nightstand. After hours of mindless scrolling, her eyes stung and her head throbbed. She turned off the light and rolled over for a nap.

***

The sun was slowly setting over the horizon when Leah awoke again. Her lower back ached, and her limbs felt weak. She yawned and rolled her neck.

You can't just lie in bed all day. Go for a run or something.

Obeying some unseen critic, Leah pulled on her running shoes and stepped out the door. Out of the corner of her eye, she saw Sarah standing next to her. Sarah waved casually, did a double take, and flagged Leah down. "Hey! How are you? I feel like I haven't heard from you in ages."

"Yeah, I'm..." Leah felt the weight of her eyelids and her lungs. "Honestly, no, I'm not great."

Sarah's eyes deepened. "Do you want to come over? I'm running out to try that new daiquiri place around the corner. We were just going to put on a movie because we don't have anything else to do, but if you need to talk..."

Relief flooded Leah's system. "Would you mind?"

"Never." She locked the door behind her and came over to wrap an arm around Leah's shoulders. "I'll come knock on your door when I get back. Want anything?"

Leah shook her head. "No, thanks."

Sarah's eyebrows furrowed, a sad half-smile on her lips. "Is this about the stuff with the clinic?"

Leah nodded, trying to hold back tears. Sarah squeezed her hand before walking to her car. Leah sat down on her patio for a moment, trying to recollect herself. Her teeth chattered in the warm night air.

Honestly, I'll probably tell Sarah and Connor everything that's happened, and they'll just hate me too. Might as well get it over with now, before we become good friends and the breakup hurts that much more.

Sarah came back twenty minutes later, drinks in hand. If she was surprised to see Leah still sitting exactly where she'd left her, she said nothing. Instead, gently laid her head on top of Leah's, just for a moment. "Whenever you're ready."

Leah stood up and wordlessly followed her inside. Sarah handed Connor their drinks and busied herself making a mug of chamomile tea for Leah. The TV was on, but Connor muted it as Leah entered.

"Hey, Leah! Good to see you!" His eyes widened when he saw the way her shoulders slumped. "What's going on?"

"She's just having a rough day," Sarah answered from the kitchen. "I told her to come by and hang out for a bit."

Connor smiled at Leah, pity in every line of his face. "I'm glad you said yes," he told her.

Sarah entered the living room and handed Leah her tea before getting settled on the couch next to Connor. Leah watched the steam rise for a moment before taking a sip. The warmth trickled down her throat and settled in her stomach. She began speaking cautiously, "I remember everything now."

Sarah's jaw dropped, and Connor raised his eyebrows.

Leah shook her head. "Yeah. Something finally clicked, and it's like the suppression never happened. Which is amazing, right? It's amazing that the suppression worked, even if I wish it hadn't happened to me. It's amazing that we were able to undo it. It's amazing that you and I, Sarah, were able to figure out so much from the breadcrumb trail left behind. The whole thing is baffling, and I wish I had time to just reflect because there are so many things that I don't want to forget."

The words tumbled out, and once she started talking, she couldn't stop. "But now I'm faced with this question that I don't know how to answer. The whole reason that Natalie and everyone tried so hard to help me recover those memories is because I had uncovered some really horrible things happening at the Institute—that's the reason Pierucci wiped my memories in the first place—and now they're all expecting me to be the one to do something with that information... and I get it, right?"

Her shoulders fell further, and a sigh escaped her chest. Sarah nodded sympathetically, encouraging her to continue.

Leah studied the wallpaper carefully. "I was the one who found out about it. I was the one who did the research and put together a case against them. I was the one who

315

submitted the tip to the FBI. But I assumed that the investigation would move pretty quickly once it got started. I wasn't trying to bring myself back so that I could swoop in and save the day. I just didn't want to... die." She didn't look up, didn't give them space to ask any questions. "But it didn't happen like that, and now they want me to jump right back in the thick of it, and I feel like I've already sacrificed so much..." She trailed off, fighting back tears.

Sarah gave her a moment and then asked quietly, "What do they want you to do?"

"Be the bait, basically." Leah threw up her hands. "We have enough material right now to get them for research fraud, easily, but if we want to have a shot at a conviction for the murders, too—"

"Murders?" Sarah interrupted in a horrified voice.

"Oh, yeah." Leah shook her head, her expression deadpan. "That's part of what I discovered. It's... gruesome. I don't really want to talk about it. But if we want to get him for everything, and not just for the research fraud, there are one or two more things we need in order to make sure our case is rock solid. And the reality is that I'm probably the only one who could get that kind of confession out of him. I told Agent McDowell I'd do it, but I just...." She trailed off, eyes locked on her mug.

"You're not a coward, Leah." Connor's voice was unexpected and decisive, cutting through the noise in her head.

Her heart skipped a beat, and she looked up. "What?"

"You're not a coward." He leaned forward and held her gaze. "I see you telling yourself that you are."

Tears filled her eyes, and her vision blurred. For a moment, she could only breathe, holding back the flood that threatened to break loose. When she got a handle on herself again, her voice was whisper-quiet around the lump in her throat. "Thanks Connor. I guess I just feel trapped by the idea that I owe them something." She sniffled and wiped her cheeks with the back of her hand.

"Owe who?" The answer to the question was obvious enough, but Sarah asked anyway.

"Everyone." Leah shrugged, a weight settling on her shoulders. "The Baileys—I haven't even told you about the part where Natalie's husband is currently in police custody for bogus reasons, and Dr. Pierucci is probably having him tortured. That's my fault too, because I was a dummy and Pierucci figured out that my memories are back... And Peter, whose brother killed himself because of his experience working with this program. He was so traumatized that he couldn't take it anymore. And the Institute itself, which I want to believe in as an organization that can do some real good if Dr. Pierucci were just not steering the ship for five minutes. And..." Leah hesitated for a moment, words on the tip of her tongue. "And all the prisoners who died because of this. And their families. I can't help but wonder how many people were killed because I didn't act faster. We lost a whole year. How many kids will never see one of their parents again?"

The question hung heavily in the air between them.

"But that's the thing—it's not just a year in the abstract... It's a year of my life. It's a year of losing touch with people I loved, of totally uprooting myself and disrupting everything I thought I'd be doing by now... Turns out my mom didn't have a stroke, and she doesn't have dementia, and I'm the crazy one, actually." Her voice sounded desperate. "It's been a lot, you know? I know

317

Pierucci isn't afraid to kill for this project, and he won't underestimate me twice."

For a moment, no one spoke. Sarah swirled her drink around, the sloshing sound cutting through the silence. Connor fiddled with the buttons on the remote. The blur of motion on the still-silent screen caught her eye. The camera panned past a brick sign in a grassy entryway.

Scarlett Bay Correctional Facility
Established 1954

Leah winced. Sarah, noticing that her attention had been diverted, motioned to Connor to turn the sound back on. The voice that floated toward them was intimately familiar to Leah, although a stranger to the others.

"—goal with the Rehabilitation Research Program is always that our incarcerated citizens are released back into the world with a new skill set and a new outlook on life. Our work is revolutionizing the local prison system, with upwards of sixty percent of inmates predicted to remain free of a second conviction after just one round of treatment. After a second or third round, those odds continue to go up. This means that our streets are safer and our fellow citizens are able to live their lives as productive members of society after their sentence is carried out."

The monologue had been accompanied by a montage of smiling men and women in orange jumpsuits—taking classes, doing manual labor, sitting down in cushioned orthodontic chairs. The frame then cut to a shot of the Pieruccis—Jude, Sr. and Jude, Jr.—in the former's office. The resemblance between the two was striking: dark hair, strong Italian features, piercing blue-gray eyes.

Sarah gasped and looked at Leah wordlessly.

Jude continued speaking. "The McNeill Institute is a family business, and we know just how important reunification can be for children and families with an incarcerated loved one. Join us as we work toward a future where rehabilitation is standard procedure, and long-term imprisonment is a distant memory."

Both men smiled, one charismatic and welcoming, one severe and frightening. The shot faded to black. As a new commercial started, Leah reached for the remote and turned the television off.

"I directed that." She stared at the blank screen, her eyes unfocused. "I think it was made after I found out what was going on. But what could I do? If I had backed out of the project..." She couldn't finish her sentence.

"You did what you thought was best." Connor stared at the black screen. "And that's all anyone could ask."

"Maybe." A sigh escaped her, and her shoulders slumped. She drained the last sip of her tea, stood up, and stretched. "You two have given me a lot to think about. I'll... I'll keep you in the loop."

She placed her mug by the kitchen sink, gave Sarah a hug, and let herself out the door, her thoughts still racing.

Chapter 27

Leah woke the next morning to a ringing phone. Eyelids heavy, she rolled over in bed and slapped the screen "Shut up. Shut up!"

It did, but only for a moment. The ringing began again, and as Leah's conscious mind processed what was happening, she pried her eyes open and forced her vision into focus. Agent McDowell's name scrolled past her.

Eyes wide, Leah accepted the call. "Agent McDowell!" It was more of a croak than a word. Her throat was dry and sticky, and her body was still half asleep.

"Ms. Harvey—" He paused. "Are you okay?"

She rubbed her eyes, scratching out the sleep that had built up overnight. "You woke me up."

"It's nine o'clock in the morning!" She thought she could hear Wilder's grin.

"I got let go from my job." It sounded harsher than she meant it.

"Oh." He sobered. "I'm sorry to hear that. I'm calling because I have news about Matthew."

She shot up in bed. "Tell me everything."

"I think it would be best if we talked in person." He paused. "I was going to offer to come by your office, but if you won't be there, why don't you meet me here instead?"

Leah nodded, holding her phone between her ear and her shoulder while she picked her jeans up off the floor next to her bed and pulled them on. "I'm there. Text me the address. I'll leave right away."

Her phone buzzed.

"Thanks." She stifled a yawn. "Okay, I thought the massive adrenaline rush you just gave me would wake me up, but apparently not. I'm going to grab some coffee on my way. Want anything?"

"A black iced coffee would be great, thanks. It's too hot for the stuff they've got at the hotel."

"Amen to that. Be there soon." She hung up and finished getting dressed, her stomach in knots.

Barely ten minutes had passed by the time she found herself seated at the wheel. She smacked her tongue against the roof of her mouth as she eased her car out of the apartment parking lot. She wrinkled her nose at the stale taste of her own morning breath.

Shoot. Forgot to brush my teeth.

She looked around her car for a peppermint or something. A single stick of gum lay nestled in the center console, and she sniffed it hesitantly. She unwrapped it and popped it in her mouth. The mint flavor was stale, but it was better than nothing.

***

Half an hour later, coffees in hand and backpack slung over her shoulder, Leah took the elevator to the fourth floor of Agent McDowell's hotel. Her mind raced as she walked the length of the hallway, looking for room 428. When she found it, she knocked gently on the door.

Here we go.

"Hang on!" His voice was muffled, and she heard quick steps toward the door. There was a long pause, and then it slowly swung open. Agent McDowell was dressed in his usual suit and tie, but his glasses were missing. "Sorry about that." He blinked a few times, seeming to look through her. "I'd shake your hand, but I can't see it." He stepped back and held the door open.

I guess Wilder must wear contacts, if he's that blind without his glasses. I never knew.

She stepped inside, taking the door from him as he walked toward the room's desk. "Well, I'd say good to see you," she replied with a grin. "But I think that'd be insensitive."

He didn't seem to hear her. Blushing, Leah turned to close the door. She closed her eyes and inhaled.

Get it together. It's not like your friend is in there somewhere just waiting for you to coax him out.

"Ah, here they are," she heard behind her. She turned around to hand him his coffee, and he took it with a slight nod. Glasses on. Back to business.

This is so stupid. Why am I upset by this?

She sat down on the couch and took a sip of her latte, trying not to think about her head on Wilder's shoulder at her last visit to the clinic. She blushed and pushed the thought away. Agent McDowell pulled his phone out of his pocket and placed it face down on the table before taking a seat on the other end of the couch.

Leah didn't waste time on formalities. "Tell me everything you know about Matthew."

Agent McDowell's voice was somber. "It's not the worst it could be, but it's not great."

She said nothing, waiting for him to continue.

"I called in a few favors and was able to find out that he got picked up for an expired vehicle registration. Texas law allows an arrest for just about any traffic violation, and it'd be easy for the precinct to claim a paperwork mishap if anyone questioned them about it. But something's definitely going on—there was no arrest report filed when he was brought in, and rumor has it that he's due to get moved to Scarlett Bay by this evening."

Leah's heart stopped. "He's going to the prison? Do you know anything more than that?"

His face fell. "No," he sighed. "It took a lot of digging just to get that much. I'm sorry."

"Does Natalie know?" Leah heard the fear in her voice.

"Not yet." He pursed his lips. "I wanted to get your read on the situation before reaching out."

Leah leaned forward, eyes wide. "You have to tell her. You can't leave her in the dark about this."

He ran a hand through his hair. "You don't think it would just worry her more? I'd rather wait a little longer and give her something definite."

"What do you mean?" Leah's brow furrowed.

He looked confused. "Didn't you say you want to get Matthew out?"

Her eyebrows shot up. "Do you think we could? You didn't exactly sound optimistic."

He shrugged. "I mean, we definitely can. It's just a question of cost."

"Cost?" Leah scoffed. "Don't you have a budget?"

"Ah, sorry. I was unclear. Not financial cost. Cost to the investigation." He hesitated a moment. "Cost to you."

She rubbed her arms, a sudden chill striking her. Agent McDowell looked at her, waiting for her response.

"Explain."

"I mean..." He shrugged with his hands out in front of him, palms up. "We've talked about this. The case you gave me last year is more than enough to convict Pierucci on research fraud a dozen times over. I'm confident he'd get his license revoked. He'd never be allowed to practice medicine again. And there's a chance we could get him for murder on the circumstantial evidence alone. There's precedent." He grimaced. "But without a body, it's not easy to convince a jury that there's no other possible explanation, especially on a case of this scale."

"But how does that relate to Matthew?" Her leg bounced rapidly, and she set her latte down on the table to avoid spilling it.

"If you're going to insist that we get Matthew out first—and I'm willing to give it my best shot—then we're going to have to show a lot of our hand. It'll be that much more difficult to get the information out of him that we need to secure the murder conviction." His expression was serious. He sat back, holding her gaze. She looked away, watching a fly tap-tap-tap against the window.

"I'll do whatever it takes to get Matthew out." Her voice was quiet but unwavering. "I know it might make things harder later on. I'm willing to take that risk. Walk me through what you're thinking."

"There she is." He smiled quietly, his eyes sparkling. "I knew you'd come around eventually. I tried to tell the others, but they didn't listen. You're not one to give up that easily."

Leah rolled her eyes and huffed a disapproving laugh. "We've known each other for, like, two months."

"Excuse you," he retorted. "We met almost a year ago."

"Excuse you," she shot back, pushing down a surge of anger. "I met Wilder Frederick almost a year ago."

"Fair enough." He looked down at his coffee.

Leah opened her mouth to apologize, but decided against it and remained silent. The clock on the wall loudly ticked out the seconds. Agent McDowell set down his drink and picked up a clipboard that had been resting on the floor.

He sighed. "Okay, before we do anything else," he said. "I do need you to fill out some paperwork. Standard protocol, but I don't want to risk this thing getting snagged on a technicality.

Leah nodded, reaching a hand out for his clipboard, but he held onto it himself instead.

"Full name?"

"Leonora Nicole Harvey."

"Date of birth?"

"April 23, 1995."

The rest was pretty standard for consent and liability release forms. She watched as he carefully copied down her answers for each question, reading them back to confirm he had everything correct. Finally, they reached the bottom of the form.

"Lastly, who do you want me to list as your emergency contact?" he asked, staring intently at his clipboard. "Someone you trust implicitly, preferably in town. It doesn't need to be someone who could make medical decisions, just someone you'd want me to call if anything happened." There was something in his voice she couldn't quite identify.

Leah raised one eyebrow and flared her nostrils. "I know what an emergency contact is." She glanced up at the ceiling as she thought. "I guess you can put my Mom? She's not in town, but she's probably the person I'm closest to." She listed off her mom's cell number before adding, "Oh, and you know what, go ahead and put Sarah Winfrey down as well. That's my neighbor."

Leah reached for her phone to find Sarah's contact information and read the number off to him.

"Is that it?" he asked. "Nobody else?"

"Who else would I have?" She shrugged. "Wilder was— well, I guess, you were–the only other person I trusted this year." She said it without thinking. Blushing, she looked over at the coffee table, avoiding his gaze.

He didn't look up from his paper, but she thought she heard him smile. "Glad to get that sorted out." He nodded and turned to a fresh sheet of paper. "So... let's start from the top. What does Pierucci know already?"

Leah sighed. "He knows my memories are back, which means that I know all about what's been going on at the prison. And he's not going to let me go twice." She heard the tremor in her voice and began tracing a slow figure-eight on the rough fabric of her jeans as she steadied her breathing.

It's going to be okay. This time is going to be different.

Agent McDowell nodded, scribbling intently before looking up at her. "Do you know if he's aware that you reached out to the Bureau last year before your memories were suppressed?"

Leah looked down at the carpet through half-closed eyes. "Honestly, if he has Matthew in custody, we have to assume he knows everything Matthew knows: not just that I contacted the FBI, but that someone is actively working on the case, and that that someone is you."

She looked up briefly and found Agent McDowell watching her. She glanced back down and began studying a smudge of dirt on her shoes. "There's no outsmarting him," she added. "It just doesn't work like that."

I swear, if he says "not with that attitude," I'm going to get up and walk away.

"Hey," he replied instead. Leah looked up and met his eyes, her shoulders hunched. "I know you're scared. But trust me—we're in a good spot. I've seen sting operations succeed with a lot less to go on than this." He pointed to his clipboard with a quiet confidence. "Plus, he's never met me. It doesn't matter if Matthew tells him my name—he knows me as Wilder Frederick. It wouldn't be the first time it's happened on an undercover assignment."

Leah ran her hand through her hair. "Matthew has seen you, though. If they get him to Scarlett Bay, Pierucci will see your face and put the pieces together."

"See my face?" He cocked his head to one side.

Leah exhaled. "Did no one tell you how this all works?"

"How what works?" he replied slowly.

"The MentaLink console." Agent McDowell still looked confused. "The technology that's being abused at the prison? They hook you up and scan your brain, and they can send those images to the simulator and walk around in them like a real place..." The end of her sentence trailed off as she thought back to her visit to her library with Valerie.

She blinked and looked back at Agent McDowell, whose eyes were wide.

"Yeah," she continued. "If Pierucci finds Matthew's memories of you, he'll be able to see your face and figure out who you really are. Your glasses don't make you look all that different." She flared her eyes and shrugged.

Agent McDowell ran his fingers through his hair. "I see." He took off his glasses and rubbed the bridge of his nose. "So we're just all in, then. Everything on the table."

"Everything on the table," Leah echoed, leaning forward to grab her coffee. "And getting Matthew out is our first priority."

"I know, I know. You've made that very clear." He studied his clipboard intently, chewing absentmindedly on the end of his pen. "But I wonder—can we turn that into our opening move?"

"What?"

"Think of this like a chess game." He looked up from his clipboard. "We lead with a bold opening move, and we just keep hounding him until we've got him in checkmate."

Leah nodded, her eyes narrowed. An impish grin broke out across Agent McDowell's face.

"Oh no," Leah groaned. "What's that look for?"

"You say he's got cops on the payroll. Is it beyond the realm of possibility that he'd have someone at the Bureau too?" His voice had changed, growing confident and almost conspiratorial.

The wheels in Leah's head began to turn. "Who are you trying to convince?"

Agent McDowell shrugged, smirking and raising his eyebrows. "If Matthew is already scheduled to be moved, who's to say that Pierucci didn't assign an FBI Agent to do the transfer?"

Leah gave a half-laugh. "I mean, it's worth a shot."

"But the second he finds out that Matthew didn't arrive at Scarlett Bay, he'll start making countermoves. Are we ready to commit to that?"

"Do we have another choice?"

"No," he shook his head sadly. "I guess not. So, assuming we can get Matthew away from him, we've effectively taken away his hostage—what's his next move?"

"He's going to start getting desperate. We'll have to make sure Natalie and the kids are somewhere safe. And I wouldn't be surprised to see him lashing out at Peter, just since he's been handling my case."

"He knows Peter's in on it?"

"He has to. My treatment results have been fudged, and he knows my memories are back. Someone has to be tampering with the files."

McDowell nodded slowly, reading over his notes. "Okay, so getting Peter to safety has to be another top priority. That cuts down another one of Pierucci's possible moves. What next?"

Leah shook her head, glancing out the window. The sunlight streamed in, not a cloud in the sky. Traffic noise from the nearby highway drifted faintly into the room. An airplane flew past, leaving a puffy white trail in its wake.

She looked back at Agent McDowell, a sudden exhaustion creeping into her bones. "Look, all of this is good, but I feel like we're just circling around the real question. If he knows that the FBI is investigating him, he's going to be on his guard against anything out of the ordinary. How are we going to get him to talk—to anyone, let alone to us?"

"We'll get there." His tone was encouraging, but his face looked tired. "This is how we make our plan—we cut down all the variables until there's only one option left."

Leah's head swam and her thoughts felt clouded. "I just don't think we'll be able to pull this off unless he's confident that he's already won."

Agent McDowell nodded, watching her thoughtfully. "So how do we convince him of that?"

"We give him someone to conquer." Her teeth chattered, and she clamped her jaw shut to stop them.

He took a long sip of his coffee and ran a hand through his hair again. He said nothing, but looked at Leah with a gentleness that surprised her.

She waited for him to speak up, and when he didn't, she continued. "It's going to have to be me. We both know that. We can stop dancing around it."

She saw the disappointed resignation on his face, the slump of his shoulders. "I know. I was hoping to find another way, but I can't see one."

"It was always going to be me. That's... that's why I ran away. There was never going to be any other option."

"I'm sorry, Leah." His green eyes were heavy.

"Don't be," she responded, her resolve growing. "Even before this stuff with Matthew, I knew it was going to come to this. It is what it is. Let's just figure something out—we're running out of time."

He nodded, his lips pursed tightly. "So we start from the end and work backwards."

Leah hesitated a moment before blurting out the thought she'd been holding back. "I think we're going to have to get Jude involved." She glanced down at her half-empty coffee, swirling the ice around in the cup.

"Pierucci's son?" He scoffed. "To what end? He's the carbon copy of his father. There's no way he'd help us."

"That's... not exactly what I mean." She saw the question in his face and looked away, studying the pattern on the carpet. "Jude and I were engaged, back when... it all happened."

Those bright green eyes grew to the size of dinner plates. "No one mentioned this to me before."

Leah winced. "Natalie probably didn't want to bring it up. It's... a sensitive subject. But he and I met when we were kids... we have a lot of history."

McDowell raised his eyebrows. "That feels like an understatement."

"Yeah," Leah responded "I... it's complicated. We never actually broke up. His father suppressed my memories—at Jude's suggestion, I might add, although I had been trying to plant the idea in his head for a couple days before, I think Natalie told you that—but anyway, when it happened, there wasn't any time to talk about it or anything. It was straight from the interrogation in Pierucci's office down to the console room."

Agent McDowell's face had changed. His initial shock had been replaced by genuine remorse. "Leah, I am so sorry."

She smiled sadly and shrugged. "It was a long time coming. I doubt that I would have gone through with the wedding. But even so, there's been some grieving recently."

"Of course." He hesitated. "Why... I guess, why do you bring Jude up now?"

"I'm not sure that I could convince him to tell me anything behind his father's back. She gave a sad half-laugh and smiled. "But if there's anybody who can throw Dr. Pierucci off his game, it's Jude. It might seem like he's just a carbon copy, but they honestly could not be any less alike."

Her eyes glazed over and her vision blurred. A dozen tiny memories of Jude pushing his father's buttons floated past her mind's eye.

"*Spooky.*"

They sat in companionable silence for a few minutes, each deep in thought. The sounds of traffic from the highway were interrupted occasionally by the clatter of ice down the hall or padded footfalls as Agent McDowell stood up and paced the room.

Half a plan began to form in Leah's mind. She didn't like it, necessarily, but she didn't hate it. She turned it around in her mind, trying to see it from every angle, to anticipate every contingency, but there were too many variables.

Maybe he'll be able to fill in the gaps.

"Agent McDowell?" He turned to face her. "I have a crazy idea. It's a long game, and it's not safe, but I think it could work."

He sat down next to her on the couch, his eyes bright. "Hit me with it."

Chapter 28

An hour later, Leah found herself seated in the passenger seat of Agent McDowell's rental car, her hands folded in her lap as they turned out of the hotel parking lot. Erratic thoughts flew through her mind rapid fire as she struggled to process the enormity of what was happening.

Are we really going to do this? Are we really going to take him down? Is it possible that this will actually work?

She looked over at Agent McDowell again, watching as he glanced down at the directions on his phone and then back up at the road. He must have felt her eyes on him, because he turned toward her expectantly.

"What's up?"

She shook her head, still lost in thought.

He looked away before speaking again. "I was sorry to hear about your job."

Leah blinked heavily. His words felt like gibberish in her ears. "What was that?"

He glanced over at her again. "I said, I'm sorry to hear about your job."

"Oh, that. Yeah. I mean..." She trailed off. "I honestly haven't even had that much time to process it. I was kind of beat up about it yesterday, but it's not like I really enjoyed it. I'm sure I'll find something else."

"If there's anything I can do to help, please let me know. A reference or a letter of recommendation or..." He trailed off, his eyes darting back and forth between cars as he changed lanes.

"Thanks. I appreciate it." Leah's gaze drifted back to her window as her thoughts began to wander again. She scanned billboards as they flew past her. Injury lawyers. Dating sites. Restaurants.

There's just no way that we've thought of everything. What are we missing? What didn't we plan for?

She didn't notice the rest of the drive, and when Agent McDowell pulled the car into a spot and shifted into park, she shook her head and looked around as if she were waking from a dream.

There were only a few other patrons at the thrift store at midday on a Thursday, and no one greeted them as they walked in. Leah wandered up and down the rows for a few minutes, flicking through racks absentmindedly.

"Agent McDowell," she began.

"Robert's fine in public." He spoke quickly and quietly. "No need to attract any extra attention."

"Oh, yeah." Leah looked up from the shirt she'd been examining. "That makes sense. So, Robert." His name felt foreign in her mouth. "Remind me what we're here for?"

He nodded. "Distraction attire. We talked about a couple different characters you could play, but you seemed drawn to the crazy cat lady stereotype." He cracked a grin.

Leah smiled. "That's right. Let's go see what they've got by way of sweaters. I know it's August, but maybe they'll have a few in stock."

It didn't take long for them to find the women's winter attire. There were only a few options, and most of them were very tame. As she flipped past one solid color sweater after another, Leah began to despair. And then she saw it. Agent McDowell's poorly stifled laugh beside her confirmed her intuition.

She pulled it off the rack and held it up to her chest. The body of the sweater was knit in a chunky white yarn with slouchy patchwork sleeves in bold colors and funky patterns. They should have been the focal point of the sweater, but neither Leah nor Agent McDowell could tear their eyes away from the scene embroidered on the front, where two cats frolicked with a ball of yarn between them. It was clearly not original to the sweater, and it looked like it had been added by someone who was still learning the craft. Eerie beaded eyes glistened on each cat, and beaded snowflakes fell around them.

Leah ran her hand over the red yarn that danced between the kittens. "It's perfect."

"That," Agent McDowell said, awestruck, "is the single most magnificent article of clothing that I have ever had the misfortune to behold."

Leah cackled. "It's going to be way too big on me, but that's so okay. We will not find anything better than this. No one at the station will be able to tear their eyes away from this beauty."

He didn't respond, and when Leah looked over at him, he wore a pensive expression.

"Everything okay?" She hesitated.

"Oh, yeah," he responded quickly. "All good."

"Anything you need while we're here?"

He glanced over at her. "Okay, actually. Now that you mention it, I should grab a Hawaiian shirt. I know that sounds so dumb, but I bet you've got better options down here than we do up in DC. Some of my buddies at work have this thing with Hawaiian shirts on casual Fridays, but I haven't been able to find one I liked."

"Lead the way," she said with a snicker.

There were an overwhelming number of short-sleeved floral button-downs, and Robert and Leah paced up and down two full aisles before he threw up his hands. "This is too many choices. I'm just going to pick one and call it good." Eyes closed, he reached out and grabbed a blue one with red hibiscus flowers all over.

"I love it," he said without looking at it.

Leah laughed. "It's a Hawaiian shirt, alright."

"Exactly. I'm going to go try it on real fast. No use getting something that doesn't fit." He started walking toward the back wall of the store and, unsure what else to do, Leah followed.

A few minutes later, he stepped out of the dressing room and looked down at his shirt with a goofy grin. "What do you think?"

Leah shrugged, "I mean, if you're going for tacky Hawaiian shirt, it definitely hits the mark."

"Perfect." He adjusted the collar of the shirt, and Leah noticed the long scar running up his right arm.

"Went mountain climbing up in Colorado last week, got this gnarly scratch on my arm."

As he closed the door behind him, Leah spoke up. "Your arm looks like it's healed up nicely."

"What?" he said, his voice muffled. "Oh, yeah. It's doing great. Thankfully."

"Glad to hear it."

There was silence for a few moments until he stepped back out, suit and glasses on, floral shirt in hand.

"Was there anything else you wanted to look for?" he asked, glancing around the rest of the store.

Leah pursed her lips and hesitated. "Maybe we could just do a quick walk through and see if anything jumps out. I feel like some really thick glasses or something would add to the effect."

Robert laughed, a warm hearty laugh.

As they turned and walked toward the jewelry and accessories, Leah screwed up her courage. "So Robert, I have to ask. How much of Wilder's whole personality is just an act?"

His face changed, and Leah wished she'd kept quiet.

"I'm sorry," she backtracked. "I wasn't trying to... I don't know, be weird about it."

He smiled sadly at her. "No, no, it's not that. I..." He sighed. "What you said at the Baileys' house a few weeks ago about feeling manipulated... and then I tried to smooth things over at the clinic and definitely made it worse. I've been trying to find an angle that doesn't make me look like the bad guy, and I keep coming up empty."

"Robert, you're not the bad guy for doing your job." Leah didn't meet his eyes, staring instead at a wall of gaudy costume jewelry. "You're just good at your job, that's all."

"Maybe." His voice was quiet. "But I can't stand the thought that you got caught in the crossfire."

She wanted to respond, but couldn't find the words.

"But to answer your question," he continued a moment later. "Wilder is the alias I use most often, by a long shot. He's someone I can slip into easily if the need arises, and so as I've come to flesh him out over the years, he's become a lot like me. Sometimes too much, probably. I should be more careful."

339

"Fair enough." Her voice sounded colder than she meant it, and she looked over at him, feeling a need to gauge his reaction.

He grinned. "It's actually really funny—you remember when you said that an epilepsy diagnosis seemed too tame?"

She blushed and nodded.

I wish I never had to think of that night again.

"So, when I was planning out my first visit to the Institute, my supervisor and I were talking through possible diagnoses to include on my patient inquiry form. My immediate instinct was to go with something big and bold and intriguing—Dr. Pierucci has a reputation in the online forums of only giving interesting patients the time of day, and I wanted to make sure that I'd fit that bill—I think I proposed paranoid schizophrenia, but I can't remember. Anyway, Steve sat me down and gave me a talking-to about keeping a low profile, said he could pull some strings if he needed to, and we ended up settling on adult-onset epilepsy and everything worked out in the end. But I didn't even remember that conversation with Steve until after I'd left the Baileys' place, and I could not stop laughing about it." He chuckled a little as he talked, glancing between Leah and the rack of costume jewelry.

"That's really funny." Leah spun the display of reading glasses, looking for the thickest pair they had. "I stand by my statement that Wilder deserves a more fitting diagnosis, but I guess I understand the reasoning."

"It was kind of a surreal moment, honestly," Robert added quietly. "Like you somehow knew him better than I do. Or at least as well as I do."

In spite of herself, Leah smiled. She pulled a pair of thick-framed purple glasses off the rack and perched them precariously on the bridge of her nose. Everything became blurry smears of color.

He laughed again, and she joined in.

"Can you see anything out of those?"

She snorted. "Absolutely nothing. It's all fuzzy. I don't think I can make these work—I won't be able to see where I'm going at all." She pulled the glasses off and blinked as the world came back into focus. "What a shame."

Before she could hang them back in their place, Robert reached out and took them from her, replacing his own glasses. He bit his bottom lip and snickered.

She opened her mouth in shock. "Don't tell me you can actually see through them!"

"This can't be much weaker of a prescription than mine. It's a little blurry, but not that much."

"Is your eyesight really that bad?" Leah raised her eyebrows, her mouth agape.

"Oh, yeah. I think I got glasses when I was six years old, maybe younger. When you showed up this morning and I couldn't find them?" He slipped the purple glasses back onto the rotating display and put his own back on. "That was no joke. I had to get like six inches from the door to even find the handle."

Another question occurred to Leah, and she spoke before she could talk herself out of it. "So what's the deal with Wilder and the contact lenses, then?" They turned to walk toward the cashier, but at the last second, Leah grabbed the purple glasses and held them tightly. "I'll just take the lenses out and wear the empty frames," she explained when Robert raised an eyebrow. "The whole point of the distraction is that I'm crazy. It'll be fine. I can't pass them up. They're just too perfect."

"Fair enough," he nodded. "And I actually prefer contact lenses, but at some point in college, I realized that people take me a lot more seriously with the glasses, so that's what I wear for work. I don't need people taking Wilder too seriously—he doesn't take himself all that seriously—so I take advantage of the opportunity to ditch the glasses when I can. Plus, contacts are safer in the field."

"Yeah, you definitely look more professional with the glasses. It kind of threw me off when I first found you on LinkedIn a few months back."

He looked over at her as they paid for their things and walked back out to the car. "LinkedIn?"

Leah grinned sheepishly. "Oh, yeah, did I not tell you about that? Whenever you called and asked me to coffee, I looked you up. I didn't think about it after you visited my office because I was pretty convinced that you were just a hallucination. But when you called, I thought maybe it was just Wilder playing some bizarre practical joke."

Or asking me out on a date.

She pushed the thought away as she opened the door of the sedan. "But anyway, I couldn't find a social media profile for Wilder anywhere, but I found yours quickly. I think my running theory was that you were twins, but maybe twins separated at birth? Because you had different last names? It was a stretch."

"Twins separated at birth is a new one for me," Robert laughed and sat down behind the wheel. "I gotta say, I like it." He looked over at her. "So, the glasses threw you off, then. Good or bad threw you off?"

She opened her mouth to protest but found herself laughing instead. "I mean, I met you without glasses, so I feel like I'm partial."

He grinned. "Good to know."

As they drove back to the hotel, Leah began to notice a few familiar landmarks. Her face settled into a serious expression, and she grew quiet. Curious, she picked up Robert's phone and checked something on the city map.

"What is it?" he asked. "Everything okay?"

"Yeah, I..." Leah raised her hand to her face, rubbing her cheeks slowly. "I thought this place looked familiar. My dad is buried not too far from here. I haven't been since before everything happened last year."

Robert pulled the car to a stop at a red light and looked over at her, his eyes heavy. "I'm so sorry, Leah. I had no idea." He glanced at the clock on his dashboard and then back at her. "Do you want to stop by while we're in the area? We've got time before we really need to start moving."

A lump formed in Leah's throat and she ran a hand through her hair. "Could we?"

"Absolutely. Pull the directions up?"

Wordlessly, Leah did so, situating the phone back in the center console. The area became increasingly familiar. A weight grew in Leah's chest, and her hands fidgeted with her phone in her lap. As they pulled into the gate of the cemetery, Leah pointed down a left-hand path, directing Robert to the plot where her father's body lay. When they arrived, he slowed to a stop and shifted the car into park.

Leah climbed out, noticing with gratitude that Robert remained in the car. She walked to the headstone with measured steps. The little wrought iron bench was still there, and the tree behind him had grown since the last time she'd come for a visit.

Someone had left her dad fresh flowers. At the sight of them, Leah could no longer hold back the tears.

"Hi Dad." She heard her voice wavering. "I'm sorry it's been so long. I didn't mean to... well, anyway. I'm here now. Jude and I broke up last year, and things have been chaotic since then. I wish you were here."

Leah tore her eyes away from the headstone and glanced around her. The place felt foreign, somehow, and intimately familiar at the same time. The names she could read from her seat were etched into her memory. A sparrow hopped around in the grass, pecking for seeds or worms, and a squirrel prowled off to her right.

"I can't stay too long. Robert and I still have a lot of work to do before this evening, but I'm so glad I was able to come and say hi." She took a deep breath. "I think you'd like Robert, Dad. I think you two would get along."

Wiping her eyes with the hem of her shirt, Leah stood up and kissed her hand, placing it gently on the headstone. She paused for a moment at the stone next to his, where the birth and death dates were just five years apart.

Taking another deep breath, she turned and walked slowly back to the car. Robert said nothing as she slipped inside. For a long moment, they sat side by side in silence.

"This is a beautiful cemetery," he offered finally.

Leah nodded. "It is. It's a historic landmark, too, which Dad would have loved. He was big on that stuff. History, archaeology, genealogy, all of it..."

Robert's voice was soft. "When did he die?"

"My senior year of high school. Cancer. It was the second time he'd had it, and it spread too quickly to do anything about it." She looked out her window for a long moment. "You know, I'm not sure I've been here since Jude and I got engaged."

"Oh yeah?"

When she responded, her voice was quiet. "A few days before he proposed, I came for a visit and found him here by himself. He'd never done that before, and he kind of dodged my questions about it. But later he told me that he'd already talked to my mom, but couldn't bring himself to pop the question without talking to my dad, too."

Robert looked over at her, his green eyes soft, the smallest frown on his face. "That's sweet."

Leah nodded. "Kind of weird, but sweet."

"No, I mean, I get it. Really." He shrugged. "As a man, there's something about talking to her father that feels like an important milestone."

A knot grew in the pit of Leah's stomach as a new fear occurred to her. She forced her voice to remain calm and tried to toss out her question casually. "Are you... I mean, have you ever..."

Robert looked over at her with a smile, and she felt her face flush a deep red. He didn't say anything, didn't rescue her by anticipating her question.

"Are you speaking from experience, or just in theory?" she finally managed to stammer out.

He made no effort to stifle his grin, and something in Leah squirmed. "No, I've never had that conversation. I've never gotten that far." He sombered. "Thought about it once, but we parted ways instead. She wasn't ready to marry someone with a dangerous job. Her words."

A weight lifted off Leah's chest. "I'm sorry."

"I'm not," he said, turning back to the steering wheel and shifting the car into gear. "I love my job, and I'm good at it. I wasn't ready to give it up for her."

"Fair enough," Leah responded. "I'm glad you were able to figure that out before things got more serious."

"Yeah." He nodded, turning the car around and taking the road they'd used on the way in. "Me too."

As they pulled out of the gates and back onto the street, Robert pushed a button on the steering wheel, and the screen in the center of the car blinked to life. "Call Peter Bennet," he said slowly.

The line began to ring, and Peter picked up quickly.

"Roberto, my man. What's up?" His tone was casual, and Leah's chest ached at the memory of their most recent interactions.

"Hey Pete. Need to ask a favor."

Roberto? Pete? How close are they?

"Anything. Name it."

Robert glanced over at Leah, who nodded but remained silent. "Can you grab me a sheet of the Institute's letterhead and bring it by the hotel when you get off work? I need it for a thing."

Peter paused. "Sure? Is this... is everything okay?"

"Everything's great. I'll explain more when I see you."

"If you say so, man." He didn't sound convinced. "See you this evening."

Robert moved to end the call, but before he did so, Leah jumped in. "Peter, grab a couple sheets. Just in case."

Peter's tone betrayed his confusion. "Is that who I think it is? Is she... Are y'all...?"

Leah blushed.

"Yeah, man, it's been a busy couple days. Like I said, I'll fill you in later. Don't want to risk too long of a call, and I know you're limited on what you can say at work."

"Okay. I want the whole story when I see you."

"Absolutely. But I'll let you go. See you later."

"Later, Roberto."

The call ended.

"Roberto?" Leah asked with a laugh.

"It just kind of happened." He shrugged. "We hit it off pretty quickly. He keeps trying to convince me to go on a backpacking trip with him once the weather cools off."

"Oh, yeah, he's intense. I think he uses all his vacation days every year for to go kayak some river out in west Texas." Leah laughed. "I've always been more of a tent camper than a backpacker, but I haven't gone in ages."

"Why's that?"

Leah frowned. "Jude isn't much of a camper. My dad used to take us all the time growing up, and I went in college a couple of times, but once Jude and I finally started dating, I wasn't able to make much time for it."

"That's a real shame." He hesitated. "I know there are sacrifices in every relationship, but I always hate to hear of someone giving up old hobbies."

"I guess you're right," Leah nodded. "I hardly even noticed it at the time, but I do miss it looking back."

Robert flipped on his blinker and turned onto the street where his hotel was located. He hesitated before speaking up again. "I hate to pry, but I'm intrigued. You said that you and Jude finally started dating. Finally just seems like an odd choice of words."

Leah barked a harsh laugh.

He looked over at her, brows knit, curiosity on his face.

"We met when we were kids," Leah explained. "Went on a couple of dates in high school, and then my dad's cancer came back, and Jude didn't want to force anything while I was grieving. We lost touch for a few years in college and reconnected when I was applying for a job at the Institute. I think I'd been working there for close to a year

347

when he finally decided to ask me out again." She smiled, lost in thought. "Back then, it felt like I'd been waiting for him to do it for forever."

Robert huffed. "How long were you two together?"

"Oh gosh," Leah said, looking up at the ceiling as she wracked her brain. "Probably something like three years." She gave a wry chuckle. "Him proposing was also something I felt like I waited a long time for."

She would have sworn that Robert snorted as he turned into the hotel, but his expression remained neutral.

"But obviously things worked out for the best," she added. "Like I said earlier, we wouldn't have made it to the wedding even if it hadn't been for all this."

"I'm not going to say you dodged a bullet," Robert responded. "But..." He shrugged, a grimace on his face.

Leah pointed out her car, and he parked next to it. "Did you leave anything in my room?"

She shook her head.

"Great, well then I'll let you go so you can get to work on that letter of introduction from Dr. P, just in case we need it at the precinct tonight. You can just email me the file when you're done, and I'll get it printed up once Peter brings me the paper. If you need a higher quality scanner, I can probably find one for you."

"No, mine at home is pretty good. Should be enough for this project, at least."

"Then I'll see you at seven o'clock at the precinct. We'll get through tonight, and assuming everything goes according to plan, we can talk tomorrow about next steps. I know you've got a pretty clear idea of what all needs to happen, but it'll be good for me to make sure I can have my team in the right place over the next week or so."

"Of course." Leah opened the door and stepped one foot outside. The humidity hit her like a wall.

"Oh, and one more thing." Robert stopped her, reaching into his pocket. "This is an earpiece. It's already synced to mine. You'll be able to hear what's going on around me so you can come in at the right time. Leave it in the car when you go inside—we don't need to make anyone suspicious—and I'll give it back to you before Saturday."

She took the small plastic box and slipped it into her backpack. "Thanks Agent McDowell. I'll see you tonight."

Her drive home was uneventful, but Leah opened her front door with her head swimming. It felt like an age had passed since she'd left that morning, but it was barely four o'clock, and she still had hours left before her day would be over. Thoughts racing, she filled her electric kettle and picked out a teabag without even reading the label. Then she walked to her desk and pulled out the manila envelope she'd retrieved from her lockbox. Nestled in the middle of the papers was a stack of handwritten letters and cards that she hadn't wanted to see destroyed in the aftermath of her meeting with Dr. Pierucci. She'd rifled through them, scanning each page and setting them aside.

This, at least, I know I can do.

Chapter 29

The sun drifted toward the horizon, casting long, spindly shadows down the street. Leah rubbed her eyes. She took a swig of her canned coffee, smacking at the chemical taste before placing the can back into her car's cup holder. It was all the thrift store had carried, but she began to wish that she hadn't purchased it.

Agent McDowell's blue sedan rolled past her, turning into the police station about a block ahead of her. She fiddled with the earpiece he'd given her, still unused to the feeling of it in her ear.

He stepped out of the car, and she watched as he approached the door of the precinct with a swagger that seemed exaggerated, even for him.

"Testing, testing," she heard in her earpiece. The sound was grainy but audible.

"Testing, testing," she responded.

"I see you're in position," he said. "I'm going in."

She watched from her car as his back disappeared into the building, wishing she could see what was going on. Her sweater was itchy—not to mention hot in mid-August—and the hand-embroidered, beaded scene covering the front was uncomfortable. Even with nothing but a cami underneath the sweater and the air conditioning in the car blowing at full blast, she was drenched in sweat. She pushed the thick purple frames up the bridge of her nose and ran a hand through her hair. Her fingers got stuck in a tangle, and she groaned loudly.

"You should wear rollers in it," Robert had said earlier that day, trying to hold back a grin. "Just for the full effect."

She'd refused, opting instead for a teased-out frizzy look, tied back in a messy bun.

I wish I'd thought to get a pair of costume earrings at the thrift store. Would have really completed the look.

Her thoughts were interrupted by an unfamiliar, muffled voice over her earpiece. "Hello, sir, how can I help you today?"

She fiddled with the beads on her sweater as Robert responded. "Hi, I'm looking for a man who was brought in on Tuesday morning, a Matthew Bailey?"

"Oh, uh, he's not available right now. Can I take a message?" The audio wasn't clear enough to pick up on nuances of tone. One of the beads fell off into her hand.

"Oh, he's available." Robert said, dropping his voice to a whisper. Leah could imagine him leaning in with an insufferable self-importance. "I'm his ride to Scarlett Bay."

She rolled her eyes.

"Is that supposed to mean something to me?" She didn't need to hear the other man's tone to know that he was unimpressed.

For a moment, no one spoke. Leah wished that she'd been able to convince Robert to use the camera glasses so she could see what he was seeing. He'd thought it too risky of a move, and it was agonizing to have nothing but audio.

There was a crinkle of paper and a whispered, "Oh."

Robert cleared his throat. "That's right."

"Very well, then. I'll take you back there, sir."

It worked.

The success brought little comfort.

So Pierucci really is behind all this. I hope we're ready.

Robert had brought in his FBI badge and the letter that Leah had put together from the samples of Dr. Pierucci's handwriting she had at home. With some effort, she'd been able to craft a convincing memo introducing Agent Frederick to 'his' cops and informing them that Frederick was operating under his direct orders.

"Thank you, mister...?" Leah prompted aloud, hoping that Robert would hear her implied request for the cop's name. She held her breath Robert repeated the phrase.

"Inglish," the other man replied. "Detective Austin Inglish. I'm not head detective yet, but I will be one day."

"Love the confidence, Detective. Special Agent Wilder Frederick, FBI. Pleasure to make your acquaintance."

I don't know why he insisted on using Wilder's name for this. Feels like a moot point.

"F-B-freakin'-I, man," Detective Inglish mused. "Must be nice."

"Better than you can imagine." A beat passed before Robert spoke again, his tone hushed and confidential. "Hey, man, are there cameras in these interrogation rooms? This Bailey fellow might need some, ah, encouragement, you know, to come along quietly, and I guess I just don't want to get you good folks in trouble."

"You know, now that you mention it, I think the camera in that room is broken. Has been for a while now, but no one has gotten around to replacing it. Shucks." The officer's voice oozed a confident sarcasm that was obvious even with the poor audio quality. Leah wanted to vomit.

Mathew had sworn up and down that some of the local police were in Pierucci's pocket, but she had found it difficult to believe.

No longer.

"Man," Inglish continued. "You must be real high up in his good graces. He never lets me do the fun stuff."

Robert chuckled. "Oh yeah. I get called in for all the tough cases."

The note of machismo and even cruelty in his voice as he bantered with the cop churned Leah's stomach. It was disarming to witness the ease with which he mirrored the other man's mannerisms, molding himself to become exactly the type of person to earn his trust.

This is all part of the plan.

She didn't allow herself to wonder whether Wilder's personality had been carefully calculated to charm her into cooperation.

The sound of footsteps in her earpiece ended abruptly.

"Well, here he is, Frederick. Hasn't said a single word since he arrived, other than to demand a lawyer and to call his wife. Course, once you get him over to Scarlett Bay, it won't matter whether or not he's talking, but he don't know that yet. Best of luck in there."

"Thanks, man. Appreciate your help. Go get yourself a cuppa. On me." The rustle of paper indicated a bill changing hands. Just a last little something to leave Inglish with a favorable impression.

"Oh, and one more thing," Inglish added. "There's a door marked 'Emergency Exit' just down the hall here, but the alarm needs repair. Every time we've asked maintenance to take care of it, they've ignored us. This hallway is only really busy when the administrative staff are here, and seeing as it's almost twenty-one-hundred hours, well..." There was silence. "But rest assured, sir, we'll make sure maintenance takes a look at it as soon as possible."

"Good man."

Footsteps pattered away, and Leah heard a door creak open. She pictured Matthew sitting alone, staring at his reflection in the obvious two-way mirror, lips sealed resolutely.

I wonder if he'll recognize Robert.

The door slammed in her ear, and she yelped.

"So, buddy." She could feel the spray of spit that must have accompanied the words. "I hear you're not cooperating with the locals. Special Agent Wilder Frederick, FBI. You'd better get talking because I do not have time for games today."

"Ro—" Matthew's voice was little more than a hoarse whisper. Robert hissed, and Matthew changed course. "I've already told the police that I won't be speaking until I can consult my lawyer." He sounded tired.

I hope they've let him sleep.

Robert's voice dropped to a whisper. "We're going to get you out of here." When he spoke again, the bravado had returned. "Things will go much more smoothly for you if you just cooperate, Mr. Bailey."

Matthew remained silent. Robert remained silent. Leah became suddenly aware of her heart pounding in her chest. She began to worry that the battery on her earpiece had died, so she fiddled it out and tapped on it.

"Leah," a sharp whisper emanated from the earpiece and she quickly shoved it back in. "You're going to give me hearing loss."

"Sorry," she mumbled back.

Robert was back in character. She winced as he slammed his hand on the table, his voice raised in feigned irritation.

Poor Matthew.

And, as if in the same breath, another thought.

I'm glad I'm not there to see this.

She forced herself to remember Robert's words from their conversation earlier in the day. "Leah, are you sure you want ears on this? It's going to be worse to only hear and not see—your imagination tends to run away with you. It's going to sound bad, but I wouldn't put myself in this situation if I thought I would have to actually hurt him."

She silently formed the words without speaking, scared of throwing Robert off his game. Over and over again: "I wouldn't put myself in this situation if I thought I would have to actually hurt him."

Focus on that, Leah. Don't let yourself get sucked into the sounds. Focus on the fact that you trust him to take good care of Matthew, no matter what it takes.

Leah heard the sound of handcuffs clicking into place. That was her cue.

She scrubbed her cheeks for a moment, glancing into the rear view mirror to ensure they were sufficiently reddened. Then she dropped some eye drops in, blinked the tears out, and ran all the way from her car to the door of the precinct, sobbing. The lights along the walkway were just starting to flicker on.

"My cat!" She burst through the doors screaming. "My cat! Can someone please help me with my cat?"

"How can I help you, miss?" The man who approached her wore a name badge reading 'Inglish'.

You no good, horrib—

Focus.

Leah sucked in a deep breath and let out her most hysterical wail. "My cat is stuck in a tree and has been trying to get down for hours, and she just can't figure out a way down! And she's all I have left of my sister, and I just need someone to get her out of that tree—I've always known it was a safety hazard for her ever since my sister broke her leg falling out of that same tree, but Mother wouldn't let me cut it down! And now sweet Cleopatra is stuck, and if you don't come help me she's going to die up there, and I don't know what I'm going to do! It's just too much to bear!" She finished with another sob, wiping tears from her cheeks as she gave her best pathetic sniffle.

Detective Inglish rolled his eyes. "Ma'am, this is a police station. I'm not sure we're the best people for the job. Can I get you a glass of water while you calm down, and then we can figure out who to call about your cat?"

Calm down! Is that all you have to say? Calm down?

Rage began to build in her chest.

Focus, Leah. Three more minutes. That's all they need.

She whimpered, forcing a tremble into her voice. "What do you mean you can't help me? To serve and protect, isn't that what you vowed to do? You can't take a vow and then just break it willy-nilly when there's a sweet, precious Sphinx cat who's about to get eaten alive by a pack of red-shouldered hawks! She's all I have!"

Inglish rubbed his face, exhaling heavily and making pointed eye contact with a colleague standing nearby. "Ma'am, that line isn't actually in our—"

"Don't give me that! I see that look in your eye! You think that my precious Cleopatra is too ugly to be saved! You don't want to help her because you don't believe that she deserves to live! Mother told me I should go to the fire department instead, but I didn't listen!"

The detective opened his mouth, his face reddening. However, mid-wail, Leah felt her phone buzz in her pocket. Without giving him time to respond, she pulled it out and saw the word 'Mother' scrolling across the screen. "Please hold on," she said frantically, holding up a finger and looking down to her phone. "I need to answer this. Hello? Mother?"

Robert's voice answered her, all business. "Take two more minutes and then meet us around the corner."

Leah replied in a pitch that bordered on falsetto. "Oh, are you serious? She's climbed down on her own? Oh, Mother! I knew she could do it if we just stopped fussing over her! You know how you can be sometimes. Always so dramatic! How is my precious baby?"

"Not great. Hurry, please. We need to get him home."

She wasn't actually expecting an update on Matthew, and it took every ounce of self-control not to break character.

She doubled down on her falsetto and continued. "Oh, me? Well, I'm just over at the police station asking for assistance, but if she's been such a clever kitty and gotten down on her own, I'll be right home to give her some kisses and a tuna fish sandwich!" She held the phone out in front of her and made smoochy noises as loudly as she could before putting the phone back to her ear.

She heard the call end, layering on a few more gushy admirations before faking a goodbye.

Fighting back genuine tears and swallowing down a lump in her throat, Leah turned back to Detective Inglish, whose face was red. "My sweet Cleo has solved the problem all by herself, and she says that she wouldn't want a no-good smelly cop like you touching her anyway. You're lucky I'm not filing your name in the Sphinx Cat Discrimination Index. Good day!"

She whirled around on her heel and found herself wishing she'd worn a skirt or a long coat just for the dramatic twirl. Her footsteps pounded on the marble floor as she marched herself out the door of the precinct, keenly aware of all the stares following her. She ignored them and kept on marching down the sidewalk and around the corner. Her heart pounded, and she drew each breath like she'd just finished a sprint. Only when she was out of sight of the building did she pull off her thick purple glasses, untie the messy bun in her hair, and pull the embroidered sweater over her head.

"Good riddance," she said as she stuffed it all in a trash bin. She caught the smell of her own sweat, pungent after she'd been trapped in winter attire for an hour, and looked down at her cami.

I wish I'd thought to bring an extra t-shirt.

Ducking into a bookstore, Leah navigated around the stacks and let herself out a back exit. There, waiting in the parking lot, was Robert's sedan. He and Matthew were standing outside, chatting quietly over paper cups of coffee. Matthew's eyes were dark with purple bags, and his shoulders slumped forward. When she exited the building, they both looked up, and she made beeline to Matthew, wrapping him in a hug.

"Thank God you're okay," she exhaled, tears streaming down her face. "I would never have been able to forgive myself if something had happened to you." He gave the faintest hint of a smile as she helped him into the backseat of the car. He noticed the pillow they'd left for him and gratefully laid down.

Robert handed Leah the keys to his car, and she tossed him her keys in return. "You saw where I parked?"

"I did. I'll meet you at their house. I'll give Natalie a call on the way."

"Better you than me," Leah said ruefully as he walked away. She went to open the door, but Agent McDowell's voice stopped her.

"Hey." She turned around to face him. "You did good in there. I mean it."

A tension in her shoulders released. She hadn't even been aware of it. "Thanks, Robert."

"And hey," he added before she could turn away. He had an impish grin on his face, and she rolled her eyes in advance. "I left you an extra shirt on the passenger seat. Figured you'd get a little toasty in your crazy cat lady get-up—which, by the way, where is your magnificent sweater?"

"Get going, slowpoke," she teased back, watching him for a moment as he walked away.

Leah slipped on the navy blue shirt and inhaled deeply. It smelled like him. She tried not to think about it as she drove silently, obsessively observing the speed limit. Her fingers tapped out a broken rhythm on the steering wheel.

Bright stars twinkled in a cloudless sky. The tranquility that felt out of place after the florescent lights and burnt-coffee smell of the precinct. As per their plan, Leah and Robert took different routes to the Baileys' house, each roundabout in its own way, to throw off any possible tails.

"Matthew," Leah said quietly as they pulled into the neighborhood. "Are you awake?"

He made a small affirmative sound.

360

"We're going to tell Natalie this as well, but if you guys have anywhere you can disappear for a couple of days, maybe a week... I think that'd be prudent. Don't tell anyone where you're going—even me or Robert, if you can help it—and we'll let you know when it's safe to come home."

He grunted quietly. Her car was already parked outside when she pulled up, and she saw Natalie's frightened eyes peeking through the blinds.

Leah helped Matthew out of the car, allowing him to lean on her as they made their way up the walk. The second they crossed the threshold, Natalie gasped and embraced him. Robert and Leah watched as she helped him down the hall to their room.

When they were out of earshot, Leah whispered the question that had been haunting her since she'd laid eyes on Matthew. "He looks broken, Robert. What did they do to him in there?"

She was frightened by the haunted despair in Robert's eyes. "I don't know the full story. I'm hoping it's just sleep deprivation. But you're right. He didn't look well."

Leah nodded, picking at a flap of dry skin on her lip and studying Matthew's smiling face in the family portrait that hung in the entryway. "I'm glad we got him when we did. Scarlett Bay...well, I'm not sure he would have made it back in one piece, even if they didn't harm him physically. He's not in any shape to be going back there."

Robert didn't respond, but she felt his gaze on her. She turned toward him, but before he could say anything, Natalie stepped back into the entryway. Her eyes were heavy, her face tear stained.

"Thank you both," she said, her voice trembling. "You didn't have to do this, but we'll be forever grateful."

Leah opened her mouth to say something. The words didn't come. Instead, she leaned forward and wrapped Natalie in a hug. Natalie stiffened, and Leah loosened her arms, but before she could step away, she felt Natalie embrace her back.

"I'm so sorry for the last couple of days," Natalie whispered. Leah felt her shoulders heave. "I was so scared. But I clearly underestimated you."

"No, Nat, I'm sorry too," Leah responded, choking back tears again. "I'm the one who let you all down and got us into this situation in the first place."

They stepped back and exchanged a heavy glance. Unspoken words lifted a massive weight from Leah's chest. Natalie glanced at Robert, who had turned to admire the family portrait.

"How did you... I mean... did everything go... smoothly? Did you guys put yourself in harm's way for him?" Her voice was timid. "For us?"

Robert turned around, his green eyes soft and sad. "We did what we had to do. We've made our opening move, so there's no turning back. We're hoping this will all be wrapped up by the end of next week, but Natalie, I think it would be best if your family took some time away while we wait for this arrest to be made. Let Matt get some rest, but the minute he's feeling well enough to move, get out of town as fast as you can."

She nodded quickly, eyes wide, shoulders tense.

"We'll get out of your hair. We've got some work to do before this next stage of our plan unfolds." Robert reached out as if to shake Natalie's hand, but instead, he passed her a handful of bills. "For dinner tonight, and any expenses you have this week."

Natalie closed her eyes and exhaled heavily, as if she were about to cry again. She mouthed a silent 'thank you' as Leah squeezed her hand. Leah and Robert walked toward the street, switching car keys once again. A few steps before they reached the curb, he rushed ahead and opened her door. She thanked him as she slid into the driver's seat, ignoring the squirm in her stomach.

"Peter called me on the way here," McDowell offered, his hand still on the door. "He's going to take the day off tomorrow and try to lay low over the weekend. He refused to leave town, which..." He trailed off, rolling his eyes.

"Classic," Leah replied.

"Have you texted Jude yet?" His voice was barely above a whisper.

"I'm just about to," she replied. "Hardly had a free moment all afternoon."

"I know what you mean." He nodded and stifled a yawn. "Further up and further in. You're doing great."

She smiled, feeling the weight of exhaustion in the corners of her eyes. "I'll be glad when it's over."

"You and me both. See you tomorrow." He closed her door and made his way over to his own car. She watched him pull away before taking out her phone and typing in Jude's name.

> Hey, we need to talk. Saturday Morning Coffee at Common Grounds? For old times' sake?

When she finally pulled her own car out into the street and drove away from the Baileys' house, moments from the day played on repeat in her mind. The pit in her stomach when Robert had been playing the role of dirty cop. The way Matthew's eyes had brightened, just a little, when she'd stepped out of the bookstore. Robert's horror at the way Jude had treated her last year. Natalie's arms pulling her in for a hug. Robert's thoughtfulness in bringing an extra shirt, just in case she needed one.

Once home, she was asleep in minutes.

Chapter 30

When her alarm went off at six o'clock on Saturday morning, she felt a mixture of relief that the night was over and terror at the prospect of facing a new day. She dressed quietly, observing the way that the not-yet-risen sun slowly illuminated her room.

Further up and further in.

She locked the door of her apartment and glanced over at Sarah and Connor's door. A squirm of regret curled around her stomach—she hadn't told them anything of what was going on. She hadn't told her mom either.

I can talk to them afterwards, when this is all over. It'll be easier than trying to explain things while they're still happening.

She refused to dwell on the possibility that there wouldn't be an afterwards. Instead, she stepped into her car, turned the key in the ignition, and shifted into gear.

Here we go again.

Leah arrived at Common Grounds an hour early, hoping that the cozy atmosphere would help calm her nerves. Robert's earpiece was snug in her ear, and her hands naturally found her pockets as she walked across the green.

The line was long—par for the course on a weekend—and while she waited, Leah pulled up Jude's Facebook page. She had checked it several times since her memories had returned, and his name was still at the top of her recent search history.

Still blocked, I'm sure.

She looked around her as she waited for the page to load, and when she glanced back down at her phone, she was shocked to see his profile appear normally.

Is this a good sign or a bad one?

"Next customer! Oh, hey Leah. Long time no see. What can I do for you?" The barista smiled as her fingers tapped at the keys of her cash register.

"Hey Rocky, how's it going?" Leah responded "The pink hair is a bold choice."

"Isn't it fun?" Rocky laughed. "Gosh, I'm glad it's actually you! You wouldn't believe it–a few months ago, I had this customer who came in, and she looked exactly like you, and I tried to be clever and guess her order..." Rocky grimaced. "Poor thing, I think I scared her off. Haven't seen her around since."

Leah felt her eyes widen but said nothing, instead ordering her usual iced latte and an early-season pumpkin chocolate chip muffin. While she waited for her order to be ready, she staked her claim at the back corner table. The same table where she and Jude had sat, coffees in hand, every Saturday morning for two years. It had been his weekend ritual before they started dating, and she had joined in until it had become a cherished part of her own weekend plans as well.

So many memories in this place. I wonder if I'll ever be able to come here without thinking of him.

It was the same back table where she had sat on a hot July morning a year previously, uncertain why she had felt such urgency about showing up. She shuddered as she remembered the feeling of bugs on her skin and the pounding of her heart as she'd run away.

Her coffee and muffin arrived promptly, and she quickly lost herself in the pages of the novel she'd packed. Every so often, she looked up, rolled her neck and stretched her shoulders, and glanced around at the ever-shifting crowd. Some regulars, like herself, had unpacked at tables— a few chatting, a few working. Mothers broke off bites of breakfast to hand to their young children. Important-looking business men in crisp suits showed online order numbers to the baristas without interrupting their calls.

"Leah?"

Her heart skipped a beat.

Well, no turning back now...

"Hey Jude."

He wore a white button down and jeans, and she could tell he'd done his hair. "Holy cow, Leah. It's so good to see you." He sat down in the chair across from her.

She smiled, trying to ignore the flutter in her chest. "It's good to see you too, Jude."

His eyes were wide with shock and delight as he looked around the room. "I never in a million years thought that we would do this again. Gosh, it's been too long. I've missed you. How have you been?"

"Is that really the question you want to lead with?" She grinned, but she could feel the sadness in her own eyes. Jude's reaction made it obvious that he saw it too.

"You're right. Let's start over." He winked, stood up, turned a full circle, and sat back down. "Leah! It's so good to see you. I've really missed you this year. It seems like we have a lot to catch up on!"

A half-laugh escaped her as a weight sank onto her shoulders. "Hi Jude. Thanks for coming. It's really good to see you, too." She sighed deeply. "I just wanted to talk about us... about that day in your father's office. I want the truth. No more games–not between us."

Robert's voice crackled in her ear. "Laying it on a little thick there, aren't you?" She jumped at the sound. She'd forgotten he was there.

Does he think this is all a performance?

"No games. I want that too." There was a note of affection in Jude's voice. "Oh, I've missed you, Leah. I've missed you so much. I've envisioned this moment in my head so many times—if I got the chance to talk to you again, what would I say?"

Leah could feel her pulse racing, and her eyes gravitated toward her cup as she spoke. "We dated for a long time, Jude. We got engaged. We were planning a wedding. And then it was all gone... and it took a year for me to realize it, so I didn't even get the chance to grieve it and move on. I'm really trying to understand how you... I guess—we never got a chance to talk after everything that happened, and I just wanted—needed—to know what was going through your head during that whole conversation." Her words got away from her. She found herself wrestling down an unexpected lump in her throat.

Jude looked away, watching a pickup soccer game through one of the coffee shop's windows. "I guess we never did get a chance to sort things out, did we? It all happened so quickly, and then you were gone."

"Something like that." She pursed her lips.

"It's funny," he began, still gazing out the window. "Well, not funny. But you know what I mean. In my head, the break-up was a totally separate thing from the fight we had in Father's office."

Leah watched him carefully. His shoulders were relaxed, but his fingers were tapping away at his knee under the table. Typing something on an invisible keyboard–an old habit he'd developed in grade school that had never disappeared.

I wonder what word it is today.

He broke his muffin into careful pieces while he spoke. "I know they were all one and the same, in real life, but we were fighting so much already... After you and Father walked out, my first reaction was... relief." He looked up at her, his gray-blue eyes downcast. "That surprised me. And then after that, I just had this overwhelming sense of shame. I thought I should have been sad or angry or... well, anything, you know? Just not relieved."

I felt that relief as well, if we're being honest." She smiled sadly. "I think our breaking up was for the best."

Jude's face fell, and her instinct was to jump in and comfort him. She held back.

"It probably was for the best." He glanced back out the window behind her. "It probably was."

She looked at his face for a long moment. The stubble he hadn't shaved that morning. The way his hair swooped to one side. The faint scar through one eyebrow from when he'd fallen out of a tree as a kid. She noticed for the first time the lines between his brows. "That doesn't make it any easier, though."

He returned her gaze, just for a moment, before looking down at the floor. "Moving on was hard. It was the worst parts of a breakup and the worst parts of a death, you know? Normally, when you break up with someone, you at least get the comfort of telling yourself all the terrible things they did to you. And when someone dies, you can reassure yourself that they're in a better place. But I didn't really get either consolation—all I could think about in the aftermath was how good you'd been to me, and how much I'd ruined your life."

This is not how I expected this conversation to go.

He took a long sip of his coffee before continuing. "I sort of... envied you, you know? I would have given anything to be able to just forget you. To not have had to do any of the hard work of getting over you."

"I hate him," Robert growled in her ear.

I wish I could hate him. But I don't think I ever will.

"Do you thin—" She started.

But Jude wasn't finished speaking. "And, of course, Father didn't get it. At all. Our relationship really took a turn for the worse for a few months."

"What do you mean?" She tried to keep her voice gentle.

"Oh, I don't know," he said, shrugging. "It was subtle. He and I fought a lot more than we ever had before. I think I blamed him, and he blamed me, and we just got stuck in this endless circle."

A loud shout of 'surprise!' erupted at the other end of the coffee shop, and Leah glanced over to see a group of four or five middle-aged women with balloons. She watched them exchange hugs and sit down.

Jude's voice drew her attention back to their table. "But he came to regret it eventually. He really did like you, and he saw a lot of himself in you. I think that's what made your betrayal hurt so much. It didn't feel professional to him. It felt personal."

She swallowed hard and clenched her jaw.

"He let slip one day—maybe, oh, six or eight months after the fact, you know how he can be—that he recognized that he'd overreacted. That was a comfort. At first, I couldn't stop replaying it in my head, just trying to see if there was anything I could have done to get the two of you back on the same side. I was the one who suggested the suppression, as I'm sure you remember. And in the moment, it seemed better than, well, you know... That probably would have wrecked him once he'd calmed down. And, of course," he added, looking back at her. "I didn't want to lose you. I wouldn't have been able to live with myself."

He took a sip of his coffee before adding as an afterthought, "But I just couldn't shake the feeling that you hadn't totally understood the whole situation at the prison."

Leah's heart sank. She opened her mouth to say something, but Jude had already looked away again, and he didn't give her a chance to cut in.

"Especially after those first couple of weeks, once he'd shown me all the documents and taken me for a site visit, I just..." He sighed. "I couldn't help wondering if you'd gotten your facts and your crazy internet theories all mixed up. I mean, really, Leah-killing people just because they didn't act a certain way in the sim? Surely you know Father better than that." He shifted in his chair and looked back at her with a long, familiar gaze. "You and that genius brain of yours—gosh, Leah, you amaze me... but sometimes you're too smart for your own good. You don't always know when

371

to stop, and then those hyperfixations become obsessions, and it's really hard to talk you out of them."

She swallowed down the lump in her throat and blinked tears out of her eyes.

He groaned and rubbed his face with his hand. "Oh, I'm sorry, Leah. I'm not trying to bring up old fights. Forget I said anything. I just... I really wished that I had been able to help you and Father meet in the middle. But I tried and tried for months to think of something else I could have done—and I came up empty every time."

WHY AM I DISAPPOINTED BY THIS?

"But, hey." He lowered his head until his eyes were level with hers, drawing her gaze back toward him. "In some weird, twisted way, I guess it all worked out."

Leah took a deep breath, willing herself to speak calmly instead of giving free reign to the anger building in her chest and limbs. "Jude, you said that you envied me not having to do the work of dealing with the break-up. Do... do you think this has been easy for me?"

"Not this line again!" He groaned, rolling his eyes.

Surely, we can have one conversation that doesn't end in one of us storming off.

"No, Leah, I don't think any of this has been easy for you." His tone was exasperated, desperate. "You don't have to always see the worst in me."

"It was a genuine question, Jude!" She felt her temper rising. "I'm sorry if it came out defensive—I'm really trying to meet you halfway. You've told me a lot about the last year of your life, and I'd like to do the same."

He raised his eyebrows and his eyes lit up. "Yes! Yes, of course. Please do. I want to hear all about it. I want to hear all about how your memories came back, too."

A sickening feeling spread through Leah's body.

Do you? Or does he?

"It's been..." Leah started, her shoulders slumping and her heart sinking. "It's been really hard. I worked a boring marketing job. I struggled to make friends. Things got weird with my mom. I hallucinated my dad's voice a half a dozen times, and it tore that wound open again every time."

Jude's face fell, and he seemed to shrink in his chair.

"For the first six months, I had migraines so frequently that I got in the habit of checking the drive time to my apartment every hour, just in case. I got my driver's license revoked for a while because of all the seizures I was having, so I had to Uber everywhere." She glanced at the ceiling with an uncomfortable laugh. "Your father really was a lifeline for me. I know that was all part of y'all's plan, but... he was one of the few people I looked forward to seeing." Leah sighed. "One of the few people who didn't seem scared of me." The words had tumbled out of her mouth before she'd fully processed them... but they weren't untrue.

Jude's voice was quiet. "I know he always looked forward to seeing you, too. He never told me when you were coming in—I think he was worried that I'd say something dumb if I saw you—but I could always tell. There's a look in his eyes."

A smile played on her lips. "I know the look you mean. He and I really did get along so well, until..." She trailed off and fiddled with a loose thread on her skirt.

"Hey." Jude extended a hand across the table, palm up. A gesture of goodwill and affection. She rested her hand in his, painfully aware of her empty ring finger. He smiled at the colorful plastic beads encircling her wrist. "I know things are weird now. I don't know if Father ever really planned for this, and I'm not sure he knew what to say when y'all talked most recently. He and I stepped out of the room, and he just gave me this look, like 'did you see that?' Talking about that bracelet that Nat's kids must have given you. Neither of us even knew you'd reconnected with them, so it was just bizarre–it felt so out of place... and yet so natural, at the same time."

Leah nodded, bracing herself. "I know what that's like."

"How did you end up getting in touch with them, anyway?" He pulled his hand away from hers and leaned back in his chair, rubbing the back of his neck. She felt one of his feet tap one of hers.

"Steady, Harvey," Robert said in her ear. "Steady."

"Oh, you know, it's really funny you should ask," Leah responded, scratching an itch on her nose. "I ran into Nat here one day, actually. I, uh," she hesitated. "I hadn't been here in ages, but I saw her across the room and just really felt certain I knew her. So we struck up a conversation."

"Oh, by the way–am I mistaken, or did I see you at Common Grounds a few weeks ago? I would have sworn it was you, but an old coworker wanted to catch up, and by the time she'd walked away, you were gone."

"And I guess that's how..." Jude prompted slowly. "That's how everything started to come back? Getting to know the Baileys again?"

How much does he know?

"I guess so." Leah forced a chuckle. "It honestly is kind of hard to remember, ironically."

She cleared her throat, looking down at the quickly-melting ice in her glass.

"I hope Nat and Matthew are well?" Jude said, his words stilted.

374

Does he have any idea at all what his father did to Matthew two days ago?

Robert's words mirrored her thoughts. "Is he playing you, or is he just that clueless?"

"Well enough," Leah responded, unable to say more through the tightness in her chest.

Jude changed the subject abruptly. "But he wants to see you again. Father, I mean. I know he does. And not just professionally, but... the way things used to be."

Leah smiled and held her hand out across the table for him to take. "I'd like that, too."

Jude's eyebrows shot up, something like hope in his face. "Really?" He placed his hand in hers.

"Yeah," Leah said, blushing a little. She rubbed the side of his hand with her thumb. "That was a lot of why I reached out. I just wanted to see you. I just wanted to see your face and hear your voice and..."

Rein it in, Leah.

She blushed. "If I'm being totally honest, Jude, I wanted to ask you if you'd be willing to give it another shot." She looked down at their hands on the table. "Give me another shot."

"Leah, I—" His eyes were wide and one corner of his mouth was raised in a half-smile.

"I know it would be a ton of work," she interrupted. "And it might not go any better this time than it did last time. I know that. But we have a whole year of life experience since we were together. A whole year of knowing just how lonely it can be when you don't have people on your side." She looked into his blue-gray eyes and held back tears. "And for all the things we fought about... you were always on my side. Always."

375

The color rose in his cheeks.

Her voice dropped to a whisper as she tried to choke out one more thought around the lump forming in her throat. "That's part of what was so shocking and painful about that day. It was the first time since we were kids that I realized that maybe you weren't on my side after all." She couldn't look at him.

Robert's low growling voice whispered in her ear again. "It's a good thing I'm not there. I would punch the living daylights out of that that son of a—"

She pretended to tuck a few stray, wispy hairs behind her ear. Using two fingers, she quickly tugged the earpiece loose and palmed it, slipping it into the pocket of her skirt.

I don't want him hearing this. He has no idea...

"I felt that too, Leah." Jude said, his voice faltering. "I really did. And I would be honored if you would give me the chance to make it up to you."

He stood up.

Leah blinked—it felt abrupt.

"Leah, I really hate to do this, but I do need to get going. I'm so behind at work. I wasn't even planning on coming at all today before you reached out. But I'm so glad you did—it was really good to see you. Can... can I walk you to your car?"

She stood up, one hand holding her empty cup, the other nestled into Jude's hand. "I would like that."

Her pocket buzzed. No doubt Robert wanted to know why her audio had gotten so quiet and muffled. She ignored it, focusing instead on the feeling of Jude's hand in hers, the familiarity and comfort of it existing alongside a question.

What if this is a terrible mistake?

But the walk to her car was a short one, and the thought didn't have time to develop. Jude opened her door for her and pulled her in for a hug. Her body tensed up, and she willed herself to relax.

"Thank you, Leah," he said, still holding her close. "For reaching out, of course, and for being willing to give me the chance to make things right. I know I've said it before, but... I'm sorry for how everything went down. It... You deserved better than that."

She inhaled deeply before muttering the words she never thought she'd say. "I forgive you."

The moment ended. Jude released her, and she climbed into her car. He waved as she backed out of her spot and drove away. Robert's earpiece started vibrating in her pocket again, but she left it alone, choosing instead to sit in a silence so deep that it felt tangible.

What am I doing?

Chapter 31

Leah couldn't stop thinking about Jude all weekend. She replayed their conversation in her mind, analyzing her every word and movement, trying to understand why she'd reacted the way she had. She fought off mental images of Jude in an orange jumpsuit, lining up for a cafeteria meal. Jude, his eyes wide, as FBI agents stormed into the clinic, guns drawn. Jude, sitting alone in a courthouse waiting room, his suit sleeves just a half-inch too short, as they always were, wondering what he had done to her to deserve this kind of retribution.

That would have been enough to keep her mind busy, but as Saturday evening turned into Saturday night, her phone buzzed with a text message.

> Told Father about our conversation today. He said he'd love to see you soon. Any chance you're free early Monday morning? Maybe we could have breakfast together and then you could come by the office for a few minutes? I'm sure you've got work to do, but maybe not first thing on Monday?

Her heart sunk in her chest as she read it, and for a few minutes, she couldn't formulate a response.

I thought I was going to be the one to reach out to him.

She fretted as she tried to compose an affirmative response that struck the balance of excited-but-not-too-excited. Her stomach knotted up a little.

> That sounds great, Jude! Thanks for the invite.
> Please tell him hello from me, and I'm really
> looking forward to seeing you both on Monday.

She made herself a cup of ginger peach tea and sat on the couch in her apartment, trying to quell the churning in her stomach.

I don't know how I'm going to do this.

***

The setting Sunday sun cast a golden-hour glow through the window. Leah sat on her bed with the orange shoe box from Natalie set to one side, its contents splayed out in front of her: photographs, pamphlets, papers. Memories. She thumbed through the papers from her lockbox quickly and then slid them into a manila envelope. On the front she wrote the words 'The Harvey Files.' She slipped the envelope in her backpack and tossed the pen into the shoe box. Then, one by one, she examined each of the remaining items before placing them in the box.

I really hope I'm making the right call.

She slipped the shoe box—now full—into her backpack and set it down by the door.

All ready for tomorrow.

The thought brought her no comfort.

Early Monday morning, Leah stepped out the door and into her car, her fingers tingling with a mixture of apprehension and excitement. The earpiece Robert had given her on Saturday still sat in her cup holder. Its battery was long spent, and dust and crumbs surrounded it. She glanced at it ruefully, her stomach in knots as she wrapped it in a tissue and tucked the whole bundle into her car's center console.

The least I can do is keep it from getting totally ruined. In case I ever get a chance to give it back to him.

Breakfast was good—sweet, even. Jude seemed more comfortable and less on edge than he had been at Common Grounds, and in many ways, it felt like nothing had changed. They swapped stories from the past year, a year full of difficult moments for both of them. Leah told Jude about the investigation Agent McDowell had been leading, about the trouble they'd had finding the bodies; Jude told Leah about the ways the research program at the prison had matured since she'd left the Institute. They reminisced about the past, cackling at old jokes and fondly remembered pranks. Leah felt her own anxiety lessen as they talked—her shoulders relaxing, her breathing regulating, her rapid thoughts slowing.

How did I forget this feeling so easily?

They didn't have time for a long meal, and they soon made their way to the Institute's office. Jude opened her car door for her, kissing her on the forehead briefly before getting into his own car. She followed him to the clinic, and he met her on the way in. Leah entered the building keenly aware of the large orange shoe box in her backpack that left it awkward and misshapen. The first drops of a promising summer rainstorm danced around her, and a breeze whipped the leaves of the trees.

Jude took her hand in his as soon as they were past the main reception area. Together, they made their way down the labyrinthine halls of the Institute to Dr. Pierucci's office. Jude knocked quietly before opening the door, and Leah took a deep breath.

Inside, Dr. Pierucci was seated at his ancient mahogany desk. He stood as they entered, and his face broke out in a wide, warm smile as he came around to give Leah a two-handed handshake. She returned it, unable to keep herself from smiling in response.

"Leonora! What a delight it is to see you. Please, come sit down." He gestured to a round table with three chairs that stood in the opposite corner of the room, bookshelves lining the walls around it.

Jude pulled out a chair for her as his father began to speak. "I am so grateful that you elected to come by for a visit, now that there are no more secrets between us. Jude informed me of your conversation this weekend."

Jude pushed her chair in and walked around to take his seat next to his father.

Leah smiled, feeling the corners of her eyes crinkle, even as a melancholy ache built in her chest. She looked Dr. Pierucci in the eyes as she spoke. "I wouldn't have missed it, truly. After my memories returned, I realized how much grieving I still had to do, and after everything that happened on Saturday, I really was hoping that you and I would have a chance to see one another again."

"Indeed," he agreed. "Your monthly visits have been a great consolation to me over this last year, but of course, it was not the same." His voice was slow and sweet.

"Absolutely." Leah swallowed hard, hoping to clear the lump in her throat.

Here goes nothing.

"Dr. P—I also... I have something I'd like to speak with you about. Now that we're all here together again."

He raised his eyebrows and glanced at Jude before returning his gaze to her. "Please elaborate."

She pulled the shoe box out of her backpack, setting it down on the table with a soft thump.

I really hope this isn't a mistake.

"I won't mince my words," she began. Goosebumps rose on her arms, and she wished she'd thought to bring a sweater. "Seeing Jude on Saturday was the last straw for something I've been considering for a while now. I'm sure you know about the FBI investigation into the research program. I was recruited to participate..." She took a deep breath. "But I'm not going to assist any further. I want out."

She heard the rain pick up, becoming a torrential downpour that filled the sky. The antique floor lamp behind the table emitted a circle of warm light, shrouding the rest of the room in darkness by contrast.

Dr. Pierucci said nothing. A cruel smile tugged at the corners of his mouth, and he opened the box with an air of victorious curiosity, laying its contents out on the table: her McNeill ID cards, the photos and promotional pamphlets, the sticky notes she'd pulled from her planner, the silver pen she'd used the night before, and the large manila envelope on which she had written the words 'The Harvey Files'. He slid out the stack of papers from her lockbox and surveyed them disinterestedly.

This is it. All the cards on the table.

Her thoughts raced and her teeth chattered, and she clenched her jaw to stop them. She didn't realize that Dr. Pierucci was speaking until he was halfway through his sentence. "—what changed your mind?"

She blinked and shook her head. "I'm sorry. I got distracted. Could you repeat yourself?"

His left eye twitched. "I said that I'm very pleased to hear that you've come around, but I would be interested to know what changed your mind."

"Oh! Of course." Leah's eyes drifted to the bookshelf in front of her, and she found herself skimming the titles. *Brain on Fire. The Man Who Mistook His Wife for a Hat. Thinking, Fast and Slow. The Brain that Changes Itself.*

She continued staring at the shelves as she began speaking again. "Obviously, last year when I found out about everything that was going on, I was really shocked. From what I was reading, it all seemed really terrible, and I felt like I had a certain duty to stop it. It's funny—it sounds so prideful now... so foolish. What did I think I was going to be able to do?" She looked back at Dr. Pierucci, then at Jude. He watched the rain slide down the window panes, apparently lost in thought.

Dr. Pierucci watched her closely. "Indeed."

She looked back at Jude's face, his pensive expression reflecting her own mood. "But then everything happened last year, and then my memories returned, of course... And pretty much ever since then, I've just been wrestling with this question of 'Is it worth it?' Natalie was instrumental in all of my memories returning, and I was grateful to her for that. I'd really love—" she added as an aside "—to write a paper for you one day detailing what the suppression was like. The whole texture of life feels different."

She watched Dr. Pierucci's face for any sign of emotion but saw none. He sat perfectly still, his back rod-straight, his lips closed in a tight line. All of his former warmth had vanished. Jude was still preoccupied with the rain; she wondered if he'd heard anything she'd said. Her heart pounded in her chest, but she forced herself to continue.

"I wasn't exactly over the moon when Nat and the agent who'd been working on the case expected that I would jump back in right where I'd left off. My first response, honestly, was to run away. I was struck by how much my investi—my meddling had cost me already, and I couldn't escape the question of what more I was willing to sacrifice, if anything... and whether or not I really wanted to lose the two of you."

She gestured to the things on the table, certain that Dr. Pierucci would notice her trembling hands. "All of this... It all felt so important before my memories were suppressed. But afterwards—after coming back from such a huge perspective shift?—it just seems... meaningless, somehow. And that's not even getting into the ways the program has matured and improved over this past year, which Jude was telling me about over breakfast. When it comes down to it, I just want to go home and live a quiet life and stay out of all of this."

She closed her eyes and a tear ran down her face. She heard a shuffle of papers and glanced up to see Jude's hand held out for her. She quietly took it for a moment before tucking both her hands beneath the table.

"I want that for you, too, Leonora," Dr. Pierucci responded. "I never wanted you to get involved with this project, in part because I knew that the rumors would move you. I knew that, without the proper context, you might come to inaccurate conclusions. Prisoners having a portion of their memories suppressed, punishments for offenses committed in a simulated environment, even the unfortunate demise of a prisoner, on occasion... These things happened from time to time, but not in the ways that your online dramatists would insist. It's not as if the on-site incinerator were operating at full capacity around the clock to dispose of a veritable heap of corpses. I thought you knew me better than that. But perhaps I overestimated our relationship." He paused, letting the words hang in the air for a moment before concluding. "Indeed, I quite regretted the way that events transpired. I was hoping to spare you."

Hoping to spare me?

"Thank you," Leah replied, her expression bittersweet. "And eventually, as you said, I came around. I realized that maybe I did believe random strangers on the internet too quickly... And for a little while, I was working with the FBI agent they sent out here, just because I felt like I had to, you know? I'd come that far already, so it didn't seem like I had another option. And when Matthew was released from custody at the police office—I wasn't thinking straight, and I came up with this crazy idea that you were behind his arrest—it turned out he just owed a fine for his vehicle registration or something..."

She shrugged sheepishly, a nervous laugh escaping her chest as she looked between the two of them. Jude's brow was furrowed, skepticism writ large across his face. Dr. Pierucci remained stoic, listening carefully.

"I just didn't want Matthew or Natalie or the kids to get hurt because of me, you know? They don't deserve that— they don't want to hurt you or hurt the Institute or anything. They just want some peace and quiet. And, really... that's all I want, too. I think I was just so scared that I wouldn't be able to get that. I felt trapped by my own past. So I figured I could at least help the Baileys out."

She stared at the bookshelves. Outside, a peal of thunder crashed, shaking the whiskey glasses on Dr. Pierucci's bookshelves. Leah shivered again, glancing over at

Jude, who mouthed the word 'spooky'. The corners of her mouth twitched with the hint of a smile.

Dr. Pierucci coughed and rolled his eyes.

The back-and-forth was intimately familiar, but even so, a new sense of dread seeped into her bones. She forced her clenched jaw to relax.

"A couple days ago," she continued. "Agent McDowell asked me to get together with Jude, just to see if there was any information we could get out of him. I didn't really think I had a choice, so I reached out, and then..." She relaxed her shoulders and looked down at the table. "Gosh, Jude, the second you walked in, it was like my heart just stopped. I didn't realize how much I had missed you. Halfway through our conversation, I decided I was done. Done with Agent McDowell and the sting operation and this case I don't even believe in anymore." She gestured to the papers in front of her. "I don't know if you saw it, Jude, but McDowell sent me to Common Grounds with a wire, and at some point I just took it out. I didn't want to be working with him anymore."

Jude smiled at her, but his eyes were wide and sad. A pang of guilt shot through Leah, and she looked away from him. His father's eyes met hers. Dr. Pierucci's gaze was unwavering, emotionless.

Her confidence faltered. "So I guess I was just hoping that you two could help me get out of this mess I've made."

She shrugged sheepishly, glancing back and forth between father and son.

Dr. Pierucci sat silently for a long moment, his piercing gray eyes on Leah's face. "We will be happy to assist you, Leonora. Of course."

A rush of relief washed over Leah's body.

The room momentarily lit up with a flash of lightning, and another peal of thunder echoed around them.

Jude chimed in. "What do you need from us? If I know you, you've got three-quarters of a plan already."

That smile in his voice melted Leah's anxiety, and she grinned back at him, her whole face smiling.

What a wonder it is to be known.

But the weight slowly settled back across her shoulders as she responded. "You're right. I do. I thought a lot over the weekend, and I think it'd be simplest if I could manage to convince Agent McDowell that it was all a lie. The story I sent him last year is outlandish enough that I could just pretend I made it up... but I want to be able to explain it to him in a way that feels believable."

Dr. Pierucci nodded, his eyes still fixed on her. "That does seem the ideal scenario, if you are able to accomplish it. I assume that without your testimony, his case has no foundation on which to stand."

"Exactly," Leah responded, all her energy focused on keeping her restless legs still. "All he has is the information I sent him, and even that isn't a complete case on its own. If I recant, he's got nothing."

Dr. Pierucci looked out the window. "This... Agent McDowell." He spat the name out. "Is he aware of your involvement with my son?"

Leah nodded.

"Then perhaps you could attribute your actions to a spat between the two of you—claim that you acted out of malice but have since repaired the relationship."

If someone had told me two years ago that Jude Pierucci, Sr., MD, PhD would unironically suggest a lovers' quarrel gone wrong as an explanation for anything...

388

She tried to keep her expression neutral. Jude nodded along as his father spoke. "People have definitely done stupider things for love. And as long as you're adamant that the story is a fiction, he wouldn't be able to base any legal action on your testimony."

"That's a good idea. I'll—" Leah's voice faltered. "Could I... could I just call him now? I'll feel better if you two are here to encourage me and back me up."

Jude smiled. "Of course, babe."

Babe? We reconnected two days ago, babe.

Leah picked up her phone, hands trembling as she made the call. Turning on the speaker phone, she placed the phone in the center of the table. Agent McDowell answered on the third ring.

"Special Agent Robert McDowell speaking."

She inhaled deeply. Exhaled. "Hello, Agent McDowell? This is Leonora Harvey."

"Good morning, Ms. Harvey. What can I do for you?" His tone was nothing but professional, and in spite of herself, Leah frowned.

"I, um..." she began. I need to tell you something."

Her chest tightened. For a long moment, she focused on her breathing, and when she finally found her voice again, it cracked and faltered. "This is difficult for me to say, and it's going to be difficult for you to hear, but I need to be honest with you. I... I have to recant the story that I sent in last year. I made it up. It's all false."

He didn't respond. Leah's pulse pounded in her chest, her ears, her fingers. Dr. Pierucci stared at the phone; Jude stared at Leah with concern in his eyes.

"Did... did you hear me?" Leah forced the words out.

"It's all false?" Robert scoffed.

"All of it," she confirmed. "I think I told you that Jude and I were engaged last year, and that things had been difficult. We were fighting a lot, and I was angry."

She looked at Jude, who gave her a thumbs up. She screwed her eyes shut and focused on each word as it tumbled out of her mouth.

"I didn't feel like I was more important than his job, and no matter how much we talked and fought, it didn't feel like anything was changing—at least, not in the way that I wanted. So I lashed out. I wanted him to prove to me that he would pick me. I made up this whole story about the Institute committing these terrible abuses to convince him that his precious job wasn't as important as I was. I wanted to punish him by taking away something he'd loved more than me. The more I worked on making the story convincing, the angrier I got, and eventually I decided that I wanted a break from Jude for a while... maybe forever. So I forged all the documents and I sent them to you, just because I was still so furious... and then I cut myself out of his life."

She looked down at the papers laid out on the table. "I was out of my mind with rage."

There's no way this is going to work. There's just no way.

Leah glanced at the two men seated across from her. She could feel the panic building in her chest as the call went on. Jude gave her a sympathetic smile. Dr. Pierucci sat still, his large gray eyes observing her carefully.

"And that was that. I moved. I got a new job. I tried to cut ties, and for a while, I was okay. I told myself I was okay. I kind of forgot that I'd actually sent something to the actual FBI." She tried to force a light-hearted chuckle, but it came out sounding more like a dry-throated cough.

"But Ms. Harvey, you…" Agent McDowell stammered. "Everything that Natalie told me about your memories being suppressed. The way that your personality completely shifted after you told us that you remembered everything. How do you explain that?"

He saw a difference in me after my memories came back?

For a moment, Leah couldn't think. Her head swam, and it took all her effort to return her focus to the conversation.

It's probably just something he made up.

She shook her head, collected her thoughts, and spoke slowly, her eyes focused on the spidery network of cracks in her phone screen. "I made the mistake of mentioning something to Natalie, and she didn't know it was all a ploy. I wanted a clean start, so I acted like I expected Dr. Pierucci to suppress my memories. I didn't really want to hear from anyone at the Institute. A clean start."

She bit down on the back of her tongue to stop her teeth from chattering. "I really never thought anyone would look at the stuff I sent in, but when you reached out to Natalie, I think it seemed like maybe this was her chance to help Matthew get over his own issues… get some closure, you know? He wasn't well during the time he worked at the prison, and it was really hard on her. I don't know. I should have known that getting her involved was a bad idea, but I can't undo it now."

Almost done. Just land the plane and hang up.

She concluded, trying to add a note of finality to her voice. "But my statement stands either way. You have no case. It's all made up."

"Ms. Harvey," His voice was pleading. "I find this extremely difficult to believe. You gave me so many details,

391

so much direct evidence... We saw each other in the lobby of the Institute every month for almost a year. Do you really expect me to believe that you wanted a clean start, and then showed up at the office regularly?"

Leah's eyes widened, and she looked to Jude in a frenzy. He tapped his forehead a couple of times, his face calm. When she didn't understand what he was trying to say, he mouthed the words 'migraines'.

A wave of intense relief washed over Leah.

"Agent McDowell, I've been seeing Dr. Pierucci since I was a child—I've lived with migraines my whole life. Dr. Pierucci was very accommodating and didn't make me see Jude during any of my appointments." She looked at him, and for a split second, he was once again the kind doctor who'd sat by her bedside during her childhood. A faint throbbing began along one side of her head, and she groaned.

I'm so ready to be done with all of this.

"The story I told you is all fake," she insisted. Her fatigue was audible even to her. "I'm a graphic designer! A marketing specialist! It was all a scam. I conned you. But I'm recanting because things have changed." She softened her voice. "You sent me to go talk to Jude on Saturday, and we talked, and I realized that I really did miss him. I want to give him another chance. So I'm calling off the dogs. It was all a lie. Go home, Robert."

She felt the color rising in her cheeks. She shifted her weight and tucked one leg up underneath herself.

"Leah, I don't know what to say." He sounded broken.

She frowned. "I'm sorry I wasted your time."

He started another sentence, but she ended the call. Sweat beaded along her hairline, and her heart pounded in her chest. She glanced back and forth between Jude and Dr. Pierucci, desperate to hear their thoughts.

"Adequate," Dr. Pierucci said, his tone blasé. "Room to improve. Oversharing and over-explaining always give the impression of lying, regardless of the veracity of one's communication. And you would do well to temper your frankly excessive displays of emotion." Leah would have sworn he rolled his eyes. "However, he seemed to receive the message, and that was the objective."

His rebuke stung, and Leah felt herself shrining in her chair. She looked at Jude, desperate for reassurance.

He did not disappoint. "Father, you're too harsh! She did a wonderful job. This whole morning has been wonderful, and it's such a relief to have that behind us once and for all."

She smiled at him, her eyes heavy. Her head was still throbbing, and she glanced around the room for a couch or anywhere she could lie down.

Finding nothing, she looked back at Jude and whispered. "I'm so sorry—I just got this pounding headache. Is there somewhere I could take a nap? Or, even," she hesitated, weighing the question in her mind. "I don't know, does the Institute still have that old house for out-of-town patients to stay in? Could I... could I stay there for a few days?"

Dr. Pierucci was visibly startled by the request. His eyes widened and he looked over at Jude, as if for explanation, but he quickly regained composure. "I must admit that I'm confused by the request." A frown played about the doctor's lips, and his heavy, graying eyebrows furrowed.

Leah shivered, her teeth chattering. "It's just that, well, Agent McDowell has my home address, and so do the

Baileys, and I'm a little scared that they'll try to track me down and... I don't know what, I guess. I got let go from my job last week, and I don't love the idea of just sitting around in my living room, waiting for someone to come knocking. I'd feel safer staying in a place where they couldn't find me, but you could if I needed you."

She couldn't make eye contact with either of them. She turned her gaze to the stack of papers spread out across the table, but her eyes refused to focus enough to make out any of the words.

Jude spoke up, reaching a hand across the table. His eyes were soft and kind and sparkling in the light that filled the room in the aftermath of the storm. "Of course you can, Leah. For as long as you need. No one is staying in the house until next Tuesday, so you have plenty of time." He pulled out his phone, flicking through screen with determination. Leah wanted to be offended, but she could hardly muster the energy. After a moment, Jude looked back up at her, his eyes suddenly tired. "It looks like I could even let you take the company van, if you'd like? It's got GPS tracking, so I can keep an eye on you and keep you safe. You're welcome to leave your car here, and I'll bring it to you this evening."

Leah's whole body tensed up, and she stared at Jude in stunned silence. She couldn't get her expression under control quickly enough, and his face mirrored her own terror for a moment.

She blinked heavily. "I would appreciate that. Just for a day or two until this blows over. Natalie has been pretty angry with me lately, and I'm worried about her reaction when McDowell tells her he's having to pull the plug on the investigation. And McDowell himself, well, I don't know him well enough to trust that he wouldn't try to force a confession out of me."

Pierucci twitched. "I'm sorry—my mind was elsewhere. I hope that Jude has been able to assuage your concerns?"

"He has." Leah tried to keep her tone measured. "Thank you, sir."

The doctor stood. "Well, Ms. Harvey, it has been truly delightful to see you this morning, and I trust that we will have ample opportunity to renew our friendship, in light of certain conversations you have had with my son." He nodded toward Jude with a knowing smile. "And I hope that you feel better soon."

"Thank you, sir." She stood as well, offering him a hand to shake. "I look forward to seeing you again soon."

They shook hands. The doctor's grip around her fingers was firm, and she noticed gratefully that her hands no longer trembled. She took a long look at the papers spread out across the table, slung her empty backpack over her shoulder, and turned to leave.

"Let me walk you out!" Jude practically jumped toward the door, holding it open for her with one hand while placing the other around her waist. They were crossing the threshold when Dr. Pierucci spoke again.

"Leonora." His voice was softer than she'd heard it in years. "In light of everything that has transpired today, I trust you know that all is forgiven. We can allow the past to remain in the past. I hope that you can say the same...?"

It was the closest she'd ever heard him come to an apology, and she suspected it was the best she'd ever get. "I'm touched, Dr. P. Of course."

Jude closed the door behind them, and they made their way to the back door of the clinic.

"Here, let me take your backpack," he insisted, fiddling with the zippers and closing the pocket that still hung half-open. She handed it to him and leaned her fatigued body into him as they walked. Her legs felt wobbly, and she was grateful for the support.

Oh, how things have changed since the last time we spoke in this hallway.

"Thank you for doing this for me." Her voice was weak, and for a moment, she worried that he hadn't heard her.

"Of course, Leah. Anything." He held her tightly for a moment before pulling the staff exit open. "I want to prove to you that I'm on your side. I'll always be on your side—and Father will be too, if you'll let him. He was shocked when I told him about our coffee date, but he was so glad. Giddy, in his own way."

Leah wrapped him in a hug, hoping he didn't notice her racing heart. "I'm just glad everything has worked out."

"Me too." They stopped in front of the company van, which was immaculately clean, as always. The blue and gold of the Institute's logo glinted in the sunlight. "Do you need me to send you the address? Or do you still know how to get there?"

She chuckled softly. "I think I can still find it. I'm pretty much as good as new, other than this headache."

He kissed her forehead, unable to suppress a warm smile. "Well, then I'll see you when I get off work. Make sure you turn your location off on your phone; we don't need anyone finding out where you're staying."

He held the keys out to her, and she took them. "That would kind of defeat the purpose, wouldn't it?"

"Exactly." He patted the side of the van affectionately. "But she'll take good care of you, and I'll make sure your car is ready for you whenever you want it back. We're here for you, Leah."

Does he have any idea what's happening?

She pushed the thought down. "I'm going to stop by the grocery store and get a few things for dinner, and then I'll head straight to the house. Do you think you could come by for dinner?"

He grinned. "I think I could." He opened the door for her and watched as she slipped into the car.

She took a few minutes to adjust the seat and mirrors, fiddle with the radio settings, and acclimate herself to the buttons and levers. When she finally shifted into reverse, she saw Jude still standing off to the side, watching her. His eyes were sparkling, filled with admiration.

She waved at him as she pulled out of the parking lot, and he waved back. Her head and heart were both still pounding as she navigated to her favorite grocery store and found a spot.

You're safe. Everything is going to be okay. There's nothing to worry about.

Chapter 32

Leah sat in the parking lot for a few minutes, breathing deeply and counting the birds whose flights crossed her windshield. Her heart slowed, and she stopped shivering. She stepped into the sweltering heat and took measured steps toward the entrance of the store, where she grabbed a cart and made her way to the produce section. The atmosphere of the store—the soft ambient music, the chatter of other shoppers, and the patter of feet—calmed her. She didn't get much—some Mike & Ikes, a bag of pizza rolls, a half-gallon of iced tea—but she methodically walked through every aisle all the same.

As she rounded the last turn, someone caught her eye—a dark-haired man in a gray suit. He stood with his back to her, looking at the cakes in the bakery case. She pushed her cart until it stood alongside his, and she joined him in looking at the offerings.

"Which one do you like best?" he asked.

She grinned, trying to keep her voice from showing it. "Chocolate. Definitely."

"Noted," he replied, all business. "When did you say your birthday is, Harvey?"

"April. You've got time." Her boldness surprised her.

He turned toward her, grinning widely. "Is that so?"

Relief spread over her like a hot shower after a chilly day. "We made it." Something fluttered in her stomach. She wanted to wrap him in a hug.

She shoved the thought down and looked away.

"We made it," Robert said, sighing deeply. "Good job in there today. I know that wasn't easy."

Leah released a breath she didn't realize she'd been holding in. "You think I did okay? Were you able to hear everything?"

"Crystal clear. Great call to slip the bug into a pen."

"He mentioned the incinerator—" she began.

"I'm already working on a warrant." He shrugged, stifling a yawn. The bags under his eyes had deepened since the last time she'd seen him. "We'll see if it pans out. It's not the most solid lead, but it's a lead. I'm not sure we could reasonably have expected more. How did he seem in person—do you think he bought it?"

"Ehhh," she waffled, looking back at the bakery display before adding sarcastically, "He did condescend to offer me some feedback on my performance after we got off the phone, and it sounded a little... pointed, I guess. But we got a lead, and that's all we can ask for."

"Exactly," he said, standing up straighter and pushing his cart forward a couple inches. "Alright, let's get out of here. You can take my car, and I'll take the transit van."

Leah felt her shoulders relax. "Thanks, Robert."

Everything is going to be okay.

He took another step, then stopped, absentmindedly picking at a faded sticker on the handle of his cart. He glanced back at her. "Jude won't be stopping by for dinner for another few hours. Do you want to grab a cup of coffee or something?"

Her stomach flipped.

"Yeah," she said, surprised by the enthusiasm she heard in her own voice. "Yeah, I'd really like that."

He grinned and winked at her. "Yeah, you would."

Leah stared, her mouth open in shocked laughter, as he walked away. She followed a few paces behind him, unable to hide her grin. They both stepped into the self-checkout area, where they found adjacent open registers.

He scanned the contents of his cart—a couple energy drinks and a large bag of generic trail mix. "Stakeout diet," he commented, noticing her gaze. "I'm not proud of it."

Leah snorted. Robert tapped a few buttons on the screen and reached into his pocket. "Hey, before I forget—text me the address of that guest house, and then you can just come pick me up or something. That way the van GPS doesn't make them suspicious."

He held his car keys out for her to take, and she traded him for the keys to the van. For a moment, Leah felt her rib cage tighten around her lungs. "You don't think one of us should be there for the rest of the day? Just in case someone stops by early?"

Robert shook his head, "I'd rather you not be there at all, honestly. They can't hurt an empty house, but I can't guarantee your safety if they show up and we're sipping espressos on the back porch."

"I guess you're right," she acknowledged, although something in her stomach still didn't sit quite right. She scanned her items and tossed them haphazardly in a bag, pulling out her wallet. "I'll run these home and put them in the fridge, and then I'll head over."

"Sounds good," he replied. "I'll be there." He grabbed his bag, pushed his cart to the return area, and vanished.

Leah watched him leave, shaking her head ruefully as she finished paying and walked toward the exit herself. His blue sedan was parked right at the front of the store, and she watched as the Institute's van pulled away.

Almost there. I cannot wait for this to be over.

Sitting at a stop light just outside the store, she put on some instrumental music, lost in thought.

I should call Mom. She'd want to hear about everything.

A car behind her honked, and she looked up to see that the light had turned green. She eased off the brakes and pulled forward, watching as the car behind her pulled into the next lane over and sped past her.

But I'll call her when it's finished.

She pulled into her apartment, threw her pizza rolls in the freezer and her iced tea in the fridge, and took something for her headache before stepping back out. For a little while, she just sat in Robert's car, keys in the ignition, eyes closed, oblivious to the world around her.

I'm glad Agent McDowell wanted to get a cup of coffee. That'll be better than just of sitting here by myself all day waiting for dinner with Jude. It'll be nice to spend some time with him...

She blushed at the thought, but didn't push it away.

To her surprise, Sarah and Connor walked past her, hand in hand. She leaned into him as they walked. Leah raised a hand in greeting, but they didn't look her way. It took her a second to remember that she was in Robert's car.

Soaking up the last few days of summer break, I guess.

She watched them wistfully as they made their way home. Her heart twisted in her chest, and she felt a squirming deep in her stomach.

It's probably just the sleep deprivation and the constant stress from the last few weeks.

As she pulled up to the Institute's guest house a little while later, her stomach fluttered again. She turned off the car and walked up to the house, her mind filled with memories of the first time she'd crossed its threshold.

"You're going to be okay, pumpkin. The doctor is going to run a few tests, and we get to stay in this fancy house all week. It'll be fun! Like a vacation."

She looked up and saw her dad's smiling face, his hand wrapped around hers.

"I love you, daddy."

"I love you too, princess."

Her heart ached as she knocked on the door.

I miss you, Dad.

Robert answered quickly, indicating towards the car. He still wore his suit, but he'd swapped his glasses for contacts. He stepped out and locked the door behind him, holding out a hand for the keys. Leah gave them to him, a little confused by the reception.

"I don't want my car sitting here for too long," he said, noticing her expression. "No need to draw attention to ourselves. Not sure if we can trust the neighbors."

"Fair enough," Leah replied, following him to the car. She slung her backpack into the passenger seat and climbed in as Robert got behind the wheel and readjusted the steering wheel and mirrors.

He turned to look at her. "So, coffee? You know this area better than I do. Where do you want to go?"

"I know this great place called Common Grounds," she replied in her best ditzy voice. Robert threw his head back with laughter. "Okay, but for real," she continued. "How do you feel about board games?"

He squinted at her, that impish grin on his face. "Oh, you're so on."

She looked away, trying not to let him see her smile. "There's a great boba place not too far from here that's got games."

"Heck yes," he nodded. "Let's do it!"

The drive wasn't long, and they soon found themselves sitting across from one another at a small table. Their drinks left rings of condensation on the waxy wood surface amid steaming paper boxes of eggrolls and sweet potato fries. A game of rummy was laid out between them.

Leah glanced at her cards, a Queen and King of spades. The eight through Jack of spades were already down on the table. She studied his face carefully as he considered his own cards—he, like her, only held two. She tallied their scores in her head.

I've got this in the bag.

With a grin and a wink, Robert laid down a king and ace of hearts, playing off a run that she'd laid down a few turns earlier.

"And I'm out!" he said, throwing his hands in the air.

"Dang, really?" She placed her last remaining cards down on the table as well. "I was this close!"

"Oohhh, two face cards?" Robert exclaimed with a sympathetic grimace. "Bad luck!"

They counted up points, and Leah's remaining face cards, combined with Robert's last hand, left him in the lead. She took a sip of her drink, absentmindedly chewing on a piece of tapioca while she shuffled the deck. Robert dipped an eggroll in the pink-orange sauce and took a bite. He grinned around full cheeks as she dealt out another hand to each of them, counting off cards under her breath.

"Coming back for more?" he teased, picking up his cards and arranging them carefully.

She raised her eyebrows. "I'll have you know I was the rummy queen at Swarthmore back in the day."

"Oh-ho-ho!" He bowed low in his seat, waving his hand theatrically for emphasis. "I had no idea I was in the presence of royalty!" He drew a card before adding with a smirk, "You coulda fooled me with that last game. Are you just letting me win so your triumph is that much bigger when you crush me in a few rounds?"

She gave him her best stink-eye, aware that its effectiveness was lessened by a grin she couldn't suppress. Turning her attention to the cards in her hand, she took a moment to arrange them before looking down at the card Robert had discarded. She picked it up and pulled out two others, laying them down on the table in front of her.

"Three kings. Come at—"

A familiar voice interrupted her. "Leah. Wilder. I thought I might find the two of you here."

Leah blanched. Across from her, the color had gone out of Robert's face as well. As he stood up, his right hand hovering over his hip, she thought she saw a glint of metal under his jacket.

How long has he been armed?

Leah's eyes widened, and she turned around slowly.

Of course he's armed. Why would he not be armed?

"Please, sit down. There's no need to make a scene. Agent McDowell, was it?" Jude's face wore an expression that Leah found difficult to read. He pulled a chair up to the side of their table and began gathering their playing cards back into a deck. He picked up a sweet potato fry and examined it, his eyes narrow and his lips pursed tightly.

Holding it out with two fingers, he placed it back in the box and pushed the box away.

He opened his mouth as if to speak, then closed it. She watched as he formed a cruel sneer. For a moment, he was the spitting image of his father twenty years prior.

Leah shuddered and looked at Robert, who said nothing, staring at Jude with unflinching eyes. His jaw was clenched, and his every muscle seemed tense. Sweat beaded along Leah's hairline, and she tried to glance around the room without moving her head.

"It's no use," Jude interrupted. "There's only one exit, and the front wall is made of glass. We're completely surrounded by innocents. It would be impossible for you to run, and Agent McDowell wouldn't be able to discharge his weapon without casualties." He slipped the cards back into their box and placed it on the table in front of them.

She knew he was right. Her pulse racing, she looked at Robert, whose eyes were wide.

"Well, then." Jude stood, indicating that Leah and Robert should do the same. "Shall we?"

How did he find us? The van is still at the guest house.

Leah hesitated, waiting for Robert to move. He didn't budge. His eyes still darted left and right, trying to find some alternative to being escorted out.

"They can't hurt an empty house, but I can't guarantee your safety if they show up while we're sipping espressos."

Jude coughed gently. Robert stood. Leah followed suit. She packed up the boxes mechanically and walked to the counter to ask for a to-go bag. Her legs trembled.

Returning to the table, Leah placed the rest of their food into the bag, picked up her drink, and took a step toward the door.

406

"After you, Jude" she said, struggling to keep her voice from shaking.

"No, no. I insist." His tone was firm. There was no trace of the affection or familiarity he'd shown earlier.

Leah glanced at Robert again. He gave the tiniest of nods, and she took a hesitant step forward. He followed right behind her, closing the distance between them with each step.

"When I give you the chance," he whispered, his voice barely audible. "Run."

Her heart pounded in her chest. She wanted to protest, but there was no time. In seconds, she'd reached the front door of the shop, and she reached out a hand to pull it open. She stepped across the threshold. Robert followed her. Jude brought up the rear.

Out of nowhere, Robert whirled around. Leah didn't stop to see anything more—she broke out into a sprint. Time slowed down. She darted off to her left without knowing why she'd made the choice, only realizing as her feet pounded the pavement that the parking lot straight ahead had been packed, and the path to her right had been blocked by a white transit van.

Shouts erupted behind her, and she fought every urge to turn around and see if Robert was okay.

He can take care of himself. He's trained for this.

Each breath was an effort. She felt a stitch in her right side. The sound of her footfalls was all that she could focus on. Her eyes were locked on the road she'd need to cross when she reached the end of the shopping strip.

A door opened a few yards ahead of her, and she tried to swerve out of the way as a man stepped out of the shop. She almost collided with him.

She lost her footing, tripped, and tumbled to the concrete sidewalk, skidding to a stop just past the door he'd emerged from.

Her hands throbbed, and a dull pain in her knee worried her. Even so, she scrambled back to her feet. As she did so, the man who had opened the door took a few steps in her direction. She glanced up at his face.

It was Dr. Pierucci.

Her heart sank. She turned to run again, but he grabbed her by the wrist and held her firm. She winced.

"Ms. Harvey," he said, as if they were two old friends running into each other by chance.

She stood there panting, doubled over with her hands on her knees. He simply watched her, an expression of mild amusement on his face. As Leah caught her breath, she stood back up. Her palms stung and her calves ached. She rolled her neck and looked back at Dr. Pierucci, but before she could do anything else, the slow tap of footfalls caught her attention. Her stomach knotted as she saw Jude walking toward them.

Robert was nowhere to be seen.

Jude approached silently and took Leah's hand, his fingers a vice grip. "Do come along, dear," he said in his gentlest voice.

She didn't respond. His eyes drifted to the shop from which his father had emerged—a veterinary clinic, by the looks of it. A woman and her young son stepped out of the clinic carrying a bird cage. The moment they passed by, Dr. Pierucci's eyes shot fire at Leah.

"You will follow me, Ms. Harvey." He didn't leave any room for questions, and even if she had wanted to run, her exhausted limbs and throbbing knee wouldn't have carried her far. Dr. Pierucci turned around without another word and began walking back.

She felt Jude's gaze on her face, but she refused to look at him. There was no way she would give him the satisfaction of seeing the fear in her eyes.

"Please, Leah," Jude whispered. "Don't make this harder than it has to be." He led her by the hand, and they walked back in the direction they had come.

When they passed by the boba place again, Leah noticed her drink and the bag of leftovers splattered across the pavement. They'd gone flying in her sprint, and she hadn't even noticed. One of the employees stood on the steps with a broom, sweeping up the food that had spilled across the storefront.

He looked with a withering glare, but when he saw her, breathless and scraped up and drenched in sweat, his expression changed. She tried to whisper an apology, but the words caught in her chest.

"Is... is everything okay?" he asked, eyeing Jude and Dr. Pierucci suspiciously.

Jude gripped Leah's hand even tighter, and she winced in pain.

"Everything is fine, sir." Dr. Pierucci didn't even bother to turn around before responding.

"I wasn't asking you." The man stood up taller and sized Jude up. "I was asking the young lady here."

Jude released his grip on her hand, and her fingers began to tingle. The employee was a tall, muscular man—he had the build of a football coach, and Leah didn't doubt that he could tackle Jude without breaking a sweat. She opened her mouth to speak–

But they've got Robert.

Her resolve faltered, and she fought back tears.

"Yes, I'm okay." She couldn't bring herself to look him in the face, staring instead at his shoes. "I'm sorry about the mess."

He harrumphed, still not convinced. Jude grabbed her hand, his grip softer than before, and led her around to the side of the large white van. As they turned the corner, Leah saw the man's eyes following them. He leaned on his broom like a staff.

Please, she tried to say with her eyes, *help us. Call someone. Call the police.*

The man with the broom raised one eyebrow and held her gaze. But a memory from her visit to the precinct—it felt like forever ago, but it had only been a few days—echoed back through her mind.

"Detective Austin Inglish. I'm not head detective yet, but I will be one day."

Leah's heart sank. She looked away from the man with the broom. Her shoulders slumped.

What's the point?

Dr. Pierucci slid the door of the van open, and Leah gasped. Inside, Robert sat curled up in one of the seats, his hands held together with duct tape. The interior of the van was dark—there were no windows in the back—but she thought she saw a purple bruise circling Robert's left eye.

Jude leaned in close and whispered in her ear. "If you come quietly, Father might not tie you up."

"Please, Leah. Don't make this harder than it has to be."

With a vacant stare, she stepped into the van. Robert looked up and saw her, and she watched as his expression turned to despair.

"I'm sorry," he whispered.

She wanted to weep. The seat next to him was empty, and she moved toward it.

"Not that seat, Ms. Harvey. Please select another," Dr. Pierucci ordered before slamming the van door shut. She stepped back a row, placed herself immediately behind Robert, and fumbled with her seat belt. Her hands shook. The empty bench around her felt like an endless void. Dr. Pierucci took the passenger seat while Jude walked around the van to the driver's side.

"It's a pity," Dr. Pierucci mused quietly as he fastened his seat belt. "I would have been so lenient, had your offer been genuine. I was prepared to move heaven and earth to reconcile with you..." He adjusted the rear view mirror, twisting it so that she could see his face. "But you spat upon my mercy."

Jude climbed into the driver's seat and clicked his seat belt. The engine rumbled to life and Leah watched, her stomach in knots, as Jude navigated toward the highway.

With no windows near her, Leah could only stare out the front windshield, her eyes glued to the road signs. Exit after exit flew past them until she couldn't deny it.

They were going to Scarlett Bay.

Chapter 33

Leah leaned into the side of the van, trying to reach one arm around Robert's seat without being noticed.

What did he do that he needed to be restrained?

She stretched and scraped, willing her arm through the narrow margin between the side of the car and the edge of the seat. Her jaw clenched tight and tears formed in the corners of her eyes. Finally, she exhaled a deep breath, realizing that she wouldn't be able to tap Robert.

What are we going to do?

Pulling her arm back through the gap, she changed tactics, driving her knee into the back of his seat as hard as she could. A sharp pain radiated up her leg, and she bit down on her tongue to keep from crying out. She geared up to try again but worried it wouldn't be enough—her angle was awkward, and her legs were still shaking after her unexpected sprint.

In front of her, Robert's head turned ever so slightly until she could see him looking at her out of the corner of his eye above the back of his seat.

She shifted her head so that she could no longer see Dr. Pierucci's face in the rear view mirror, and then widened her eyes and raised her eyebrows as much as she could.

Robert nodded a fraction of an inch.

So he knows, at least. I hope he's got a plan.

It wasn't much, but it would have to be enough. It was all she was going to get. Her chest grew tight with anxiety, and she shifted her position, drawing one leg up under herself. In front of them, the highway stretched on. The strip malls and gas stations and restaurants began to give way to open fields of crispy brown grass, parched and sun-dried in the August heat. Leah shifted in her seat again, placing both feet firmly on the floor of the car. Her right foot began bouncing rapidly.

In front of her, Dr. Pierucci cleared his throat. "Ms. Harvey, I must know—did you truly believe that your charade this morning would fool me?"

Leah said nothing. Her heart sped up.

"Do you think I've forgotten you, Leonora?" He didn't turn around, but he made eye contact with her in the rear view mirror. "No—it is you who have forgotten me."

Next to him, Leah noticed Jude's fingers endlessly tapping the steering wheel. The vice grip around her chest loosened at the sight of it, and she closed her eyes to better focus on the faint tap-tap-tapping sound.

"Of course, Leah. Anything for you. I want to prove to you that I'm on your side. I'll always be on your side."

Dr. Pierucci continued speaking. "It was obvious to me from the beginning of your romantic involvement with my son that the two of you were not a natural match, in spite of your closeness since childhood. But the two of you seemed stubbornly unwilling or unable to see it. After all your petty fights last year, there was no way you would willing re-enter the relationship."

Jude had stopped tapping. His hands clenched around the worn faux leather of the steering wheel.

"I'll always be on your side—and Father too, if you'll let him."

Dr. Pierucci groaned. "And then, to add insult to injury, your performance was sub-par. I explained as much in my office—you are a naturally steady woman, Leonora, and intense displays of emotion do not become you. You give yourself away when you try to act the way you think others want to perceive you. You forget that I know you better than you know yourself."

All she could see in the mirror was his eyes, stormy gray and haughty. She couldn't see any of Jude's head or shoulders behind his seat, but his fists still gripped tightly to the wheel. She imagined him sitting perfectly still, jaw clenched, eyes locked forward.

I'd give anything to know what's on his mind right now.

Pierucci did not continue speaking, and they made the rest of the drive in silence. All told, nearly two hours passed before they slowed to a halt at the security checkpoint.

***

"ID and badge, please." The guard's voice was monotone, and although Leah couldn't see his face from her vantage point, she imagined him with one hand held out of his window as he stared down at his cell phone.

Dr. Pierucci didn't respond. He merely sat, waiting, looking at the gate house.

"I said, ID and badge, pl—" Fear entered the guard's voice. "Oh! My deepest apologies, sir. We weren't expecting you today. I'll let Mr. Fernandes know that you're here."

"I will not be requiring a meeting with the warden today. I'm here on... personal business." Although he spoke across the width of the van, he didn't raise his voice at all.

"Understood, sir." The guard's voice trembled.

Ahead of them, the arm of the gate lifted, and the van lurched forward onto the prison grounds. Jude navigated around the main building and selected a parking spot on the far side of the campus. He shut off the engine and stepped out onto the black asphalt of the parking lot. The interior of the van grew lighter as Jude slid the door open, and heat radiated from the concrete. A red brick building filled Leah's vision, interrupted only by a door marked 'STAFF ONLY.' Leah blinked heavily as her eyes adjusted to the daylight.

Jude held out a hand for her, and she leaned on him as she stepped out of the car. But when she went to release his hand, he gripped hers tighter, spinning her around. Confused, Leah followed his lead.

She felt the cold touch of metal on her wrists and heard the telltale click of handcuffs. Her heart dropped, and as Jude turned her toward the door, she glanced up at him. He averted his gaze the moment she met his eyes.

Robert, his wrists already taped together, stepped out of the van tentatively. He looked around, taking in the scene, before landing his gaze on Dr. Pierucci, who was waiting silently by the staff door.

"This way." Dr. Pierucci's voice was eerily calm as he scanned a security badge on the pad next to the door. A green light flickered on, and the door clicked open.

The air inside the prison was frigid, and goosebumps rose on Leah's arms as they stepped across the threshold. They entered a hallway of yellowed linoleum that seemed to stretch on for miles, the visual monotony only broken by an occasional gray-green door.

Leah shivered in her short-sleeved blouse, wishing she'd packed a sweater. The absurdity of the thought struck her, and she almost laughed, until a lump formed in her throat. Robert's footsteps beside her drew her out of her thoughts, and she looked over at him. She thought she must look like a spooked animal, but his face was calm.

What do you know?

Her heart raced as Dr. Pierucci led the way. His usual air of authority felt absolutely dictatorial within the walls of the prison. Robert followed him, his suit coat wrinkling awkwardly. Leah limped along behind Robert, and Jude took up the rear, his fingers once again tapping away on the leg of his pants. Leah thought she heard the telltale smack of his lips that indicated he was engaged in an intense silent conversation with himself.

What I wouldn't give to see inside his mind right now.

A few burly guards in white shirts and navy pants passed them, but each gave Dr. Pierucci a wide berth. Leah stared at each of them intently as they passed by, allowing her face to reveal the panic clawing way inside her. But none of the guards returned her gaze; each of them studied the floor carefully as they stepped quietly past the group. Leah didn't need to see the doctor's face to know that a storm was brewing on his brow. She didn't blame the guards for keeping their distance.

They continued walking—a left turn here, a right turn there, another left after that. Her knee throbbed, and the scrapes on her palms were tender. The fluorescent lights beat down on her, shattering her sense of time and direction. The linoleum floors stretched on endlessly. Chips and scrapes in the pale yellow paint on the walls told stories of aggression and resistance.

How many times did Matthew walk this hallway? Is this where Jorge Rodriguez...?

417

Dr. Pierucci stopped in front of one of the gray-green doors, inserting a key into the lock and turning the handle. A room appeared before them: in one corner, a bulky computer console and a swivel chair; in the other, a well-worn orthodontic chair and a coat pole draped with equipment and cables.

"Jude, I will restrain Ms. Harvey." He stepped away from the door. "Please do the same for Agent McDowell, and I will be with you in a moment."

Leah's breathing shallowed as she watched Dr. Pierucci unlock another room, turning the key and holding the door open for Jude and Robert to step inside.

No, no, no, no, no!

Jude grabbed Robert by the arm and jostled him through the doorway. Leah tried to catch a glimpse of Robert's eyes as he walked away from her, but he didn't turn around. Leah wanted to scream as the door clicked shut behind Jude. Her heart pounded in her ears, and tears welled up in the corners of her eyes.

Dr. Pierucci held the first door open again and gestured for her to step through.

"They'll have him spirited away, memory wiped, and back on the streets within a month if Pierucci is really convinced that we're a threat. And that's the best case scenario."

She walked across the threshold of the room mechanically.

Dr. Pierucci closed the door behind her, then turned and unlocked her handcuffs. She massaged her wrists gently and rubbed her arms, which were still riddled with goosebumps. She looked around the room expectantly.

"I expect you know why we're here, Ms. Harvey?" There was no emotion in his tone.

"I believe so." She felt her voice shake, and she willed herself to remain strong.

Dr. Pierucci stepped toward the orthodontic chair and indicated for her to take a seat. Legs shaking, she did so.

What other choice do I have?

She pivoted in her seat. Dr. Pierucci offered her one hand to stabilize herself and placed the other on her back to guide her down into the incline of the chair.

"I will not make the same mistake twice," he said quietly as he strapped the velcro cuffs around her wrists. At the foot of chair, he unfurled another long strap, which he wrapped tightly around her ankles. He double-checked the restraints and powered on the desktop computer.

Then, wordlessly, he left the room.

Leah's vision blurred. The tick of the wall clock measured out the seconds, the only sound audible in the sterile white room. Her heart pounded in her chest, her ears, her fingers. She forced her frantic brain to focus on the clock, counting out each successive second as she screwed her eyes shut against the disorienting glare of the fluorescent lights.

Slowly, her breaths lengthened—in for four counts, out for four counts. In for eight, out for eight. Her heart began to return to its normal pace, and her vision cleared.

To her left, a set of metal double doors gleamed. Although she couldn't see through them, she knew that a simulation chamber sat on the other side. Suddenly the room began to feel crowded, as if every inmate who had ever been strapped into that chair were inexplicably present in memory.

The image of Robert, strapped down in the next room over, wrapped itself around her like a whip, sharp and painful. She couldn't hear the sounds of a fight through the shared wall—no thumps, no grunts or screams, no crashing of furniture and metal instruments.

The silence terrified her.

The clocked ticked on as Leah tested the straps around her wrists and ankles. Tied down tight, as she'd expected. There would be no escape. She drew her fingers together, trying to make her hand as narrow as possible.

The door creaked open, and Leah started, her wrist scraping against the edge of the cuff. She winced. Dr. Pierucci and Jude filed in wearing grave faces. Jude carried a blue plastic tray lined with medical equipment. Leah thought she saw a spent syringe among the other paraphernalia he carried.

Her heart stopped.

She couldn't breathe.

The door whooshed shut behind them. Dr. Pierucci pulled the swivel chair from the computer console over to Leah's side and sat down, taking the tray from Jude as he did so. Jude stationed himself at the computer and began to work silently.

"It is regrettable that we have come to this point, Ms. Harvey," Dr. Pierucci began, setting the full tray on the retractable table attached to the side of her chair. "I do not relish the task at hand."

Once again, Leah tugged at the straps that held her down. They didn't budge. Her brain began to feel fuzzy.

I hope Mom isn't mad at me for not telling her about any of this before...

"Now," Dr. Pierucci continued as he carefully filled a syringe in front of her. "This injection will be administered first. It will sedate you and mitigate any pain you might otherwise feel. Even if this were the only drug I were to administer, your breathing would eventually stop."

Leah's mouth filled with warm saliva as an acrid sting moved up her throat.

I'm going to choke on my own vomit before he can even touch me. That seems a pleasanter way to go.

Jude began pacing up and down the length of the room. His footsteps were out of sync with the ticking of the clock, and Leah felt her brain go into overdrive trying to discern a pattern. Dr. Pierucci set the first syringe down, then the vial, before picking up another vial and another syringe. He inserted the needle and turned the bottle over, watching intently as it filled up with a blueish liquid.

Is Robert... could they have gotten to him already? Was that really enough time to...?

"This injection will paralyze your body. Even I if were to forego the third injection altogether, your lungs would be unable to inflate."

Leah couldn't see Jude until she could. His fists were clenched, his eyes locked forward. He did an about-face, and for a second, she could see a wild panic in his eyes.

I think I left all the lights on in my apartment this morning. I wonder if Sarah will see them tonight and knock on my door.

Dr. Pierucci repeated the ritual a third time, filling a third syringe from a third vial. "This is the final drug you will receive. It will stop your heart."

She thought her heart might give out before he even got to that point. The restraints felt tighter with every passing second, closing in on her. She gritted her teeth and tugged at them again. Her fingers and toes were numb. Dr. Pierucci observed her with calm disinterest.

Is this what they did to Jorge Rodriguez?

"What story do you think Detective Inglish will come up with?" Jude asked of no one in particular. "More victims of that serial killer he made up?"

Leah heard the strain in his voice before she heard the words he said. She turned toward him, her neck craned at an unnatural angle in the orthodontic chair. He looked at her with his eyebrows slightly raised, his head tilted forward just a little.

What is it, Jude? Why is that significant?

Dr. Pierucci stopped abruptly at Jude's words. He didn't look up, didn't make eye contact. The syringe in his hand clattered onto the tray.

All of the sudden it hit her.

The bodies. He knew they were still looking for the bodies. Rage built in her limbs as she considered the implications of his words.

I wish Robert were here to hear this.

Dr. Pierucci breathed deeply and picked the syringe back up, turning it over several times in a methodical examination.

But it's too late for any of that now.

Dr. Pierucci stood, his lips drawn tight, his eyebrows furrowed. He picked up a small square packet and a long blue strip of rubber. The latter he wound around Leah's upper arm. He tied off the tourniquet with a loose knot and cradled Leah's hand in his own. Then he ripped off the top of the packet and removed an alcohol wipe, swabbing Leah's inner forearm methodically.

Jude's feet continued to step out a rhythm at the back of the room as his father unwrapped an IV cannula and threw the paper covering in the trash can next to him.

I wonder if Dad will be there to greet me.

"Squeeze your fi—" Dr. Pierucci looked up from his work, but didn't turn around to face his son. "Jude, what have I told you about the pacing?"

Poor Jude. Always doing something wrong.

Jude didn't acknowledge his father, but he stopped walking. His face was deep red. His eyes were screwed shut, and his lips formed inaudible words.

He's about to blow. Too late, of course. Always too late.

With no warning, Dr. Pierucci plunged a needle into her arm. She winced in pain but couldn't bring herself to look away. He secured the line with a clear adhesive pad and handed the trash to Jude to throw away. A large bag lay on the tray next to her, and Dr. Pierucci picked it up, hanging it on the metal pole behind her and taking a moment to connect various parts before clicking the end of the tube into the port on her arm.

I wish Robert were here.

Her head swam and her vision blurred as the saline began coursing through her body. She thought she might pass out. When her vision stabilized, Dr. Pierucci stood next to her, holding a full syringe. A small flick released a bubble trapped at the bottom, which danced its way upward toward the needle.

Suddenly, Jude stepped closer. "I won't let you do this."

His father scoffed, his voice whisper silent and razor sharp. "As if you could stop me." He didn't look up.

Jude's voice shook. "I've stopped you once befo—"

"Yes," his father interrupted, glaring at him. "And look where that got us. You must be so proud."

The color rose in Jude's face, and he stammered a response. "Father, you can't do this." His voice cracked and his shoulders slumped. "You can't do this."

Dr. Pierucci looked back at the syringe in his hand. "We will discuss this at a later time. Please step out of the room so I can complete the procedure."

Jude tensed. His eyes widened, darting around the room. "I want to be here for it... for her."

His father didn't look up. "That is out of the question. Please excuse yourself."

Stiff as a corpse, Jude stepped toward the door. He reached for the handle. Turned it. Pulled it open.

Is he just going to let this happen?

Jude gasped. Leah craned her head as far upward as she could. Dr. Pierucci whirled around.

A cacophony of voices surrounded them as the room filled in a flash of sound and motion. A blur of navy and white and black flew all around her. She heard the shattering of glass, the click of handguns being cocked, and the barking of orders from two separate male voices, until over the clamor rose words she thought she'd never hear.

"FBI! Get down!"

Chapter 34

Leah's eyes widened, and she struggled to turn her head and shoulders to get a better vantage point. She tugged frantically at her restraints, desperate to be free of them. Every nerve in her body screamed that it was too much—too much noise, too much movement, too much everything.

She felt herself shutting down. She squeezed her eyes tight and tried, against all reason, to pull her hands up to her ears to block the sounds. Her inability to do so only added to the panic and confusion building in her head.

And then Robert's voice in her ear, his tone deadly serious. "Leah, are you okay?"

Her eyes flew open and her jaw dropped. There he was, standing at her bedside. "I—" she wheezed. "You— how did you— you're not dead. I thought you were dead."

Relief washed over his face, and his trembling fingers fumbled with her the cuffs on her arms. A black woman with close-cropped hair stepped to her other side, calmly undoing one cuff, then gently pushing Robert's hands away to unfasten the other. Leah felt a push and a pull on her ankles as well, and suddenly she was free.

Robert helped her sit up and placed his hands squarely on her shoulders. Those bright green eyes looked her over with concern, and all of the sudden, he pulled her toward himself, his arms around her. She could feel his heart pounding. He smelled like sweat and deodorant, and his chest rose and fell with deep breaths.

He's alive. He's really alive.

She closed her eyes, breathing deeply. The muscles in her back slowly relaxed, and his arms loosened around her. After another long moment, he released her. His face was red, his expression sheepish.

"Sorry," he said, rubbing the back of his neck. "I was so worried that we were going to be too late."

Leah held his gaze for a long moment. She tried to say something, but the words just wouldn't come. She shook her head, watching with wide eyes as chaos still unfolded around them. Dr. Pierucci was on his knees, his hands cuffed behind his back. An agent at his side spoke quietly in his ear. The black woman who had been at her bedside a moment before placed the three vials in large plastic bags.

"How did you—?" Leah couldn't finish her sentence.

"It was all Jude," Robert responded, his voice reverent. "If you can believe it."

"Jude..." She repeated the word in a distant tone, but it didn't mean anything to her. She looked around. Jude was nowhere to be seen. She hadn't noticed his absence in the fray. After staring at nothing for a long moment, she blinked and looked down at her hands, still tingling as her blood flow returned to normal. Tears welled up in the corners of her eyes, and she shivered. Out of nowhere, a blanket materialized around her. She looked around and saw another one of Robert's agents walking off. She tried to call out a thanks, but her words caught in her throat.

"Hey," Robert said. He looked directly into her eyes. "I think you need to get out of here and get some rest."

426

"But you—" she said, looking around the room. "How did they... You're okay? Everything is going to be okay?" The words tumbled out of her mouth.

Robert nodded. "Everything is going to be okay." He turned away from her. "Imani, can you get Leah out of here and make sure she gets some water?"

"Sure thing," a woman's voice replied.

Suddenly, Leah felt herself being helped off the orthodontic chair, an arm around her as she was led out of the room. Imani, the woman who had helped her before, guided Leah gently as she tried to turn and look around. Together, they stepped over the threshold into the yellowed linoleum hallway.

How long was I in there?

She continued to glance around her, looking for a clock, but her eyes were heavy and her brain swam. She shivered, even with the blanket, and her teeth began to chatter.

"Let's find you somewhere to sit," Imani said, leading Leah down the hall.

"Leah," someone called from behind her. It was a voice she knew. It was important. She couldn't place it, but she knew she needed to remember. Frantically, she tried to turn to face them, but Imani held a firm grip around her waist.

"Leah!" came the voice again.

It was Jude. She felt her knees give out, and suddenly the ground rushed up to meet her. Her wrists protested as she hit the floor, swollen red scrapes still lining her palms from her earlier fall.

Jude rushed toward her, his gait awkward, his eyes concerned. Imani scooped her up and waited as she found her footing again. It wasn't until Jude got close that Leah

427

noticed that his hands, like his father's, were cuffed behind his back.

"Leah, I just—" Jude began.

Robert peeked his head out of the door. "Everything okay out here?"

He saw the three figures clustered in the middle of the hallway, and his expression changed. Nodding to someone in the room behind him, he stepped out and made his way toward them.

"Sir, I'm sorry, I—" Jude began.

"Mr. Pierucci," Robert interrupted with a frown. "Ms. Harvey needs to rest. She's been through a lot."

Jude nodded, his eyes wide and sad.

"I know you want to talk with her," Robert continued. "But for now, I need you to hang tight until we get all this wrapped up."

Jude nodded again, still silent. Robert placed a hand on his shoulder, and they turned back toward the room.

"Jude," Leah stammered. The two men turned around, one curious, one desperate. "Thank you."

Jude's frame melted in visible relief. His shoulders relaxed. His jaw un-clenched. Robert smiled at her sadly.

As they walked away, Imani offered Leah a hand, and the two women walked down the hallway until they reached a door marked 'Infirmary'. Imani pushed the door open and helped Leah inside.

"You can rest here," she said, pulling out two chairs. "I know Agent McDowell wants to debrief with you, and I'm sure you have questions too. He'll be by in a few minutes, but for now, I'mma get you something to drink, and we're just gonna sit here and enjoy the peace and quiet. You've been through a lot, and we want to make sure you're okay."

"Thank you," Leah muttered. Imani offered her a cup of orange liquid, and the salty sweet taste of electrolyte drink filled her mouth.

The two women sat in companionable silence for a few minutes as Leah sipped her drink. Slowly, her body stopped shivering, and her head began to clear. She wasn't sure how much time passed—it felt at once like an eternity and only a moment.

"Hey," a quiet voice called from the doorway. "How are we doing in here?"

"Come on in," Imani replied, pouring another cup.

Robert stepped in, looking around tentatively. He'd taken off his suit jacket and wore a black vest over his white button-down, his sleeves rolled up to his elbows. The handle of his gun was visible in its holster.

"Here you go." Imani handed him the paper cup of orange drink, which he downed before handing the empty cup back to her.

He turned to face Leah. "Ms. Harvey," he said with a brief nod.

Leah's heart sank. "Hi Agent McDowell," she replied quietly, pulling her blanket tighter around her shoulders.

"How are you feeling?" His eyes were wide and gentle.

"I've been better." She shrugged. "But I've been worse."

He didn't look convinced. "I'm going to have one of my guys come give you a quick check-up, just to make sure you're good to go home, and then what do you say you and I have a little chat?"

She nodded. He placed a hand on her shoulder and smiled at her before walking back out the door. She watched him leave, a disappointment she didn't fully understand settling like a weight on her chest.

Robert's voice called out down the hall, and the doctor walked in a moment later. He made friendly small talk with Imani for a few minutes before checking Leah's blood pressure and temperature. Pulling out a pen light, he looked closely at her pupils, and he watched her drink another cup of water.

"No sign of any physical trauma. Obviously very glad that he didn't have time to get anything in your system other than saline," he said as he carefully peeled back the adhesive around the IV cannula in her arm. "I'm going to go ahead and remove this now, and we'll get you patched up and on your way."

Leah looked away while he slid the thin tube out of her vein. Her head felt light, and she leaned on Imani as the doctor held a cotton ball over the site. He wrapped a strip of neon green bandage around her arm, securing the cotton ball in its place.

"No lifting anything for a couple hours," he said. "You may see some bruising over the next few days. That's totally normal. Otherwise, everything looks good, and you should be fine to go home. Get some rest, and let us know if anything else comes up."

Leah nodded slowly, and he stepped out of the room as quickly as he'd entered it. She stared at the bandage on her arm, flexing slightly to feel it tighten. Already, the first hints of a bruise snaked down her arm.

The doctor's absence left a void, and the relative silence was tangible. Leah looked around, wishing the room had a window. She glanced up at the lights before tentatively standing up. Her legs felt steadier, and she stepped over and flicked the light switch off. Only a few dim round bulbs remained lit. The darkness of the room was comforting.

Imani watched her quietly as she returned to her seat, still shivering. "How are you feeling?"

"Still not great," Leah grimaced. She held up her empty cup. "But this helped."

"Good. That's what we're hoping for." She paused. "You think you're ready to talk to Agent McDowell now? Or do you want a few more minutes?"

Leah's stomach fluttered. "Now is fine."

Imani nodded. "I'll go let him know. You hang tight here. There's more juice in the cabinet if you need it."

"Thanks."

When Imani had left the room, Leah glanced around at the posters and cabinets in the pale glow of the emergency lights. It looked like every doctor's office she'd ever visited, and for a moment, the whole day felt like a bad dream. She scuffed the toe of one shoe against the floor, listening to the squeak of her sneaker sole on the linoleum.

Someone knocked on the door and cracked it open. "May I come in?"

"Of course, Rob—" Leah looked down at her shoes. "Agent McDowell."

He stepped in and sat down in Imani's chair. "Hey."

"Hey," she replied, wishing she could quell the butterflies in her stomach. She wanted to lean her heavy head on his shoulder and close her eyes for a few minutes.

His tone kind but strictly professional, and he didn't comment on the darkness of the room. "Would you prefer to chat in here? Otherwise, we could go out to the courtyard and get some fresh air."

"Fresh air," she nodded, standing up slowly. She didn't feel shaky anymore, but she didn't make a fuss when Robert wrapped an arm around her waist and let her lean on him

431

for support. They made their way out of the infirmary and down the hall. Conversations hushed as they passed, and Leah felt the weight of every eye on her. He led her around a corner to a heavy metal door. When he pushed it open, Leah gasped.

A tiny garden greeted her—two cast iron benches, a small fountain surrounded by purslane flowers, the constant hum of honey bees. Overhead, the sun shone in a cloudless blue sky.

"Wow," she exclaimed hoarsely. "Why is this here?"

She heard a smile in his voice. "I don't know. But one of the guards told me about it, and I thought it might be a nice place for us to debrief."

She nodded, still watching with wonder as the bees bustled around from one flower to the next. She stepped forward and crouched down, observing everything with bright eyes. After a moment, she stood back up and made her way to the bench where Robert had taken a seat.

"So," he heaved a deep sigh. "How are you?"

"I—" Leah started. Words failed her. She examined the fountain in the middle of the garden, watching the water tumble down. It jumped and burbled into the wide basin at the bottom, and little drops splashed out on the concrete sides.

"Why don't I start?" Agent McDowell gently interrupted her thoughts.

She nodded. The words caught in her throat, and she blinked back tears.

"Obviously, things didn't go according to plan." He looked over at her, but she didn't meet his gaze. "But that's okay—that's something we always try to anticipate. That's why we have backup plans."

Leah continued nodding, her eyes still locked on the fountain and the flowers and the bees.

His tone sobered. "But I'll be honest with you, Ms. Harvey—we'd be dead in the water if it weren't for Jude."

Leah turned toward him, her eyes wide. "What?"

He raised his eyebrows, all seriousness. "I thought I'd already told you that, I'm sorry."

She squinted and cocked her head, trying to remember.

"Don't worry, don't worry," he reassured her. "It's okay if you didn't hear me. There was a lot going on. When we walked out of the boba shop, you ran, just like I told you to. I was mid-swing at Jude when he blurted out that he needed to get away from his father." Agent McDowell met Leah's eyes. "He helped me make sure that my team would be here on time. He convinced his father to leave me unattended in the console room so that they could come release me. He made sure I got my gun back. And he told me all about—"

"The bodies!" Leah interrupted. Her heart started racing again, and her body tensed up. "Detective Inglish, from the precinct! He takes them and makes up serial killer stories to explain how they died."

Agent McDowell nodded. "Exactly. I told Jude that his sentence would be lighter if he could help us get his father on the murder charges." He looked away from Leah, watching a bumblebee flit around the garden. "I don't know the man at all, but I would have said he seemed relieved by the offer."

Leah felt a tear streaming down her face. "He was," she whispered. "He's been ready for years. He just didn't think he'd be able to do it."

For a moment, neither of them spoke. Water cascaded down the fountain, casting a shimmering light on the ground. Leah was painfully aware of how close Agent McDowell was to her. She scooted away from him an inch or two and then immediately regretted it. He looked over at her, a look on his face that she couldn't quite read. There were so many things she wanted to say.

"Ms. Harvey," Agent McDowell said eventually, and she turned to meet his eyes. "I meant it when I said we'd be dead if it weren't for Jude. I had no idea Dr. Pierucci would move in so quickly, and my team wasn't scheduled to be on site at the prison until tonight. It was irresponsible of me to put you in so much danger, and I'm sorry."

Leah shivered. "It all worked out in the end."

They sat side by side on the cast iron bench for a few minutes longer. Leah played their conversation back in her head, aware of every formality between them. Once again, the question filled her mind of whether Agent McDowell might intentionally manipulate her emotions in order to ensure her cooperation.

Surely, he wouldn't. He's not really like that. Right?

The mental image she'd conjured of Agent McDowell and Detective Inglish exchanging friendly punches wouldn't leave her alone.

I don't even know anymore. And what's the point, anyway?

Eventually, Agent McDowell stood, dusted off his pants, and turned back toward the door. "I probably ought to check in and see how things are going inside. You're welcome to stay out here as long as you'd like." He took a few steps toward the door before adding, "I know Jude would like to talk to you, if you're feeling up to a conversation."

Leah turned around on the bench, nodding slowly. "I think I ca—"

He interrupted her. "If not, there's no need to force it."

She shook her head. "No, I think I need to talk to him as well. Can... can you send him here? Or do I need to come inside?"

Agent McDowell tilted his head from side to side, his lips pursed. "He is technically in custody, so I really shouldn't let him be alone with you. But I know you might want some privacy." He placed a hand on the doorknob and sighed. "Tell you what, I'll send him out here, and I'll just prop the door open and stand in the hall."

Leah nodded her thanks and watched as Agent McDowell stepped back into the bustling hallway of the prison. When the door clicked closed, she turned her attention to the purslane flowers—reds and yellows, pinks and oranges dancing among waxy green leaves. A few of the flowers had begun to close for the day, and Leah found herself wondering how much sun the garden got.

A few minutes later, Agent McDowell returned with Jude, whose hands were no longer secured behind his back. His left wrist still bore the metal cuff, and Agent McDowell fastened the other end around the arm of the bench. Jude said nothing, studying the red bricks of the garden walls.

As promised, Agent McDowell left the door open but remained standing inside the building, out of earshot. The chatter from the hallway had begun to die down, but an occasional shout still drifted into the otherwise tranquil garden.

"Jude," Leah began. "Agent McDowell told me what you did."

He turned to face her, his blue-gray eyes wide and sad. "I wish it hadn't taken me so long to do it." His shoulders fell. "When we got coffee on Saturday, I was still so sure

435

that he was right and that you would come around eventually... He was listening to the whole conversation, of course, and we both thought that you'd come around eventually."

Something twisted in Leah's gut, and she looked away.

He continued. "But then the way he talked about you this weekend, it just... It killed me. I finally came to the realization that no matter what he said, he didn't actually care about you, maybe didn't even respect you anymore. It was always about him."

Leah didn't know what to say. She sat quietly beside him, waiting for him to speak again.

When he did, his voice was quiet. "I'm sorry about last year, Leah. I'm sorry I didn't stand up for you."

Leah swallowed down the lump in her throat.

"I can't change the past," he continued, looking down at his shoes. "But I hope I can make up for it."

"What you did today—" She stopped mid-sentence. "Thank you, Jude. You did a good thing."

He smiled at her sadly, then turned around and waved at Agent McDowell. Leah watched as McDowell silently unlocked the handcuff from the bench and led Jude back into the hallway.

"Goodbye, Jude," she whispered as the door closed behind them. Her heart ached, and each breath felt heavy. Slowly, the tears that had been building up inside her began to trickle down her face.

The shadows had lengthened when she wiped her eyes and looked around her again. She was seated on the darker side of the courtyard, the shade a welcome reprieve from the summer's heat. Turning around, she glanced at the door through which Agent McDowell and Jude had left.

I'm sure the door is unlocked. I could just leave.

But she didn't stand up. Turning back to the fountain, she watched the water trickle downward, the light dancing as the sun shifted in the sky.

A soft whoosh behind her caught her ear, and Agent McDowell sat down next to her on the bench again. He'd put his glasses back on, the bruise around his eye magnified by the lens. She was suddenly very aware of her own puffy red eyes and splotchy face.

"You ready to go home?" If he noticed that she'd been crying, he said nothing.

Leah breathed deeply. "Yeah."

"Great. I told my team I'd give you a ride." He gestured in the direction of the door. "They're going out for drinks... I'm trying to decide if I want to meet up with them, or if I just want to go back to the hotel and crash for the next fifteen or twenty hours."

Leah chuckled quietly.

"There she is." He smiled, but his eyes looked heavy. "I'm sorry that today took such a toll. You being strapped down on that table... Pierucci having all those needles loaded..." He took his glasses off and rubbed the bridge of his nose. "I keep asking myself what would have happened if we had come in thirty seconds later."

"Yeah." Leah's voice was flat. "When Jude came back into my room with Dr. Pierucci, I thought you were dead. I just kept wishing I'd had a chance to talk to you..." She didn't finish her thought.

He stared at his shoes. "I wish I'd had a chance to tell you about Jude before we got here."

"Yeah." Leah shook her head watching an ant crawl across the gravel. "There just wasn't, though."

"Still," he insisted. "This isn't how I like to treat my informants."

Her heart twisted in her chest, and she swallowed hard. A single butterfly flitted through the garden, black and blue and orange and white. It landed on a flower and slowly stretched its wings.

"Well," Agent McDowell said, standing up. The butterfly spooked and darted off. "Let's get out of here."

They stood up, and Leah rolled up the blanket she'd been wearing like a shawl. "Can I give this back to... what was her name, your friend who was taking care of me?"

"Imani?" Agent McDowell put a hand on the doorknob and pulled the door open. "I don't think that's ours–I think it belongs here. But yeah, just give it to one of my team, and they'll take care of it for you."

Leah's heart started racing as she stepped across the threshold back into the hallway. "Is... Are they still..." Her feet froze in place.

Agent McDowell took a few more steps before he realized she was no longer beside him. He turned around, and his eyes softened. "They're gone. Jude and Dr. Pierucci were both taken into custody and left the premises about half an hour ago."

Leah nodded, shivering. Her eyes darted up and down the hall, following a few employees who were cleaning up the rooms she and Robert had been held in. She handed the blanket to one of them, who accepted it silently and walked away.

"Come on, Ms. Harvey," he beckoned. "You're going to be okay."

There was something in his voice. Compassion? Impatience? She took a tentative step forward.

"That's it. Here we go."

The walk out seemed to last an age, and Leah jumped at every sound and every person who crossed their path. It wasn't until they were walking through the front door of the facility that Leah realized they weren't going out the way they'd come in.

Stepping out of the prison and into the warm evening air left Leah's toes feeling icy. A black SUV was parked in the spacious circle driveway. Agent McDowell pulled a set of keys out of his pocket and opened Leah's door for her before walking around to the driver's side.

"Hey Robe–Agent McDowell?" Leah asked as she fastened her seat belt. "Do you always carry a gun?"

He clicked his own seat belt and looked at her, one eyebrow raised. "Yes. I always carry my gun when I'm on the job. Just like I wear contacts instead of glasses. It's part of the uniform."

She turned and looked out the window, saying nothing.

"Why do you ask?"

"I just... didn't think about it." The engine rumbled to life, and Leah added. "I saw you reach for it at the boba place, and I..." She hesitated. "I got really scared that you were going to shoot Jude."

He grimaced and said nothing. Leah began rehashing the conversation in her head, wondering what she should have said differently.

As the scenery changed and the pastures gave way to shopping centers, Leah blinked out of her thoughts. "Do you know how to get to my apartment?"

He paused for a moment to consider her words, as if he too had been lost in thought. "No. Can you tell me where to get off the freeway?"

She pulled the directions up on her phone and nestled it in the center of the car where he could see it. For a few minutes, the exits flew past in silence. Leah recognized more and more of their surroundings, and the afternoon at Scarlett Bay felt more and more like a nightmare.

"How did Jude know where we were?" she blurted out before she could stop herself.

Agent McDowell glanced over at her before turning his eyes back to the road. "He slipped a GPS tag in your backpack at the clinic. When your location didn't match the van's, they decided to move in."

Leah's heart sank. He glanced over at her again, his eyes sad. "My team is looking into the lead Jude gave us about Inglish as we speak. We're going to get him, too. We're going to get all of them."

She nodded, unconvinced.

They rode the rest of the way in silence. When Agent McDowell eased the SUV into a parking spot in her apartment complex, he unlocked the door and let her leave without getting out to say goodbye.

"We'll figure out picking up your car in the morning," he said. "I'll shoot you a text."

"Sounds good." Leah struggled to keep her voice steady. She shut the door of the SUV, and it thumped closed before he could say anything in return. He waved as she turned and walked toward the door of her apartment.

Ten minutes later, still in her clothes, Leah was fast asleep.

Chapter 35

When Leah awoke, light danced on the walls of her bedroom. She yawned and stretched, her blouse stiff around her shoulders.

Why am I still in my—

And then it hit her. Fear and relief crashed down like a wave, and she sat on her bed, feet on the floor, paralyzed.

Then, slowly, she stood up. One foot in front of the other, she made her way over to the kitchen, where the coffee maker was still full of damp grounds from the last time she'd used it. Rinsing it out and soaping it down felt like an act of thanksgiving—what would her landlord have thought if he'd come to clean out her empty apartment and found moldy coffee grounds growing by the sink? What would her mother have said?

I need to call Mom.

She filled the coffee grinder with fresh beans and let the machine rumble away.

She's going to be livid when she hears how much danger we were in.

Leah poured filtered water into the bottom of the moka pot, then filled the basket with coffee grounds and gently set it in place.

I hope she doesn't think it's all Robert's fault.

Her cheeks reddened as she screwed the top half of the espresso maker onto the bottom, set it on the stove, and turned on the heat.

Not that it matters, I guess.

Sighing, she pulled out her phone and made the call.

"Hi," her mom's voice greeted her. "You've reached the voicemail box of Donna Harvey. I can't get to the phone right now, so just leave a message, and I'll call you back whenever I get around to it."

Leah's heart sank. "Hey Mom," she said. "I was just calling to chat. I had a big day yesterday, and I guess I just wanted to talk about it with you. Hope you're doing well." She paused, wracking her brain for anything else to say. "I love you. Call me back. Bye."

She ended the call and pulled out two eggs, scrambling them in a bowl with her favorite spice mix. Examining the contents of her refrigerator, she also pulled out a wilted bunch of green onions and an orange bell pepper that had seen better days. Working around the spoiled parts, she chopped the veggies up and let them sizzle in the pan for a few minutes.

Her phone rang.

Mom!

She raced to pick it up.

"Ms. Harvey, how are you feeling this morning?" Agent McDowell's voice greeted her.

She exhaled heavily and hoped he couldn't hear the disappointment in her voice. "Fine, how are you?"

He didn't sound convinced. "I'm doing well. I was wondering if you'd like some help retrieving your car."

"I, um..." She hadn't thought about the car at all. "I guess that'd be helpful."

"I'm guessing you're at home? I'll head out in a few minutes. Would you send me the address?"

"Of course. See you in a little bit."

"Lea—"

She'd already ended the call before she heard him speaking. Her phone beeped and the screen went dark.

If he needs something, he'll call back.

Turning back to the stove, she pulled the coffee off and glanced at the chopped veggies into the pan. For a few minutes, the process of preparing breakfast was all she could focus on. Salt, pepper, garlic on the veggies. Honey in the coffee. Stir. Add milk and ice. Pour the eggs into the pan. Stir. There was something freeing in it.

When she sat down to eat, her hand compulsively reached for her phone, checking to see if maybe she'd missed a call from her mom.

Nothing.

She ate slowly, tasting each bite and letting it warm her from the inside out. The crepe myrtle outside her window waved in the breeze. A stray cat mewled as it walked past.

Everything is going to be okay.

She was down to the last sip of coffee when Agent McDowell knocked on her door. Setting her cup back on the table, she walked over to let him in. He was dressed in his usual suit and tie, his left eye purplish and swollen behind his glasses.

He looked her up and down when she answered the door. "Sleep well?"

Leah looked down at her wrinkled blouse and rubbed her face. "Something like that. Give me ten minutes."

"Can do." He sat down on the couch and looked around at the empty walls of her living room.

Leah changed quickly and ran a toothbrush over her teeth before grabbing her backpack and walking back toward the living room. His eyes widened when he saw her, and he held out a hand. Leah furrowed her eyebrows and extended a hand as well.

"Backpack?" he said.

"Oh." She drew her hand back and gave him the backpack. "Here you go."

He unzipped each pocket and rummaged around for a few minutes before pulling out a small white square. "Jude's GPS device. We'll give it to Peter at the clinic."

She nodded, eyes wide. Agent McDowell stood and walked to the door, glancing at her expectantly. She followed behind him, locking the door and walking out into the parking lot.

His navy blue sedan was parked in her unofficial spot. "I had one of my guys drive me back by yesterday," he explained as they climbed in. "I wasn't sure if they'd tow."

The drive to the clinic was uneventful, and Leah breathed a sigh of relief at the sight of her car sitting in the same place she'd left it. As they pulled into the spot next to it, Leah was struck by how unchanged everything was.

Do they even know yet? They have to know, right?

Peter opened the clinic's front door as Agent McDowell shifted the car into park. His hair stood straight up, and his eyes looked tired. Leah waved slowly, and they both stepped out of the car as Peter raced toward them.

He skidded to a stop right in front of the sedan. "Did you get them?"

Leah nodded, suddenly emotional.

"Hell yes. Well done, Harvey." Peter ran his fingers through his hair. "I started panicking when I saw your car

444

in the parking lot as I was leaving yesterday. I couldn't stop thinking that our last conversation was going to be a fight. I'm so sorry—"

"Don't worry about it, Peter," Leah interrupted him. She heard the exhaustion in her voice.

"No," he insisted. "I'm sorry. I was being cruel, and I knew it."

Leah cocked her head.

"Come on, Harvey. I knew deep down that you'd come around eventually... but somehow that makes it worse." He clapped Agent McDowell on the shoulder. "Roberto here tried to talk sense into all of us, but we didn't listen. Much obliged to you, man."

Agent McDowell waved a hand. "All in a day's work."

"I can't believe y'all pulled it off." Peter shook his head, running his hands through his hair again. "One of these days, you've got to tell me the whole story."

"One of these days," Leah nodded. Her eyes felt heavy.

"And Jude?" Peter's voice was quiet. "Did he... I mean, did you get to talk to him after everything happened? To either of them?"

Leah shivered and crossed her arms. "I talked to Jude for a few minutes. He..." She glanced at Agent McDowell, who nodded. "He's the reason we walked out alive. Had a change of heart at the last minute. I still... I don't know. It's a lot."

Peter stared at her, wide-eyed, but didn't press the matter further. He looked over to Agent McDowell.

"One of these days," McDowell reassured him. "But not today."

Wordlessly, Leah walked around to her car door and climbed inside, feeling the pull of exhaustion deep in her bones. Peter winked at her and smiled sadly, and she waved at him. Agent McDowell visibly started when he noticed that Leah was no longer standing beside him, but he stepped out of her way and let her drive off.

***

Back at home, Leah climbed into bed and pulled the covers up over her shoulders. She closed her heavy eyes and fell right asleep.

Her clock read ten past noon when she awoke to a knock on the door. Bleary-eyed and stiff, Leah pulled herself out of bed and walked to the door with clunky steps. She peered through the peephole and gasped. Her fingers fumbled with the lock, and she pulled the door open.

Her heart leapt. "Mom?"

"Hi, Leah," her mom said. She wore a garnet and white Swarthmore t-shirt that Leah had given her, and her hair was grayer than Leah remembered it.

"Mom, what are you doing here?" Tears formed in Leah's eyes as she wrapped her mom in a hug.

"Well, I got an email from the Institute last night about Dr. Pierucci and decided to come right down instead of waiting until the fall."

Leah gulped as she took the handle of her mom's rolling bag and pulled it into the living room. "Come in, come in. How was your flight? Did you rent a car? How long are you staying?"

"Fine, yes, and through Friday, if you'll have me." She sat down and adjusted her sunglasses on top of her head. Leah sat down beside her and pulled her legs up onto the couch, leaning against her mom's shoulder. Her mom wrapped an arm around her and kissed her hair.

"So, what did the email say?" Leah asked hesitantly.

"Oh, Leah, it was the most bizarre experience. I opened it up on accident—I don't normally read their emails anymore, but someone I found myself on this one—and I tell you what, I almost dropped my phone right on the floor when I read it."

"Yeah?"

"Why don't I just read it to you?" She pulled out her phone and tapped the screen a couple of times. Leah sat up and read the email over her shoulder.

Dear Friend of the Institute,

We are shocked and disheartened by the news coming out of Scarlett Bay Correctional Facility this afternoon regarding Dr. Jude Pierucci, Sr. His actions were unknown to the board and do not reflect the values or mission of the McNeill Institute that he helped to found. In an emergency session, the board voted to remove him from his position, effective immediately. We are beginning the search for a new President who will lead the Institute into an era of healing and transparency.

If you have an appointment scheduled at an Institute clinic, your local staff will reach out if there are any disruptions in the schedule. We are working diligently to minimize the day-to-day impact of this transition, and we appreciate your patience during this challenging time.

Sincerely,
Alice Zhang
Chairwoman, Board of Directors
McNeill Institute for Neurological Development

Leah sighed, and her mom put the phone back in her pocket. "After that, it didn't take much time to find out what was going on. I rescheduled my flight before I went to bed and landed about half an hour ago. I think I missed a call from you this morning when I was on the plane, but I didn't tell you I was coming because I didn't want you to convince me not to."

Her mom laughed, and Leah couldn't help joining in. "That is exactly the kind of thing I would do, isn't it?"

Her mom stroked her hair gently. "So I've got to know—did you get that email too, or is this the first you're hearing about it? The timing is so odd," her voice faltered. "Just with everything you were telling me on the phone recently."

Here goes nothing.

Leah grinned sheepishly. "I was... actually... there. At the prison. It was my lead that tipped the FBI off to everyth—"

"Leah!" Her mom's jaw dropped, and her eyes grew huge. "You're not serious, are you? Oh my gosh, you are serious." She covered her mouth with her hand. "Why didn't you tell me what was happening?"

Leah grimaced, covering her mouth with her hand. "I didn't want to scare you!"

"What happened? I mean, is everything oka—? Are you okay? Everything I saw on the news sounded like it was a huge operation—how did you even get involved in it?"

"It's a long story." Leah scratched at her scalp just above her ear. "And you're not going to be happy about it."

"Leah, you tell me right this instant." There was urgency in her mom's voice, but no anger. "What happened?"

"Well, so last year, right before Jude and I broke up—"

Another knock on the door interrupted Leah. In spite of herself, she breathed a sigh of relief.

"Who's that?" her mom asked, still breathlessly waiting for Leah's story.

"I don't know." Leah frowned and shrugged, moving the blinds a fraction of an inch so she could peek through.

It was Robert.

She barely recognized him in a t-shirt and blue jeans, his hands in his pockets as he rocked back and forth and stared at her door. He was more muscular than she'd realized, and for a second, she just watched him.

What is he doing here?

"Hang on, Mom, I've got to get this." Leah hoped her mom couldn't hear her heart pounding as she turned the lock and cracked the door open.

"Hey, Leah. I—" He looked past Leah and blushed. "I hope I'm not interrupting anything."

"Who is it, Leah?" her mom called from behind her.

Leah laughed and stepped aside.

"Mom," she said as he crossed the threshold, stifling a smile at the surprise on her mom's face. "This is Special Agent Robert McDowell. He led the whole thing yesterday."

She turned to Robert, who also looked shocked, and felt the color rising in her own cheeks. "Agent McDowell, this is my mom."

He recovered quickly, and without missing a beat, he extended a warm handshake. "A pleasure to meet you, Mrs. Harvey. Your daughter is a very special woman."

"I'm glad I'm not the only one who sees it." Leah's mom gave her a pointed look before standing up and shaking Robert's hand. "And please, call me Donna."

"Well, Donna, I'm about to hop on my flight back to DC, but I wanted to check in with Leah first and see how she's feeling after yesterday. We'll have a doozy of a trial here in the next couple months."

"Is that so?" Donna glanced at Robert, then back at Leah. "I actually just got in from a flight myself and really need to use the restroom. If you'll excuse me." She nodded to Robert and walked down the hall. Leah blushed and watched her go.

"Hi Agent McDowell." She turned back toward him.

"Hi Leah."

Her heart fluttered in her chest, and she tried to stop it. "So you're off to DC? Another big sting operation next week? Or are you off to climb the mountains of Colorado?" She regretted her words as soon as she said them. They were too friendly, too familiar.

He furrowed his brow for a moment before a light bulb went off. "Oh, that scar. Yeah that was definitely not from mountain climbing."

Leah's eyebrows shot up, her mouth agape. "What? How did you get it?"

He winked at her. "A story for another day. We'll be seeing a lot of each other until we get Pierucci behind bars."

She looked away from him and glanced around the room. Her eyes landed on her mom's purple rolling suitcase. The fabric on one corner was frayed, and she knew from experience that one of the wheels didn't turn.

I don't know why she doesn't just replace it.

"Well," she replied eventually. "Just let me know what you need for the trial, and I'll be there."

"I will. Thanks Leah." He stood next to her silently, studying her face.

She looked away, fidgeting with a hangnail. When she glanced back up, his eyes were still on her.

"What?" A nervous laugh escaped her chest.

He sighed and looked away. "Look, Leah, I know we've been through a lot lately. And not just yesterday, right, but this whole year. I know you might not be ready to trust me, after the whole Wilder thing—I..." He paused and rubbed the back of his neck. When he looked back up at her, his green eyes sparkled. "I've really enjoyed getting to know you, and I would love for you to get to know just plain Robert. Not Wilder Frederick, adrenaline junkie. Not Special Agent Robert McDowell... well, okay, I guess adrenaline junkie was a bad example." He laughed. "There is a reason I got into this line of work."

Leah couldn't stop smiling.

"I..." He paused again, watching her face. "I can't be super friendly during the trial. Yesterday at the prison, with my whole team there, I freaked out, and... well, anyway, I don't want you to be caught off guard if I have to be a little distant during the legal proceedings. I don't think either of us wants to risk things getting derailed by claims that we have a conflict of interest..."

She nodded, a hand over her mouth to hide her grin.

"But afterwards, I'd really like to give you a chance to get to know, well, Robert." He gestured to his t-shirt and his messy hair.

"I would love that." Her cheeks hurt from smiling.

He winked and elbowed her. "Yeah, you would."

Before she knew what she was doing, she stepped forward and threw her arms around him, holding him tightly. He did the same, and for a long moment, they stood silently in her living room. His t-shirt was softer than she'd expected, and he smelled good. She closed her eyes and breathed deeply, feeling the week's tension release.

After a long moment, he pushed her away. "Ms. Harvey!" he exclaimed in feigned shock. "Please, let's keep things professional." He couldn't finish his sentence without laughing.

She saluted him, trying and failing to maintain a serious expression. "Sir, yes sir."

He groaned. "Now I don't want to leave."

Leah raised her eyebrows. "Oh yeah? You want to be here when I tell my mom how you almost got me killed yesterday? How Jude totally saved the day?"

He snorted and looked at the ceiling. "Never mind, Harvey, I'll see you around."

They laughed again, and Robert glanced at his watch. "I do need to get going, though. My flight leaves in two and a half hours, and I have no idea where I'm going."

She gave him a playful smack on the arm, blushing when her hand touched his skin. "Get outta here!"

He opened the door, turning to look back one more time. His whole face smiled, and Leah's stomach fluttered.

"Do you play Murdle?" he asked, one foot out the door.

"You literally know that I play Murdle! We've talked about this!"

"Oh, it's so on." He winked and closed the door.

Leah watched through her window as he walked back toward the parking lot. His absence left her sick to her stomach, and she sat down on the couch, her eyes closed. A moment later, her mom stepped back into the living room.

"He seems nice." She said, trying to sound nonchalant. After another moment, she added, "Cute, too."

Leah rolled her eyes and groaned. "Mom!"

Chapter 36

Leah and her mom spent the rest of the day catching up and running errands around town. When Leah's fatigue began to overwhelm her, they stopped for coffee at Common Grounds and sat on the patio watching the after-school crowd climb around on the playground.

While they were sipping their coffees, Leah's phone buzzed with a text message. She was surprised to see Valerie's name pop up on the screen.

Are you free tomorrow for lunch? Lots to talk about.

How sweet of her to check in on me.

She responded with an affirmative, silenced her phone, and slipped it back into her pocket.

"Is this the place you used to come with Jude every weekend?" Leah's mom asked, her voice quiet. "I don't think I've ever been here before."

Leah nodded. "Yeah. We'd sit at the back corner table for a couple hours and just catch up. It was always nice to have some time together that wasn't work-related."

She took another sip of her coffee and looked out over the grassy field. A runaway preschooler was cackling and sprinting as fast as his little legs would carry him, his mother not far behind.

She kept watching the child and added, "It's also where I had my breakdown."

Her mom's gaze felt heavy, but Leah didn't meet her eyes. "I came here, just force of habit, I guess... and Jude was here, and he was so surprised to see me—he came over to say hello, and I got spooked and took off running... It was frankly a miracle that he found me at all, and then he called the clinic to get me an overnight room." She looked over at her mom, her shoulders slumped. "I don't know. I keep thinking about him today." She sighed. "I just wish things had been different."

Her mom didn't say anything, but she reached over and gave Leah's hand a squeeze.

They left Common Grounds and made dinner at home, laughing and crying over a bottle of wine and a side of salmon they'd splurged on. As the sun began to set, Leah lined her couch with clean sheets and pulled out her extra pillows.

"Sorry I don't have a guest bed or something." She grabbed a blanket from the basket next to the couch and handed it to her mom. "But I'm really glad you're here."

Her mom gave her a hug and sat down on the couch, smoothing out the pillowcase. "I'm glad to be here too, honey. Sleep well."

Leah walked back to her room, flicked off the lights, and curled up in bed. The sounds of her mom puttering around—brushing her teeth, tidying up in the kitchen, watching her show—lulled Leah into a deep sleep.

Wednesday morning dawned, cloudy skies keeping the light low as Leah and her mom drank their coffee on the small patio of her apartment. Connor waved at them on his way out to work but didn't stop to chat—his untied tie and uncombed hair gave Leah the impression that he'd overslept—and Leah told her mom all about her neighbors.

Finishing her coffee, she took one last breath of the fresh morning air before heading inside. Her mom had made plans with some old friends in town, and Leah had some time before she needed to start getting ready for her lunch with Valerie. She deep cleaned the bathroom, swept under the couch, and threw away all the trash that had built up in her car. A couple hours later, worn out and satisfied with her work, she sank into the couch and put on a show.

When lunch time rolled around, she drove to the address Valerie had sent her, pulled into a parking spot, and stepped inside the restaurant. Valerie was already there, looking radiant in a bright yellow top, her hair loose and curly. She stood up and waved Leah over, smiling widely.

"Leah! Thanks so much for meeting me. How are you?"

"Doing okay," Leah replied. "My mom heard the news about the Institute and came to visit, and it's been really great to spend some time with her. I'm still super tired, but I guess that's not totally unexpected."

"I'm glad to hear you have some support. I'm sure it'll take time for the dust to settle, but it's much easier with someone close by."

"Yeah," Leah nodded. "How are you doing?"

Valerie looked around slowly. "I'm feeling a lot of relief that Dr. Pierucci is no longer running the Institute. My father would be happy to hear it."

"I'm sure he would. And I'm sure he'd be proud of you for the role you played in making it happen." Leah leaned in and took a sip of water.

Valerie raised her eyebrows. "I don't know. I could have done more... I should have done more." She held Leah's gaze as she added, "As I told you that night at Natalie's house—when I had the chance to act, I ran away. I'm not proud of that."

Leah didn't know how to respond. She picked up a piece of bread from the middle of the table and slowly spread butter across it.

"My father," Valerie continued. "He worried about Dr. Pierucci, you know. They founded the Institute together when Dr. Pierucci was just a resident, and I always got the sense that Dad regretted bringing him on board at all. But when Dad asked me to take over his role as President, I said no, and then Dr. Pierucci forced his way into the position instead... I left the Institute for good shortly after Dad's death, as you know."

"You couldn't have known what Pierucci would become" Leah offered, fiddling with her fork.

"I did know." Valerie's voice was heavy. "Or, at least, I had my suspicions. I knew he shouldn't be practicing medicine." She took a sip of her water and smiled at the waitress who brought their plates to the table. For a few minutes, both women focused on their food, and the conversation lulled.

When Valerie looked back at Leah, her eyes seemed brighter. "You asked me a few weeks ago if I'd ever go back to the Institute..."

Leah looked up from her food, eyebrows raised.

Valerie waited silently for a moment before responding deliberately, considering each word. "I got a call from the Chairwoman of the Board late Monday night asking if I would consider stepping in as the new President."

A wide smile broke out on Leah's face. "Valerie! That's amazing! Truly, I can't think of a better person to take the helm." She raised her eyebrows. "You are going to accept the position, right?"

Valerie smiled, her eyes revealing something between pride and exhaustion. "It's an honor, certainly... although part of me wonders if they've only asked me because I'm my father's daughter. DeLeon is a well-known name in the Institute's circles, and my stepping in will really boost confidence for their donor base."

Leah waved the thought away. "But even so—even if that were true, which it's not—you'll be able to do so much good in that role." Excitement built in Leah's chest as she thought about the Institute's future under Valerie's leadership.

"I hope so." Valerie watched as a couple sat down at the table next to them. "The wheels of change don't move quickly, but I have a unique perspective and a lot of ideas... And I'm committed to making things happen."

Leah leaned forward, her eyebrows arched. "So you're going to accept it?"

"I already have." Valerie smiled. "I'll go in to complete the paperwork before the end of the week."

Leah released a sigh. "I'm glad to hear it. The Institute will be in good hands."

"Better than some, at least." Valerie's face grew thoughtful. "But I want someone by my side who also knows what it's been like in the past... someone else who's committed to making the changes that are necessary." She looked at Leah pointedly.

Leah's heart skipped a beat. "What are you saying?"

"Would you come back with me?" She asked the question plainly, as if it were the most natural thing in the world. "I have high hopes of re-opening the Children's

457

Ward, and I can't think of a better Director than you. You have the experience, the knowledge, the passion..."

"You're offering me a job?" Leah felt her jaw drop.

Valerie nodded, laughing under her breath. "I am. I know you might need some time to think ab—"

"No, I'm in." Leah shook her head, her eyes wide. "I don't have anything lined up right now... I think I told you that I was let go last week?"

Valerie's face revealed that Leah had not told her, but she didn't interrupt.

Leah continued. "With everything that's been going on, I haven't been able to get more than a handful of applications submitted... and besides, you know how much the Children's Ward means to me. I couldn't pass up an opportunity like this, even if I did have another offer on the table." Her heart swelled.

"Well, that's settled, then." Valerie nodded decisively. "When can you start?"

Leah laughed. "How soon do you want me?"

Valerie shrugged. "I want you involved from the get-go, helping with interviews and hiring contractors to spruce up the building." She took another bite, chewed, and swallowed. "We'll start small—probably one pediatric neurologist and a couple of technicians, and then an administrator or a hospitality director, just someone to keep the place running and welcoming. You've been through treatment at the Children's Ward, so you know better than I do what's necessary and what's not."

"You call that small?" Leah's eyes were wide. "Is there room in the budget for all that?"

Valerie laughed. "We'll find room. With the Scarlett Bay program on pause, we'll be able to divert the funds back to the kids." She raised her eyebrows and pursed her lips. "And I think we'll be able to find some donors to help build the place back up. Yours wasn't the only family that was disappointed when the Children's Ward shut down."

A realization dawned on Leah. "The in-house funding for Scarlett Bay came from the Children's Ward budget?"

Valerie nodded, her eyes downcast. "Father was so disappointed—he really felt like his vision for the Institute was abandoned. He couldn't bear to see everything he'd worked for being taken down brick by brick, and so he left. I'm grateful for the chance to help rebuild it."

They spent the remainder of the meal chatting about their hopes for the organization and reminiscing about their parallel experiences growing up around the Institute. Leah had a new spring in her step when she returned home, and she talked her mom's ear off all afternoon. She jotted down renovation ideas, researched possible hires, and daydreamed about programming she'd like to implement for her future patients and their families. By the time Friday morning rolled around, when both Leah and Valerie signed their contracts, Leah was ready to start making things happen.

She wanted to set her start date for the following Monday. "I just dropped my mom off at the airport! My weekend and next week are totally empty."

"You need to rest, Leah," Valerie insisted. "You've been through a lot, and jumping into the next big project to distract yourself from the discomfort won't serve you well." She added quietly, "Believe me. I know that from experience."

Leah acquiesced, accepting a full week of down time. She promised Valerie that she'd do her best to keep her mind off the Institute, the Pieruccis, and the preliminary preparations for the trial. And, as best as she could, she stuck to her word. She went for a run every morning, relishing the first rays of sunshine on her face and shoulders. She pulled out her favorite old cookbook and whipped up a few family recipes. She raided the craft store and came home with knitting needles and yarn, committed to teaching herself how to knit.

***

Three days into her rest week, she received an unexpected text from Natalie.

> We're home. Matthew is feeling loads better. I know
> he'd like to see you if you're free.

Leah made her way over to their house that afternoon, lugging along a double batch of cookies. Before she had even climbed out of her car, the kids were running out toward her, clamoring for her attention and then asking her for a cookie. Natalie stood in the doorway, granting a nod of permission, and Leah offered her a sad smile. She handed a cookie to each child, and they took off back into the house.

When Leah finally reached the door, she spoke in a hushed tone. "How is he? Was he ever able to tell you what they did to him?"

Natalie nodded slowly. "He's doing much better. Most of it seemed to be simple exhaustion, which I consider an enormous blessing... and which I attribute in large part to you and Robert's quick thinking. I spoke with Robert a few days ago, and he said that rumor around the precinct was that Matthew was headed for Scarlett Bay." She shuddered. "That would have shattered him."

460

Leah exhaled heavily. "I'm so glad we got to him when we did. He already looked so broken when we picked him up, and I know Pierucci would have been ruthless if they'd gotten him hooked up to a console. He was absolutely unhinged on Monday."

"Leah, about that—" Natalie wiped something out of her eye.

"Please don't worry, Nat. Everyone came out safe, and that's what matters. Pierucci is going to be put away for a very long time, and all the horrible things he was doing are going to be exposed and stopped." Her cheeks flushed, warm and red. "I'm only sorry that it took Matthew getting kidnapped before I was ready to step up."

Natalie squeezed Leah's hand and was about to respond when Matthew walked slowly out of the hallway. "Leah? Is that you?"

She wanted to weep at the sight of him. "Matthew! How are you feeling?" She didn't comment on the obvious weight he'd lost since she'd seen him last.

"Doing alright, all things considered." He extended an arm and gave her a side hug. "We stayed at some friends' house out of town for a few days, and I think I slept for fifteen hours the first day we were there. Been recovering slowly. Finally getting my appetite back, which wasn't something I expected to lose." He paused for a moment before adding quietly, "McDowell old us that you guys got Pierucci."

Leah nodded. "We got him."

"Praise God," Matthew sighed. "I want to hear the whole story, but maybe in a few days. It's still a little too real right now." He hobbled past them, toward the kitchen. "I'm going to make some coffee. Do either of you want any?"

"Let me do that, Matthew! You sit down and eat some cookies." Leah tipped the open container toward him.

He grinned and plopped down on the couch. "Ah, well, you've convinced me."

Leah handed him a few cookies on a napkin before setting about making some coffee. The three of them chatted for another few minutes until the kids came back inside to ask for another round of cookies. Natalie shook her head discreetly, and Leah launched a tickle attack on Josephine. Nat took advantage of the moment to hide the sweets, and Leah spent most of the next hour playing hide and seek or pushing Victor on the tree swing he and Matthew had set up outside. By the time she was ready to go, her sides hurt from laughing.

As she made her way out the door, Matthew stopped her. "Hey, I don't think I ever got a chance to thank you for everything you did. For the Institute, yes, and the prisoners, and all that... but for me and my family as well. You went above and beyond to make sure we were taken care of, and I don't know that I'll ever be able to repay that debt."

Leah didn't know what to say, so she just wrapped Matthew in a hug.

**

A few days later, bright and early, Leah showed up at the clinic that had been her home-away-from-home in so many capacities over the years. She was welcomed with open arms... and donuts and coffee. Peter greeted her with a fist-bump. Valerie introduced her to the staff, showed her to her office, and laid out a tentative onboarding plan. The first item on her calendar was a strategy meeting about the Children's Ward—a chance to think practically about next steps, draft a timeline, and set goals for the coming year. While both women shared a long list of dreams and ideas, Leah went in with one specific ask, and she was pleased to walk out with a green light to move forward.

That evening after dinner, brownies in hand, she knocked on Sarah and Connor's door.

Connor answered, surprised but happy to see her nonetheless. "Leah! Come on in! We were just saying that it feels like ages since we've seen you. What have you been up to lately?"

Leah laughed. "Oh, man, that's the million dollar question. Lots to catch up on. How have y'all been?"

"We've been busy here as well." He stepped out of the doorway. "Come on in and sit down."

They walked into the living room, where Sarah was curled up on the couch, half-asleep and cradling a can of ginger ale. She sat up as they entered, a smile on her face and bags under her eyes.

"Hey." Leah sat down next to her, eyebrows raised. "You doing okay?"

"Yeah. A little tired, that's all." Her voice sounded more than a little tired. "What's up?"

"Well," Leah began with a nervous chuckle. "I have a big question for you. You might need some time to think it over, so I don't expect an answer now, but I do want to go ahead and put it on your radar."

Sarah furrowed her brow. "Oh yeah?"

"So, we had this insane sting operation on Monday, and we got him. We got him on everything." Leah heard the note of disbelief in her own voice. "So he's obviously not in charge of the Institute anymore... and the new President asked me to come on as the Director of the

Children's Ward—that's the pediatric division where I was treated as a child."

Sarah's face lit up. "Amazing! I hope you accepted!"

"I did! Today was my first day, actually." Leah nodded and smiled. "I'm really, really excited about everything we've got planned. And, well... we're going to need a business development person... Would you consider leaving your current job to come work with me?"

Sarah grinned and exchanged a knowing glance with Connor. He gave a tiny nod.

"I will," she said. "With only one question... What does the Institute's maternity leave policy look like?"

"I have no id—" It took a moment before Sarah's words registered. "Are you...?"

She smiled again, and Leah noticed the bags under her eyes for the first time. "I am."

Leah's jaw dropped. "Sarah! Congratulations! How far along? How are you feeling?"

"Early. Probably only six or seven weeks. I'm so tired," Sarah groaned. "And so sick. But we're really excited, too." She looked over to Connor with the sweetest expression. He smiled and took her hand in his.

They chatted about this and that—pregnancy, the sting operation, Connor's first week of school, Leah's mom's visit. Only as Leah stood up to leave did Sarah bring up the job offer once more.

"Leah, go ahead and send over the information for that development position, will you?"

Leah smiled, gave her friend a hug, and promised to send the paperwork over in the morning. She let Connor walk her out in comfortable silence. He closed the door behind her, and she set her steps toward home.

Epilogue

Eighteen months later...

Leah awoke before her alarm went off. Her stomach was in knots and her mind racing.

Today's the day!

She slipped on her favorite pair of slacks, her most flattering blouse, and her most comfortable blazer. All the while, she ran through the schedule for the day in her head.

Three appointments in the morning, one in the afternoon, and then the open house in the evening.

The skillet sizzled as the smell of sautéed onions and bell peppers filled her kitchen. Leah cracked two eggs and scrambled them, throwing in some leftover ham from the housewarming brunch at her mom's new place the day before. When it was all cooked, she sprinkled some cheese on top and sat down to eat. She considered making a cup of coffee, but refrained when she remembered the message her mom had sent before she'd woken up.

> Today's the day! I'll be there around 9:00 with a cup
> of coffee and a scone for you.

Breakfast eaten, teeth brushed, and lunch packed, Leah slipped on her flats and headed out the door. She had to intentionally counteract her muscle memory as she drove to the Children's Ward instead of the main clinic. Alicia's car was already parked in the back; as hospitality administrator, today was a big day for her as well, and Leah wasn't surprised to see that she'd arrived early.

The red ribbon from the Grand Re-Opening Ceremony still hung around the pillars. Leah smiled as she gently peeled the tape off and slipped the pieces of ribbon into her bag. She found the door unlocked and let herself in. The smell of Alicia's cinnamon oil diffuser met her as she stepped into the lobby.

"Is that you, Leah?" Alicia called from the kitchen around back, where she had stowed all the food and drinks and flatware for the open house later in the day.

"It's me! First day!" She was giddy with excitement.

Alicia peeked her head through the doorway of the staff lounge. "First day! I can't believe it's finally here!"

"Is Dr. Vallagomesa here yet?"

Alicia shook her head. "He texted me about ten minutes ago saying he was on his way."

Leah nodded, looking around the entryway and blinking back tears. "Everything looks beautiful, Alicia. You've done a great job making this place feel like home. I know the families who come in are going to be so grateful for all your hard work the last few weeks."

"I hope so." She turned to go back to her task, but stopped. "Oh, before I forget! I brought the mail in; it's on the reception desk. And someone had flowers delivered for you. I put them in your office."

Leah walked back to her office and set her backpack down on her desk. A vase of blue and yellow tulips greeted her, and she picked up the card that had been slipped in among the blooms.

I am so proud of you, Leah. I hope today is perfect!
Here's to new beginnings. I can't wait to see you this
weekend.
Robert

She smiled and balanced the note against the frame that
contained a picture of her and Robert. They were each
'leaning' against one side of the Washington Monument,
the obelisk between them seeming small on the other end
of the reflecting pool. The photo had been taken on Leah's
first visit to Washington DC after they'd finally started
dating. She'd groaned and protested halfheartedly when
he'd suggested they take it—"It's such a tourist thing to
do!"—but he'd insisted, telling her she'd be glad of it later.
He'd been right, of course.

The mail!

She slipped out of her office and made her way over to
the reception desk. Alicia's laptop was open, but she was
nowhere to be found. A stack of envelopes lay next to the
computer. Leah picked it up and flipped through it: a
couple ads from pharmaceutical companies; a note from
Valerie; an invitation to Jorge Rodriguez' memorial service,
on which was written, "Leah, we'd love to see you if you're
available." This last paper she tucked under her arm to
ensure she remembered to add it to her calendar. She'd
become quite close with the Rodriguez family during the
trial, and she didn't want to miss the memorial under any
circumstances.

At the very bottom of the mail stack was a letter
addressed to her in a handwriting that looked familiar. She
didn't recognize the return address, some place in
Hopewell, VA.

What could this be?

In spite of herself, Leah felt her heart speed up. Glancing at the clock, she set the rest of the letters down absentmindedly before returning to the privacy of her office.

I've got a few minutes before our first patient shows up.

She opened the envelope and slipped out a bulky bundle of paper lined with the same handwriting. She couldn't quite place it until she started reading, and then it hit her like a ton of bricks.

Dr. Pierucci.

Dear Leonora,

I hope this letter finds you, and finds you well. We don't get much news here, but rumors have reached me that the McNeill Institute is re-opening the Children's Ward with you at the helm. I do hope this is true, as I don't have another address at which to attempt to reach you. I have gotten settled here and, I must admit, have been severely disappointed by the general culture. Now that I have time to read again, I finally acquired a copy of *Kristin Lavransdatter*, which you recommended to me several years ago. My original aspiration was to begin a weekly discussion with several of the other men in residence, but none has expressed any interest. Indeed, many have shown outright disdain.

Nevertheless, I have persisted, and I admit I'm quite surprised to enjoy a novel as much as I am enjoying this one. If you ever find yourself in Virginia on a weekend, I understand that guests are permitted on Friday evenings, as well as most of the day on Saturdays and Sundays. I would welcome the chance to discuss *Kristin Lavransdatter* with you, as it's been

468

quite some time, and I no longer remember the particular insights you shared.

I have come to the realization, especially since coming here, that I quite missed your presence around our office and our home during the year you were out. There was one day in particular—you'd been gone for several months already—I found myself standing in the door of your office, words all but out of my mouth to describe some article I'd just read that I wanted to share with you... and yet, seated in your chair was the woman we'd hired to replace you. It was a jarring moment, and a revealing one. It struck me then that the families of our incarcerated research participants likely felt something similar. I began to consider that perhaps I had allowed my rage to become disproportionate, that there might have been a solution we could have reached together. Your intellect and empathy would have brought a lot to the table at Scarlett Bay. I must acknowledge that I wished (not infrequently) that my son had discovered the details of the research program instead of you. Perhaps things would have turned out differently, at one point in the process or another. Perhaps it would have been for the best.

He absolutely worshipped you, you know. I, of course, thought you could have done much better for yourself, and often wondered what you saw in him... but I was reticent to cause a rift between us, so I said nothing. And then to lose you after all! Once you were gone, there was simply no one to talk to. Even after you began your monthly visits to the clinic, I was unable to speak with you, at least as freely as I'd become accustomed to. As you might

469

imagine, the initial purpose of the treatment was observation; we wanted to be able to follow your progress for at least two years. However, after the first visit or two, I found myself falling into our old conversations, trying to establish a rapport with this young woman whom I knew so well, but who didn't know me at all.

That was another terrible thing—the suppression does tend to dull people out. I could sense from the start that you had lost some of your edge, and it saddened me. Not to a point that I no longer felt an affinity for you, or that I no longer wanted to see you personally each month, but enough to feel I had inflicted a great loss on the world. It is a true consolation to know that all was not lost—your actions last August certainly proved that beyond my farthest-flung expectations. I do hope, if you don't mind my saying it, that you are making an effort to sharpen that mind of yours. It would be a shame to waste it. I hope I am not being too upfront in this little note. It is difficult to gauge without you seated in front of me, especially in light of how much time has gone by since we were able to speak candidly.

I'll ask the guard for a leaflet about visiting hours, just so you have it. If you are able to stop by, I would appreciate a few words from you ahead of time, if possible. I will be thrilled to see you, but it would be best if I had time to prepare Jude. He hasn't taken any of it well, you know, all the recent proceedings. I suppose I had long accepted the possibility of something like this, but Jude had not. He's been rather sulky, especially on the rare occasion when I have slipped and let your name be spoken between us. I think it would be good for

470

him to see you, but it would not be easy. I, of course, would be delighted. It's quite quiet here, and a rousing, stimulating conversation would be most welcome. Even the act of writing this letter has brightened my day considerably. Do consider a visit, if you will.

Sincerely,
Jude Pierucci, Sr. MD, PhD

Sure enough, tucked behind the last page of the letter was a flyer advertising visiting hours and procedures at a medium-security prison in Virginia.

There was another page, too—smaller and filled with Jude's scrawling hand.

Leah's heart skipped a beat as she skimmed his words.

Leah,

I saw Father writing to you, and I'm sure he's going to give you the same tired old nonsense about how heartbroken and angry I am. I don't know where he's getting that idea. Just another story he's telling himself. I'm doing about as well as you'd expect, for someone in prison. Most of the guys here are pleasant enough, but it's a chore to be cooped up with Father and his novel. I'd enjoy myself more if I could spend less time with him.

I'm going to try and slip this in with his letter so he doesn't see it. He mentions you about every other day. Lately, he's been informing me that you'll be coming to visit him soon, so I need to make sure I'm ready to see you again. It's everything I can do not to just massively roll my eyes at him. He's been absolutely insufferable lately.

I've been thinking about you a lot, and I hope you're doing well.

Jude

Leah set the pages down, her stomach churning. She reread Jude's words, then scanned Dr. Pierucci's letter again, laughing anxiously at the discrepancies between them. Part of her wanted to sit down and pen a response. Part of her wanted to burn the whole thing, or rip it to shreds, or flush it down the toilet.

Alicia's voice from the other room roused her. "Leah, there's a car pulling up outside!"

"Eep!" A squeal escaped her, and she dropped the letters on her desk. "Will you let Dr. Vallagomesa know?"

"Already done!"

Leah glanced at the clock. Three minutes until eight. She straightened her blazer, ran a hand through her hair, and stepped back out into the entryway.

***

The rest of the day passed in a blur. Her mom came by with a gallon of coffee and a dozen scones for her team. She teared up when she walked through the door, and as Leah gave her a tour, she pointed out everything that had changed and everything that had remained the same since Leah's childhood visits. After her mom left, Leah spent most of the day chatting with the families who were bringing their children in for evaluations. Sarah didn't work on Mondays, but she brought little Nate to the beginning of the Open House all the same, and Leah took advantage of the opportunity to show him off to everyone. Finally, just after seven o'clock, Alicia ushered the last guests out the door. As the car drove off, Leah and Alicia drained their plastic cups of red wine, equally exhausted and exhilarated. They chatted for only a moment before Alicia left, asking Leah to lock up.

Heading back to her office to grab her things, Leah was confronted by the letters still lying on her desk. With the thrill of a good day behind her, they no longer turned her stomach sour, and she read both notes again with something bordering on amusement. Coming to Jude's signature, she pulled out her phone and called Robert. He answered on the second ring.

"Leah!" His excitement was palpable, and Leah felt a warmth in her chest. "I'm so glad you called! How was your first day at the Ward?"

"Oh, Robert, it was so lovely. We had four families come in, and they were each just a delight to chat with. Dr. Vallagomesa is going to be amazing with them, I can already tell. And Sarah and Nate came by for the reception, so I got to squish his little rolls and give Sarah a hug." She sighed. "I wish you could have been here."

"I know. I can't wait to come and visit."

Leah smiled. "But wait, that's not why I actually called! You're not going to believe the letter I got this morning."

"Oh, yeah?" She could see him in her mind's eye-one eyebrow raised, a goofy grin on his face.

Leah read both letters to him aloud, and when she finished, he was quiet. She gave him a moment to think before speaking again. "What's up? You look like you're thinking something."

"No, I mean..." He hesitated. "Hopewell can't be more than a couple hours away from me. You're already coming up this weekend. Would you want to go?"

Leah felt her eyes widen and her cheeks flush. "Oh my gosh, Robert! I wasn't telling you so that we could go visit them. I just wanted to laugh about how ridiculous the whole thing is!"

"Sure." She could see him shrugging, unconvinced. "We could still go."

"Ah, yes, such a romantic weekend." Leah rolled her eyes and laughed. "Let's go to jail to see my ex-fiancé and his psycho father."

"What could go wrong?" Robert's usual grin had come back into his voice. "But I'm serious, Leah! I think it would be good for you to get some closure."

"The trial was closure enough, Robert!" she protested. "It was more closure than I ever wanted. Fifteen months of nothing but closure."

He snorted. "Okay, you say that, but remind me how many letters you've written to Jude in the three months since the trial ended? Six?"

"Seven," she muttered, looking at the carpet.

"And how many of those have you actually sent?"

"None." She dragged the word out. "There's just so much I want to say to him, and I can never quite figure out how I want to say it."

Her phone buzzed with a FaceTime request. Laughing, she accepted.

All she could see of Robert was a quarter of his face, his eyebrow raised. "Does that sound like closure to you?"

"How did I know you were making that exact face?" Leah cackled.

Robert laughed back, pulling the phone away from his face so he could see her better. "Dang, you're beautiful. Come see me already. We can go visit a prison together. Isn't that the kind of romantic date you wanted to go on when you agreed to go out with an FBI Agent?"

Leah laughed. "I..." She was going to vehemently oppose the plan, but something stopped her. "You know what, Robert? I'll think about it."

THE END

About Fire & Feast Books

Fire & Feast is an independent author cooperative committed to telling stories that nourish the baptized imagination. We publish primarily character-driven stories across a wide variety of genres and strive to offer beautiful, well-designed books. Our focus is primarily on building connection and relationships between authors and readers directly. When you purchase a book from Fire & Feast, you can rest assured that you are directly supporting the storytellers you love!

To learn more, visit us online at fireandfeastbooks.com.

About the Author

Sara Hayes Dietz lives with her husband and two daughters in a century-old farmhouse in Texas. She started writing stories at six years old, and although she'd like to think she's improved since then, the jury's still out. When she's not writing, you can usually find her pushing the preschooler on the swings or reminding the toddler that no, she's not big enough to pick up a cow.

If you'd like to stay in touch with Sara, you can find more of her work online at mcneillinstitute.com or subscribe to her newsletter at blinkingblueline.substack.com.